Longbourn

www.transworldbooks.co.uk

Longbourn

Jo Baker

Doubleday

LONDON · TORONTO · SYDNEY · AUCKLAND · JOHANNESBURG

TRANSWORLD PUBLISHERS
61–63 Uxbridge Road, London W5 5SA
A Random House Group Company
www.transworldbooks.co.uk

First published in Great Britain
in 2013 by Doubleday
an imprint of Transworld Publishers

A CIP catalogue record for this book
is available from the British Library.

ISBNs 9780857522016 (hb)
9780857522023 (tpb)

Addresses for Random House Group Ltd companies outside the UK
can be found at: www.randomhouse.co.uk
The Random House Group Ltd Reg. No. 954009

The Random House Group Limited supports the Forest Stewardship Council® (FSC®),
the leading international forest-certification organisation. Our books carrying the FSC label are
printed on FSC®-certified paper. FSC is the only forest-certification scheme supported
by the leading environmental organisations, including Greenpeace.
Our paper procurement policy can be found at
www.randomhouse.co.uk/environment

Typeset in11.5/15pt Adobe Garamond by
Falcon Oast Graphic Art Ltd.
Printed and bound in Great Britain by
CPI Group (UK) Ltd, Croydon, CR0 4YY

4 6 8 10 9 7 5 3

MIX
Paper from
responsible sources
FSC® C016897

For Clare, with thanks
for her attention, forbearance, patience

*'What praise is more valuable than
the praise of an intelligent servant?'*

VOLUME ONE

CHAPTER I

The butler . . . Mrs Hill and the two housemaids . . .

THERE COULD BE no wearing of clothes without their laundering, just as surely as there could be no going without clothes, not in Hertfordshire anyway, and not in September. Washday could not be avoided, but the weekly purification of the household's linen was nonetheless a dismal prospect for Sarah.

The air was sharp at four thirty in the morning, when she started work. The iron pump-handle was cold, and even with her mitts on, her chilblains flared as she heaved the water up from the underground dark and into her waiting pail. A long day to be got through, and this just the very start of it.

All else was stillness. Sheep huddled in drifts on the hillside; birds in the hedgerows were fluffed like thistledown; in the woods, fallen leaves rustled with the passage of a hedgehog; the stream caught starlight and glistened over rocks. Below, in the barn, cows huffed clouds of sweet breath, and in the sty, the sow twitched, her piglets bundled at her belly. Mrs Hill and her husband, up high in their tiny attic, slept the black blank sleep of deep fatigue; two floors below, in the principal bedchamber, Mr and Mrs Bennet were a pair of churchyard humps under the counterpane. The young ladies, all five of them sleeping in their beds, were dreaming of whatever it was that young ladies dream. And over it all, icy starlight shone; it shone on the slate rooves and flagged yard and the necessary house and the shrubbery and the little wilderness off to the side of the lawn, and on the coveys where the pheasants huddled, and on Sarah, one of the two Longbourn housemaids, who cranked the pump, and filled a bucket, and rolled it aside, her palms already sore, and then set another bucket down to fill it too.

Over the eastern hills the sky was fading to a transparent indigo. Sarah, glancing up, hands stuffed into her armpits, her breath clouding the air, dreamed of the wild places beyond the horizon where it was already fully light, and of how, when her day was over, the sun would be shining on other places still, on the Barbadoes and Antigua and Jamaica where the dark men worked half-naked, and on the Americas where the Indians wore almost no clothes at all, and where there was consequently very little in the way of laundry, and how one day she would go there, and never have to wash other people's underthings again.

Because, she thought, as she fixed the pails to the yoke, ducked into it, and staggered upright, really no one should have to deal with another person's dirty linen. The young ladies might behave like they were smooth and sealed as alabaster statues underneath their clothes, but then they would drop their soiled shifts on the bed-chamber floor, to be whisked away and cleansed, and would thus reveal themselves to be the frail, leaking, forked bodily creatures that they really were. Perhaps that was why they spoke instructions at her from behind an embroidery hoop or over the top of a book: she had scrubbed away their sweat, their stains, their monthly blood; she knew they weren't as rarefied as angels, and so they just couldn't look her in the eye.

The pails slopped as Sarah stumbled back across the yard; she was just approaching the scullery door when her foot skidded out from underneath her, and her balance was gone. The moment extended itself, so that she had time enough to see the pails fly up and away, off the yoke, emptying themselves, and see all her work undo itself, and to realize that when she landed, it would hurt. Then the pails hit the ground and bounced, making a racket that startled the rooks cawing from the beeches; Sarah landed hard on the stone flags. Her nose confirmed what she had already guessed: she had slipped in hogshit. The sow had got out yesterday, and all her piglets skittering after her, and nobody had cleared up after them yet; nobody had had the time. Each day's work trickled over into the next, and nothing was ever finished, so you could never say, Look, that's it, the day's labour is over and done. Work just lingered and festered and lay in wait, to make you slip up in the morning.

After breakfast, by the kitchen fire, feet tucked up under her, Lydia sipped her sugared milk, and complained to Mrs Hill.

'You don't know how lucky you are, Hill. Hidden away all nice and cosy down here.'

'If you say so, Miss Lyddie.'

'Oh, I do say so! You can do what you like, can't you, with no one hovering over you and scrutinizing you? Lord! If I have to listen to Jane thou-shalt-notting me one more time – and I was only having a bit of fun—'

Next door, down the step into the scullery, Sarah leaned over the washboard, rubbing at a stained hem. The petticoat had been three inches deep in mud when she'd retrieved it from the girls' bedroom floor and had had a night's soaking in lye already; the soap was not shifting the mark, but it was biting into her hands, already cracked and chapped and chilblained, making them sting. If Elizabeth had the washing of her own petticoats, Sarah often thought, she'd most likely be a sight more careful with them.

The copper steamed, a load of linen boiling away in there; in front of her the fogged window was laddered with drips. Sarah stepped neatly from the duckboard by the sinks to the duckboard by the copper, over the murky slither of the stone floor. She slopped the petticoat into the grey bubbling water, lifted the laundry stick, and prodded the fabric down, poking the air out of it, then stirring. She had been told – and so she must believe – that it was necessary to wash a petticoat quite white, even if it was to be got filthy again at the next wearing.

Polly was elbow-deep in the cold slate sink, sloshing Mr Bennet's neck-cloths around in the rinsing water, then lifting them out one by one to dunk them in the bowl of cold rice-water, to starch them.

'How much more we got to go, d'you think, Sarah?'

Sarah glanced around, assessing. The tubs of soaking linen; the heaps of sodden stuff at various stages of its cleansing. Some places, they got in help for washday. Not here, though; oh no. At Longbourn House they washed their own dirty linen.

'There is sheets, and pillowslips, and there is our shifts, too—'

Polly wiped her hands on her apron and went to count the loads off on her fingers, but then saw how startlingly pink they were; she frowned, turning them, examining her hands as if they were interesting but unconnected to her. They must be quite numb, for the time being at least.

'And there are the napkins to do, too,' Sarah added.

It had been that unfortunate time of the month, when all the women in the house had been more than usually short-tempered, clumsy and prone to tears, and then had bled. The napkins now soaked in a separate tub that smelt uneasily of the butcher's shop; they'd be boiled last, in the dregs of the copper, before it was emptied.

'I reckon we have five more loads to do.'

Sarah huffed a sigh, and plucked at the seam under her arm; she had already sweated through her dress, which she hated. It was a poplin described by Mrs Hill as *Eau de Nil*, though Sarah always thought of it as *Eau de Bile*; the unpleasant colour itself did not matter, since there was no one to see her in it, but the cut really did. It had been made for Mary, and was meant for pastry-soft arms, for needlework, for the pianoforte. It did not allow for the flex and shift of proper muscle, and Sarah only wore it now because her other dress, a mousy linsey-woolsey, had been sponged and dabbed and was patchy wet, and hanging on the line to air the piggy stink out of it.

'Dump them shifts in next,' she said. 'You stir for a bit, and I'll scrub.'

Save your poor little hands, Sarah thought, though her own were already raw. She stepped back from the copper to the duckboards by the sinks, stood aside to let Polly pass. Then she scooped a neck-cloth out from the starch with the laundry tongs, and watched its jellied drip back into the bowl.

Polly, thumping the stick around in the copper, plucked at her lower lip with blunt fingernails. She was still sore-eyed and smarting from the telling-off she had had from Mrs Hill, about the state of the yard. In the morning she had the fires to do, and then the water to take up, and then the Sunday dinner was underway; and then they had ate, and then it had got dark, and who can go shovelling up hog-doings by starlight? And hadn't she had the pans to scour then anyway? Her fingertips were worn quite away with all the sand. And, come to think of it, wasn't the fault in the person who had let the sty's gate-latch get slack, so that a good snouty nudge was all it took to open it? Shouldn't they be blaming not poor put-upon Polly for Sarah's fall and wasted work – she glanced around and dropped her voice so that the old man would not actually hear her – but Mr Hill himself, who was in charge of the hogs' upkeep? Shouldn't *he* be obliged to clean up after them? What use was the old tatterdemalion anyway? Where was he when he was needed? They could really do with another pair of hands, weren't they always saying so?

Sarah nodded along, and made sympathetic noises, though she had stopped listening quite some time ago.

By the time the hall clock had hitched itself round to the strike of four, Mr and Mrs Hill were serving a washday cold collation – the remnants of the Sunday roast – to the family in the dining room, and the two housemaids were in the paddock, hanging out the washing, the damp cloth steaming in the cool afternoon. One of Sarah's chilblains had cracked with the work, and was weeping; she raised it to her mouth and sucked the blood away, so that it would not stain the linen. For a moment she stood absorbed in the various sensations of hot tongue on cold skin, stinging chilblain, salt blood, warm lips; so she was not really looking, and she could have been mistaken, but she thought she saw movement on the lane that ran across the hillside opposite; the lane that linked the old high drovers' road to London with the village of Longbourn and, beyond that, the new Meryton turnpike.

'Look, Polly – d'you see?'

Polly took a peg out from between her teeth, pinned up the shirt she was holding to the line, then turned and looked.

The lane ran between two ancient hedges; the flocks and herds came that way on their long journey from the north. You'd hear the beasts before you saw them, a low burr of sound from cows still in the distance, the geese a bad-tempered honking, the yearlings calling for mothers left behind. And when they passed the house, it was like snow, transforming; and there were men from the deep country with their strange voices, who were gone before you knew they were really there.

'I don't see no one, Sarah.'

'No, but, look—'

The only movement now was of the birds, hopping along through the hedgerow, picking at berries. Polly turned away, scuffed her toe in the dry ground, turfing up a stone; Sarah stood and stared a moment longer. The hedge was thick with old tea-coloured beech leaves, the holly looked almost black in the low sun, and the bones of the hazel were bare in stretches where it had been most recently laid.

'Nothing.'

'But there was someone.'

'Well, there isn't now.'

Polly picked up the stone and lobbed it, as if to prove a point. It fell far short of the lane, but seemed somehow to decide the matter.

'Oh well.'

One peg in her hand, a second between her teeth, Sarah pinned out another shift, still gazing off in that direction; maybe it had been a trick of the light, of the rising steam in low autumn sun, maybe Polly was right, after all – then she stopped, shielded her eyes – and there it was again, further down the lane now, passing behind a stretch of bare laid hedge. There *he* was. Because it was a man, she was sure of it: a glimpse of grey and black, a long loping gait; a man used to distances.

She fumbled the peg out of her mouth, gestured, hand flapping.

'There, Polly, do you see now? Scotchman, it's got to be.'

Polly tutted, rolled her eyes, but turned again to stare.

And he was gone, behind a stretch of knotted blackthorn. But there was something else now; Sarah could almost hear it: a flicker of sound, as though he – the scotchman that he must be, with his tally-stick scotched with his accounts, and a knapsack full of silliness and gew-gaws – was whistling to himself. It was faint, and it was strange; it seemed to come from half a world away.

'D'you hear that, Pol?' Sarah held up a reddened hand for quiet.

Polly swung round and glared at her. 'Don't call me Pol, you know I don't like it.'

'Shhh!'

Polly stamped. 'It's only 'cos of Miss Mary that I have to be called Polly even at all.'

'Please, Polly!'

'It's only 'cos she's the Miss and I imnt, that she got to be called Mary, and I had to be changed to Polly, even though my christened name is Mary too.'

Sarah clicked her tongue and waved for her to shush, still peering out towards the lane. Polly's outbursts were all too familiar, but this was new: a man who walked the roads with a pack on his back and a tune on his lips. When the ladies were done with his wares, he'd come down to the kitchen to sell off his cheaper bits and pieces. Oh, if only she had something nicer to wear! There was no point wishing for her linsey-woolsey, since it was just as ugly as her *Eau de Bile*. But: chapbooks and ballads, or ribbons and buttons, and tin-plated bracelets that would stain your arm green in a fortnight – oh, what happiness a scotchman represented, in this out-of-the-way, quiet, entirely changeless place!

The lane disappeared behind the house, and there could be no further sight or sound of anyone passing by, so she finished pegging out the shift, snapped out the next and pegged it too, clumsy with haste.

'Come on, Polly, pull your weight there, would you?'

But Polly flounced away across the paddock, to lean on the wall and talk to the horses that grazed at liberty in the next field. Sarah saw her rummaging in her apron pocket and handing over windfalls; she stroked their noses for a while, while Sarah continued with their work. Then Polly hitched herself up onto the wall and sat there, kicking her heels, head bowed, squinting in the low sun. Half the time, Sarah thought, it is like she has fairies whispering in her ear.

And out of tenderness for Polly – for a washday is a fatiguing thing indeed, while you are still growing, and while you are not yet yourself quite reconciled to your labours – Sarah finished off the work alone, and let Polly wander off unreprimanded, to go about whatever business she might have, of dropping twigs into the stream, or collecting beechnuts.

When Sarah carried the last empty linen basket up from the paddock, it was getting dark, and the yard had still not been cleaned. She slopped it down with grey laundry-water from the tubs, and let the lye-soap do its work on the flagstones.

Mrs Hill was burdened with a washday temper; she had been alone at the mercy of the bells all day: the Bennets made few concessions to her lack of assistance while the housemaids were occupied with the linen.

When Sarah came through from clearing the scullery, hands smarting, back aching, arms stiff with overwork, Mrs Hill was laying the table for the servants' dinner. She slapped a plate of cold souse down and glared at Sarah, as if to say, *Abandon me, and this is what you can expect. You only have yourself to blame.* The pickled brawn was greyish pink, jellied, a convenience when cooking was not to be contemplated; Sarah regarded it with loathing.

Mr Hill sidled in. Beyond him, in the yard, Sarah caught a glimpse of one of the labourers from the next farm along, who tucked in his neckerchief and raised a hand in farewell. Mr Hill just nodded to him, and shut the door. He wiped his hands on his trousers, tongue exploring a troubling tooth. He sat down. The souse wobbled on the table as Mrs Hill cut the bread.

Sarah slipped into the pantry, where she gathered up the mustard pot and the stone jar of pickled walnuts, and the black butter and the horseradish, and brought this armful of condiments back to the kitchen table with her, setting them down beside the salt and butter. The feeling was returning to her hands now and her chilblains were a torment; she rubbed at them, the flank of one hand chafing against the other. Mrs Hill frowned at her and shook her head. Sarah sat on her hands, which was some relief: Mrs Hill was right, scratching would only make them worse, but it was an agony not to scratch.

Polly ambled in from the yard with a cloud of fresh air, rosy cheeks and an innocent look, as though she had been working as hard as anybody could be reasonably expected to work: she sat at the table and picked up her knife and spoon, and then put them down again when Mr Hill dipped his grizzled face towards his linked fists. Sarah and Mrs Hill joined their hands together too, and muttered along with him as he said Grace. When he was done there was a clattering and scrabbling of cutlery. The souse shivered under Mrs Hill's knife.

'Is he upstairs then, missus?' Sarah asked.

Mrs Hill did not even look up. 'Hm?'

'The scotchman. Is he still upstairs with the ladies? I thought he'd be done up there by now.'

Mrs Hill frowned impatiently, slapped a lump of the jelly onto her husband's plate, another onto Sarah's. 'What?'

'She thinks she saw a scotchman,' Polly said.

'I *did* see a scotchman.'

'You didn't. You just wish you did.'

Mr Hill looked up from his plate; pale eyes flicked from one girl to the other. Silenced, Sarah poked at the pickled brawn; Polly, feeling this to be a victory, shovelled hers up into a grin. Mr Hill returned his baleful gaze to his plate.

'There's no one called at the house at all,' Mrs Hill said. 'Not since Mrs Long this morning.'

'I thought I saw a man. I thought I saw him coming down the lane.'

'Must have been one of the farmhands.'

Mr Hill scraped the jelly up to his mouth, his jaw swinging back and forth like a cow's, to make best use of his few teeth. Sarah tried not to notice him; it was a trick to be performed at every meal time: the not-noticing of Mr Hill. No, she wanted to say; it was not one of the farmhands, it could not have been. She had *seen* him. *And* she had heard him, whistling that faint, uncatchable tune. The idea that it could have been one of those rawboned lumpen boys, or one of the shambling old men you'd come upon sitting on stiles, gumming their pipes – she was just not having it.

But she knew better than to protest, in the face of Mr Hill's silence, Mrs Hill's brittle temper, and Polly's general contrariness. Mrs Hill, though, seeing her disappointment, softened; she reached over and tucked a loose strand of Sarah's hair back inside her cap.

'Eat your dinner up, love.'

Sarah's smile was small and quickly gone. She cut off a small piece of souse, smeared it with mustard, and then horseradish, then blobbed it with black butter, spiked a slice of pickled walnut, and placed the lot cautiously between her lips. She chewed. The stuff was hammy, jellied, with melting bits of brain and stringy shreds of cheeks and scraps of unexpected crunch. She swallowed, and took a swift gulp of her small beer. The one good thing about today was that it would soon be over.

After dinner, she and Polly and Mrs Hill sat, silent with fatigue, and passed the pot of goose-grease between them. Sarah dug out a whitish lump and softened it between her fingertips. She eased the grease into her raw hands, then flexed and curled her fingers. Though still sore, the skin was made supple again, and did not split.

Mr Hill, out of kindness to the women, washed up the dinner things ineffectually in the scullery; they could hear the slapping water, the scraping and clattering. Mrs Hill winced for the china.

Later, Mr B. would ring the library bell for a slice of cake to go with his Madeira wine, making Mr Hill start bad-temperedly awake and shamble off to give it to him. An hour or so after that, Mrs Hill would fetch away his crumby plate and smeared glass, and Sarah would gather the ladies' supper things from the parlour and carry them down on a chinking tray, and that would be that. On washday, the supper dishes

could wait for tomorrow's water. On a washday, too, Sarah did not
have the attention necessary to read whatever book she had borrowed
last from Mr B. Instead she had a lend of his old *Courier*, and read out
loud, for Mrs Hill's benefit, the news from three days ago, soft with
folding and refolding, the ink smudging on her goose-greased hands.
She read softly – so as not to disturb the sleeping child or the drowsy
old man – the account of new hopes for a swift victory in Spain, and
how Buonaparte had now been put on the back foot, and would soon
be on the hop, the notion of which made her think of the war as a
dance, and generals joining hands and spinning. And then there was
a noise.

Sarah let the paper hang from her hand. 'Did you hear that?'

'Eh?' asked Mrs Hill, blinking up from the edge of sleep. 'What?'

'I don't know, a noise outside. Something.'

A soft whinny then, and the bump and thud of horses unsettled in
their stalls.

'I think there's someone out there.' Sarah set the paper aside, went
to lift the child's sleeping head off her knee.

'It's nothing,' Mrs Hill said.

Polly sat up, still three-quarters asleep. Mr Hill muttered, blinked,
then reared up suddenly, wiping his chin. 'What is it?'

'I heard something.'

They all listened for a moment.

'It might be gypsies—' Sarah said.

'What would gypsies want here?' Mr Hill asked.

'Well, the horses.'

'Gypsies know horses; gypsies would have more sense.'

They listened again. Polly leaned her head against Sarah's shoulder,
eyes closing.

'It's nothing. It's probably a rat,' said Mrs Hill. 'Puss'll see to it.'

Sarah nodded, but still listened. Polly's breathing softened again, her
body going slack.

'All right, then,' Sarah said. 'Bed.'

*

As Sarah stripped the lacing from her stays, moonlight seeped underneath the curtains, and soaked right through their weave. In her shift, she drew back the drapes and looked out across the yard, at the moon hanging huge and yellow above the stables. All was clear, almost, as day; the buildings stood silent, the windows dark; there was no movement. No gypsies certainly, not even the slip-scurry of a rat.

Might it be the scotchman? Might he be bedding down for the night here, and away at dawn before anybody knew? His pack empty, he'd be off to restock at one of the market or manufacturing towns. Now that would be a thing indeed, to live like that. To be there and gone and never staying anywhere a moment longer than you wanted; to wander through the narrow lanes and the wide city streets, perhaps even as far as the sea. By tomorrow, who knew: he could be at Stevenage, or maybe even London.

Her candle guttered in the draught. Sarah blew out the flame, dropped the curtain, and crept into bed beside Polly's sleeping warmth. She lay looking across at the veiled window: she would not get a wink, not tonight; she was quite sure of it, not with the bright moonlight and the knowledge that the pedlar might yet be out there. But Sarah, being young, and having been on her feet and hard at work since four thirty, and it now striking eleven, was soon breathing softly, lost in sleep.

CHAPTER II

'Whatever bears affinity to cunning is despicable.'

T HEY WERE LUCKY to get him. That was what Mr B. said, as he folded his newspaper and set it aside. What with the War in Spain, and the press of so many able fellows into the Navy; there was, simply put, a dearth of men.

A dearth of men? Lydia repeated the phrase, anxiously searching her sisters' faces: was this indeed the case? Was England *running out of men?*

Her father raised his eyes to heaven; Sarah, meanwhile, made big astonished eyes at Mrs Hill: a new servant joining the household! A *man*servant! Why hadn't she mentioned it before? Mrs Hill, clutching the coffee pot to her bosom, made big eyes back, and shook her head: shhh! I don't know, and don't you dare say a word! So Sarah just gave half a nod, clamped her lips shut, and returned her attention to the table, proffering the platter of cold ham: all would come clear in good time, but it did not do to ask. It did not do to speak at all, unless directly addressed. It was best to be deaf as a stone to these conversations, and seem as incapable of forming an opinion on them.

Miss Mary lifted the serving fork and skewered a slice of ham. 'Papa doesn't mean your beaux, Lydia – do you, Papa?'

Mr B., leaning out of the way so that Mrs Hill could pour his coffee, said that indeed he did not mean her beaux: Lydia's beaux always seemed to be in more than plentiful supply. But of working men there was a genuine shortage, which is why he had settled with this lad so promptly – this with an apologetic glance to Mrs Hill, as she moved around him and went to fill his wife's cup – though the quarter day of Michaelmas was not quite yet upon them, it being the more usual occasion for the hiring and dismissal of servants.

'You don't object to this hasty act, I take it, Mrs Hill?'

'Indeed I am very pleased to hear of it, sir, if he be a decent sort of fellow.'

'He is, Mrs Hill; I can assure you of that.'

'Who is he, Papa? Is he from one of the cottages? Do we know the family?'

Mr B. raised his cup before replying. 'He is a fine upstanding young man, of good family. I had an excellent character of him.'

'I, for one, am very glad that we will have a nice young man to drive us about,' said Lydia, 'for when Mr Hill is perched up there on the carriage box it always looks as though we have trained a monkey, shaved him here and there and put him in a hat.'

Mrs Hill stepped away from the table, and set the coffee pot down on the buffet.

'Lydia!' Jane and Elizabeth spoke at once.

'What? He does, you know he does. Just like a spider-monkey, like the one Mrs Long's sister brought with her from London.'

Mrs Hill looked down at a willow-pattern dish, empty, though crusted round with egg. The three tiny people still crossed their tiny bridge, and the tiny boat crawled like an earwig across the china sea, and all was calm there, and unchanging, and perfect. She breathed. Miss Lydia meant no harm, she never did. And however heedlessly she expressed herself, she was right: this change was certainly to be welcomed. Mr Hill had become, quite suddenly, old. Last winter had been a worrying time: the long drives, the late nights while the ladies danced or played at cards; he had got deeply cold, and had shivered for hours by the fire on his return, his breath rattling in his chest. The coming winter's balls and parties might have done for him entirely. A nice young man to drive the carriage, and to take up the slack about the house; it could only be to the good.

Mrs Bennet had heard tell, she was now telling her husband and daughters delightedly, of how in the best households they had nothing but manservants waiting on the family and guests, on account of everyone knowing that they cost more in the way of wages, and that there was a high tax to pay on them, because all the fit strong fellows were wanted for the fields and for the war. When it was known that the Bennets now had a smart young man about the place, waiting at table, opening the doors, it would be a thing of great note and marvel in the neighbourhood.

'I am sure our daughters should be vastly grateful to you, for letting us appear to such advantage, Mr Bennet. You are so considerate. What, pray, is the young fellow's name?'

'His given name is James,' Mr Bennet said. 'The surname is a very common one. He is called Smith.'

'James Smith.'

It was Mrs Hill who had spoken, barely above her breath, but the words were said. Jane lifted her cup and sipped; Elizabeth raised her eyebrows but stared at her plate; Mrs B. glanced round at her house-keeper. Sarah watched a flush rise up Mrs Hill's throat; it was all so new and strange that even Mrs Hill had forgot herself for a moment. And then Mr B. swallowed, and cleared his throat, breaking the silence.

'As I said, a common enough name. I was obliged to act with some celerity in order to secure him, which is why you were not sooner informed, Mrs Hill; I would much rather have consulted you in advance.'

Cheeks pink, the housekeeper bowed her head in acknowledgement.

'Since the servants' attics are occupied by your good self, your husband and the housemaids, I have told him he might sleep above the stables. Other than that, I will leave the practical and domestic details to you.'

'Thank you, sir,' she murmured.

'Well.' Mr B. shook out his paper, and retreated behind it. 'There we are, then. I am glad that it is all settled.'

'Yes,' said Mrs B. 'Are you not always saying, Hill, how you need another pair of hands about the place? This will lighten your load, will it not? This will lighten all your loads.'

Their mistress took in Sarah with a wave of her plump hand, and then, with a flap towards the outer reaches of the house, indicated the rest of the domestic servants: Mr Hill who was hunkered in the kitchen, riddling the fire, and Polly who was, at that moment, thumping down the back stairs with a pile of wet Turkish towels and a scowl.

'You should be very grateful to Mr Bennet for his thoughtfulness, I am sure.'

'Thank you, sir,' said Sarah.

The words, though softly spoken, made Mrs Hill glance across at her; the two of them caught eyes a moment.

'Thank you, sir,' said Mrs Hill.

Mrs Bennet dabbed a further spoonful of jam on her remaining piece of buttered muffin, popped it in her mouth, and chewed it twice; she spoke around her mouthful: 'That'll be all, Hill.'

Mr B. looked up from his paper at his wife, and then at his housekeeper.

'Yes, thank you very much, Mrs Hill,' he said. 'That will be all for now.'

CHAPTER III

When first Mr Bennet had married, economy was held
to be perfectly useless . . .

SARAH CARRIED A chamber pot down from the Bennets' room, crossing the landing towards the narrow back stairs. She went carefully, head turned aside. Just nightwater, thankfully; not the dreadful slopping thunk of solids.

It was pissing it down outside, and confined by bad weather for the morning, the young ladies made the house rattle with noise. From upstairs came the sound of Mary practising on the piano – it seemed, to Sarah's untrained ear, rather pleasant: lots of notes, in quick succession, and most of them sounded like the right ones – a laugh from Lydia, hammering footfalls, and then an angry outburst from poor Kitty – 'Too many people in this house! Just too many people!' – and then Elizabeth's calls for peace, and then Jane's emollient tones, and then, for a while at least, calm. Oil on troubled waters, Jane was: a blanket over flames.

Sarah clumped down to the ground floor, past the open door onto the hall, where she caught the low mutter of Mr B.'s voice coming from the library; he'd often address himself to the empty air, or rather to his book: it was the only way, he'd say, that he could be sure of a decent conversation in that place.

Just past the open doorway, Sarah stopped, mid-step: there was another voice. It was as though the book that he'd been talking to had spoken back. It was a woman's voice, pitched low, so that the words themselves could not be distinguished, but Sarah recognized the speaker instantly. It was Mrs Hill. And she just kept on talking.

Sarah took a step back and peered down the hallway. The library door was shut. The glossy wood, the polished brass doorknob: all was as it ever was, and as it should be. And yet the door seemed somehow quite particularly, pointedly shut.

The pot was growing heavy in her hands, and she could hear the rain hissing down outside, and the gutters dripping, and Mrs Hill still talking, low, urgent, insistent, the words themselves teasingly unclear. It was a cardinal sin to eavesdrop; Mrs Hill herself had impressed this upon both Sarah and Polly in their training, but this was just too much. Sarah set the pot down on the bare boards, slipped out of the servants' corridor and crept, breath held, along the main hall.

A hand on the cool wood of the library door, she listened. She still could not hear *what* was being said; she could only hear that *something* was; so it wasn't really eavesdropping, was it? And still Mrs Hill talked, and talked, and the longer she talked the stranger it became that she was still talking. Mr B. would lend you a book, but he didn't want to hear what you thought about it. He'd say thank you for any service you performed, but he wouldn't even catch your eye. How could she have so much to say to him, and why – and this was the truly baffling thing – was he just letting her go on saying it?

Then something changed. Three words from Mr Bennet, like dropped stones: *You may go*, Sarah guessed. She raced on tiptoe back down the hall, slipping through the open door into the servants' corridor. Heart pounding, she crouched to lift the chamber pot, then peered back the way she'd come. But Mrs Hill did not emerge. And from inside the library it was like when the ginger beer went wrong – the top burst off the bottle, the contents foaming out until what must be spilt was spilt: a torrent from Mrs Hill. Sarah's eyes widened. How could she be so angry? How could she *dare* to be?

And then – Sarah nearly dropped the chamber pot, had to clutch and steady it – Mr Bennet did not simply send Mrs Hill away, but instead raised his voice over hers, and then there was a tangle, the voices spiralling up and growing louder, then suddenly hushed, to be followed by a furious hissing, which stopped abruptly, like a cut thread. There were footsteps, and then a fumbling at the inside of the door, and the handle turned. But Sarah had already slipped away, out through the side door, and was closing it behind her, and turning to face the rain; she did not see Mrs Hill come out of the library, shut the door, and stand there a moment, chest heaving, to calm herself, struggling with the constriction of her stays.

As Sarah headed away from the house, she could hear Mary still picking out her music, and another squabble brewing between Kitty and Lydia, and in a moment Jane and Lizzy would intervene again, and the rain fell thick and heavy on Sarah, who crossed the gravel and heaved open the door of the necessary house, and leaned into the cold stinking little room to slop the contents of the chamber pot through one of the holes, down into the foul pit below. Everything was as it always was, and yet everything was different.

Seven years old, heartsick, and all alone in the world, Sarah had blinked up at Mrs Hill, a person of substance with her clean apron and her white cap and her vast kitchen. Mrs Hill had chivvied the Parish Overseer out of the door, and clapped it shut behind him, and said he was a fox set to guard chicks, and then had drawn up a stool at the kitchen table for Sarah, and then produced bread-and-milk in a pretty blue-rimmed china bowl, and grated sugar over it. Then she had sat down to watch Sarah eat. All shyness flown, Sarah, straight from the poorhouse, had scraped the bowl clean in a trice. And so Mrs Hill, tutting and shaking her head, calling it criminal the way they starved these poor children, had taken the bowl, and filled it again with good bread and sweet creamy milk, and set it down in front of Sarah, and then scraped more sugar over the top of it.

And for that second bowl of bread-and-milk with sugar on the top, and for all the uncountable kindnesses since, to her and then to Polly when she had joined them – similarly saucer-eyed and starving – Mrs Hill deserved better than this. Sin or no, Sarah knew she would not eavesdrop again: nothing good could come of it.

27

CHAPTER IV

. . . the entrance of the footman . . .

SARAH'S THOUGHTS WERE tugged away across the courtyard by the sound of old furniture being shifted, of wood crumping down on flagstones, all of it accompanied by a faint whistling. The rain had stopped now, and the new man was hard at work clearing out the stable loft. The tune seemed familiar but she couldn't quite catch it. It fluttered around her like a moth, distracting.

Not that the task in hand required particular attention. She was elbow-deep in the slate sink in the scullery; condensation beaded the lead water-tank, its tap dripped, and the washing-up water had become grey and cool and greasy. Polly, having dried up a stack of plates, wandered through into the kitchen with them; Sarah could hear her dragging a stool over, then clambering up on it to reach the shelves and put the plates away. And all the time, all that Sarah could actually think about was the man across the way.

Of men, she had scant experience. She steered around Mr Hill: he was old and worn-out, and offered nothing by way of interest or engagement. She had very little to do with Mr B., who was, after all, only really present in the physical sense. She kept her distance from the farm lads; it was kinder to ignore them than to pay them any attention at all – say good morning and they'd be blushing and mumbling and wiping their hands down their britches and staring off out across the fields, as if there was something of great interest on the horizon.

The egg pan sank deep into the sink; Sarah watched the glair whiten and lift. Jane did well with men – with gentlemen. One of them had even written her some poems. How did you get a man to do a thing like that?

Jane, well, she sat nicely, and smiled, and she listened with her head tilted, and replied politely when spoken to, and she always seemed quietly pleased to be spoken to, and to dance if she was asked to dance. But Jane was really very lovely indeed – a beauty, in fact – and she was dealing with *gentlemen*, not *men*. An ordinary girl, Sarah thought, such as herself, would be taking quite a risk with that approach – she straightened her shoulders, smiled, tilted her head – on an ordinary man. Only a gentleman would have that kind of time on his hands, would have the leisure to devote his hours to winkling a female out of herself.

Sarah looked down at her sore, pruney fingers, and the limp folds of her bile-coloured dress. She lifted her hands to sniff them: grease and onions and kitchen soap. This must be the smell she carried with her, wherever she went, whenever it was not something worse. Sarah was not confident that she was lovely at all; far from it.

She lifted the ham pan, dipped it into the sink. Water bubbled up over the copper sides and cascaded in.

'These done?' Polly asked.

'Yes, take them.'

Elizabeth. She was a different, much more active, creature, when it came to dealing with gentlemen. Sarah had seen it at dinners, and at supper-and-cards, when she handed round the anchovy toasts. Elizabeth was always ready with a what-do-you-call-'em, a *witticism*. Bright-eyed and quick and lovely, making the young men blush and stammer, and the old fellows smile and wish they were half their age, and that bit sharper in their wits.

Sarah bit at what was left of a nail. She wasn't up to that.

Lydia and Kitty – who Sarah sometimes struggled to think of as two separate persons, but saw instead as one collective creature of four limbs, two heads, and a bundle of frocks and ribbons – Kitty and Lydia always had a hum of men around them. Curl-tossing, a bold look: it wasn't hard to copy – she copied it now, as there was no one to see her do it. They pitched themselves at every unmarried man who came their way, which made for rowdy card-parties and dances. Their approach required nothing more of a girl than enthusiasm, stamina and a copper-bottomed sense of self-importance. But really, did it amount to anything? Any man at all, gentle or otherwise, would surely be squeamish about attaching himself to a woman who had already flirted with every other man of her acquaintance.

Sarah lifted the copper milk pan, tilted it, watched her reflection spindle up and down the side: tadpole head, tapering body; swelling body, shrinking head. Bringing the pan close up, she regarded herself with a bull's eye. There was little benefit in making a show of yourself, when you were a wrung-out dishrag of a thing.

She could not model herself on Mary, either; she was unfledged still, a shabby nestling, her plumage not yet grown.

Mr and Mrs B., then. Married love. No good in that at all. The mistress had no understanding of her husband; she persisted in tackling him head-on, when, as everybody else already knew, you were better off taking a more circuitous path, and weaving your way around the obstacles.

If anything, the Hills were a better model of understanding between the sexes. Mrs Hill maintained a calm and mild demeanour towards her husband, and Mr Hill was always respectful, and deferred to her in all material things, and insisted too that others show deference and respect. Sarah had had plenty of cross words off both of them in her time, but she had never once heard a cross word between them. Maybe that was just what it was like, when you had been married for ever: all fell still as a pond, and passionless.

She was, she realized, entirely on her own, and without example or a guide.

The best that she could think of – and it did have a pleasing simplicity to it – was to be civil. To be civil and polite and welcoming; natural manners were always considered the best – she'd heard Miss Elizabeth say so.

So she would say, 'Good Morning.' That would start things off.

She rubbed the mist from the window and looked out. Low sun now, after all the rain. The light was golden: it caught on the damp flagstones and made them brilliant. And there he was. He was wiry, of middling height, his shirtsleeves rolled back and his forearms bare and weather-tanned, and he moved with a pleasing briskness about his work. His shirt, she supposed, had once been white, but was greyish now with wear; he kept his long dark hair tied back in a queue. She noticed all this through a welling sense of delight.

'Polly!' she called. 'Polly, come and see.'

Polly came down the step from the kitchen, wiping her hands. They both leaned in against the sink, and peered out through the clear patch in the misty window.

'Oh my—'

Sarah put her arm around Polly's waist. The girl rested her head against Sarah's shoulder.

'That,' said Sarah, 'is one job we won't have to do now.'

They watched in silent happiness as the new man swept the yard.

When she went out – cap neat, cheeks pinched, teeth rubbed shiny with a corner of her apron – to feed the gallinies, she could hear him moving around in the stable loft. Could she go inside and call 'Good Morning' up the ladder to him? Then he might look – or even climb – down, and she could say thank you for all his hard work, and he'd have to reply to that, and that would be almost a conversation in itself.

Mrs Hill came bustling out of the house; Sarah looked down at the bowl of chicken scraps, and then up at the housekeeper: she could summon no excuses for loitering there. Mrs Hill, though, was too busy to notice Sarah's dawdling. She had a sheaf of old clothes slung over her arm, and was dragging the clothes-horse out behind her. She thumped it down, then set about battling with its wooden rungs.

'Can I help you there, missus?'

'I can manage, thank you, Sarah.'

Mrs Hill heaved the clothes in a heap on the stone bench, then lifted a jacket off the top of the pile. She shook it out, and turned it round, inspecting it. She snapped it out again, and draped it over the top rung of the clothes-horse. Seeing Sarah still lingering there, she said, 'Them chickies do need fed, miss, though. Hop to it.'

The rest of the morning Sarah kept crossing the yard. He could not stay in the stable loft all day, she told herself; he *must* come out at some point, and when he did, she would say 'Good Morning,' and he would say 'Good Morning' back. Then she would thank him for sweeping up the yard for them, and he would say 'You're welcome,' and it would go from there, and that would be that.

But if he did emerge at all, in the middle part of that day, she missed him. She caught the smell of fresh whitewash, though, and from time to time the sound of him whistling.

The afternoon stretched out like catgut. She thought he might come across to the kitchen to beg a cup of tea. She wondered if she ought to take a cup over for him, but then she'd have to ask Mrs Hill to brew up, and dinner preparations were now in full flood, and Mrs Hill would not welcome the suggestion that she pause in the middle of all that, just to put the kettle on.

Sarah was chopping the fennel, the aniseed-smell of it sweet and clean, her lip caught between her front teeth while she considered the likeliness and otherwise of tea; Mrs Hill was gutting the carp, with Puss twining and coiling around her ankles, demanding notice; she dropped the innards for it to catch. Polly, meanwhile, pumped the bellows at the fire, watching as the fuel flared and sparked. They could hear Mr Hill thumping around below them, down in the cellar, where he was selecting the wine. Mrs Hill took up her scaling knife and set to scraping the milky-silver scales from the flank of the fish. Then her hands went still.

'The apple pie!'

'Apple pie?'

'I forgot all about it.'

'I thought it was to be gooseberry.'

Sarah had seen the pastry made the night before; she'd topped and tailed the gooseberries with her own hands. She had watched Mrs Hill grate the sugar over the berries.

Mrs Hill flapped a fishy hand. 'It was to be apple, and I forgot all about it.'

'What's to do then, missus?'

'You run and pick the apples; I'll make the pastry.'

Sarah was on her feet and heading for the door before Polly could realize what was happening, and volunteer herself for a jaunt down to the orchard in Sarah's stead.

'How many do you need?'

Mrs Hill looked down at her fists, uncurling one finger then another in an attempt at calculation. Though she must have been distracted by the state of them, red and thick, and slippery with oil from the fish, because the numbers themselves continued to elude her.

'Just fill that trug with them nice Broad-eyed Pippins, they're good cookers and they're ripe. They'll do just fine.'

Sarah undid her apron, and grabbed the gallon trug from the low shelf by the door. She was half in, half out when Mrs Hill called out to her, 'And thank you, lovey. I don't know what's wrong with me today.'

Basket on her arm, Sarah was out of the fug and fluster of the kitchen, and into the autumn cool. She dawdled past the stable door; dust motes hung in the air, along with the limey smell of whitewash. The top half of the door was open. Inside, it looked warm; she got a glimpse of the chestnut mare's glossy flank, and sun shafting through a high window. Of the new manservant, still no sign.

Every step she took was as slow as a step could possibly be. And still he did not come out.

The ladder had been left against the pippin tree. Head and shoulders amongst the leaves, she stretched out for the heavy blushed fruit, taking whatever was within easiest reach, with little thought to size or ripeness. As soon as she had filled the trug, she scrambled straight down the ladder, skirts gathered. She hurried up to the house, the basket handle hooked over her folded arms. The apples might bruise a little, knocking about like that, but they'd hardly have time to spoil.

As she strode along the side of the stable block, the basket bumping against her thighs, feeling bright with possibility, the new manservant was at the same moment striding along the front of the stables, pushing a heavily laden wheelbarrow before him. The two met as they swung round the corner from opposite directions: the corner of the wheelbarrow hacked into Sarah's shin; she grabbed at her basket; he stumbled to a halt, clutching the barrow handles.

They stood face to face. She was wide-eyed, lips parted; he was a mess of loosened hair. The barrowload of ripe and stinking stable-muck steamed faintly in the autumn cool between them.

'Sorry!' she said.

He pulled the barrow back, then pushed the hair out of his eyes. His skin was the colour of tea; his eyes were light hazel and caught the sun. He peered down at her skirts, where he'd hit her.

'Does it hurt?'

She bit her lip, shook her head. It really did.

'I didn't see you—'

'You should be more careful.' She could feel the trickle of heat where her shin bled. 'I nearly dropped my apples.'

'Oh yes,' he said. 'I see that. Apples.'

'Yes. Well, you should really—'

'So, if you're all right—' He jerked his head: 'Kitchen garden down this way?'

She nodded. He wheeled the barrow back another step and swerved past her.

'Right, then. Thanks.'

Then he was away, rattling down the track and round the bend, his waistcoat hanging loose around him, britches gathered in at his middle like a flour sack, one boot sole flapping half off. So this was the fine upstanding young man. This was the great addition to the household. As far as Sarah could see, he was no great addition to anything at all.

'And a good afternoon to you, too!' she yelled after him.

Sarah's shin was bloodied, red seeping through her black worsted stocking. Not really a cut, more a split in the skin, all blue with bruise and oozing blood. Her stocking was not torn, however, and for that she was not

34

entirely grateful. If it had been ruined too, then she could have allowed herself to be proportionately more cross. She shook down her skirts.

'I finally met the new man, missus,' she said.

'Oh yes?' Mrs Hill, her forehead beaded, was rubbing lard into flour, but paused at this. 'Pleasant lad, I think.'

'He ran smack into me. With a barrowload of dung.'

'And were you running too, by any chance?'

'You needed the apples, so I was, perhaps.' She looked pointedly down at her shin. 'He hurt my leg.'

'Could you get on with the peeling, do you think?'

'It's really sore.'

'Oh dear.' Mrs Hill still did not look round.

'I think my leg's going to fall off altogether.'

'What a shame.'

'It's only hanging on by a bit of gristle.'

'Well, never mind.'

Sarah got up from her seat and limped emphatically to the kitchen table. She took up a paring knife. Mrs Hill glanced up at her then; she ran the back of her hand across her forehead, leaving behind a fine dusting of flour.

'Are you all right, though, Sarah, love?'

'No. And he's not either. Not in the head. I'll bet that's the only reason we could get him. That's why he's not in the service of some earl or away fighting in the war. Because nobody else would have him. Nobody wants him because he's a cack-handed lummox who's a danger to everyone around him.'

Mrs Hill gave Sarah a warning look.

'Well—'

'Sarah. Don't you dare go blaming others for what you've brung upon yourself.'

Sarah lifted an apple and chunked her knife into it. She peeled away a ragged strip of skin and watched it coil onto the scrubbed tabletop, her lips pressed tight. Everything was wrong. This was not how things were supposed to be at all.

CHAPTER V

'I cannot see that London has any great advantage over the country for my part . . .'

JAMES SMITH HAD presented himself in the kitchen for Mrs Hill's inspection some hours previously, as Mr Bennet had required him to do. Mrs Hill took one long assessing look at him. He was thin. He was very thin. You could see his skull through his skin, at the edge of his eye sockets; you could see the ridge of his jawbone and its joint by the ear. And he was dirty: his fingernails were black, his hair filthy, there was a rime of grey about the skin and clothes. And the clothes themselves looked as though they'd been stolen off half-a-dozen different washing lines. He had a beard. It was straggly and unkempt, but it was certainly a beard. He had been on the tramp a while.

'What's first to do, then, ma'am?'

She lifted the kettle from the range, and jerked her head towards the scullery.

'Let's get you sorted out.'

She poured him hot water from the kettle into the scullery sink and let it down with water from the tap; she gave him a slip of soap and a linen towel and a comb, then fetched Mr Hill's razor and stropped it for him. She left her scissors on the drainer, for his nails.

In the kitchen, she scrubbed down the table with salt, and set out the bread, and butter, and cheese, and listened to him huff and splash. When he had rolled back his sleeves at the sink, his arms had been twisted rope, just bone and muscle. These were hard days indeed, to be between employments.

The table laid, she sat and waited. He came up the step from the scullery, his hair still damp and dripping around his ears. His beard was gone, and his skin was pale and soft where it had been. He was ill at ease, moving awkwardly in the confined space of the kitchen, with its obstacles and hurdles, its clutter of stools and chairs, tubs and fire-irons and skillets. He was one of those men, it seemed, who are not quite at home indoors.

'So, what's to be done now, ma'am?'

She drew out a chair for him at the kitchen table. He looked down at it.

'Sit.'

She poured him a cup of tea, set the milk jug beside it, and placed a bit of sugar on the edge of the saucer. She cut the bread and the cheese, then went to the pantry to shave a few slices off the ham. When she had set all this down in front of him, he was still just looking at the cup; the drink itself was untouched. His lips – he rolled them in, bit down on them – were cracked and peeling.

She sat down opposite him. 'You don't drink tea?'

'No, I—'

'Would you prefer milk?' She pushed her chair back. 'Or we have beer. Would you like a mug of beer?'

'I do drink tea, it's not that.' His gaze was uneasy; it scudded around the room.

'What is it, then?'

'To earn it. I should work first.'

'No,' she said. 'Not here. You eat first here.'

He looked at her then, with his clear eyes.

'There will always be food for you here. Breakfast, dinner and tea. You eat, and then you work,' she said. 'You don't need to worry about that any more.'

He smiled then, and it was a transformation; all unease gone, he softened and seemed young. He picked up the sugar lump and set it aside, then lifted the cup and sipped.

37

'It's good,' he said. 'Thank you.'

'But you don't like sugar?'

'I do, I suppose. But I don't take it.'

She shunted the plate of ham a little closer, watched his Adam's apple roll down, then back up his throat. She dug a knife into the butter, slid it towards him too. He smeared the bread with butter, laid on ham and cheese, folded it in half and bit. When he had finished, she was ready with a broad wedge of gooseberry tart, and a dish of thick yellow cream with the little silver spoon stuck in it.

'Go on,' she said.

He looked up at her. Then he shook his head, and softly laughed.

'What?'

'Nothing. Just. Thank you.'

He dug a spoon into the fruit, and ate. When he had finished the first slice, she gave him a second. And when, after that, she thought he still looked hungry, she just shunted the pie dish towards him and let him get on with it.

'I wonder . . .' she began, as he picked up the pastry crumbs from the tabletop with a fingertip. 'Mr B. didn't mention where you've worked before.'

'Oh, here and there.'

'Have you come far?'

'Not very far. Been all over, really.'

'Always in domestic service?'

'That kind of thing. And horses. I do know horses.'

'Well,' she said, after a moment, when nothing more was offered. 'You're here now.'

'Yes.'

'And that's all to the good.'

'Yes,' he said. 'And thank you, ma'am, for that fine meal.'

'"Missus" will do. I hope you will be happy here.'

She took his empty cup, with its thin strewing of leaves at the bottom, and his cleaned plate, and stacked them all on top of the empty pie dish. She pushed back her chair.

'We are glad to have you.'

'What now, though, missus? What shall I be getting on with?'

'You could go and sort that room out for yourself, above the stable.'

He wiped his mouth, and was on his feet.

'You'll hear the church clock strike,' she said. 'Come back over at four. You'll be waiting on table with Mr Hill at dinner.'

He nodded.

'Oh, and – do you have any other clothes?'

He glanced down at his loose waistcoat and hitched-in britches, and then up at her; a smile. He shook his head.

'I'll sort something out for you.'

'You are very kind.'

'Mrs B. will have you kitted out in due course, but you'll need something decent for everyday; can't be mucking out the horses in livery.'

'Livery?'

She nodded. He pulled a face. It made her smile.

'Well then,' she said. 'Get along with you.'

When he had gone, Mrs Hill climbed heavily up to the attics. She picked her way through old banded trunks and chests and boxes that were labelled with long-lost maiden names and the careful print of young boys heading off to school. She swept off dust and brushed away cobwebs, teased straps out of buckles, and flung back lids, making the dust roil away in billows. She lifted out long-outgrown shirts and nightshirts, narrow and unfashionable suits of gentlemen's clothes, and held these up to the light, assessing their size and degree of decrepitude, remembering the long years ago when they had still fitted, had been fashionable, and had still been worn.

The kitchen was hot, the new pie baking and the fish bubbling gently in its copper kettle, the door standing open to let out the stour. Polly clambered on and off her stool, lifting down the china; Sarah filled a tray with glasses while Mr Hill scrutinized the silverware, brow furrowed, lifting one fork and then another to the light. He held one out for Sarah's notice; there was a crust of something stuck between the tines.

'I'm very sorry, Mr Hill. It won't happen again.'

He shook his head at her, then spat on the fork and polished it up to a satisfactory shine with a corner of his waistcoat.

'Where's the new fellow, then?' Polly asked.

Mrs Hill looked up, over towards the window. 'Here he comes right now.'

He slipped in quietly through the kitchen door. Dark hair combed and tied back, he was rigged out in a narrow brown coat, black knee-britches and worsted stockings. His appearance was very decent and neat, but the clothes were antique in cut, like in a portrait of a gentleman made thirty years before.

'Coo,' said Polly. 'You look like a ghost.'

He rippled ghostly fingers at her; she giggled. Mr Hill came to look him over; he brushed a lapel, nodded.

'Well,' said Mrs Hill. 'You'll do.'

It was to be a simple family dinner, Mr Hill informed him, an easy introduction into the proper arrangement of knives and forks, plates, platters, decanters and glasses, so that by the time that company were invited, James would be able to set these items upon a tablecloth in a manner that would not offend the neighbourhood.

He was as silent as one of the candlesticks. He shadowed Mr Hill, watching every move of his white-gloved hands, nodding whenever the old fellow looked round at him to check he had been understood. Between them they laid the table, so that all was in readiness for when the family sat down.

Then, at half past four, Mr Hill went out into the hall and rang the dinner bell. From all around the house came the sound of doors being opened and shut, the clattering of footsteps, and voices animated in anticipation of another of Mrs Hill's good dinners.

The two men, with Sarah to assist on this first attempt of James's, carried the dishes up to the dining room, and if she had not had a tureen of buttered leeks in her hands, she would have tugged on his queue – it bounced along on his back so temptingly – just to get some kind of notice out of him.

She could see, though, that Mrs Bennet already looked upon him with considerable satisfaction. He didn't have to do anything very much at all, just set the sauce boat upon the table without splashing the tablecloth or jostling anyone, and the mistress would gaze around the assembled family to gather up their admiration, her eyes wide, as if to say, *See what a clever fellow we have got ourselves here!* Sarah would admit that he was an improvement on the rustics they had been obliged to rope in on occasion in the past, but that was all she was prepared to admit. His hands might be nice, and his nails neat and clean, but that hardly made him Beau Brummell.

When the servants were dismissed, Mrs B. very pointedly said, 'Thank you, James.'

Unseen in the hallway, Sarah rolled her eyes. First Mr B., and then Mrs Hill, and now Mrs B.: why was everyone so bowled over? The only thing of note about him was that he was a *man*. And under fifty, and with nice hands.

'So how do you like it here, Mr Smith?'

'I hardly know yet.'

He slipped past her, and kept on going, his stride long. She skipped a step to keep up.

'You will find us very dull, I expect, after the kind of thing that you are used to.'

He did not reply.

'I doubt you'll find anything of interest to you here.'

They were at the kitchen door now. He pushed it open, then stepped back and held it for her. She was utterly wrong-footed. Already a good way gone towards being properly out of humour with him, she had fully intended to continue in that course until she loathed him heartily. Now, she was obliged to shuffle past him, and nod her thanks, and consider to what degree she had already been uncivil, and if he had warranted it or not. Her discomfort was not, however, sufficient to

41

prevent her from pushing home her point: 'You will hardly think us worth the trouble of talking to at all, I should say.'

He looked at her now. She met his look, and raised her eyebrows. Then she spun away, and strode off to help Polly lay the kitchen table. She had succeeded in drawing his attention at last. It gave her surprisingly little satisfaction.

Mr Hill said Grace, and they started dinner.

Polly watched from under lowered eyelids: James ate as though each mouthful was a thing of great importance that must be considered with all seriousness and respect. It was very interesting, Polly thought, that he should eat like that, when most men of his sort ate as though they were shovelling coals into a furnace, or hay into a barn.

Mrs Hill passed him the bread, and the butter, and the salt, and kept refilling his cup with small beer.

'May we have more milk, please, Mrs Hill?'

Mrs Hill pushed the jug across to Sarah; Sarah filled Polly's cup and then her own with thin blue buttermilk. Polly did not notice, so fascinated was she by this new manservant. She peered at him; she asked questions; she nodded eagerly along with the answers.

Where had he learned his craft?

He had done similar work before.

What work exactly had he done, though, Polly wanted to know, and where had he done it?

Mrs Hill shushed her.

He said he didn't mind, and that Polly was a clever girl, and this made her blush and smile, and slowed down her questioning for a little while. He had worked on a farm, he said, and then as an ostler, and then as a general servant in a house much the same size as this.

'Which house, though – I mean, whose? Maybe we know them – maybe the Bennets visit there.'

The house was beyond the neighbourhood, of course; the farm was just over the distant hills; the inn where he'd worked as an ostler was out past Ashworth, and on a few more miles. All of it was just out of reach, Sarah noted: all the places he mentioned were just a little too far away, for there to be any connection or shared acquaintance between his previous situations and his new one, here at Longbourn.

This was what Sarah had always wanted: something – anything – to disturb the quiet, to distract her from the sounds of Mr Hill's revolving mastication, and the prospect of another spiritless evening, and the monotony of her own voice reading three-decker novels and three-day-old news. But now change had come to Longbourn, and Polly was staring at it as if she was a simpleton, and Mrs Hill kept topping up its glass, and even Mr Hill was smiling and glancing at it and then shyly away, and Sarah was left heartsunk and ignored, and wishing that this change, with its dark hair and its hazel eyes, and its skin the colour of tea, had never come to Longbourn at all.

Sarah felt even lower the following morning, when she stumbled her way down to the kitchen, Polly dragging along three steps behind. The warm glow of her candle illuminated the stairway, the bare treads and the green distempered walls, the candle's own greasy drips, and her cracked hand carrying it, the skin dark with dried blood and patched with chilblains that she must not scratch however much they itched.

First chores: fuel and water to be fetched, the hearths swept and the range to be blackleaded, and then her hands scrubbed free of blacking and soot before the day's work could properly begin. Outside, the iron chill of the pump-handle awaited her: she'd almost rather pluck hot coals from the fire.

Polly sat down at the table and rested her cheek on her folded arms. Sarah, still dozy herself, took up the hearth brush and was about to hunker down and sweep the fallen cinders, but then she stopped short. The hearth was clean, the range gleamed, the fire was bright and crackling with new wood. She glanced at the log basket: it was full.

Someone had been up early.

Water next. She leaned into the scullery to lift her yoke. Candlelight fell through the open doorway, and caught on the inner shells of the wooden pails. She crouched to touch: her fingers came away wet.

Straightening, she brushed her hand down her apron, then crossed over to the water-tank and laid her hand on the lead. She could feel the cold weight of water pressing out against the metal skin. Someone had mended the fire, and then fetched the water; they had filled the tank right up to the brim.

A brownie. A helpful little lubber fiend. They'd never had one of them at Longbourn before.

'Polly—'

But back in the kitchen Polly had fallen asleep again, head on her arms, curls falling across her face. Sarah stood, hands on hips, looking around the room. For a moment she was lost. Because there was nothing, for the next little while at least, for her to do. An hour had been freed for her, had been presented to her like a gift.

She grabbed the old pelisse that hung by the back door, and ducked out into the peppery-cold morning. Pulling on the coat, her fingers fumbling with the frogging, she strode out of the yard and across the paddock, the frosted grass crunching and the rime kicking back up over her toecaps. She slipped through the side gate and turned up the lane; birds hopped and peeped in the hedgerows. She ducked into blue-black woods, and then back out into the starry morning. The sleeves hung low over her hands; she tugged up the collar and dipped her face into it; the old velvet smelt musty. She came to where the lane crested the hill, and met the drovers' road.

The drovers' road was ancient. It swept along the ridge, and was not surfaced or shaped like modern roads were, with their gravel and their ditches. The drovers' road was just a ribbon of grass worn short by the passing of the herds. The openness, the prospect here was striking; you could see steeples, villages, woods and copses miles away, and the smooth distance of far hills. And she knew that if she just turned that way, and kept on walking long enough, she'd end up at the first city of all the world, and that in itself was a kind of miracle. London was everything that could be imagined; and plenty more, no doubt, that as yet could not.

She wrapped her arms around herself. A curlew cried. The sun nudged itself up above the hills, flushing the blue morning through with orange. A sheep called; a lamb replied. Shadows reeled out like ribbon; there was green now in the meadows and on the trees. Somewhere, off down the valley, a cockerel crew, and there was a whiff of woodsmoke on the air. And at Longbourn the kettle should be filled and put on to heat because soon enough everybody would need a cup of tea. And she could hardly expect the pixie, however helpful he might be, to think of that.

As she made her way back down the lane, the house was still dark, its windows glassy and blank. A few sheets hung on the line; the linen was a white flicker through the hedgerow's weave. And she felt a little inward shift: she saw herself standing down there where the washing lines were slung, saw the flicker of movement that she would be making now, as she passed behind the hedge.

It hadn't been a scotchman, of course, she saw that now: it had been James Smith.

He must have been coming down from the drovers' road that day, just as she was now. That noise from the stables that evening: that had been him too, sneaking in, honey-talking the horses, like he honey-talked everybody – finding himself a nice warm spot, and bedding down for the night. And in the morning he had somehow contrived to see Mr B. before anybody had seen him. Why the master had been per-suaded to employ him in such circumstances, Sarah had already conjured: it was a matter of economy, no doubt; a bargain so tempting that Mr Bennet could not bring himself to refuse it.

But the thing was: if he had come down from the drovers' road, he hadn't come from that house out past Ashworth like he'd said, or from the farm over the far hills. He could have come from anywhere. He could have come from London. From half a world away.

The kitchen glowed with firelight when she glanced in through the window; Polly was still asleep, head on folded arms. Sarah could hear Mr Smith moving around in the stables; she should really just go indoors, wake Polly, and get started on their day. But instead she crossed to the stables, and stood on the threshold, looking in at the warm scene there, lit by a hanging lantern. He was rubbing down the mare with a currycomb, and seemed absorbed and peaceful. The horse noticed the newcomer first, and swung her head round to fix a big soft eye on Sarah, buffeting James and making him stumble back and laugh, and then glance round to follow the horse's look, his face closing when he saw her, like a box.

'Thank you,' she said, shifting on her cold feet, her arms wrapped tight around her. 'For doing all that work this morning, I mean.'

He turned back to the brushing. 'That's all right.'

'It's mine – and Polly's, really, but she finds it hard to wake up early. So.'

'I was awake anyway. I like to keep busy.'

He did not so much as glance at her.

She squeezed her arms the tighter. 'What are you doing here?'

He paused in his work. 'What?'

'I mean, why here? I mean, if I were you, I wouldn't have settled for this. Hidden away like a pike in a backwater. Hardly knowing you're alive.'

He shifted the currycomb in his palm, straightening the strap across the back of his hand. He didn't look up.

'I saw you walking down the lane the other day. It was you, wasn't it?'

He stiffened, and turned to look at her. She was struck again by those light hazel eyes, the darkness of his weather-tanned skin.

'Where did you come from?' Her voice dropped. 'You must have travelled. Have you ever been to London?'

'London's only twenty miles or so from here, you know.'

She flushed, kicking one boot heel with a hard-capped toe. He went back to his work.

'I don't know what to make of you at all,' she said.

'Please don't trouble yourself to try.'

She spun away, and clumped off back to the kitchen. He was such a frustrating mixture of helpfulness, courtesy and incivility that she could indeed form no clear notion of him. Of one thing, though, she was certain: he was lying. He was not what he pretended to be. He might have fooled everybody else at Longbourn, but he did not fool her. Not for a minute.

CHAPTER VI

The business of her life was to get her daughters married; its
solace was visiting and news.

Mrs Bennet's dressing room: her inner sanctum, her retreat from the pressing demands of family life; a place of bulging upholstery and swags and cushions and drapes and Turkey-rugs; a place heaped with worn-once gowns, abandoned shawls, spencers, pelisses and bonnets; a place of rose-petal mustiness, of striped and flowered wallpaper, of surfaces trinked out with all the porcelain her pin money could supply, and all the paper flowers and shellwork and scrollwork and embroidered panels and painted china her daughters' nimble fingers could furnish, and all of it decomposing now and peeling and gathering dust, and driving Mrs Hill's ordered, governable heart to distraction.

Mrs Hill had been summoned to discuss the menus for the week, and having committed the requests for partridge and timbales and ragouts, as she always did, to memory, she should now be off and away to knead the bread dough, which she'd left to rise in the kitchen. But instead she was kept in the dressing room to hear Mrs B.'s complaints, which concerned – as they often did – Mr B.'s failure to understand the necessity of something that was violently important to his wife. And since he seemed barely capable of hearing her voice, let alone the import of her speech, Mrs B. was resolved not to pursue the matter with him any further. Instead, she complained of it to Mrs Hill.

It was not in Mrs Hill's nature to make sympathetic noises and be idle, even though she knew from long experience that all attempts at putting this room in order were entirely futile. She dusted a japanned box with a corner of her apron, and then wiped the dust off the cabinet shelf that it stood on. She lifted a rumpled egg-yolk evening-gown from a chair, and shook out its folds.

'Oh, just leave it, Hill.'

'I'll hang it up—'

'Hang it up? Hang it all! Don't bother yourself with it! That ragged old thing!'

Mrs Hill looked the dress over: had the girls missed something? The silky yellow folds slipped through her hands. No marks that she could see, no fallen hems or pulled seams; no obvious tears. It seemed entirely as it had been when returned to Mrs Bennet's wardrobe after its last laundering; there had been a particularly soupy supper at the Gouldings'. How the girls had tutted over the gown; how they'd steeped and soaped and teased the spots out of the silk. She had been proud of them, capable little laundresses that they were. And she had felt that they were pleased with themselves, too, when it had at last come up clean, and that was gratifying: they were beginning to take a proper pride in their work, rather than just getting through it, wishing they were elsewhere.

'I must have something new,' Mrs Bennet was saying. 'Really, I must. And so must all the girls. Surely that is not too much to ask, after all these years? You shall have that hideous old thing. I don't want it any more.'

Mrs Hill laid the gown carefully over her arm; there was a time it would have quickened her heart to think of possessing something of such loveliness. But really, now, what use were yellow silk and flounces, to her? It would need taking up and taking in and all the silliness cut away or she would catch fire while she was cooking. So it was really not so much a gift as another job of work, and that was something that she did not need at all.

'It is terrible indeed, Hill. You have no notion of what it is, to be a mother, and to know your children suffer, for want of fatherly attention.'

And now Mrs B. made a great evacuation of her lungs, and heaved her softened body up from her reclining posture, waving Mrs Hill's proffered hand impatiently away. She crossed the little room, stays creaking, to glower out of the window, though her thoughts clearly were not occupied by the view of the pretty park below.

'And not just for the coming ball; we shall need new gowns for morning calls, and for family dinners, and for supper parties, and for drinking tea in, and all that kind of thing.'

Then she leaned on the windowsill, and wiped her eyes.

'But I suppose he will forbid it. He does not understand this kind of thing at all. Indeed, I do not think he cares.'

Mrs Hill gazed at her mistress's broad back. If she did not get down to the kitchen and sort out the bread, they would have bricks that week instead of loaves. She had to send one of the girls to collect eggs, and the other to beat the hall carpet, and whichever girl she asked to do whichever job, they would scowl and bicker over it. And James was away off up in the High Field, repairing fences, and she had a jug of beer set aside on a shelf in the larder, to carry up to him, and if she didn't take it soon, she wouldn't have the time to take it up at all before his work was finished there. Before you knew it, dinner would have to be got underway, and Mr Hill would be wanting his cup of tea, and it was not good to leave him wanting his tea for very long.

And yet Mrs B. was sad, and needed her; she came close, and touched her shoulder.

'I am sorry, madam.'

Mrs B. shook her ringlets. 'There is always something more pressing, as far as he's concerned. Some tenant not paying the rent. Or they want seed on the farm, or there are repairs to be done; there's always *some-thing* more important than me, and the needs of my poor girls.'

Mrs B. turned to face the housekeeper, her look grave and earnest. Mrs Hill found her hard hands caught up in her mistress's soft ones.

'Would you speak to him for me, Hill?'

'I can, if you wish, madam, but I don't think that it would have much consequence.'

'Oh, you know you have influence with him, Hill. If you tell him it is necessary he will understand that it is. If I say something he thinks it is not worth attending to. But he will listen to you. He does not listen to me. Not any more.'

Mrs Hill turned her face away. A powder-pot sat on the dresser nearby, the puff lying loose, the mahogany surface floured thick with good lavender-scented powder. There had been no more babies, and there would never be more babies now: this was what lay at the heart of this rats' nest of unhappiness. She had not provided the necessary heir, and this was a desperate disappointment. And yet, Mrs Hill thought, having been worn threadbare by all those pregnancies and torn by all those confinements, with all those lost teeth and all that shed blood and a loose belly now to lug around with her like a sack; there must be some relief for Mrs Bennet, mustn't there, to know that it was all over now, and she would not be obliged to endure it all again?

'You know that it is true,' the mistress continued. 'One word from you, and we'll have a new broom or a pan tinned or more candles or whatever it is that you want.'

'Household matters, madam, and that is all.'

Mrs Bennet released Mrs Hill's hands.

'These *are* household matters! This concerns all of us! I had thought, as a woman, you would understand. But then, you are not a mother, so you do not know. You cannot comprehend how I suffer for my girls. Mr Bingley may be married off before my dear daughters can even get a look-in.'

'Mr Bingley?'

'Oh, yes, perhaps you haven't heard!' Mrs Bennet's face was like a blustery spring day: dark clouds were bundled away, and then the sun shone. 'Netherfield Park is let at last, you know. When Mrs Long was here earlier, she told me all about it. They are to be in residence by Michaelmas.'

'Mrs Nicholls will have her work cut out, to get it all in order.'

Mrs Bennet wafted the air: Mrs Nicholls's troubles did not signify at all in comparison with her own.

'But you see, Hill. The new tenant is a young gentleman – an *unmarried* gentleman. A young unmarried gentleman of *good fortune*.'

Mrs Hill shifted on her feet; she glanced at Mrs B.'s cushion-cluttered sofa, considered collapsing into it. A young, unmarried gentleman, newly arrived to the neighbourhood. It meant a flurry of excited giggly activity above stairs; it meant outings, entertainments, and a barrowload of extra work for everyone below.

'Yes. So the girls *must* have new clothes so that they may be fallen in love with, and *I* must too, so as to show that we are a respectable family and worthy of his notice. I will not have Mr Bingley over-looking us and thinking we are nothing, for want of a few frocks. Therefore *you* must speak to Mr Bennet about it, and insist that we have them.'

At least they had James to help out this time. Another pair of hands, a young man to drive the carriage in Mr Hill's place.

'I will speak to Mr Bennet,' Mrs Hill said. 'If you really wish it, madam.'

'Good,' said Mrs Bennet, and she sank down on the sofa once again, leaving Mrs Hill standing. 'Well, as soon as you can, Hill. And pour me a dose of my balm, would you? My nerves are all aflutter.'

Mrs Hill unstoppered the bottle and half filled a glass and handed it to her mistress, who sipped and closed her eyes, and was soothed. Mrs Hill left her there, and trudged back down to the kitchen. The bread dough had risen up above the edge of the bowl; it was tight and round and streaked with stretch marks. She turned it out onto the floured tabletop, scraping it away from the bowl with her fingernails, flipping it over and slapping it down again, then pounding and hammering at it with her fists, sending out gusts of flour; when Mr Hill shuffled into the kitchen a little later, he took one look and decided it would be better not to ask for his tea, and instead sat down quietly by the fire and waited till she noticed him.

Sarah had been there, once, years ago, before Polly had even come to Longbourn. She'd been sent with a gift of a ham, after the killing of a Bennet pig. Back then the grand pillars of Netherfield had stood streaked with green and damp. The door had been opened by a desiccated footman, whose livery was moth-eaten and food-stained and who stood in the dim lobby and looked at her with his one good eye – the other being an orb of milky white – and asked her whose girl she was, and then had pulled the creaking door wide and bowed her in.

Inside it had been cold, and echoing, and full of flitting shadows: the little girl had passed down corridors lined with foxed and blistered mirrors, with furniture draped and shrouded in dust sheets. The ham, swaddled like a baby in its cotton wraps, was heavy and cold in her arms. The footman showed her into a parlour, then he sank down in a sofa and tilted his head back, mouth open, as if utterly exhausted by the small journey to and from the door.

The room was frowsty and cold, and smelt of medicaments and camphor wood and urine but also something faintly sweet; a card-table was set out with a clutter of mismatched tea things, and there was a tumbled daybed in the corner, on which lay what she first took to be a bundle of mending, but which moved and then turned, and then smiled at the child; such teeth as the old lady still possessed were black.

'Would you like a piece of cake, little girl?'

Sarah shook her head, set down the ham, and walked backwards for the door. She spun round and sprinted the length of the haunted corridor, and heaved open the huge front door herself. Then she ran, stumbling, the first mile back to Longbourn, and when she couldn't run any more she walked as fast as she could, glancing over her shoulder. The smell of the place – the sweetness that was decay – had seemed to linger about her for days.

Today, all grown up, she approached Netherfield again. This time, instead of a heavy cold ham, she was carrying an elegantly phrased invitation for Mr Bingley, requesting his company at a Family Dinner.

Crunching up the gravel drive, which had been raked and hoed and cleared of weeds, she gazed up at the stately scrubbed-clean colonnade: this was clearly no longer the kind of establishment where a neighbour's housemaid could be received at the front door. She took a path round the side of the house, looking for the servants' entrance. The sashes were lifted to let the fresh air in to sweeten the rooms – all inside was newly painted; she could smell it. She glimpsed pure-white ceilings, dust sheets, a watery mirror.

The young ladies and Mrs B. were all of a twitter about him, this Mr Bingley. There had already been a bit of to-and-fro, but the servants had had little to do with it. When Mr Bingley called at Longbourn, the gentlemen had sipped Canary wine in the library in a remarkably self-sufficient manner. James had seemed to think the care of the Bingley horse – an impressive black gelding – to be a pleasure rather than an imposition.

But now there was this, the invitation to a Family Dinner, and Mrs B. was already in a fluster about fish and soup, because a Family Dinner was of course more difficult to get right than a formal one. You had to impress, but at the same time you had to look like you were not *trying* to impress at all. It had to be excellent, and it also had to seem as though it was how they were all used to dining every day.

Mrs B. had been very particular about the note, had shaped the words carefully on the best paper in the house, tongue protruding from the corner of her mouth. Mrs Hill had been very particular about it too: when James came down from the breakfast room with the missive, she had tweaked it off the salver, squinted at it a long moment, then handed it straight to Sarah.

'Quick as you can; no dawdling, please. I need you back here to help with the pies.'

The door was small and plain and must be a servants' entrance. No one answered her knock, so she just slipped in, and followed the noise towards the kitchen. This seemed a likely place to find someone to convey a note on its onward journey to an upstairs apartment. Sarah already felt anxious, and she had not even been obliged to speak to anybody yet: it would surely look odd that she, a housemaid, had come with an invitation, instead of a footman. What was Mrs Hill thinking?

What was Mr Smith *for*, if not to dash about the countryside on the family's behalf?

Sarah sidled through a swing door, and into the vast kitchen. No one even noticed her. The place was cavernous, echoing, and bustling with activity. She saw a male cook in a blue jacket, pacing and peering into pots; three kitchen maids chopped onions and leeks; manservants swept in and out. The scents were overwhelming: beef and wine and stewing fruits. Then a footman – tall, in fine livery and powdered wig – whisked past her.

'Excuse me . . .'

He stopped, and came back. His face was quite brown. She glanced at his hands; he wore white gloves, so she could not see if they were brown too. She bit her lip, looked up at his face again – he was distressingly handsome – and then away, because it was rude to stare. Her cheeks were hot; she stared down at her feet.

'May I be of assistance?'

The words were English, and spoken in a very gentlemanlike fashion. Not daring to meet his gaze, she held out Mrs B.'s carefully constructed note, and shook it at him.

'For— For Mr Bingley.'

'And do you wait for a reply?'

She nodded. But he just stood there, so she was obliged to look up at him again. His eyes, dark as black coffee, still rested on her; he was almost smiling. She felt her cheeks get hotter.

'I am very glad to know it.' He bowed, and was gone.

So was he what they called a black man, then, even though he was brown? An African? But Africans were cross-hatched, inky, half-naked and in chains. That plaque she had seen at the parsonage, hanging in the hallway: *Am I not a man and a brother?* This fellow, though, was immaculate in his livery, and his skin was not scribbly at all, but beautifully smooth and clear. He was indeed hardly darker than Mr Smith, or any local man who worked the fields in the August sun. Though with them, the brown faded with the winter, and only ever extended as far as their shirt collar and rolled-back sleeves . . .

Sarah shrank back against the wall, so as to be out from under everybody's feet. It must be a fair old hike up to the family rooms and back. Or perhaps Mr Bingley could not make up his mind whether he could face a Family Dinner with the Bennets or could not. The lime-washed plaster was cool against her palms. She watched the busyness and hurry and was glad that she was not required to be a part of it. The Netherfield housekeeper, Mrs Nicholls, had been stopped by the male cook, and he was barracking her; he must have come up with the family from London, since they did not have male cooks around here. Mrs Nicholls was apologizing, flustered, hands spread in supplication, and Sarah looked away; Mrs Nicholls would not want to be noticed like that.

When the black footman came back, he held out a little letter, folded and sealed in a slapdash fashion, the direction written in a scruffy hand.

'I do hope there is a reply to the reply,' he said.

Sarah did not know what to say to that. She bobbed a curtsey, and she fled.

'So he's not coming?'

'He won't even be at home at all!' Eyes wide at the thrilling news: 'He's going to London!'

And at the drop of a hat, as though it were something and nothing, as though it were a thing one might do every day!

'He's fetching some people back for the ball.'

'Gallivanting about!' Mrs Hill tutted, resumed her darning. 'And I've already ordered the beef.'

'Oh, the Bingleys do have good money for gallivanting,' Polly said. 'Everybody says so. I heard their old daddy was in sugar.'

'And there's a fair deal of money to be found in sugar.'

James was cleaning the cutlery; Sarah should be grateful, since it saved her doing it. But it felt like a slight: was her work no longer considered up-to-scratch, that the new man was required to do it for her?

'It must be a very profitable trade,' Mrs Hill said. 'We can't seem to do without the stuff.'

'I would *love* to be in sugar,' sighed Polly. 'Imagine!'

'You'd go sailing out' – James traced a triangle in the air with a fork – 'loaded to the gunwales with English guns and ironware. You'd follow the trade winds south to Africa—'

Polly smiled excitedly at this. But then she blinked. 'What's ironware?'

'Shackles and chains, pots, knives,' James said. 'In Africa, you can trade all that, and guns, for people; you load them up in your hold, and you ship them off to the West Indies, and trade them there for sugar, and then you ship the sugar back home to England. The Triangular Trade, they call it. I dare say the Bingleys will be out of Liverpool, or Lancaster, since it's said that they hail from the North.'

'I didn't know they paid for sugar that way,' said Polly, shuffling her chair forward at the table.

'What way?'

'With people.'

'Well,' he said, and rubbed at the fork, and gave a little shrug. 'They do.'

'You seem to know a good deal about it.'

He glanced up at Sarah, who had said this. He shrugged again. 'I read a book.'

'Really?'

'Yes, really. Why not?'

'It just seems unlikely.'

'Why would it seem unlikely?'

'Just, it doesn't sound like you.'

'What? That I might read?'

'Well—'

The feel of things had changed, Polly noticed, though she could not quite understand why, since it had all been going so swimmingly just moments before. James and Sarah's voices shuttled back and forth, Polly's attention darting between them; Mrs Hill's hands had fallen still, her needle tucked through the loops of worn thread; Polly saw her glance at Mr Hill, saw Mr Hill raise his bristling eyebrows back at her.

'So you just assumed me to be ignorant.'

'No, but—'

'But it never occurred to you that I might read more widely than, say, you, for example?'

'I read all the time! Don't I, Mrs Hill?'

The housekeeper nodded sagely.

'Mr B. allows me his books, and his newspaper, and Miss Elizabeth always gives me whatever novel she has borrowed from the circulating library.'

'Of course, yes. Miss Elizabeth's novels. I'm sure they are very nice.'

She set her jaw, eyes narrowed. Then she turned to Mrs Hill.

'They have a black man at Netherfield, did you know?' she announced triumphantly. 'I was talking to him today.'

James paused in his work, then tilted his head, and got on with his polishing.

'Well,' said Mrs Hill. 'I expect Mrs Nicholls needs all the help that she can get.'

'But to think,' said Polly, anxious to return to the earlier ease, 'all of that loveliness, all that money, and all of it comes from sugar; I bet they have peppermint plasterwork, and barley-sugar columns, and all their floors are made of polished toffee, and their sofas are all scattered with marchpane cushions.'

'The columns are just the local stone, I am sorry to inform you.' Sarah lifted up her sewing, picked at the stray loops. 'As for the cushions, I cannot say. But marchpane would get rather sticky by the fire.'

Polly nodded, smiled dreamily, swallowing her spit.

CHAPTER VII

'If I can but see one of my daughters happily settled at Netherfield,' said Mrs Bennet to her husband, 'and all the others equally well married, I shall have nothing to wish for.'

'HERE'S YOUR DRESS, miss.'

Elizabeth looked round, her lips parting in that beautiful smile. And it was a beautiful dress, a dress to make you smile. Delicate muslin dyed duck-egg blue, which would set off the young lady's complexion perfectly. Sarah carried it through the doorway, and laid it down on Jane and Elizabeth's bed like a swooning girl.

Jane was already hooked into her evening-gown, standing carefully at a distance from the fire, so as not to scorch the fine muslin, and doing nothing, not even sitting down, so as not to crush it. Her hair was already dressed in neat, smooth bands and plaits; her expression was mild and revealed little of her inner workings. The main thing about Jane was that she could be trusted. She could be trusted not to spoil a gown, not to nag, not to scold, not to require any particular attention. Jane's composure and self-sufficiency were as balm to Sarah's frayed nerves. She was as sweet, soothing and undemanding as a baked milk-pudding, and as welcome at the end of an exhausting day.

The younger sisters' die-straight locks had had to be tormented into ringlets, which wore out Sarah's hands and everybody's patience. The smell of hot hair and pomade followed her through the upper rooms and corridors. It was, to Sarah, the smell of resentment: her hands were already blistered from the flat-irons, her feet throbbed in her boots, her back ached; if provoked at all at this stage of preparations, she might even start deliberately burning hair.

Elizabeth's hair curled naturally, though; it seemed a manifestation of her lively and obliging temperament. She had already pinned it up herself, and affixed a spray of artificial roses to it; she now waited, in shift and stays and petticoat, to be dressed. She raised her arms, exposing the dark musky fluff underneath; Sarah lifted the sheaf of muslin, and dropped it down over the young lady's head. Between them, they shuffled Elizabeth into the gown, then Sarah plucked the little silky buttons, on the inner side of the arm, through their button-holes. Elizabeth winced.

'Did that pinch?'

'A little.'

'Sorry.'

Sarah continued working in silence. She bobbed down on her haunches, straightening the hem, then was up again to fit the bodice, tugging the high waist neat beneath the bosom.

'Good?' Elizabeth asked.

Sarah nodded.

Elizabeth shuffled cautiously around, so that Sarah could settle her bodice there, and fasten the row of tiny covered buttons that ran up between the shoulder blades.

'Are we done?'

Skirts rustling, Elizabeth moved towards the dressing table, to see herself in the mirror there. Sarah followed her, smoothed the dress's yoke onto china collarbones, using only her left hand, so as not to risk staining the muslin. On her right, a blister had burst and was weeping.

'You look very lovely, Miss Elizabeth.'

'All your hard work, Sarah, dear.'

Sarah smiled and shook her head. Even to her long-accustomed gaze, Elizabeth was genuinely compelling: if she was in the room, you knew you were wasting your time if you looked anywhere else but at her.

59

'Though it is a shame for you, Sarah, dressing us up and not going anywhere yourself. And you are always so uncomplaining.'

Sarah shrugged; it did not do to talk about it. She could not go to their ball, no more than she could attend a mermaids' tea-party; but still she felt herself get blinky, her nose tickling. She turned away.

'Do you ever get to go to a dance, Sarah, dear?'

It was Jane who had spoken, revealing the gentle stirrings of her mind.

'Once in while, miss.'

'And what do you wear when you go?' Elizabeth asked.

'Whatever I have that's best.'

Which was never very good, but then who was to notice, at those dances on the village green? The farmhands lumbering in their Sunday jackets, the church players sawing on fiddles and puffing their fifes and battering at their tambours. And Polly going feral, haring around with a pack of village children in games that Sarah was now too old to play, and Mr Hill getting quietly drunk and having to be half carried home. And on the way home, the dairymaids giggling in the hedgerows with the lads, and Mrs Hill barking, *Eyes dead ahead, miss, eyes dead ahead*, in case Sarah saw something that she shouldn't see, though she had seen the bull at it with the heifers, and the boar with the sow, and so had a fair idea of what they were about.

'She shall have a new dress for the next one, I think, don't you, Elizabeth?' Jane was moving towards the closet. 'Shall we see—'

'Miss, that would be . . .' Such a delight that she couldn't even finish her sentence. Maybe the footman would come from Netherfield to the next village dance; maybe he would ask her to dance with him. Mr Smith might even be obliged to notice her then, dancing with a handsome man, in a new dress, on the village green.

'By some miracle of my mother's devising,' Elizabeth now said, 'we each have a new gown at the same time, so no one is clamouring for hand-me-downs, and you may have your pick.'

Jane lifted out an old evening-gown, in oyster-coloured satin, and laid it on the bed. Low-necked, short-sleeved. Elizabeth went to join her, shook her head.

'Or there's this . . .'

An oak-leaf-print pelisse, in twilled silk, to wear indoors on cool evenings.

'She's better with something less . . .' Elizabeth turned towards the closet, frowning. 'A day-dress perhaps, simpler, I think, for village dances on the green.'

She lifted out a sprigged poplin day-dress, with long sleeves and high neckline. The pattern was a repeat of green stems and tiny claret rose-buds on a cream background. Sarah had cut and stitched the stuff two summers ago, it was lovely then, and was pretty still; through every washing, every mangling and ironing, she had adored it. Then Elizabeth laid a sage-green tea-gown beside the poplin; it was trimmed with white velvet ribbon; you had to unpick the ribbon every time you washed it, to keep the dye from bleeding into the velvet.

'Here,' Elizabeth said, 'whichever you prefer.'

'Really?'

'But just the one, or we shall have Polly in a sulk,' Jane said. 'And none of ours will fit her yet.'

'She'd have to persuade Kitty or Lydia to give up a frock.'

Jane smiled. 'Lydia would.'

'Lyddie would give anyone anything, just for the asking.'

From Mary's room came the sound of the pianoforte, a rill of scales and arpeggios, and the muffled laughter of the youngest girls in their room across the landing. Quietly, Sarah lifted the sprigged poplin and laid it over her arm, and bobbed a curtsey, and said thank you, before anyone could change their mind. The pleasure of its acquisition made her breathless.

Elizabeth nodded to a book on the dresser. 'And you might like to borrow that.'

Sarah tilted her head to look at the spine. *Pamela*, she read.

Then, dressed and coiffed and beautiful, Elizabeth and Jane wished her a good evening. They wafted out of the room and clipped softly down the stairs. Sarah laid her new gown reverentially down on the bed; she tidied away the brushes and combs, the spilt pins and ribbons. She smoothed the rumpled counterpane. The room was dull now, and meaningless, with the young ladies gone from it. They were both lovely, almost luminous. And Sarah was, she knew, as she slipped along the servants' corridor, and then up the stairs to the attic to hang her new dress on the rail, just one of the many shadows that ebbed and tugged at the edges of the light.

In the kitchen, Mr Smith leaned by the fire and chewed an apple, looking stiff in his livery. He caught Sarah's eye, and looked away, and crunched again.

'Where's missus?' she asked.

He swallowed, spoke: 'Upstairs with madam.'

So Sarah went straight through the kitchen and down into the dim blue scullery, where Polly was sitting on the duckboard, legs stretched out in front of her, boots at odd angles, back against the wall. Sarah slid down and sat beside her. It was their mutual secret: this spot was unfrequented at certain busy times, and so here they could snatch moments of respite.

'Do you ever think,' Sarah asked, 'that it would be good if there was somewhere else you could go?'

Polly raised her eyebrows, lifted a finger to her lips: from the kitchen they heard Mrs Hill's voice, Mr Smith's reply; she had come back, and was asking where the girls were.

Sarah dropped her voice, whispered, 'That's what I mean: somewhere you could just *be*, and not always be obliged to *do*. Somewhere where you could be alone, and nobody wants or expects anything of you, just for a while, at least.'

Polly wriggled her narrow shoulders against the bare brick; it was the chimney wall – on the other side the kitchen range flared and sparked – and so was dry and warm.

'Stop moaning and shut up,' she said. 'Someone will hear you.'

Polly had herself come through a frozen January night in a basket on a farmer's doorstep, then the precarious neglect of a parish wet-nurse, and a few rough and hungry years in the poorhouse, and she had come through all of it alone; she had survived, it seemed to Sarah, simply by failing to notice how unlikely it was that she should. It also meant that Polly did not possess the capacity for nostalgia, wishful thinking or regret; it was not worth trying to solicit her sympathy in this, because to her *this* was as good as things ever got, and were ever likely to: there were no golden memories for her.

Sarah, though, could still summon her ghosts, blurred with summer sun and dim with shadow: chickens scuffing at the cottage door beside a little boy who was still unbreeched and smelt of piss and milk; of the woman in a red dress who had whisked her off her feet and kissed her; of a man who sat indoors over a shuddering loom, a book balanced on the frame, and got up from his seat so stiffly in the dark; of lying in her box bed, her brother curled warm and damp beside her, listening to her parents' voices in the night, weaving back and forth, holding the whole world together.

Happiness was a possibility for Sarah; she had a fair idea of what she missed.

Chapter VIII

The evening altogether passed off pleasantly to the whole family.

CANDLELIGHT SPILT OUT of the front door, making a warm pool in
the blue moonlight. Mr Bennet stood on the threshold, a shawl
over his powdering gown, to see his family off. James, seated up on the
carriage box, lifted his hat to his new master, who gave him a gentle-
manly nod in reply; Mr Hill was handing the ladies into the coach;
their gowns frothed up over the doorsill like breaking waves.

Mrs Hill and the two housemaids waited on the gravel, as was
expected, to watch the ladies leave; the older woman's expression was
benign and fond, Polly bounced on the spot to keep warm, and Sarah,
with her wrecked hands tucked under her armpits, was looking off into
the moonlit night, a frown creasing her forehead.

'Don't they look lovely!' Mrs Hill said. 'My beautiful girls!'

Mr Hill clapped the carriage-door shut, and stepped away. And now
it was up to James.

James clicked his tongue, flicked the reins, and the horses stirred
themselves. There was that moment's pause as the slackness in the tack
was taken up, and then the tug into movement, gravel crunching under
wheels, the carriage lamp swinging, and from inside one of the girls
gave a little shriek of excitement, and a bubble of conversation swelled,
and they were underway.

Sarah did not see it, because she avoided looking at him; and Mrs
Hill did not see it, because she only noticed how fine he looked in his

livery; even Mr Hill did not remark upon it, and he tended to be on the lookout for shortcomings; but James was all too aware of how his hands shook, and that the trembling would be communicated down the reins, all the way to the delicate flesh of the horses' mouths, and could make them all skittish and jumpy.

But they knew the way better than he did, so he let them get on with it, enjoying the comfortable sway of the carriage, and intervening only so as to keep them on the left, in case something brisker than their own conveyance might thunder through. And the horses, sensing they were trusted, held their heads high, picked up their feet smartly; and Jane, inside the coach, said to her mother what a capable young fellow James had turned out to be, and Mrs Bennet agreed that the ride was both brisk and comfortable, much more so than when old Mr Hill had driven them about.

James turned up his greatcoat collar, and tugged his sleeves down over his hands, and gazed out at the silvered landscape, at the soft slopes, dark copses, the fields studded with sheep. Everything seemed clean and clear and fresh. James smelt the spearmint growing in the wet ditch, and the sweetness of a hay barn as they passed, and these were, he realized, the old scents of home.

Below him, the ladies' voices twittered; the carriage was a cage filled with pretty birds. How could he ever show sufficient care? How could he ever repay the trust that that good man had placed in him? Things could change so entirely, in a heartbeat; the world could be made entirely anew, because someone was kind. He would do nothing to risk the loss of this. He would keep his head down, draw no attention to himself. He would not even look at Sarah, for all she was so very good to look at.

They descended through woods, into the nutty scent of beech-mast and the peaty smell of this year's first fallen leaves.

After the quiet of the road, Meryton was a bombardment. Iron-shod hooves and iron wheel-rims on cobbles; shouts, catcalls, laughter. The streets were choked. Ostlers and footmen yelled, horses whinnied;

passers-by rapped on carriage windows, passengers waved frantically at acquaintances spied across the street.

The stream of gigs and chaises and cabriolets thickened and slowed at the Assembly Rooms, where they discharged their cargoes. People pushed eagerly up towards the doorway, the young and light and keen weaving briskly around the grey, heavy older folk. Through the windows, James glimpsed the already teeming interior. He pulled up at the curved stone steps.

It was one of those strange handicaps that afflicted gentlefolk, that they could not open a door for themselves, nor get in or out of a coach without someone to assist them. An old man with a heron's stoop and full livery stepped forward and opened the door, so that James did not have to get down and do it himself.

The young ladies streamed out like chicks from a hencoop, rustling gowns, each of them clasping the unknown servant's hand for just a moment – a strange intimacy to allow him, it seemed to James – their faces radiant with the evening. And then Mrs Bennet, splendid in mauve, clambered out, and sailed away, her daughters tucking themselves in around her, talking and laughing and waving to other new arrivals. Then they disappeared into the crush, where it already seemed too full to accommodate another soul.

'God's sake, man! Get a move on! Get that old hulk out of the way!'

Someone slapped the back of the carriage. James clicked his tongue, told the horses to walk on.

Along the side wall of the Assembly Rooms a row of carriages waited, the overflow of the inn yard and the livery stables. The coachmen gathered there too, passing a bottle, calling out to him to join them for a sup, and he nodded them a good evening, but instead unhitched the horses and brought them back to a trough in the Market Square. When they had drunk, breaking the moon into shards and ripples, he led them back to the coach, to wait.

There was a hum of voices from inside the Assembly Rooms. Peals of laughter, and not words themselves but the shapes of talk in the air, the burr of it. Then the music started; voices fell away, and there was a thundering of feet on the wooden floor.

He buckled the horses up in blankets. Across the street, the coachmen sung out dirty words to the pretty tune. A pair of them performed a clumsy jig.

The mare clopped a hoof down on the cobbles. He patted her neck.

What was astonishing was the peace of this place. Like a pebble dropped into a stream, his arrival had made a ripple in the surface of things. He'd felt that; he'd seen it in the way they looked at him, Sarah and Mrs Hill and the little girl. But the ripples were getting fainter as they spread, and he himself was by now sunk deep and settled here; time would flow by and over him, and wedge him firmer, and he would take on the local colour of things.

But Sarah. Those clear grey eyes of hers; you could see she was always thinking. She peered at him like he was a slipped stitch: unforeseen, infuriating, just asking to be unpicked.

A yell startled him back to himself. One of the coachmen took a swing at another, and missed, staggering. There were shouted insults, laughter. James breathed on his hands, looked away.

There had been times, in the past years, when he had felt more acutely alive. When circumstances had conspired to keep him painfully alert, on his toes, on the *qui vive*, thinking three steps ahead. But that night, as he drove the carriage back from Meryton, the chill air on his face, the full moon low on the horizon and the call of a curlew across the high fields, he was happy not to think, and just to be.

And when the coach wheeled up the driveway and the horses stopped unbidden at the front steps, and Sarah, sleepy-eyed and holding a candle, opened the door and let the ladies in, he found himself strangely moved by it all. It was the warm candlelight, perhaps, after so long under the cool moon; it was also the girl's face, all soft and frowning with sleep, and the young ladies shivering at the night air and speaking quietly now, so as not to disturb their father. A scene of such simple certainty that you would think the world was just like this all over, always had been, and always would be.

Sarah, having presented the family with the tea things, dragged herself up to bed, the candlelight dancing off the walls; she would clear up their cups and plates in the morning. Though it was, now she came to think of it, already morning. She had sat up late so that Polly and Mr and Mrs Hill could sleep; there was no point in them all being exhausted the next day. And so that she could read alone: she had raced guiltily through her newly acquired book, which was volume one of two, and which was, she was sure of it, not quite respectable, for all Elizabeth had lent it to her. All those attempts on the young maid's honour, all that convenient fainting; the mere thought of being asked to read any of that out loud of an evening made her feel hot and bothered. *Pamela* was clearly for private contemplation.

There was, however, another reason for her taking it upon herself to wait up. Until she'd seen it with her own eyes, she could not feel quite certain of James's return. She would have lain awake half the night anyway, listening out for the carriage wheels on the gravel, the sound of the front door. Whatever anybody else might think of him, she knew him for the fly-by-night, drop-of-a-hat, here-today-and-gone-tomorrow fellow that he clearly was. And when he did finally go, flitting off no doubt just as suddenly as he had arrived, she wanted to be the first to have intelligence of it.

Polly was deeply asleep, breathing heavily, the whites showing through the slits of her eyes. Sarah blew out her candle and slid in beside her, shivering, clinging to the cliff-edge of the bed. She lay blinking in the darkness. What did it matter, anyway, if he stayed or went? What did it signify to her?

James lay awake too, cheek on his pillow, looking out sidelong at the dark. The old pain was bearable, because it had to be, because it would never be entirely gone. And it was something, was it not, to have this to come back to? A pillow, a pallet, a quilt. Four walls and a floor. A roof over his head. His breath plumed in the night air. It was something to come home.

Mrs Hill was not asleep either. She lay looking up at the cold stars through the skylight, while Mr Hill snored beside her, mouth gaping like the grave. She thought, Wherever you are in this world, the sky is still above you. Wherever you are, God still watches over you; He sees into your heart.

CHAPTER IX

. . . they were well supplied both with news and happiness by the recent arrival of a militia regiment in the neighbourhood; it was to remain the whole winter, and Meryton was the head quarters.

THE MILITIA HAD marched through the town, men on foot, officers on horseback. It was, Mrs Bennet announced while Mrs Hill was helping her off with her bonnet in the vestibule, quite as good as a circus.

'Oh, I wish you could have seen it, Hill. The officers in their regimentals, looking so handsome and brave.'

Outside, James heaped the pile of Mrs Bennet's purchases into Sarah's arms, then went to lead the coach away. Mrs Hill glanced out after him. There was something different about him; he looked – his features darkened by the shadow of his tricorn hat – quite washed out.

He had been worked hard, from the moment he had joined the household. Every time the coach was brought out, it was James that must drive it. Whenever there was company, it was James that must wait on them. Long drives, late nights, days spent darting around the place like a shuttlecock, serving dinners and teas to the Longs and Gouldings and Bingleys and Lucases; even when not actually in the presence of the family and their guests, he could never be properly at rest, but was obliged to wait in readiness for the bell; he could be summoned at any instant to supply further jam, or hot water, or another bottle of that excellent sherry wine, late into the night. The poor boy must be exhausted.

'What's the matter, Hill? I don't believe you are even listening!'

'I am, ma'am, of course.'

Sarah picked her way up the steps with the pile of packages, watching James's departure from the corner of her eye. She also had noted his changed demeanour. Sarah, though, did not think that he looked tired; she thought that he looked worried. As though something had crawled in under his skin, and left him feeling itchy and unclean.

'Well, take notice, Mrs Hill, for I am determined that Mr Bennet will call on the officers, and we shall invite them for a Family Dinner, two full courses, mind . . .'

People just kept on not saying. This was what Sarah could not understand. She slipped past Mrs Hill, who was helping Mrs B. out of her pelisse, and carried the purchases down the hall. She could not comprehend how it was that nobody, not Mr Bennet, not even Mrs Hill, both of whom could usually be relied upon for their perspicacity, had noticed anything untoward about this young man. The very fact that he was happy to work as an underservant at Longbourn, when he could have commanded better wages at a better house or in other trades, was suspicious in itself. And he had appeared out of nowhere that day, as if he'd been hiding in the cupboard under the stairs. And ever since, in all the weeks that he had been with them, they had learned nothing of him, beyond the stories – or rather the *lies* – that he had chosen to tell them.

She pushed the breakfast-room door open with a hip, crossed the carpet, and tumbled the packages down on the tabletop. *And* he slogged away like a navvy; it was unnatural, the way he went at his work: this was not the begrudging half-arsery they were used to from the local labourers; he was brisk and thorough, as though shovelling out the necessary house was a task that merited method and precision, rather than just a strong stomach and a clothes peg on the nose.

She arranged Mrs Bennet's purchases on the table, righting the paper-wrapped bottle from the apothecary's, smoothing out the haberdasher's parcel and turning the neat flat box from the confectioner's shop the right way up. So what was different about today? What had made him so distinctly uncomfortable?

He would have seen what Mrs B. had seen in Meryton: the officers on horseback, sabres glinting at their sides; the soldiers marching smartly, muskets shouldered.

Sarah, a hand dimpling the soft package from the draper's shop, went cold.

The Militia.

So he might be a criminal. He could be a *murderer*. He might have slipped the noose at Newgate, for all they knew – she'd read about it in the newspaper: those desperate men, the scapegallows and chancers who bribed or sneaked or fought their way out of gaol, dodged the hangman, and made a run for it. He'd fled London and made his way into the country, deep into Hertfordshire, where nobody would know him or know what he had done. He'd probably wrung a good character out of some poor victim or dupe, or an accomplice had written it for him, and then he'd used it to worm his way in here at Longbourn – a shiver grew at the back of her neck – and now he'd rob the house while they slept.

He'd murder them in their beds.

After all, what did anybody really know about him?

Well. She would know. She would find out. And they would thank her for it.

Her chance came one evening when James drove the family to Lucas Lodge, where there was a large party invited; the family was not expected back until after supper. This meant, as Mr B. pointed out with some degree of resentment, as he clambered into the carriage, that it was Liberty Hall for the remaining servantry until then.

Some took more advantage of it than others.

Mrs Hill took it as her chance to sort through the contents of the linen closet, which she had been meaning to do for some months; she would check for rust-mould, scare away the moths. Polly was to assist her in the folding and refolding; the child would benefit from the opportunity to practise the proper method. Mr Hill, meanwhile, found a more pleasant use for his time, though in all fairness an audit of the wine cellar was also long overdue. He had his own little chair down there, and a corkscrew and a glass, and if Mr Bennet happened to remark that his store of Canary or sherry wine had been depleted rather sooner than might have been expected, it was easily explained: a bottle had turned to vinegar, and was being made use of in the kitchen.

Sarah, finding herself thus briefly unobserved, snatched up a lantern, lit the candle with a spill and slipped out of the kitchen door. She skimmed across the yard and into the stables. In the candlelight, the empty stalls looked clean and soft. The place smelt of fresh straw. Whatever else James was, he was thorough: before he came the place had used to look – and smell – like a midden. She bundled her skirts up, and climbed the ladder into the loft.

No one had ever told her *not* to go into a manservant's lodgings. But then no one had ever told her not to fly up to the roof and perch beside the weather-cock. It was a thing that did not even need forbidding, being so very far beyond what could be reasonably expected of her.

She emerged, head and shoulders, into space, and set her lantern on the bare-boarded floor. The room was clean; it smelt of hay and horse and leather and sawn wood. She clambered fully up. Under the eaves was a neatly made bed covered with an old patchwork quilt. She recognized some of the patches: the blue sprig, the yellow stripe; it belonged to the house; Mrs Hill must have turfed it out for him. Above the head of the bed he had fixed a shelf; he'd left a few books there, and a spare set of men's linen, clean and carefully folded. She came close, holding up her lantern to read the books' spines, her skirts pressing against the edge of the bed, her head tilted. Hooke's *Micrographia*. Gilpin's *Observations* – she had read that; she had followed Gilpin up one side of the country and back down the other. These were both from Mr Bennet's library – they were bound in his tan-and-red calfskin. The others were probably stolen. *A Letter on the Abolition of the Slave Trade*. A cheap volume, well worn, by one William Wilberforce. He had not lied about that, then, at least. She turned, and lifted her light; she scanned the room. A chair, a table, his dark everyday coat hanging from a peg. Nothing of any great value or importance lying out; but if you had something you really needed to hide, you would put it – where? She ducked down and peeked under the bed. An old canvas backpack lay slumped on its side: there you go. She dragged it out, her skin prickling with anticipation. The straps were soft with wear; the bag had probably once been black but had faded out to grey. It could have been a pedlar's pack: this seemed to confirm everything.

Something rattled inside. Money.

On her knees beside the bed, she worked to open the buckles. A man like him with a bag of coin? It could not have been honestly got. She would spill it out onto the kitchen table and announce where she had found it. And Mrs Hill would be all amazement, and then she would praise her, and then thank her, and then she would beg her to run as quick as she could all the way to Meryton for the constable, or – even better – the Militia. And Sarah would return with a platoon at her heels, and everyone would be astonished by her pluck, her quick wits, and her good sense, and they'd cart him off to gaol to wait for the assizes.

He would notice her then; he would find himself obliged to notice her. And everybody else, who had thought he was so wonderful, would now see that she was in the right.

The second buckle came undone and she reached inside; the handful was strangely light and sharp. She drew it out into the candlelight.

They were pale, and fine, and cool to the touch. She had seen these things before. They were not money. The young ladies made picture frames and decorated boxes with them. They were sea-shells. She tipped them out onto the floor. One was shaped like a fan; it was pink and ridged on one side, and smooth as a saucer on the other. One was pale, chalky, and twirled out like a poke you'd get hot chestnuts in. One had had its outside worn away, and she saw a tiny staircase spiralling up inside. One – and she really wanted to slip this one into her pocket – was a deep inky blue on the outside, and sheened like pearl on the inner surface. She shifted them around on the floor, lining them up; she held one and then another to the light to study it: a fan, a spiral, a donkey's ear.

She should be gone. At any moment Mrs Hill and Polly would be finished with their linen closet, or Mr Hill would come stumbling up from the cellar, blurry with drink and wondering where everybody, and his supper, was.

She lifted the fan-shaped shell and turned it round, and ran a thumb down its ridged back. She sniffed it: it smelt neutral, clean, and a little of the canvas bag that it had been in. She touched it with her tongue and it was faintly salt. The mystery of James shifted and re-formed itself. She thought, How alone he is, that he must keep these secrets here.

She thought, I have no call to see this, not at all.

Sarah scooped up the shells, slid them back into the bag and buckled it. She bundled everything under the bed. Two rungs down the ladder, her lantern swinging, she stopped and looked round: had she left any sign that she had been there? But she had not stopped to think before she'd tugged the bag out and rifled through it, so there was now no way of knowing if she had put it back as it should be. She could only hope and pray that she had.

And that, when he returned, James would not just take one look at her and see right through her, and see what she had done.

She need not have concerned herself that James would see through her, because, in the event, he did not look at her at all. He just scrambled down from the carriage box, and helped the ladies out, and then he led the horses off. She stood in the vestibule with an armful of bonnets and cloaks, shivering in the draught from the open door, and watched the rear carriage lamp swing in the wind as the coach moved away. How could it be, that he could occupy her thoughts so entirely for hours and days together, that he could be the first notion that crossed her mind in the morning, and the last niggling worry at night, when – it was perfectly clear to her – she did not so much as wander across his consciousness from one day to the next? She dragged the discarded clothes to the cloak-room, and hung them up. She would take a leaf out of his book, she decided; she would do her best not to think of him at all.

It was Tuesday morning, and Sarah was lugging the swill bucket down to the sty, when she saw a man coming down the field path from the direction of town. She did not recognize him for a moment, and so stopped, and watched him approach, noting first his greatcoat, then tricorn hat and wig, and thinking him a gentleman, though it was strange that a gentleman would go on foot, particularly with the ground so wet and muddy.

But then he looked up – he had been watching where he placed his feet in the cattle-churned ground – and she saw that it was the black footman from Netherfield. And there was she, in her limp dress still patched with hogshit stains, carrying a swill bucket – she'd just keep going, and hope he hadn't seen her – but then his foot slithered, and stuck fast. He had to pause to pull it from the mud, and for a moment he was teetering, arms flung wide for balance. Their eyes caught, his with a look of alarm, but also laughter – it made her smile. He stumbled up to the stile and was half over when he wobbled. She scrambled to help him, clattering down the pig-bucket to offer him her hand.

'Bless you.' He gripped it in his gloved fingers, and stepped down onto the drier ground of the track.

'Are you all right, sir?'

'I find I have been sadly duped!'

She blinked up at him. He still held her hand.

'I was told it was a much shorter way by the fields. No one mentioned the mud.' He showed her his boots, tilting one and then the other for her inspection. They were very fine, and very filthy. 'I expect my friends at Netherfield are laughing heartily at me now.'

'I am sorry, sir.'

'And the beasts! Did you know? Have you seen them? Cows, roaming loose! Without so much as a by-your-leave! Would you credit it? They should be locked up!'

She laughed outright.

He really was astonishingly handsome, she admitted to herself: there was a degree of symmetry to his features that was not often seen; at least not by her. Those liquid eyes. The way they lingered on her made her feel a trifle hot and bewildered.

'What brings you here, sir?' she tried.

'Oh, please don't "sir" me—'

'Mister.'

He rifled in an inside pocket. 'I've been sent with a communication,' he said, and made a show of peering at it. 'For Miss Bennet.'

'Go on up to the house then, if you will. Everyone is at home.'

She gestured up the track. He bowed smartly, and went.

Swinging the pig-bucket, she strode on down to the sty. He was just a wonderment. His manners, his looks, the way he spoke to her; his colour was no longer a thing of note, compared with the stunning strangeness of all this courtesy. She slopped the peelings and scraps into the trough, and spun away, leaving the pigs to their snuffly munching. She raced back up to the kitchen with the empty bucket banging against her leg.

The new mister was sitting by the fire, and James had already taken the note – a folded and sealed little sheet of hot-pressed paper, very elegant, Mrs Hill remarked – upstairs, to the noisy delight of the ladies assembled there. The noise and the delight reached them, even in the kitchen; its passage there was facilitated by Polly's pushing the door open, and leaning on the threshold, the better to hear what was being said. Jane was invited to dinner at Netherfield! Unlucky that Mr Bingley was dining out with the officers, but still; this was a very good thing indeed, that his sisters were keen to show her such particular attention.

'Can I have the carriage?' This was Jane.

'No, my dear, you had better go on horseback, because it seems likely to rain; and then you must stay all night.'

The mister crossed his legs, and his boot shed a clump of mud on the hearth. Mrs Hill gave him an equally dirty look.

'I am,' he announced, 'awaiting a reply.'

He looked around him in an interested kind of way, taking in the kitchen and its appurtenances with the benign air of a person of some substance visiting the poor, to assess what relief they might be granted.

'Pleasant little place, this,' he observed.

Sarah, having seen the Netherfield kitchen, felt the undertow of condescension, but also that what he said was kindly meant.

Then James returned with a note, written on the best paper the household could supply. He offered it to the footman, who took it, thanked him handsomely, and stood to stow it away in an inner pocket.

Sarah saw the place, and them all, as he must see them. It was so small and mean and poor, compared with Netherfield. The dark cramped kitchen, Polly staring like a frog, Mrs Hill brusque to the point of rudeness, James stiff and formal and distant, and she herself a bundle of sticks wrapped in an old rag. What impression they must make, the shambling lot of them. At least Mr Hill was elsewhere, so they were at least spared his tooth-sucking and his scowls.

With another glance down at his muddied boots, and a wry smile at Sarah, he buttoned up his coat, which he hadn't taken off, and set his hat down on top of his wig.

'Back out into the mire,' he said. '*Au revoir*, then.'

'Goodbye.'

Mrs Hill's jaw shut tight like a trap; she did not so much as glance at him.

Sarah wanted to say something to him, to explain, to excuse. She wanted to tell him that she thought that he was lovely, and that she was very sorry they were not lovelier themselves. But she just bobbed her curtsey, and when he had left the kitchen, she leaned at the doorjamb, staring out after him. Mrs Hill, scraping a vanilla pod into the cooling custard, watched her watching.

'Fancy the Bingleys keeping a mulatto as a servant,' the housekeeper said. 'I wonder what Mrs Nicholls makes of that.'

'Perhaps they couldn't get an ordinary man,' said Polly.

'I hear it's quite the fashion,' Mrs Hill said. 'Though I'm not sure I would care for it myself.'

'I think he's lovely.'

Mrs Hill glared at Sarah's heedless back, then blew a puff of breath up her face. 'You wouldn't know what a man like that would get up to. You don't know what kind of grudges he would be holding. You wouldn't feel safe in your bed.'

Then James, who had been silent all this time, came and stood beside Sarah in the doorway. He stayed there a long moment without saying anything. And then he said, 'It is coming on to rain.'

CHAPTER X

. . . several of the officers had dined lately with their uncle, a private had been flogged, and it had actually been hinted that Colonel Forster was going to be married.

I T RAINED HARD. It bounced off the flagstones, bumbled down the gutters, juddered out of the down-spouts. The women sat inside over their sewing. James mended the links on an old bridle. Mr Hill hid in his pantry, cleaning glassware, and picking his remaining teeth with a long fingernail.

''Course, Jane might have beat the weather.' Polly let her darning fall to her lap. 'She might be safe and dry. She might have galloped all the way to Netherfield.'

Silence between then, and the rain hissing down. Whether wet or dry, Jane would not be returning home tonight.

'I'll take you for a ride one day, if you like, Pol?'

She grinned. She did not mind being called Pol if it was James who called her it.

'Not a gallop, mind, I don't think the old girl's quite up to it.'

And the footman – she had not yet thought to ask his name – Sarah wondered: would he have got back to Netherfield in time, or would he be soaked through to his barley-malt skin?

The rain continued all evening without a break. It was still hammering down when the servants retired for the night. James had to dash across the yard with a sack over his shoulders and head, to keep

79

off the worst of the water. He could have gone to his room earlier, and read quietly there, since he had his own allowance of candles; instead he kept to the closeness and company of the kitchen. Today had seen something of an awakening: a quiet, unshared revelation. James had seen how the new man from Netherfield had looked at Sarah. He had noticed, too, how she had looked at him. And all of this gave James an unsteady feeling, as though the ground beneath him had started to swell and shift like the sea.

He would keep an eye out for her, he told himself, just friendly-like. He owed it to Mr B. to be alert to anything that might disturb the household's tranquillity. Which is why he sat on with the women when he could have been quietly reading in his room. And there was, he had to admit it, such a pleasure in her proximity. To feel her breathe, to hear the rustle of her skirts, a sweet word or two spoken to little Polly. It was good.

The footman returned the following morning. He was mucked up to the knees, his greatcoat heavy and wet, and his wig limp, its powder running down his coat in milky streams. Sarah had an armful of eggy plates from breakfast, and cast desperately around for some way to be rid of them. Still on the threshold, he took off his hat and shook the water off it. He reached inside his coat, and produced a rather damp-looking letter.

'For Miss Elizabeth Bennet.'

James looked from Sarah to the footman and back again. Mr and Mrs Hill being occupied elsewhere, the three of them stood alone in the kitchen. It was clearly James's duty to take the missive up, but then that would leave Sarah alone with the footman.

'Will you take it?' he asked her.

'It's for you to do, isn't it?'

James bowed stiffly, took the note and strode off upstairs to the breakfast room, where Mrs Hill was serving the family their coffee. He waited, fidgeting all the time that it was being read and exclaimed over.

Down in the kitchen, alone with the Netherfield footman now,

Sarah said, 'Terrible wet, this weather . . .' and then quailed at her own dullness. Thankfully he did not seem to notice it: he flumped down in the fireside chair, and stretched out his arms and booted feet, to show her the state that he was in.

'This Hertfordshire mud has a will of its own, I'd swear to it. It latches on and climbs. In London,' he said, 'with the paving and the arcades, you can go about whatever the weather, it can rain stair-rods and you won't even get your feet wet.'

'You're from London, then?'

She handed him a cup of tea. He seemed mildly surprised by it, and glanced around the kitchen, but observing nothing more to his taste, he took the cup.

'I lived there for a time. With the old master, and then the new.'

She sat down opposite, and drew her chair a little closer.

'Tell me; what's it like?'

He told her about Astley's Royal Amphitheatre, where they performed feats of horsemanship, and juggling and acrobatics. And then about the pleasure gardens at Vauxhall, where there was music and dancing. He told her about a beggar that he knew, an acquaintance of his, quite a gentleman, who sang sea shanties and wore a model ship on his head, so that when he danced it was tossed around as though it rode upon a stormy sea.

'And there are fireworks at night, so splendid and noisy that even the old soldiers say they never saw anything like it.'

James returned more swiftly than Sarah could have anticipated.

'Do you wait for a reply?'

'If there is one.'

'Well, there isn't.'

Buttoning up his greatcoat, the footman was gone with a wink, trudging off out into the grizzling morning. Sarah went to the window to watch him go. It was such a glorious thing, to know that he was around now, that he might wander in at any time, and want to have a cup of tea with her, and tell her about London.

'Miss Jane is ill.'

James said this with more emphasis than it really merited; after all, the young lady had only caught a chill.

He was rewarded with the barest glance.

'She got caught out in the rain like we thought she would, and now has a chill, and is laid up at Netherfield.'

'Oh,' said Sarah.

'So Miss Elizabeth is going to her.'

This was, as far as Sarah was concerned, not the worst news she could have heard. If Jane must be ill, then it was better that she be ill at the Bingleys' house than at home: they had an army there to care for her, but at Longbourn sickness meant so much extra work to be shared between so few; the sickroom linen, the handkerchiefs, the special drinks and treats and little meals, the running up and down stairs with it all. It was considerate – just like Jane – to be ill away from home.

'All will be well, then,' Sarah said.

For him, the moment stretched like wool on tenters. There must be no slip, no hint, of the trouble she was causing him. The urge to speak, to touch: that must be bitten back and shoved down and locked away tight.

Sarah, on the other hand, was busily burying her guilt about going through his things, by heaping irritation and outrage over it: why could Mr Smith not take her into his confidence like this new fellow did? Why did not James tell her about all his travels, about where he had come from, and where he had been? *He* did not volunteer anything, *he* just remained taciturn and uncivil. No wonder she had misunderstood him. No wonder she had spied . . .

He drew a breath; she flinched, and looked round.

He just said, 'Well.'

And then he left, following the other man out into the rainy yard, and she tutted, and turned away, and went back to her work.

Elizabeth's departure, once the rain had stopped, caused no particular trouble to anyone below stairs. She just put on her walking shoes and buttoned up her good spencer, threw a cape over it all, and grabbed an umbrella just in case the rain came on again. Such self-sufficiency was to be valued in a person, but seeing her set off down the track, and then climb the stile, Sarah could not help but think that those stockings would be perfectly ruined, and that petticoat would never be the same again, no matter how long she soaked it. You just could not get mud out of pink Persian. Silk was too delicate a cloth to boil.

Neighbours called during the day. Sir William Lucas and his daughter Charlotte sat a while, but they were no trouble either, and did not stay to dinner. Elizabeth was expected back for the meal, but as preparations – and the clock's hands – advanced and there was still no sign of her, Mrs Hill began to despair of her returning in time to assist with the eating of the gravy-pie; if only the Lucases had been prevailed upon to remain. At half past four, when the pie was waiting on the kitchen table, and would, if not served promptly, have to be eaten cold, that same mulatto footman of Mr Bingley's flung open the kitchen door and stood there letting out the warmth while he scraped the mud off his boots. It seemed he did not find this amusing any more.

'It is blasted cold out there.'

He had brought a note from Elizabeth this time. She would not, she informed the family, be returning for dinner, but would instead remain at Netherfield to take care of Jane until she was well enough to travel. Elizabeth requested a supply of clothes for them both. On hearing this news – Mr Bennet reading it aloud over the dinner table for the benefit of the assembled family, and to shame his wife for her reckless-ness with her eldest daughter's health – Mrs Hill set off immediately to pack a bag for the young ladies. Mrs Bennet followed a little after, once she had finished up her dinner.

She arrived in the girls' room when Mrs Hill's work was almost done, and proceeded to undo it, whisking one gown away to exchange it for another, demanding that Mrs Hill cease packing and wait while she had a think, and then standing lost in calculation and a drift of clothes as she considered the benefits and disadvantages of each of Jane's bonnets, gowns, caps and capes. The contents of the valise spilt out like an over-boiling pan.

'No, no, not that gown, for Mr Bingley saw her in it at the Lucases', and will think she has not another one as good.'

What Miss Jane would want with chilly evening-gowns or worked muslin or fancy bonnets when she was confined to her room by sickness, or why Mr Bingley would be expected to concern himself with what she wore, since he would not see her anyway, Mrs Hill could not imagine, but she was too absorbed in wardrobe mathematics to pay her mistress any real attention: Jane had arrived at Netherfield in a good dinner-dress and cloak, which would have been soaked through; the servants there would have dried them out and sponged off any mud by now, and meanwhile the ladies would have lent her a gown and shawl for the evening, as well as a nightgown on seeing she was to stay the night. So what Jane needed now were nightclothes of her own, a couple of shawls and a good day-dress for when she was able to sit up again. Elizabeth, on the other hand, would have arrived muddy after her walk: she would need a good gown to dine in, a plain day-dress to nurse her sister in, and a pair of decent shoes for around the house, and linen. For all she understood Mrs Bennet's eagerness to make a good impression, anything else was just silliness, and would be seen as such by the servants over there.

When Mrs Bennet turned away, saying she would just find Jane's dancing shoes, Mrs Hill slammed the valise shut and buckled it. If she did not get that black dandy out of the kitchen sharpish, who knew what trouble would come of it. He'd have Sarah's head turned entirely.

At Mrs Bennet's outraged glare, she said, 'We'd risk spoiling the gowns, ma'am, if we crammed anything more in there.'

Then Mrs Hill hurried off with her burden, before Mrs B. could either protest, or congratulate her housekeeper on her good thinking.

The pair of them – Sarah and the mulatto – were facing each other in the chairs by the fire, he stretched out and at his leisure, she leaning forward, hands on knees, eyes bright, her kerchief falling away to reveal rather too much of her bosom. The talk stopped the moment Mrs Hill came into the kitchen. Sarah looked flushed and far too animated for

Mrs Hill's liking; the housekeeper strode over and dropped the valise in the footman's lap. He winced.

'There you go,' she said. 'Safe home, now.'

He made charmingly heavy weather of his new burden, pretending to puff and crumple under its weight, shaking his head and tutting in mock outrage. This made Sarah laugh, which seemed to satisfy him; he left, doffing his hat to her. Mrs Hill closed the door on him; then, hands on hips, she watched Sarah brushing the ashes together on the hearth, swirling them into patterns, heaps, then sweeping them out flat again. The girl's thoughts were, clearly, not on her work.

The following day, Mrs Hill dispatched Sarah to Meryton with a request for a loaf of good sugar from the grocer. There was not a scrap of the stuff left in the house. She must have it home in time for dinner, as it was needed for the baked apples. Mrs Hill was very sorry to inconvenience her, but she was obliged to ask the favour. She was far too busy to go herself. And so the girl now would be out of the way, when that fellow next came calling.

'Can I go too?' asked Polly.

'No. I can't have everyone gadding about. I need you to scrub. Get the rags out, and the cold tea. We're doing the hall and vestibule floors.'

'Bah,' said Polly. 'When Miss Jane marries Mr Bingley, there'll be no need to go to Meryton for sugar. We will have mountains of sugar-loaves, we'll build a house out of it. We'll bathe in syrup.'

'That,' said Sarah, 'would not be very pleasant.'

She took off her apron, and fetched her bonnet, before Mrs Hill could change her mind.

Sarah, with the ragged old crow of an umbrella folded under her arm, and the old blue pelisse warm on her shoulders, walked out of the kitchen light of heart: this seemed as good as a fête-day. To be out, with nothing but a mile of fresh air ahead of her, with nothing very much to carry and no one to tell her what to do, this was a pleasure indeed. Mrs Hill wouldn't notice if a crumb of the sugarloaf went missing. The walk back would be sweetened: the prospect of a dinner she had not made herself, on her return, was really quite delightful.

Her boots were soon heavy and damp, and the left one rubbed a blister on her heel, but the way through the fields was better on foot than the turnpike, where the post-chaises and mail-coaches bowled by, making you throw yourself into the ditch, or risk the pounding hooves, the flying wheels.

The handsome footman – he so dazzled her that she kept on forgetting to ask his name – didn't like the mud. He was a pretty bird, a parakeet; the weather weighed him down. And if *he* was a parakeet, then Mr Smith was a collie-dog: the weather made no impression on him at all, however much cold or dirt or rain was flung at him: his mind and soul were fixed upon the work in hand. And she – well, the weather didn't bother her that much either way. If you got wet, you'd get dry again. There was no point in complaining in the meantime.

She thought, though, how beautiful those Vauxhall Gardens must be, after the rain.

The footpath joined the riverbank, and followed it into Meryton. The river was fat and full and dimpling; the millpond brimmed and the wheel thundered round on its frothing race.

It was not raining now, but the sky was heavy and low, and it brought a strange dusk to the backstreets; the shadows were bruised and purple, the stones and walls and cobbles a queasy green.

She passed the tannery, with its death-and-dogshit reek, and the blind walls of the poorhouse, where no lights were lit despite the darkness of the day. Back-alleys opened off to left and right, where half-naked children made dams and pools in the gutters and women hunched on their doorsteps under shawls, bundled babies in their arms. The shambles, when she passed them, were deserted, but were filled with their usual miasma of terror, of ammonia-and-blood.

It was so quiet.

She moved on, through the backstreets. It was usually lively and familiar here: the weavers leaning in the doorways, talking politics; the women in a cheerful cluster at the pump. They knew who she was, whose daughter she had been. Today only those who could do no better were out of doors. Today there was just defeated silence, and the drip from patched rooves.

It started to rain again, a drenching haze; she opened her umbrella. On the corner ahead stood one of Meryton's principal inns, its half-timbered face turned towards the buying and selling of Market Street, its flank towards this damp lane. Round the corner, and she'd be out into the wider, more populated streets. She quickened her pace. She'd go straight to the grocer's and get the sugar, then she'd call at the apothecary's and see what report Mr Jones could give of Jane. And then – she'd brought her own penny with her – she'd buy a bun at the pastry-cook's and she'd march straight home along the turnpike eating it, and take her chance with the carriages, rather than come back this dark way again.

She came alongside the inn yard. Last time she had passed this way, it had been market day, and the yard had been alive with the come-and-go of farmers with their heavy, gentle horses. But today the space behind the curving lime-washed walls was different: they had been building there. The structure was rough, its unseasoned timbers streaked with damp. It looked like a cowshed. It covered half the yard.

The barracks, Mrs Bennet had said. They were building barracks for the soldiers.

There was a new sound, too; she noticed it for the first time then. A hum of gathered voices. Men's voices.

She quickened her pace, umbrella tilted to shield her from their notice. She passed the gateway, and though she could not see, she could feel that something was going on in there. That something was swelling up and ready to burst.

But a few more paces and she would be out into Market Street. She would go to the grocer's and buy the sugar and talk about the weather and the shocking state of the roads. She didn't *have* to look into the yard, where the men were gathered. She would be much better off not looking: they were all the more likely to notice her if she did. But she lifted the umbrella a little, and glanced in.

The yard was made narrow by the new building; it was now little more than a dank alleyway between the raw wood and the boundary wall. Red-coated soldiers were packed tight at the far end, corralled there by some invisible restraint. Not one of them even glanced at her. She kept on walking, though everything seemed to have slowed, every moment seemed to linger; she took a step, and the angle of her sight-line shifted, and she saw what it was that kept the men pinned back there, their faces turned aside.

It was at the hitching post, just inside the gateway. It stood between them and her.

Her senses, briefly, could not accommodate the image.

Then it was a pig. A carcass. A great slab of meat waiting to be skinned.

Then her perceptions shifted again, true patterns formed: she saw the shape of human muscle, shoulder blade, a dark slick of hair, the cable-twist of neck.

In the instant that she saw, she looked away, but by then it was too late. The image pressed itself upon her sight like a die into sealing wax. His skin was lurid in the dull light, his cheek hazed with greying stubble and flattened against the dark weathered wood. His eyes were wide and rolling, his jaw clenched. His body, held immobile by the bonds, was fiercely at work: his arm muscles shifted and twisted, his feet trod and braced against the cobbles like a horse's.

At the end of the yard, the redcoats stirred, muttered; some were very young – one, a boy of perhaps fourteen, looked as if he might cry, but not one of them could turn their gaze towards the shackled man. The crowd shuffled itself, and a man emerged; stripped to his shirt-sleeves, coiling a whip in his hand, he did not look at the prisoner either.

She was almost past the gateway now, the rain chill on her cheek, and as she passed, she saw the point to which the men's attention was fixed; the final point in this web of complicity. A clutch of officers stood to one side of the gateway, lolling by the wall, looking fine and bright in their regimentals. There were one or two of middling age, and a few who were younger. One of them was so smooth-cheeked he could almost have been a girl. He was looking green.

The officers were at their ease, engaged in discussion; the man with the whip, the prisoner, the boys in uniform, all waited on their word.

'Well, Chamberlayne, what d'you say?' This was an older man. 'Are you fit for this?'

'Yes, Colonel Forster, sir.' Chamberlayne. This was the smooth-cheeked boy.

'He does look rather queasy.'

'I do not. I just – there was something wrong with that ale.'

'You haven't got the stomach for *something*, that's for sure.'

'Give over, Denny. Twenty lashes is not nothing.'

'Yes, sir. Sorry, Captain Carter, sir.'

'They need it, you know, Chamberlayne,' said the older man – the colonel. 'They're nothing without discipline. They're incapable of self-control, and so it falls to us to control them. We would be remiss in our duty if we neglected this. Failure to salute an officer; that's rank insubordination, that is.'

Now Sarah was beyond the sight of it all, passing along the outside of the long whitewashed wall; she could still hear the voices coming clear through the quiet and the rain.

Chamberlayne's piping tones again: 'If we could but get it over with, I would be quite well.'

'Well then, Sergeant. You heard the officer, and you know your business.'

'Sir.'

She felt it in the air, her skin bristling. A breath's pause, as the men fell into alignment. Then the whip hissed. The thwack and slice of it.

The prisoner cried out. Sarah pressed a hand to her mouth.

'One,' the sergeant called.

Another hiss and thunk of the whip. The man screamed. Sarah let the umbrella fall aside. She put her hand to the wet stone wall.

Another pause. The lash snapping out again. Another cry.

She was sure she would be sick. She stood there, heart pounding.

Twenty? If they went on like that they would kill him. She should go back, put herself between him and the pain; they would have to stop. The whip cracked out again. She closed her eyes, and the darkness swam. The snap; the scream. Again, and again. His cries getting weaker now.

And she just stumbled away, feet tangling in wet skirts, hand tracing the wall, unsteady, the umbrella swinging out to one side, rain in her face.

Soon after Sarah had left, the mulatto (why always him? Did not Mr Bingley possess a single other footman to send scampering about the countryside?) arrived with another note from Miss Elizabeth.

He chucked Polly under the chin, shook James's grudging hand, looked around the kitchen with an enquiring air.

'Where's, um—'

'The skivvy?' Mrs Hill asked.

'Um, I suppose yes. The pretty chick.'

Mrs Hill handed Elizabeth's note to James, and jerked her head in the direction of the parlour. He went.

'Elsewhere,' she said.

She offered the footman nothing; not tea, not even a seat, and certainly no further information about Sarah. They could have met each other on the path, she realized; it was mere good luck that they had not. She would have to think of some other means of keeping Sarah out of his clutches. And he would have to satisfy himself with a quick reply in the form of a folded note from Mrs Bennet, and be on his merry way.

But as she watched him off the premises, Mrs Hill congratulated herself on the effectiveness of her scheme. He'd soon fix his interests elsewhere, on more likely prospects. He wasn't the kind to hang around.

In the grocer's shop, Sarah folded the umbrella and asked for a loaf of sugar, and the grocer, instead of simply parcelling it up and noting it to the Bennets' account, peered at her and said, 'My dear, are you quite well?'

'I am, thank you kindly.'

'You are as white as salt. You must take something.'

He called his daughter out from the back kitchen; a plump dark-eyed thing, she ushered Sarah through to warm herself and drink tea.

A little while later the grocer put his head round the door to inspect the two of them, and said they had succeeded in putting some roses back into Sarah's cheeks at least, which was good, because earlier he had feared that the walk back to Longbourn would be entirely too much for her, and that she would be found dead in a ditch in the morning.

James, contrary to his habits, was getting under Mrs Hill's feet, and was suddenly talkative. He had been there and back to Netherfield with Mrs Bennet and a carriage full of young ladies, and had passed through Meryton twice that day: why had she not thought to ask him to fetch the sugar, and save Sarah the trouble? He hovered at the window, and when she shifted him from there to get at the pot of parsley on the sill, he moved only far enough to get in her way when she turned back again.

'Excuse me please, Mr Smith.'

He stepped aside to let her pass, and went back to his post. He rubbed the mist off a pane. 'It's getting dark.'

'It's just overcast. It's been grey all day.'

'Yes. And now it's getting dark.'

Mrs Hill heaved the fish-kettle onto the table. 'She has another hour or so, I'd say, before the sun sets.'

He frowned, nodded. A moment later, though: 'She should be back by now, really, shouldn't she? She should have been back hours ago.'

The implications of his behaviour whirled around Mrs Hill's head like a flock of starlings as she lifted the dripping fish from the kettle and laid it on the platter. So he was taken with the little scrap. Well, fancy that. And if Sarah liked him back – so long as that mulatto could be prevented from turning her head completely – things could be very nicely settled here indeed. James and Sarah married. She would not object to that, no, not at all; and if she did not, how could anybody else?

'There,' she said, and tapped the platter with a stubby nail. 'Fish is ready. Take it up now, please.'

He glanced non-committally at the tench. Then he turned back to the window.

'She'll be back before dinner's eaten. Don't fret.'

'I'm not fretting.'

His anxiety was becoming infectious: Mrs Hill did now feel a faint stirring of unease. Could Sarah have somehow come to grief?

'The dinner's getting cold.'

He heaved himself away from the window, caught up a tea-cloth, and lifted the dish.

'She's a sensible girl,' Mrs Hill said. 'And we are very quiet around here. We are not used to any kind of trouble.'

'Yes,' he said. 'Of course.'

'And who would bother a respectable young woman, with the Militia stationed so near by?'

There was a flicker of hesitation, but he nodded his agreement.

'We are fortunate in that,' Mrs Hill said. 'We may consider ourselves well protected.'

He looked at the fish, lying dull-eyed and blistered on the plate. He'd give it until the dinner things were cleared, and if Sarah wasn't back by then, he'd go out looking for her.

He did not have to go far. From the blustery crest of the hill he spotted her. She was trudging along the low road that curved round the base of the hill. Why she'd chosen to come that heavy slow way, rather than by the footpath through the fields, he could not fathom.

The sight of her spun something suddenly loose inside him; he let a breath go, and it was borne away by the wind.

He hunkered down against the field wall and watched her labour on through the mud, skirts wind-torn and wrapping around her legs. She looked so slight and flimsy, as though she could be blown clean away.

When she was gone some twenty yards or so along the road, he got back to his feet and scrambled down the hillside. He tailed her home, keeping her in sight until she slipped through the gates; he waited by the gatepost while she trudged up the gravel drive and trailed round the side of the house; she looked deeply cold, and deeply tired. When she had passed round the corner, he scudded over to it, and crouched there to watch her reach the stable buildings and cross the yard. Then she slipped inside the kitchen, and the door closed behind her.

He took himself into the stables, where the horses were twitchy with the rattling, gusting wind. He stroked their necks, and gentled them: it soothed his nerves as well as theirs. He rubbed his hair dry, and left his greatcoat to drip from a nail.

He had been concerned for her; that was all. No one here seemed to have any real notion of the world. This was innocence as deep and dangerous as a quarry-pit. He, though, he knew. He knew that men were capable of many things, and had come to believe, indeed, that some men were not really men at all, for all that they walked and talked and prayed and ate and slept and dressed themselves like men. Give them just time and opportunity enough, and they'd reveal themselves to be cold creatures with strange appetites, who did not care what harm they did in satisfying them.

While James was toiling through the wind and mud, out looking for Sarah, Mrs Hill was climbing the stairs with a laden tray. She shouldered into the parlour; the remaining Bennet family brightened at the arrival of coffee and biscuits. Kitty and Lydia dropped their work – if picking apart perfectly good bonnets to make them up a little less well could really be considered work – and came over to the table. Mrs B. and Mary peered across to inspect the refreshments; even Mr B. folded his paper and put it aside and said, 'Good, good.' It all seemed perfectly pleasant to them. But in Mrs Hill now grew an unhappy pre-occupation: James's worry worried her. What had he seen, what had he done, what did he know that they did not?

*

Sarah was, of course, returned to them quite safe, though fatigued, bedraggled, and chilled. She set down the sugarloaf and sank into a chair by the fire. Polly came sidling through from the scullery, chewing a fingernail.

'We were just beginning to be worried, missy.'

Sarah blinked at Mrs Hill; it seemed like an age since she had left; it seemed like a different world.

'The ways are heavy, missus; slow going in all that mud.'

Sarah shivered. Polly snuck up to her and huddled in close, looking for comfort. Her thumb slid into her mouth.

'Don't do that, Polly, love. You're a big girl now.'

Polly smiled around her thumb, nudged in closer to Sarah. The words came muffled: 'You're all hot!'

'Am I? I feel cold.'

Mrs Hill frowned at this, and laid a hand on Sarah's head. Her frown deepened. Sarah made no objection to being given warm milk with honey, and sent early to bed.

When James came into the kitchen a little later, perfectly dry and tidy and looking as though he hadn't been up to anything much at all, Sarah was not there, and Mrs Hill had a stiff and defensive air about her. Polly informed him with a kind of awe that Sarah had gone and got herself tired out and frozen stiff and had had to be sent off early to bed.

The sugarloaf, well wrapped at the grocer's, kept close all the way home, was sitting on the table, nestling in its unfurled wrappings. He touched its smooth translucency with a fingertip, expecting ice, but finding it neutral, with a hint of her body's lingering warmth.

Upstairs, in the attic, stripped out of her wet clothes and ducked into her nightgown and with a shawl around her shoulders and bedsocks tugged up to her knees, Sarah lay shuddering beneath her blankets. Eyes shut tight, she saw the deathly white of the man's skin. She heard still his outraged cries, the sickening way they weakened and died away.

CHAPTER XI

Bingley urged Mr Jones's being sent for immediately; while his sisters, convinced that no country advice could be of any service, recommended an express to town for one of the most eminent physicians.

ON FRIDAY, SARAH burnt to the touch; her head rolled on the pillow; she muttered. Mrs Hill came up, or sent Polly, when she could, with broth or tea, and they would prop her up and spoon a little between her chattering teeth. But the attics were a long way from the kitchen and it was not often that someone could get away, and there was certainly little time to stay and comfort her.

If Sarah was not better in a couple of days, Mrs Hill would ask Mrs Bennet if she might send for the apothecary. Or she might beg a drop of the mistress's Cordial Balm of Gilead. That preparation had never been known to fail Mrs Bennet, but at half a guinea a bottle you didn't go dishing it out to servants without very good cause.

Downstairs, James chewed at the inside of his cheek, and got on with his work, and asked after Sarah much more frequently than either Polly or Mrs Hill were able to go and check on her. If Mrs Hill had known the truth of it – that he allowed himself to enquire only a tiny fraction of the number of times that he actually wanted to – then she would have felt her suspicions about his feelings to be entirely confirmed.

On Saturday, Sarah was cooler, and could sit up. Polly brought apples and nuts, and when Sarah couldn't eat them, Polly cracked and crunched them herself and looked at the older girl appraisingly.

'Is there anything you *would* like?'

'I can't think of a thing.'

Polly held up a finger, got up, and dashed off. She returned a few minutes later with a jar of bramble jelly and a spoon.

'Missus won't miss it,' Polly said.

As sparrows to Our Lord, so the contents of her larder to Mrs Hill. Every single item must be accounted for; Sarah knew it. She made Polly promise to return the jar unopened.

'Only if *you* promise to hurry up and get better. It's miserable with you stuck in here. I miss you.'

Polly was, for the duration of Sarah's illness, obliged to share the Hills' bedroom. She had a little pallet on the floor.

'They both snore like pigs! And he's a terrible old crack-fart.'

'Polly!'

'He *is*. He's windier than the horses.'

On Sunday, when Mrs Hill came into the kitchen to stoke up the fires and get the kettle on, for a quick cup of tea before the morning service, she found Sarah already there, up and dressed and kneading dough for the breakfast rolls. She was, though, seated at the table; she must be feeling as yet unequal to being on her feet for any length of time. And she was still waxy-looking. She would have to stay home from church.

'Well,' said Mrs Hill, laying her hand on her forehead, and finding it quite cool, 'I am glad to see you up and about.'

'I wanted to be busy,' Sarah said.

The long, dull Sunday morning was broken neatly in two by the arrival of the Bingleys' carriage, with Elizabeth and Jane inside it.

Sarah stood shivering in the thin wind, her shawl wrapped around her, as the family bustled up the steps and indoors. Jane herself was wan and weak-looking, but she withstood her mother's protests –

about the trouble she had put the Bingleys to, in using their carriage – with her usual calm resolve. The noise, the bother: it now washed over Sarah without touching her. The family's concerns, though they were flapped and fussed over and made the most of, seemed far away and tiny now; they did not signify.

The black footman handed the valise down to James, and James carried it indoors, and she, with a quick glance to see she was not observed – and everyone was gone inside – came up to him.

'I haven't seen you for a while,' he said. 'Not these past few days. And I've been back and forth like a fiddler's arm.'

'I've been poorly.'

'What's your name? No one tells me anything.'

'Sarah.'

He touched his hat. 'Ptolemy Bingley. At your service.'

His first name was strange enough, but: 'How can you be a Bingley?'

'If you are off his estate, that's your name, that's how it works.' He climbed back up to his place on the footplate, and took a long look at her. 'They've worn you out, have they?'

'I caught a chill.' She wrapped her shawl tighter, goosepimpling.

'You have to take care of yourself, chick. No one else is going to do it for you.'

She was conscious of the other Netherfield men – the second footman and the coachman – and the silent communication between them, of glances and raised eyebrows.

'Where is this place,' she asked, 'where everyone's called Bingley?'

'Ah, God, now, you wouldn't catch a chill there.'

'Is it warm, then?'

'As a bath.'

She hesitated. The coachman clicked his tongue, and the horses stepped and blew.

'I hope you'll be back to Longbourn soon, Mr Bingley,' she said.

'Ptolemy. Tol. They do seem to keep finding me good cause.'

Then the wheels started to ease round, the gravel crunched; he touched his hat to her again, and then was underway. She watched the carriage roll off, and felt an uneasy kind of gratification. The only thing of which she was certain now, was that she would not go on like this for ever. Things were cut adrift, and shifting, and nothing could continue as it had been.

End of Volume One

VOLUME TWO

Chapter I

'About a month ago I received this letter, and about a fortnight ago I answered it, for I thought it a case of some delicacy, and requiring early attention.'

WITH JANE AND Elizabeth returned to the bosom of their family, and Sarah's restoration to something like good health, Mrs Hill might have allowed herself to hope that familiar routines would be resumed, that there could be a resumption of what might be thought of as normality.

If such an expectation had indeed blossomed in her heart, it was quashed entirely the following day, by an announcement of Mr Bennet's over breakfast. His cousin, Mr Collins, was expected that very afternoon, and was to stay with them until the Saturday se'night following. Having imparted this information to his family, he left them with their crumbs and coffee dregs and retired to the library, the better to relish his *coup de théâtre*. His escape was not entirely successful, however. Mrs Hill followed him to his place of refuge. She slipped round the door without knocking.

'This gentleman is to be stopping with us for twelve days, Mr Bennet?'

Mr Bennet nodded.

'And this being the very day that he is expected to arrive?'

Mr Bennet shook out his copy of the *Courier*. 'It is exactly as you observe.'

'You must know, sir, that I am not at all prepared for this.'

'And yet,' said Mr Bennet, 'barring acts of God or bandits, he shall be with us by four o'clock.' He lifted his watch deliberately from his waistcoat pocket and examined it. 'And it wants but fifteen minutes till eleven. Tick tock, Mrs Hill. Tick tock.'

'This is most unkind, sir.'

He slipped his watch away. 'And that is unfair, Mrs Hill. This is merely a question of practicalities, not kindness. All you have to do is what we employ you to do.' He tucked his chin into the folds of his neck-cloth, shook out the paper again. 'And you had better be getting on, don't you think?'

Mrs Hill drew breath to protest, but then caught herself: it was – it always was – a waste of time to argue with him. This was a punishment. He had waited till this moment to dish it out, but she had earned it a couple of months ago by speaking her mind to him when James had first joined the household. If she made another objection now, he would just notch it up against her on that secret tally he kept, and bide his time. So let him enjoy this little victory: she would just get on with what must be done, and pretend it did not hurt her. She dropped him a curtsey and clapped the library door shut behind her, and clattered up the stairs to the guest room.

Mr Bennet well knew what Mr Collins meant to her, to all of them below stairs. They were safe at Longbourn only while Mr Bennet's heart kept ticking: beyond that, they were dependent entirely on this stranger's will. And it had always been Mrs Hill's intention that, should that gentleman ever visit, she would take a month to plan the menus, she would take a fortnight to air and iron the best linen, she would spend days getting the guest bedchamber buffed up to the highest possible sheen with vinegar and good cold tea and her best wax.

Because Mr Collins must, of course, be made to see how entirely necessary the current servantry were to the future enjoyment of his inheritance: he could, if he chose to, dismiss them all with a snap of the fingers once Mr Bennet was dead, and this secure little arrangement would be peeled into its separate parts and flung to the four winds. Poor Mr Hill would die of it, that much was certain. Little Polly would fall foul of something or someone, being far too young and far too daft to fend for herself, and Sarah was simply too trusting to be out alone in the world. James had only just joined them; she couldn't let him be flung off like that, not when they were all getting so used to having him around.

Such were Mrs Hill's thoughts as she thundered up the stairs, as she swung open the door into the guest room, crossed the carpet, flung back the shutters and heaved up the sash. The bitter November wind rushed in. No, there was nothing to be gained by protesting: the only thing for it was to spite Mr Bennet's spite. Mr Collins would be impressed by the service here at Longbourn, if it killed her. If it killed them all.

In the wintery light, the bedchamber looked sad and neglected. The pallet was bare, the dressing table was filmed with dust; there was a fall of soot on the hearth. It smelt of damp.

By four o'clock it must be warm and bright and cheerful, and an excellent dinner must be waiting. Which had yet to be started on. And she already knew that there was not a decent bit of fish to be got today. She'd kill a hen; that would have to do. Sarah and Polly would sort out the room. Light the fire, dust, sweep, make the bed. A spray of evergreen and berries in a vase. Sarah was thorough, and could be trusted to keep an eye on Polly. James could carry the wing chair up from the library; a few masculine comforts of that kind would satisfy. The room would soon look well; with her little crew at work on it, it would be warm, and pleasant, and no longer smell of damp.

She would roast the hen with some parsnips. She'd make white soup; there would be nuts and fruit for dessert. There would not be so much as a ripple on the surface of things. Try as he might, Mr Bennet would not get a rise out of her. Not again.

Sarah took her orders, and went to gather up the needful equipment: her blacklead, vinegar, the jar of cold tea leaves, her rags and broom; at

103

times like this, you just gritted your teeth and got on with it. She carried her basket upstairs, and, with Polly, got down on her knees to roll the Turkey-carpet up. She swept out and blackleaded the grate, and then between them she and Polly dragged the carpet down the stairs. It was a cumbersome thing – why carpet-weavers had never thought to sew handles on the undersides, Sarah could not fathom – and they had to lug it through pinch points and round corners, grazing their knuckles on doorframes and bending their stubby nails against the dense warp and weft. They carried it down to the paddock and heaved it over the line, where they beat billows out of it, Sarah coughing in the dust, a hand to a stitch, finding herself still weak and easily tired.

Polly wiped her eyes. 'He must be a bit special, this Mr Collins.'

'I should say he is.'

Back upstairs, they left the carpet rolled at the door, and set about cleaning the bare floor. They shoved the bed up against the wall and piled the chair and washstand on top. Then they scattered their damp tea leaves as if they were sowing seed, whisking handfuls out into the air, the dark shreds showering down onto the boards. They chased them into heaps, then swept the heaps – clotted with dust, dead spiders, and shed hair – towards the door.

'What do you think?' Sarah asked, scanning the room for missed bits.

Polly nodded. 'Good.'

James came upstairs with kindling and logs; Sarah slid past him and clattered downstairs with the sweepings. She came back up again with warm water, and poured in vinegar, for the windows and mirror. Polly continued her slow drift around the room with a damp rag.

As the clock chimed the three-quarters of the hour, Mrs Hill, blood still on her apron, climbed up to check on their work. She slid a finger over the mantel, laid a hand on the snowy freshness of the linen, and ran a fingertip around the curlicues of the mahogany dressing table. She sniffed: beeswax, the tang of vinegar, soft woodsmoke from the crackling fire.

'Well done. Good girls. You should be proud of that.'

Sarah was not proud. She was terrified. They were all mustered on the front steps to meet him, this man who would be their future master, if they could but persuade him of the necessity of it. She had conjured a Mr Collins so stern and exacting that she could hardly reconcile her notion of him with the soft, rather heavy-looking young man of twenty-five or thereabouts who clambered down from the seat of the hired chaise, performed a series of clumsy bows to the assembled Bennets, and then to Mr and Mrs Hill, to herself, James, and even Polly, who stared at him agog.

Sarah dug Polly in the ribs. 'Curtsey. And close your mouth.'

It turned out that Mr Collins was wonderfully ready to approve of everything he saw, from the size of the vestibule to the width of the staircase. He even commented on the serviceable nature of the guest-room door. He was, James was able to report, having carried his bags up there for him, delighted by the cheerful comfort he found on the other side, and had enquired as to whom he owed his thanks for all these kind attentions.

'What did you tell him?'

'That it was all the housemaids' work, Sarah and Polly, under your careful direction.'

'Good boy. Good. Sarah, don't forget his hot water. He will want to wash before dinner.'

When Sarah brought the ewer up to him, Mr Collins was at the window, hands clasped behind his back, rolling on his heels and then forward onto his toes, enjoying the view. She set her burden down on the washstand; he heard the chink of it, and looked round. He addressed her in a formal but kindly enough manner, asking if she was indeed one of the housemaids to whom he owed his thanks. She bobbed him a curtsey, nodded. He added how pleasant it was, after a long winter journey, to find oneself the recipient of such a warm – and he said this with a smile and nod towards the fire – welcome.

She was confounded by his notice of her: gentlemen did not make conversation with housemaids. At least, not in her experience; maybe they did in *Pamela* – but surely he did not intend that kind of thing? With his fat hands and his awkward gait, she could not imagine him chasing her around the room like Pamela's Mr B. Or, rather, she preferred not to imagine it.

'And the other bedchambers, tell me: are they all as handsome as this?'

She had no idea what to say. Lydia and Kitty's shared room was a thicket of discarded clothing that she attempted from time to time to hack her way through. Mary's was too small for the pianoforte that Mrs Bennet had banished there, let alone the slithering piles of sheet music and books. Elizabeth and Jane's was pretty enough, and relatively neat, but even there you'd struggle to shut the closet doors . . . And did he really, standing there in his clerical black, wish to discuss the young ladies' bedchambers with her? And Mr and Mrs B.'s – a married couple's bedroom – one did not offer one's opinions on that, surely?

'They are all much of a muchness, I suppose.'

'Indeed! Delightful.' He rubbed his hands together. 'Ah, hot water! How marvellous.'

A fox had got at the pheasants. Idiot birds: by now fully fledged, they still congregated around the nursery pens in the Bennets' woods, expecting to be fed. The fox had left a dozen dead, killing them as they scratched and pecked, oblivious; it would have carried off maybe a couple more.

The ground was sodden, poached after the recent rains. Water churned and tumbled; the stream was in spate. James gathered up the corpses into a bouquet, their dead beaks gaping, bodies dangling. The remaining birds followed him around, making their little croaking sounds. He kicked them away: they were far too trusting. They needed to be much more fearful if they were going to survive long enough for the gentlemen to shoot them.

When he had gathered them all up, he dumped the fowls on a sack, their slack and bloodied bodies in a heap. Mrs Hill would find a use for them, no doubt: they were destined ultimately for the pot, in any case; they had just arrived there rather sooner than expected. All that was lost was the gentlemen's pleasure in killing them; the fox may have that, and be welcome to it, as far as James was concerned.

So why, then, did he feel sad?

Because he had fed them, he supposed; he had let them trust him, depend upon him. He had watched them peck and scratch and flap and squabble. He had got attached.

He looked up from their little bodies, ruffled and broken, and over towards the edge of the woods, to the tree-line, and the open hillside beyond, where the cool winter light gleamed through. A glimpse of distance, of the wide world beyond.

It didn't do to get dependent. It didn't do to get attached.

He scrubbed himself at the pump, then went up to his loft and dressed in his livery, changing his shirt, lifting his chin and closing his eyes to tie the neck-cloth right. Tonight was a simple family party, and as such it was no great demand upon his nerves. There had been – and there would yet be – much more trying occasions than this. He pocketed his gloves, tugged his sleeves straight. He had not expected to encounter the Militia in this quiet place; he had certainly not foreseen such ready intimacy between the officers and the Bennet household. Neither had he anticipated how much Mrs Bennet would like to show him off.

He left the bundle of little pheasants on the cold slate shelf in the scullery. He turned round, and Polly was there, sitting with her back against the warm wall, watching him, keeping out of Mrs Hill's way. He slid down beside her.

'Fox had 'em?' she asked.

He nodded. 'You lying low?'

'It's Bedlam in there.'

She jerked her head towards the kitchen. The clatter of crocks and the rattle of spoons in pans. And then something was fumbled and dropped and hit the stone floor with a clang.

'Sarah!'

'Sorry!'

'Why can't you have more sense?'

They could hear the jostling and bustle as Mrs Hill snatched up whatever it was that Sarah had dropped, and swiped a cloth at the spill; she did not for a moment pause in her scolding. James would, he decided, leave telling Mrs Hill about the pheasants until later. It was not, after all, an urgent matter.

Sarah, flushed and cross, slunk into the scullery soon after. She flumped down on the boards in front of Polly and James, crossed her ankles, blew a huff of breath upwards, which made the fringe of her cap flutter.

'Missus is in a bloody awful one.'

He turned his head away to hide a smile.

They sat a while in silence, listening as Mrs Hill did something at the oven, rattling away just behind them, on the other side of the dividing wall. There was a waft of cooking chicken and the sweet, almost floral scent of roasting parsnips. Polly's belly growled. She clutched it, rolled her eyes, making James smile openly and Sarah cover up a laugh.

'You lot!' Mrs Hill yelled.

A collective flinch. 'Yes, missus—' Sarah called tentatively.

'Shift your lazy backsides. James, go and lay that table! Girls, get yourselves in here.'

The three of them exchanged a glance, and scrambled to their feet.

It was not so very long ago that dinner had meant swallowing down whatever you could get your filthy hands on: filched vegetables that left you crunching grit for hours afterwards, or a bit of bread that was hard as a husk and blue with mould, or scraps of stuff scraped off the bottom of the pot that you couldn't quite identify. And you pushed it down your gullet fast as you could: if it wasn't in your belly then it wasn't yours.

Dinner meant something different here. It meant half a day's work for two women. It meant polished crystal and silver, it meant a change

108

of dress for the diners and a special suit of clothes for the servants to serve it up in. Here, dinner meant delay; it meant extending, with all the complexities of preparation and all those rituals of civility, the gap between hunger and its satisfaction. Here, now, it seemed that hunger itself might be relished, because its cessation was guaranteed; there always was – there always would be – meat and vegetables and dumplings and cakes and pies and plates and forks and pleases and thank-yous, and endless plates of bread and butter.

And this was, already, becoming normal for him; he was already becoming used to this.

So when a fox – or a fox's equivalent: a keen-sighted somebody, with a nose for trouble – came creeping up behind him, what then? Would he be too habituated, too fat, too silly, his senses too blunted by this comfort, to sense the danger? Would he even realize that it was on its way before it had him in its jaws?

There were voices coming from the drawing room as he laid the dining table; the family was seated there, with the newcomer, that soft young Mr Collins. James watched the press of clean fingertips onto a wineglass stem, the pattern of the skin's ridges and the gleam of the crystal. He had thought once that his hands would never come clean again. And yet, and yet, was he not more of an animal now than he had ever been back then? Content now to trudge and pull and carry and to serve, serene in the expectation that at the end of it all there would be a full belly and a safe warm place to sleep.

Mrs Bennet was in the midst of what must pass for a discreet exchange of confidences with Mr Collins. It came through only slightly muffled by the lath-and-plaster. They would be ensconced on the sofa. James set out the silverware and tried not to hear.

'. . . a grievous affair to my girls, you must confess . . .'

A peal of laughter further off – that was Lydia – and then Kitty chiming in with her giggles a moment later.

'Not that I mean to find fault with *you*, for such things I know are all chance in this world . . .'

Did she think that her voice did not carry? Did it not occur to her that at this hour someone would of necessity be next door, in the dining room, laying the table? He rattled a handful of cutlery, but the hint seemed to go unheard.

'There is no knowing how estates will go once they come to be entailed.'

And then Mr Collins, a little lower in pitch but no lower in volume: 'I am very sensible, madam, of the hardship to my fair cousins – and could say much on the subject, but that I am cautious of appearing forward . . .'

So young Collins was there to select one of the girls, as you'd choose an apple from a costermonger's stall. A brisk look over the piled-up stock: one of the bigger ones, the riper ones – that one will do. They were all the same, after all, weren't they? They were of good stock. All the same variety, from the same tree. Why bother looking any further, or making any particular scrutiny of the individual fruits?

Idiot man. James scraped a chair back and whacked it down, hoping the noise might communicate something to the speaker, but Mr Collins burbled on oblivious.

'I can assure you that I come prepared to admire them. At present I will not say more, but . . .'

Poor virgin boy that he was; more to be pitied than despised. No notion of the strangeness of women, of how you could love and think yourself beloved, and yet find at the heart's core something so practical and cold that it would turn your blood to stone. Of love, so little notion; and of love's physical manifestations no notion whatsoever.

'. . . when we are better acquainted . . .'

James could stand it no longer. He swung out into the hallway and marched up to the drawing-room door. He flung it wide, making the whole family start and look round.

'Dinner is served.'

Mr Collins rose to his feet, taken aback by this abruptness. This would never be tolerated at Rosings, nor indeed would it be at Longbourn, when he himself was master of it. But – and this was the much more urgent thought – he was very hungry indeed after his long journey; his posting-inn breakfast at Bromley was now long ago and far away. A lack of nourishment, combined with Mrs Bennet's probing conversation, had left him light-headed, nervous, and a tad more confessional than he had really intended. The footman's announcement, though rather brusque, came, therefore, as very welcome news indeed.

CHAPTER II

. . . the coach conveyed him and his five cousins at a suitable hour to Meryton . . .

MRS BENNET'S SISTER and her husband were clearly popular with the Militia: the Philipses' house – standing right on the street, its lit windows making pools on the pavement – crawled with officers like a beggar's head with lice. James simply could not see the appeal of it himself; supper and cards at a poky townhouse in a dull provincial English town, with a frowsty old attorney and his less-than-ample missus, who'd be serving up cheese toasts and nuts and thimblefuls of sherry wine and dull conventionalities to a bunch of matrons and old fellows. There'd be knots of badly shaven local gallants glaring from the sidelines, unable to get a look-in now with dim girls who considered it their God-given right to be flirted with, but who could never possibly be touched. He'd rather be where he was, waiting outside in the rain.

These officers, though: they skipped along from their billets about town, they gathered on the pavement, they scurried up the front steps; they seemed keen as flies for jam.

A few of them glanced at him in passing, making him turn aside, but the officers were just in a social mood – one nodded to him, another said good evening – so he touched his hat brim in reply, and then occupied himself with the horses, buckling them into their oil-cloth coats, while the men sauntered past him in their regimentals. The rain fell steadily, and made the manes and long eyelashes sparkle with brilliants.

The Philipses' young scrub, a sweet little freckled child, twined her hands together and asked him if he'd like to come into the kitchen for a drink and a bite, and to warm himself, since, as she said, he must be froze to the bone. Downstairs, the kitchen was stuffed to the walls, she said; and very jolly it was too: all the other coachmen were waiting down there.

She made him smile, with her market-town tones and her shyness and her chat, but he just thanked her and said he wouldn't leave the horses.

She came back a little later with a mug of beer and a bit of pork pie for him.

James thanked her again, and ate his supper, and set the mug and plate on a windowsill when he had done. Through the rain-streaked glass, he saw the guests standing around in little knots; he watched a young officer approach Miss Elizabeth and take a chair beside her. He watched the officer speak, smoothing his moustache, one side and then the other; he watched Elizabeth's happy reply, a warmth flushing her cheeks. James could only guess at what they were talking about – the weather, no doubt; it was indeed a wet night, and yes, she did think it likely to be a rainy season – but Miss Elizabeth was clearly finding it all very agreeable. That officer smiled, exposing creamy teeth, and it might have just been the damp that caused a creeping chill at the back of James's neck, that made him rub his nape and pull his collar up, or it might have been real and knowing unease. But there was, after all, nothing to be done about these intimacies. He unhooked the coach lamp and got up inside the coach, closing the door on the wet night and the worry. He settled back into the upholstery, making the springs creak; he opened his book. He had brought Gilpin's *Observations* with him, borrowed from Mr Bennet's library. He had got as far north as Lancaster with it, and, found himself in some disagreement with the author's taste.

It grew late, and it grew cold, and the noise from the Philipses' house swelled and shrank and grew again. He was just drifting off, head back against the padding, when the girls bounded out with Mr Collins in tow, all bright chatter and noise. James stirred himself and climbed out of the carriage, folded the steps down and was there waiting with the lamp to hand them in. He felt the warm, damp, excited squeeze of five pairs of white kid gloves. Mr Collins, he left to shift for himself: the young man clambered in.

The journey back was noisy. Lydia could be heard chattering on about the games she had played that night, the fish that she had lost and the fish that she had won. From Mr Collins came a low drone about the wondrous civility of the Philipses and the dishes there had been at supper, and his losses at whist. Nobody actually mentioned the officers on the journey home, at least as far as James could make out, though that did not necessarily mean that nobody was thinking about them. Perched up on top of the carriage, wet wind in his face, he felt brittle. One sharp knock would shatter him to fragments. The horses, sensing his unease, twisted back their ears, their flanks twitching as though troubled by summer flies.

CHAPTER III

'I beg your pardon;—one knows exactly what to think.'

SARAH WAS SUMMONED from the scullery by the furious jangling of the breakfast-room bell. She traipsed up: the morning meal was done and cleared away; now was a time for peaceful pursuits, for needlework or music or reading or calling on the neighbours. For not bothering the servants. What could possibly be required so urgently of her now?

Mrs Bennet was flushed and flustered, and needed her excitement acknowledged and participated in, as well as lots of things done with all possible speed. She had, from the window, spied the Bingleys' carriage as it turned into the drive.

'Oh, this is wonderful, this is quite wonderful, do not you agree?'

Sarah peered out with her: there he was – Bingley, Ptolemy Bingley, perched at the back of the carriage, along with the other footman, and the whole equipage was rolling up the drive towards Longbourn's front steps. Her stomach did a little swooping dive. She had no name for the sensation; she had no time to pause and consider and find a name for it, either – Mrs Bennet dug an elbow in her ribs, bringing her back to the moment, the breakfast room, the next thing to be done. Her mistress wore a girlish grin, was almost bouncing on the spot with joy. Sarah smiled despite herself.

'Run and get Jane, will you? I mean: do actually run,' said Mrs Bennet. 'She's wandering out in the shrubbery, I think. Quick now; quick as you can, my dear. Go fetch her.'

Mr Bingley and his sisters were ushered along the hall. Their voices could be heard trailing after them: they had come to bestow upon the Bennet family an invitation to the ball at Netherfield, which was fixed for the following Tuesday. Mrs Hill wilted at the news.

Sarah, having fetched the girls in from their walk, now hung up the cloaks and laid the ladies' bonnets carefully on the cloakroom dresser. She ran an ostrich feather through her fingers, touched a rosebud of vermilion silk. Then she took a swift look down the hall: it was empty, though she could hear Mr Bingley's clipped tones, his sisters' chiming laughs. Sarah slipped out to the vestibule, and then out of the front door.

The Bingley coach was waiting for its owner, the coachman slipping down from his seat to check some aspect of the harness; the footmen were round the back, standing at their ease, talking and sharing a cigarillo.

Now that she had come this far – actually outside, closing the door behind her, blinking in the cold morning light – Sarah was appalled at her own brazenness. She would just stroll past him, she could be on her way anywhere: it need not mean anything. He had no particular cause to think that it was his presence that had drawn her out.

But as she passed, she saw the way his attention shifted, and focused; the way a smile dimpled his cheeks. And it was wonderful to be noticed; it was giddying. She felt the gravel crunch beneath her feet; she felt too the shush of her skirts around her ankles, the press of her stays, the tickle of a curl at the back of her neck. She felt as though she was more *there*, simply because he noticed that she was. And then he took his cigarillo from his lips, and came towards her, a cloud spilling from the corner of his mouth.

'Pretty round here, isn't it?'

'It is, sir, I suppose.'

'You'll have time for a stroll, show me around, while the big folks are indoors.'

He offered his arm. She laughed.

He held out his arm still, nodded to it. 'Go on.'

She looked at it, then up at him. 'I can't.'

''Course you can.'

'I'm working.'

'No, you're not. You're skylarking. It's written all over your little face. And you've got this far; why not do it properly?'

'If I get caught—'

He smiled fully then; it was sunshine. 'Don't.'

She slipped her arm through his. It was warm and solid. His sleeve, lying against her own, was good blue twill. He moved off, and she, laughing nervously, was drawn after him, off the drive and onto the grass plait; she saw them as others would see them now, their figures jaunty and almost comically ill-matched: the bulk of him in his good blue greatcoat, her slight figure in wilted linsey-woolsey, tagging along, a faint wisp of tobacco smoke following after them.

'This way—'

'Oh, I don't—'

But he drew her along into the little wilderness, and they followed the path through the tangled dead grass. He lifted a low-hanging branch to let her pass. The rowans still had a few scarlet berries unpecked by the birds, and everything was hung with raindrops, and smelling of rot. Behind her, in her absence, the house was grinding along, its cogs turning and teeth linking, belts creaking, and there must come a moment – any moment now – when a cog would bite on nothing, and spin on air: some necessary act would go unperformed, some service would not be provided; the whole mechanism would crunch and splinter and shriek out in protest, and come to a juddering halt, because she was not there. And all the time she was pulling further and further away, like a spindle twisting out upon a thread of flax. Pull far enough, twist and stretch it too thin, and the thread would snap.

She squinted up at the grey clouds, conscious of the bulk of him so near to her, the scent of smoke. To think that it was the same sky that blanketed the whole world, that skimmed all across America and the Antipodes. That he had come from so far away, himself.

'Do you find it miserable here?' she asked.

'England has its own particular charms.'

She blinked round at him. 'Really?'

'I was trying to be gallant.' He looked at her a long moment, which made her look away. 'But, one thing about this country is that once you set foot here, you are not a slave.'

'You weren't a slave?'

'I was born a slave.'

'Your mother—'

'Was one of Mr Bingley – Senior's – slaves.' Ptolemy lifted his cigarillo to his lips and sipped on it.

Sarah did not know where to put herself, or what to say. She felt hot. 'I'm sorry.'

'It's not your fault, sweetheart.'

They walked on together, silently, through the rough grass.

'Mr Bingley, Senior, God rest him, brought me back here,' he said, after a while. 'He was always very fond of me. And of my mother, too, though he left her there. I was just a boy.'

He proffered the smouldering cigarillo. She looked at it, uncertain. He jerked it closer: *Go on*. Out of shyness more than anything else, she took it off him, and tried it at her lips. The smoke was treacly and rank; it turned into a lump in her throat. Coughing, she thrust the cigarillo back towards him.

'You have to practise.' He patted her back. 'Don't suck it in like that.'

She nodded, feeling sick. They continued on along the path, and his hand lingered on her back, where the stays stopped and the shoulders were just thinly covered by her shift and dress.

'Tell you a secret?' he asked.

'Go on, then.' Her head was spinning.

'I'm going to set up my own tobacco shop one day. Only the very best, oh yes indeed. Only the very finest Virginian tobacco.'

He stopped in his tracks; she had to turn back to him. He stood there, brilliant in that shabby little wintery wilderness. He examined the neat scroll of the cigarillo, turning it between dark fingers. Then his face broke into one of his miraculous smiles, and he looked up at her.

'They can't ever get enough of it, your proper London gentlemen. Men of that calibre, they love their tobacco almost as much as they love their sugar.'

She felt suddenly giddy with it all: the novelty, the transgression, the thrill of his difference; the way that all awkwardness with him had seemed to dissolve and drift away with the tobacco smoke. She took the cigarillo from his hand, to show that she approved of him and his tobacco and his grand plans, and was herself a creature of his ilk, and willing, as he had said, to practise. This time, she huffed the smoke out into the air with a shade more composure.

He said something that she did not quite hear.

'Mm?' She peered at him through narrowed eyes.

'She going to give you grief?'

He nodded over towards the edge of the wilderness: Mrs Hill was marching up towards them, arms swinging, face like a quince.

'Oh, good Lord.'

She fumbled the cigarillo back into his hand.

'Trouble?'

She nodded, prickly with terror. How on earth could she excuse this to Mrs Hill? She turned to go.

'We could go walking out,' he said. 'When you get your afternoon off.'

She flashed him a look, half fear, half delight; then she gathered up her skirts, and raced back to Mrs Hill.

Fortunately Mrs Hill required no explanation or excuse. Indeed, she offered Sarah no opportunity to give one. She just met her with a cuff round the back of the head – 'Ow!' – then a shove at the small of her back, which sent her staggering towards the house.

'Missus, please—'

'Don't you "missus" me! When I think – with Mr Collins in the house, and the Bingleys! And you out where anyone might see—'

Mrs Hill gave her an extra shove to impel her up the front steps, then

119

she grabbed Sarah's arm and dragged her through the door, and into the vestibule.

'Fetch the Bingleys' things. They're leaving.'

'They've not stayed long.'

Mrs Hill's voice dropped to a hiss. 'I was calling you, Sarah, and you were not here. I was so ashamed. Now get on with your work. Jump to it, girl. Quick as you like.'

Quick as I like, Sarah thought, is actually a good deal slower than I am going now. But her cheeks burnt with misery, at the thought of shaming Mrs Hill.

CHAPTER IV

*The prospect of the Netherfield ball was extremely agreeable to
every female of the family.*

WITH THE DEPARTURE of the Bingleys the heavens opened, and
there followed such a succession of bad weather as prevented
the ladies from walking out at all.

It also prevented Sarah from sleeping; the rain clattered on the attic
roof, and pattered on the little skylight, and burbled in the guttering,
and whirlpooled down the drainpipes. Polly snored through it all, arms
flung back and wide above her head. Sarah lay awake, thinking of Tol
Bingley; his twining smoke, his dark eyes, his hand warm on the top
edge of her stays.

The rain also fell on the stable roof, and dripped, and dripped, and
dripped, somewhere off outside the lamplight's glow, outside the realm
of James's book. It distracted him; he found that he turned the pages
without reading the words. He was obliged to mark his place, throw on
his coat and tread into his boots, and go out into the streaming night
with a storm lantern and a ladder, and climb up onto the stable roof,
and listen, in the drenching rain, for that particular drip amongst all
the other drips. He found the loose slate and slid it back into place; this
would serve until a dry day and daylight, when the job could be com-
pleted properly.

And Mrs Hill, stark awake at her window while her husband
wheezed behind her, looked out across the puddled yard, at the

moving storm lantern that seemed fringed around with crystal where the raindrops caught the light, and watched James climb the ladder up onto the roof, and watched him fix the loose slate, and watched him climb safely down again, and watched until he had carried the ladder back into the stable, and watched the door shut on his light, and watched the light return to his window. Inside, he settled down again to his solitary night.

When his light went out, she realized that she was cold, and drew her shawl tighter around her, and went to her bed, and knelt beside it, and said her prayers silently to herself. And when she had said them through once, the rain drumming on the skylight above, she said them through again, shivering, her lips shaping the unspoken words. She held each phrase for a moment in her thoughts, to try to give it full and proper attention. There was so much to be thankful for: there was pleasure in her work, in the rituals and routines of service, the care and conservation of beautiful things, the baking of good bread and the turning of rough, raw foods into savoury and sustaining meals. There was pleasure, too, in the little clutch of people that she now had clustered around her. If she could but be certain that they would continue in this manner, that James would settle, that Sarah could be made to see sense, that Polly would become steady and useful; if she could but know that this would tend towards continuance, and not towards dissolution, then she could be quite content.

And yet, and yet, the feeling still could not quite be quelled: there was also the fact of her, herself. Would she, at some time, have the chance to care for her own things, her own comforts, her own needs, and not just for other people's? Could she one day have what she wanted, rather than rely on the glow of other people's happiness to keep her warm?

Work, Mrs Hill knew, might not be a cure for all ailments, but it was a sovereign remedy against the more brooding kinds. With Sarah buried deep in a drift of gowns and petticoats, harried by demands for miracles of rejuvenation and embellishment, she would have little time to daydream, and was conveniently hidden away from that trouble-some mulatto.

He was, thankfully, less present in the kitchen than of late. The rain, and the pre-existence of a significant social engagement in the near future, meant there was a temporary falling-off in communication between the households. It was a pleasant sensation, Mrs Hill felt, to be locked up tight and snug at Longbourn. The rain streaming down the windows, the countryside beyond sheathed in grey, the roads awash, the footways mired, no one approaching the place, no one leaving: it was like the Flood, and Longbourn was their ark; whatever happened to the world beyond, they few were safe inside.

But it was a temporary situation at best. It could not be for ever.

And so Sarah must be spoken to: behaviour of that kind could not be ignored. But how to speak on such a subject without risking damage to the girl's innocence? Innocence was a sheet of pristine glass, a screen from the harshness of the weather; one slip and Sarah would do terrible, bloody damage to herself, and others, and the glass would be all in pieces on the floor.

Best to keep it simple. Simple rules for a simple girl to follow.

'I forbid you to see that mulatto man again.'

'What?' The girl's face was gaping shock. 'You mean Ptolemy? Why?'

'Do I really need to tell you? Really?'

Her lips pressed tight, Sarah nodded.

'You were *smoking*, Sarah. You were out walking the grounds – not *your* grounds, need I add; your master's property – when you should have been at your work. And with this man – a – a stranger to us here, and quite unknown. You could be dismissed for less, and fined, into the bargain. When I think of the harm it could do, to the reputation of the household—'

Mrs Hill folded her arms under her bosom, conscious that she could stand up to only about three-fifths of what she was saying. Conscious, too, of her husband looking up from his work, and James coming in from the hall but halting on the threshold, and of Polly sloping off into the scullery before anybody could start blaming her for anything, and realizing that this much should have been allowed Sarah at the very least: that she be scolded in private.

Because Sarah was bristling now; she rolled her shoulders, planted her feet, rearranging herself. 'And when he's sent here?'

Mrs Hill did not like this. The defiance. She bristled too. 'Absent yourself.'

Sarah raised her eyebrows, and just looked at Mrs Hill.

'What do you expect me to say?' Mrs Hill's voice rose with her temper. 'Do you think I should give you permission to make an exhibit of yourself? To make us all a laughing stock?'

'So I can't even have a friend? Is that what you are saying?'

'He is not your friend.'

Sarah hesitated. Then she nodded. 'Will that be all?'

'If you will take heed and mind it, I think that it will do.'

Sarah curtseyed. Biting her lip, she turned to get on with her work, since it was all that she was allowed to do. She carried the teapot through to the scullery, poured the slops into the bucket for mopping floors with, straining out the dregs and slapping them into the stone jar where they were kept for sweeping. She fumbled them, scattering wet leaves.

Her hands shook. She wiped them on her apron, then rubbed her face, her callouses scratching against her cheeks.

Whatever was done with bad grace was done badly: how often had Mrs Hill told her that?

Back in the kitchen, Mrs Hill was frowning over her sponge cakes, which had not risen, and looked like biscuits. She only meant the best for Sarah, but of course the girl would not see it that way: she could not. She did not know what she was risking.

When Sarah brought Mr Collins his hot water the following morning, he was already awake, and sitting up in bed. She was just going to set the heavy jug down on the washstand and slip out – there were four more of these ewers to convey to the other bedchambers, and of course one did not speak unless required to do so – but he cleared his throat and asked her, with an unconcerned air, and as if apropos of nothing, 'Have they been brought up very high, the young mistresses, would you say?'

'Sir?'

'It turns out that they have nothing to do in the kitchen, which is something of a concern, and a surprise, if I may say so; but I think they must have *some* responsibilities about the house, some actual *work* to do. A family of this size, with Mr Bennet's income, I don't see how they could all be idle. Or, indeed, what good it would do, to bring up a child to be of no practical use to herself or anybody else.'

He busied himself fussily with the sheets across his lap. He looked like a little boy.

'They are kind and sensible, clever girls, sir,' she said. It was true in some measure of some of them.

'But are they biddable?'

She hesitated. Nobody ever bade them do anything that went against their own desires, so it was hard to say; but still, she hated to disappoint him. She nodded.

He brightened. 'And Miss Elizabeth: is she an active, useful kind of person? She would be able to make a modest income go a good way?'

Sarah tilted her head. She wished she could be more encouraging. *Think of Mary*; that might be the most helpful, and kindest, thing to say. In interests and temperament, and degree of personal loveliness, Mary and Mr Collins were a far more likely match; but if he could not see that himself, it was not her place to point it out to him.

'It is a matter of some importance. You must speak your mind to me, child.'

Elizabeth did have Sarah making over her evening-gown for the Netherfield ball. And she was always fashioning flowers and head-dresses out of offcuts for herself. Not a bit of twist or a slip of Persian or a scrap of Irish ever went to waste.

'They are *thrifty*,' Sarah suggested. When it came to matters of their own adornment, this was true. They were obliged to be.

He grasped this eagerly, hitching himself more upright in the bed. 'And Miss Elizabeth, is she as amiable as she seems to be?'

Elizabeth's hair curled naturally, which was vastly in her favour. And they being of a similar age, and having grown up alongside each other, Elizabeth always had an ear for Sarah, and an interest in her, and a book to lend her; but Elizabeth also had a core of ivory, and Mr Collins should really realize it for himself, because there was no way on earth that he could be told, not by Sarah, that Mr Collins would never do for Elizabeth.

'Miss Elizabeth is as amiable as anyone could wish her to be.'

He nodded again, rubbed his hands together, and seemed satisfied; heaving back the covers, he swung his legs out of the bed. His feet padded pale and bare across the carpet; he tugged back the curtains and gazed out, and seemed to have forgotten that she was there. Sarah remembered the billowing dust as she and Polly had beaten the carpet that he was standing on now, the choke and sneeze of it. Then she remembered the heavy ewers waiting for her in the scullery, their water cooling.

'Sir?'

He turned, looked at her, startled but benign.

'Sir, might you advise me, too? As a man of the cloth, I mean.'

He fluffed himself up like a winter bird at this. 'What troubles you, my child?'

'I work hard.' She shifted on her feet. 'I try to be good. I do as I am told.'

'Well, you do your duty then, and that's just as it should be. Work is sanctified and sanctifying. Consider the Parable of the Vineyard.'

She nodded, though uncertain. That story was about being as well rewarded for doing very little as you were for doing a great deal: it always made Sarah feel dispirited, and hopeless.

'But what about Martha?' she asked. 'From Martha's story don't we learn that there must be pause, that there must be time to listen and be still, and to learn.'

'Ah, yes—' His eyes narrowed at her.

126

'And what about the Lilies of the Field, that neither toiled nor spun nor did anything very much at all?'

'Yes, yes, but – you must see that to work is your duty, and like all of us you will find satisfaction in doing your duty.'

'But it does not make me satisfied—' Sarah wanted to stamp. 'It makes me feel tired and sore, and though I work so hard, it seems I cannot even take a moment, even a moment's pleasure, but I am scolded, I am found to be in the wrong.'

'*Pleasure?*' Mr Collins moved towards her, eyes wide now. He smelt of bed, and hair-oil and bad teeth. 'Have you committed some error, my child?'

Sarah took a step back. She had run away with herself, and now was far beyond what she had intended.

'I'm sorry, sir, I should not have spoke.'

He stayed her with a soft hand. 'What error is it, child? Upon your soul. You must tell me.'

All that had been done and seen and thought and felt, since James's arrival in the household – the collision with the barrow, the chalky disks and spirals in his bag, his spare clean room; Tol Bingley and day-dreams of Vauxhall Gardens and Astley's; the dark and dirt of the back lane in Meryton, the soldier's naked skin and his cries; the dizzy sick feeling of tobacco smoke – it all came down upon her at once, and was too much, was far too much to make sense of and explain and offer up to Mr Collins, tied with a neat bow.

'I spoke to the neighbour's footman.'

He recoiled, his features squashing up together in a frown. 'Is that all?'

She nodded.

'Just – spoke?'

She nodded again.

'Well, I expect that must be necessary from time to time.' She watched as his thoughts shifted and fixed. 'Did you experience an unwonted pleasure in speaking to him?'

She'd experienced something; that much was certain. But what she'd felt had not been an unwonted pleasure. It had, perhaps, not even been pleasure at all, but, rather, the dawning realization that pleasure was a possibility for her.

'Not unwonted, I don't think so, sir.'

'Well then,' he said, 'you would be better speaking to the house-keeper, I think, than to me; it seems more a matter of domestic discipline, than a religious or moral concern.'

He waved her away, and turned back to the window, looking out across the wide green lawns, the shrubberies and woods of his inheritance. As she was leaving, Sarah lifted his chamber pot out from underneath the bed, and carried it out, her head turned aside so as not to confront its contents too closely.

This, she reflected, as she crossed the rainy yard, and strode out to the necessary house, and slopped the pot's contents down the hole, *this* was her duty, and she could find no satisfaction in it, and found it strange that anybody might think a person could. She rinsed the pot out at the pump and left it to freshen in the rain. If this was her duty, then she wanted someone else's.

Chapter V

. . . the very shoe-roses for Netherfield were got by proxy.

SARAH SEWED BY the window. Elizabeth and Jane talked low, their heads close together by the fire; they were sewing too, wrapped in their dressing gowns and shawls, the firelight glowing through their hanging curls.

It was Monday, the day before the ball. Sarah had a blister on the soft flesh between her index finger and her thumb, where the flat-irons had worn the skin away. Whenever she closed her eyes, she saw the minnow-dart of her needle through muslin, the drag of thread through the open weave.

Wickham, she heard, and *Wickham* and *Wickham* and *Wickham*. It sounded like the clack of knitting needles.

The wind buffeted the chamber window; outside bare branches rattled. The shrubbery beyond was glistening and wet, and all the gravel walkways were pooled with rainwater; the little wilderness was sodden, and the sky low and laden with clouds, and the wind just brought more clouds, more rain. It matched Sarah's mood – grey, with no glimmer of better things to come, now that she was forbidden to see anything of Ptolemy Bingley.

Then the door slammed back, and Lydia tumbled into her sisters' room; she could not, it seemed, be trained to knock. There had been no opportunity for her to run off any of her natural ebullience for days: confinement to the house was a perfect torment for her. Lydia needed

129

to be taken out for a wild gallop; she needed someone to throw sticks for her to chase, poor love.

'No morning visitors, no officers, no news, nothing! Lord! I don't know how I shall bear it.'

She flopped down on her sisters' bed, kicking her feet against the patchwork. All pent-up and fiddly-idle, she picked up a length of pink ribbon and ran it through her fingers.

'Put the ribbon down, please, Lydia, you'll spoil it.'

She pulled a face, let the ribbon slip and coil onto the quilt. 'You two have done well, hiding yourselves away up here, out of Mr Collins's way.'

'Lydia! That's not true. We're working.'

Lydia shrugged, kicked off her slippers and trod into Jane's dancing shoes, which were lying out on the floor.

'Oh, it's only Sarah to hear, and she's as good as gold, she won't tell a soul, will you, Sarah?'

Lydia flashed Sarah a grin, making Sarah smile back. Then she turned her feet this way and that, appraising the shoes. 'Anyway, I'm not staying down there to be read sermons to, and that is that.'

There was a moment's pause, and then Jane said gently, 'He follows Papa into the Library, you know.'

'And that,' said Elizabeth, 'is trespass indeed.'

'There, you see! Even Papa tries to escape the dreary fellow, so I don't see why I should not. Lord! What a bore he is. I don't know how anyone can stand him.'

Sarah peered closer at her sewing, her lips pressed tight: Mr Collins could not help his awkwardness. He could not help where he had come from, or what chances nature and upbringing had given, or failed to give, him. And if he did not know the by-laws of the household, it was because nobody had told him; he was expected to intuit them, and then was blamed for his failure.

'Papa never receives company in there.'

'If he can help it, Papa never receives company at all.'

'Yes, but the *library*. My goodness.'

Sarah glanced up at the pretty, plump faces, so delighted with their own daring; she was transported back to that morning before Michaelmas, to the cold hallway and the smell of urine, and the tangled voices coming through the firmly shut library door. Mrs Hill was allowed in there, she thought, though obviously Mrs Hill did not count as company.

Lydia sniffed, kicked her heels, swinging Jane's shoes out in front of her. 'Mr Collins is his cousin, so if anyone must suffer the fellow, it should be Papa.'

Then she peered harder at the shoes, as if somehow struck by them. She looked up.

'Did we order new shoe-roses?'

Every gaze now turned to the dancing shoes dangling from Lydia's toes. One rose hung loose, ragged and greyed, its sorry state a testament to Mr Bingley's enthusiasm for dancing with Jane at the Meryton ball. The other one was gone.

'Oh goodness, did we?'

'I didn't.'

'Nor I.'

'Did you mention it to Mother?'

'No.'

'We must have some left over.'

Jane went to the dresser, opened a drawer and began to sort through its contents, a frown on her pretty forehead.

There were, indeed, shoe-roses, but they were of such varying vintage, colour and degree of wear, that only two sets could be made of them. One pair was blue, the other yellow; and even then, the yellow pair matched only in the loosest sense of the word. They were much the same size, but were conspicuously different shades: one was lemon and the other was, as Lydia observed, more of a custardy colour.

Whilst all this was going on, Sarah sat, and sewed, and kept her eyes on her work. She was listening to the wind in the chimney, watching the way it made the fire shudder and the light dance, and feeling her skin already beginning to tighten in the expectation of cold.

'I shall need pink ones to match my dress,' Lydia said.

Sarah closed her eyes. She let a breath go softly. She looked up.

'Big as cabbages! Big as you can get, anyway. You know the shade of pink, like my good muslin. You can take the sash with you if you like, to get as close a match as you can. Thank you, Sarah. You *are* good as gold, you know.'

Sarah set her sewing aside.

'Yes,' Elizabeth said, with a sorrowful glance at the misted window, and the rain beyond that spattered it. The panes shook in the wind. 'I'm afraid the shoe-roses will have to be got by proxy.'

It was a slow, reluctant trudge along the turnpike, the rain coming down with a drenching fullness that seemed to cut her off from all the world. The umbrella soon let water through, and drips gathered on the inside and fell heavily on her shoulders, the damp penetrating to her skin. Her skirts became weighty with water. For the time being, there were no carriages, which was a blessing.

She tried imagining herself striding down a London street, paved, and lined with glowing windows. Then she was wandering along a glimmering arcade, which was warm and bright and dry. She dawdled at displays of fancy bonnets, glossy jewels, and mountains of confectionery. But then there was a lady walking ahead of her, and the lady – who was, it seemed, Elizabeth all grown up and in a fancy orange spencer and bonnet – handed her a package, and then another, and then a bandbox, and heaped more and more parcels on top of it, and when Sarah tried to refuse the packages and hand them back, grown-up Elizabeth scolded her for being clumsy and not paying proper attention.

Then the mail-coach came thundering up, startling her awake, making her leap the ditch and press up against the dripping spiky hedge. The coach tore past, the horn blaring, a flurry of hooves and wheels; it sprayed up behind itself a fountain of mud that spattered her from head to foot. She wiped her face and hands with her sodden handkerchief. She bent to dab at her skirts, but then just gave up: what was the point? She was stupidly wet; a spray of mud made little difference now.

In Meryton, the haberdasher spread an oil-cloth for her to stand on. The fire made her skirts steam.

Wet to the skin, she stood for a half-hour, while the haberdasher and the haberdasher's boy made up six pair of shoe-roses, in the required colours, bringing the different ribbons and braids over for Sarah's approval, so that she did not trail her wet and mud across the nice clean shop. She nodded at everything she was shown, profoundly un-concerned by the differences in shade and texture. The ladies could like the shoe-roses or they could lump them. Indeed, she would rather like it if they lumped them. She rather looked forward to their having to lump them.

Other, dryer customers came and went, having just stepped out of their conveyances or popped down the street from their houses in the town. They left their umbrellas dripping at the door, and looked at her with that particular combination of sympathy and amusement that the soaked seem always to elicit in the dry.

The finished shoe-roses were wrapped in tissue, then brown paper, then canvas, to keep them safe. She took the package under her arm, and set off back into the murk.

She had just passed the toll-house and slipped round the turnpike, when she heard a carriage approaching behind her, and the coachman addressing the keeper, then the click and chink of a coin tossed and caught, and the call of thanks. The fastening rattled, and the hinge creaked as the pike was swung round to let the carriage through.

She gathered up her skirts and stepped back out of the way, up against the wooden palings of the fence. More mud hardly signified now, but she could do without getting flattened to the bargain. She glanced over her shoulder to watch the carriage approach.

The lamps glowed warm in the grey afternoon. The keeper leaned on the pike, hat sodden, a sack over his shoulders. The coachman clicked his tongue, flicked the reins, and the coach rolled forward. She recognized the livery; and she felt a flicker of – what – excitement, unease . . . guilt? Because there was Ptolemy. And she was supposed to absent herself from Ptolemy. But she was stuck there, back pressed against the rough fence, and the state that she was in, oh Lord – the coach trickled past her: warm horseflesh and supple leather, then a glimpse through the glass of Mrs Hurst and Miss Bingley, beautiful and bored inside. And then the footmen, up on the footplate, in their rain-streaked greatcoats and tricorn hats. Tol Bingley saw her, and he tipped his hat, making the water pour from its brim.

He spoke a quick word or two to the other footman, who nodded in reply. Then he turned back to Sarah, and beckoned. Eyebrows up, he hooked his fingers back towards himself, then gestured at the perch where he was standing: would she like a lift?

It all happened in a moment: she stepped forward; he reached down and she reached up. He grasped her arm above the elbow, and she was lifted into the air. One foot found the step, and the other was on the ledge, and then she was perched on the end of the footplate beside him; he was all warmth and old smoke and wet wool and substance.

'Light as a feather!' he puffed.

She laughed, glanced sidelong at him, anxious.

'Hold on here.'

She grasped the handrail, her raw hands beside his neat gloved ones.

The coachman, with a complicit half-glance back, snapped the reins again, and the horses broke into a high-stepping trot, and the movement of it flung her backwards, and Tol's arm came around her waist to hold her steady.

The wind was on her face, and the wet wrapped itself around her. The horses surged along with easy strength, and the roll of the carriage made her sway against him, hip to hip. The ground blurred with speed. It was an elevation indeed, from the clinging misery of the mud.

Landmarks – the hay barn, an ancient witchy oak with its limbs broken back to stumps, a stretch of bog – were reached and passed before she knew it. So this was the luxury of speed, the ability to compress the world into folds and slip through them like a needle.

Already the Longbourn crossroads emerged from the rain, and grew close. The carriage slowed.

'Just hop down as we make the turn.'

She turned to him, eyes wide. 'You're not stopping?'

He gave a sympathetic half-shrug. 'They can't know I've been picking up strays.'

She glanced down at the blurring ground: she would break her leg, her neck; she'd break something. She felt him fumble for her arm again. He gripped it just where he had before, above the elbow.

'Now,' he said. 'Step off.'

The horses slowed as they skimmed the bend, but they were still going far too fast. She could not step off.

'Now, Sarah. Now.'

She stepped off.

For a moment she was dangling, and the ground was hurtling by. Then her feet hit the road, and he let go of her, and she was running, stumbling to catch up with her own speed. The coach was away; she staggered to a halt.

Looking back over his shoulder, Tol Bingley tipped his hat to her again, and she raised her hand to wave. Then the coach made the turn and he was gone.

She trudged up the village street, huddled into herself; it was like a poke of hot chestnuts to carry with her, the knowledge that she had done this. She had done what she had been forbidden to do, and she had got away with it unseen, and nobody at Longbourn would ever know! She was so wrapped up in gleeful contemplation of her misdeed, that she did not notice the figure on the high path through the fields, who stood in a sodden coat, watching her from beneath a dripping hat brim.

He had watched the coach slow and make the turn and, with a lurch of fear that she would be hurt, her small figure detach itself from the back of the conveyance, and stumble along a little way, and come to a standstill, apparently unharmed. He had watched her wave after the disappearing carriage. He watched as she wandered up the village street, slow and dreamy, as if this were a sunny day in May.

Only when she had passed through the main gates, and was out of sight, did he turn and stride back to the house.

He was in the kitchen when she came downstairs in her dry clothes, the wet ones bundled up in her arms. She went straight through into the scullery, where he heard her sloshing them in a tub to soak away the mud. She came back through wiping her hands. She had missed dinner; the kitchen was in chaos: she did not seem to care. She seemed somehow outside it all now, and unconcerned.

He set out the coffee things. He wondered if she'd notice that his cuffs were damp, his wrists goosepimpled, that he had an outdoor chill about him. He gave her a long assessing look, taking in the fresh-air flush of her cheeks, the bright sheen of her eyes, thinking how lovely she was, now that she was happy. But she gave him only the briefest of glances.

'Will you take those up to the drawing room when you go?'

She dropped the package on the kitchen table and peeled off the outer layer of damp canvas.

'Of course.'

And then a moment later, when she had begun to sort through the muddle of fine china and kitchenware, he asked, 'So, what's in it?'

He lifted the haberdasher's parcel, and set it on the tray between the coffee cups.

'Hm?'

'The package. What's inside?'

'Shoe-roses,' she said.

'Shoe-roses?'

'Shoe-roses. Roses for shoes.'

'I don't understand.'

She puffed impatiently. 'Dancing shoes, they have to have roses on them. You fasten them on.'

'Why would you do that?'

'To look pretty.'

He raised his eyes to the heavens.

'What?'

'Only, if they send you on a fool's errand in foul weather again,' he said, 'you come and find me, and I'll go instead.'

She planted her hands on her hips, her eyes brilliant.

'And why must you dictate what I may and may not do?'

He held up his palms. 'I didn't mean—'

'What if I *want* to go? What if it is a *pleasure* to me to go? What if I do not want you to poke your nose in where it's not wanted?'

'I meant no harm by it,' he said. 'I would not deprive you of any pleasure.'

He bowed, lifted the tray, and left the kitchen.

Sarah was left with the unwelcome sensation that she had spoken unfairly, and that Mr Smith had unluckily reaped what Mrs Hill had sown.

James had no intentions; he could not afford to have any; he could not afford to rope another person to his saddle. All he could do was keep his head down and get his work done. Which was why this stirring in him, the prickle of desire in his belly, the twist of jealousy there too, was so very unwelcome indeed. It must be quashed; it did not, after all, mean anything. It was a shame: that was the most that could be said of it. A shame to have to turn his head away, when he would very much prefer to look; a shame that Sarah would of course go and fall in love and it would not be with him. But the sorrow of it came as something of a surprise: he should by now have been perfectly accustomed to doing what he did not want to do, to letting things happen that he did not want to happen. But this? No; he could not reconcile himself to this. The idea worried at him as a dog worries at sheep: he knew it would not kill him to see her happy with someone else; these things were not fatal, no matter what poets and novelists liked to pretend. He might not *like* it, he might not like it one little bit; it might make his chest constrict with something very similar to fear, but it would not *kill* him; he knew perfectly well that it would not.

It was with all this in mind that he set to drying up the coffee cups. It gave him the opportunity to be near her, her sleeves rolled back on bare and downy arms, as she rinsed the fine china. Polly crouched like an imp on the scullery floor behind them, polishing the lined-up dress shoes and muttering bad-temperedly under her breath. It was all perfectly innocent; Sarah could not imagine that because he dried the cups that she had washed, he meant to impose upon her interest in any way.

His nails, she noticed, were like pale moons – and she was distracted by the movement of muscle in his forearm as he twisted the cloth inside the china – but he remained as silent as a stone. Then she remembered Tol Bingley's arm around her waist, the rain prickling her skin, the miracle of speed, and how *he* noticed her, how *he* paid her those attentions, while nobody else in all the world ever paid her any attention at all. She dipped another saucer under the water, and turned it over, and lifted it out dripping, and handed it to James, and wondered how far Tol Bingley had gone on that day, and what he might have seen from the back of the Bingleys' carriage. If she unpicked the distance of her own day, the back and forth to Meryton, the up and down of stairs and the pacing along corridors, if you unravelled all that, how far would it reach? Would it go those twenty miles or so to London? Or even further, through the twisting country lanes, to the sea?

James worked on with deliberate slowness, drying each cup and saucer to a squeak, staying next to her, enjoying her frown, her stubborn silence. This doggedness, this bloody-mindedness: it charmed him in a way that he could not quite fathom. When he had offered to go to Meryton in her stead, she had rounded on him, sparking, self-possessed, glinting steel; she had been brilliantly bad: *What if I want to go? What if it is a* pleasure *to me to go?*

She was tougher than she knew. She wanted nothing from him. She brushed him aside like a fly.

He found this quite delightful.

CHAPTER VI

. . . nothing less than a dance on Tuesday, could have made such a Friday, Saturday, Sunday, and Monday, endurable . . .

THE DAY THAT simply could not be waited for did arrive, as they all eventually do. The house was in a flurry all afternoon, and Sarah, as she finished curling Kitty's hair, could have wept with the pain from her chilblains: they throbbed red and tight, and grew worse each time she crouched to heat the hair irons at the fire. Even Mr Bennet, usually blithely indifferent to appearance, had been prepared with particular care: he had James play the valet, and brush down his ancient evening gear and powder his wig.

It was a different order of a thing, Mr Bennet remarked as James buttoned up his straining waistcoat for him, to those God-awful public dances at the Assembly Rooms at Meryton, with their crush, their noise, and their vapid conversation. He would never be persuaded to subscribe to them, though his wife and daughters did so most assiduously. Some crowding and noise were still to be expected, even at a private ball, but neighbourly courtesy outweighed these inconveniences.

James, nodding along, helped him shoe-horn his corns into his old dancing pumps.

Mr Bennet would never have admitted this to any living person, but the most pressing reason for his attendance at Netherfield was that if he did not go, he would never hear the last of it from his wife. It was easier to suffer the discomforts of a ball than his wife's disgruntlement that he did not. As James helped him clamber into the coach, Mr Bennet gave him a sympathetic look. James had been obliged to wear a wig and tricorn hat as well as his stiff and creaking livery, just to drive the three short miles to Netherfield.

'I see they have you trussed up like a partridge too,' Mr Bennet said.

''Deed they do, sir,' said James, who was ready always to humour the good old man.

Mrs Hill – having pressed Mr Collins's evening wear with particular care, and hung it up for him to notice particularly that particular care, and having checked Polly's work on that gentleman's dancing shoes, and having, on his descent to the lobby, curtseyed as he passed – did not receive a single word of acknowledgement from him. She stood, somewhat lowered in her spirits, on the front steps with her husband and the maids to wave the coach away.

'Thank the Lord,' said Polly, turning back to the house. 'I'm glad that's over.'

They trooped through the vestibule and into the silent lobby. For a few hours at least no one would require anything of any of them, and that was a blessing to be savoured. Without a word, Mr Hill set off up the back stairs. He was an old man, and worn to a rag. He needed his sleep.

'You won't mind, Sarah,' Mrs Hill said, 'sitting up tonight. I am all done in. Come on, Polly.'

Sarah, eyes narrowed, waited till Mrs Hill, her rump swinging, had gone round the turn in the stair, with Polly dragging along behind her like a tired pup. She dug into the rug with a toecap, tucked her sore hands into her armpits. She was left with a candle flame, and the clock's tick, and a long empty night ahead of her. This was an outrage: she had sat up last time. This time Mrs Hill did not even know that Sarah had misbehaved, and still she was punishing her.

She had the house to herself now, though: there was that. She eased a hand out of the warmth under her arm, lifted her candle from the console, and shouldered through the door into the drawing room. She lifted a china shepherdess to look at her painted eyes, her painted lips, the rounds of rose painted on her cheeks. She tipped the thing over to peer at the rough underside, and into the dark opening of its hollow interior. She set it back in its place, then wandered over and picked up an embroidery hoop from the work-table: Jane's fancy work was stretched tight in the frame's beechwood grip. By candlelight, Sarah examined the time-devouring birds, and flowers, and leaves, and set it down again, as something she would never do, while there were still hems to be sewn and seams to be joined and stockings to be darned. At the card-table by the window, she put down her candlestick and took out a pack of playing-cards. She tried a game of Patience, but soon found that she had none, and gave up, scooping the cards together, tamping them neat, and slipping them back into their wooden box.

She sat down in Mrs Bennet's chair and wriggled into the upholstery, stretching out her legs and resting her feet on the fender. The cat slouched in and leapt onto her lap. It purred and stretched, kneading her leg; then it dug its claws in hard. She lifted it off and set it down on the floor. It stalked over to the hearthrug, where it folded itself into a sphinx, and closed its eyes.

The clock ticked. She should draw the curtains: beyond the glass, the park and countryside were wide and empty. But that meant getting up. An owl called across the silence. She could go and fetch her book, but it was three flights of stairs away, and that was just too far. She sat and scuffed the carpet and the cat rolled onto her back, and Sarah dreamed of fireworks and dancing bears and feats of strength and agility, of the flounces that she had unpicked and then re-stitched and the hair that she had curled, and the dresses that now were skimming over polished toffee floors, between peppermint columns and under peardrop chandeliers. She thought of Netherfield and of London and the sweep of the world beyond the dark panes of the window.

She heaved herself up and crossed to the sideboard and poured herself a glass of Canary wine. She may as well be hung for a sheep as a lamb, or, as things currently were, merely the suspicion of a lamb. She sipped the wine. It was sweet and tickly.

So she was in bad odour with Mrs Hill – and Mrs Hill was, of course, perfect. Mrs Hill had never put a foot wrong in all her born days because she never put a foot, not even a toe, anywhere. She had never lived, had never stepped outside this little soap-bubble of a place, and yet she always knew best, always had an opinion on everything. And was always so self-righteous about it. But when it came down to it, what did Mrs Hill know of the world, or of people in general, or of anything at all, apart from housekeeping, and her ramshackle old husband, and the care of the Bennets?

And – pouring another glass, this time of sherry wine, so that no great quantity would be missing from any particular bottle (they would blame Mr Collins, if they did notice: they were very ready to find fault with him) – Mrs Hill stood so in thrall to the Bennets, it was as though she considered them some species of little god. Well, Sarah would not turn out like *her*. No question of it. She would not settle for so little. Settle for nothing, really, or worse than nothing, since everything Mrs Hill made – everything she cleaned, baked, broiled, darned, knitted, crocheted and stitched, everything she ever laid her hands on – already belonged to, or was intended for, somebody else.

She emptied her glass, refilled it from a third decanter.

The clock chimed the half-hour. Would the young ladies be dancing already, or only just arrived at Netherfield? Their muslins light as egg-white, shoe-roses flicking in and out of sight, heads twined with braids and coils and ornaments. Like confectionery they were, all daintily decorated, and perfectly wrapped.

Sarah took another sip. This stuff burnt.

And take it all away – the shoe-roses, the muslins, all that fancy packaging – and then what? Would a gentleman look twice, if they had rough hands and chilblains and chapped lips and wooden pattens on their heavy boots? And if he did, would it be the way that a gentleman looked at a lady – appraisingly, but detached – or would it be the way

142

that in *Pamela* the greasy little master looked at his maid? As something he could get his hands on and peel the wrappings off?

Sarah drained her glass, wiped it dry with her apron and set it back on the tray.

Back in the kitchen, she attempted the remaining business of the day. She swabbed down the table, then clattered out everything for the family's return: milk, biscuits, a bowl of sugar flaked off the loaf.

We could go walking out. When you get your afternoon off.

CHAPTER VII

Attention, forbearance, patience . . .

IT WAS A BLOWY, scuddy night; a big bright moon hidden then revealed by clouds. Sarah raised her face to the sky, stumbling through the cow-churned fields. She thought, How lovely to be out; she thought, I should have done this so much sooner; she thought, I should do this much more often. It was not so cold out after all.

She would see Netherfield lit up and decorated for the ball; she would hear the music, see the dresses; she would watch the dancing through a window for a while. She could not go to the ball, but she could see it at least. Then she would find Tol Bingley – she did not concern herself for the time being with the practicalities of finding Tol Bingley – and maybe take a walk and have a smoke with him. She could quite fancy a smoke right now. And hadn't he asked her, after all, to walk out with him? It wasn't afternoon, she'd admit that quite freely, but why shouldn't she take her pleasures where she could, just like anybody else?

The three miles passed in determined, blustery self-justification, swaddled in the old blue pelisse and snaffled drink, bonnet jammed on her head and knotted tight under her chin. She reached the boundary wall of the Netherfield demesne and blundered on through the little gate into the woods.

The path, broad enough by daylight, was strangely narrowed by the dark; the undergrowth crowded close and the boughs above creaked against each other in the wind. Her outstretched hands fumbled over the waxy leaves of laurels and the springiness of privet, but at any moment, she felt, they might touch something else. She'd heard things whispered – uneasy things – dark tales of girls who went out on some silly spree, and just never came back, or who came back strange, or with a baby in them, and she was beginning to feel a little uneasy for herself. But then she heard the music. A trail of it on the wind, there and gone and there again. And then the shrubs were thinning, and there were lights glimpsed between the branches, and there was the music again. This time it was clear, and it made her forget that she had been afraid.

The trees here stood wide apart, bare branches hanging low and clattering in the wind. She came out to the edge of the shadows. Beyond, in the moonlight, was a sweep of grass, then the carriage circle, and the house itself.

The marble façade was swept with shadow as clouds bundled across the sky; the windows were uncurtained, and figures moved past inside, silhouetted against the candlelight. The guests' carriages must have been wheeled away round to the back of the house to wait, since the drive was clear and the carriage circle white and empty in the moonlight. James would be there, in the servants' hall. Drinking beer and playing dice. For who knew what James got up to, who knew what he was even *like* when he was away from Longbourn.

She crept out beyond the edge of the trees, across the lawn, and stood on the gravel in a patch of light, looking up at the high window. The wind snatched at her pelisse, dragged her hair out from under her bonnet. It was crowded inside, milling: she recognized Charlotte Lucas strolling past with Elizabeth, and then Kitty and Lydia go laughing by with a pair of red-coated officers, and then Mr Goulding stopped right in front of the window to talk to Mr Long in his clerical black, and she could even hear what they were saying, they were so close. The fox had had his birds; the hunt would be through soon. The roads. The awful weather, the certainty that it could not continue.

The plaster was not peppermint, of course it wasn't. And the floors were not made of polished toffee. And the light came from conventional, crystal chandeliers, and not from peardrop ones. And that was, after all, what she had expected, because a house cannot really be built of sugar, and it was all very fine and lovely, of course. But the people! She could just not get over how dull the people were. Granted, there were the officers, and the Bingleys were new and rich, and that was no doubt thrilling. But otherwise it was just the Longs and Lucases and Gouldings, the same old neighbours who passed through the doors of Longbourn year after year, and through whose halls the Bennets passed too, and had done for all eternity, and who had played the same old card-games and eaten the same old suppers and danced the same old dances and worn the same old gowns; and any new gowns – aside from Miss Bingley's and her sister's – were made of fabric Sarah had seen fading in the draper's shop for months. And all of them with the same old freckles and wrinkles and bad breath and smallpox scars and limping gout; all of them airing the same old opinions, having the very same conversations, about the hunt and the roads and the weather, year after year after endless year.

How could they possibly stand it?

Her envy puffed up into smoke and was gone on the wind. She turned away. So what if she could not have this? She did not want it. She felt light of heart and almost giddy with the sense of release.

She was just passing the shadow of the first trees, when she saw a red speck in the darkness. She could make no sense of it, could not tell the distance; it seemed to be hanging all by itself. Then – making her start – it swung up a foot or two higher, glowed brighter, hotter, for a moment, then fell, fading, and hung again just a couple of feet from the ground.

Then it clicked into sense: the burning tip of a cigarillo, held in a man's hand, lifted up to his lips. As she realized this, the man himself came towards her. Tol Bingley, peering at her out of the darkness.

'Hel-lo. Who is that?'

'Good evening, Mr Bingley—'

'Is that young Sarah?'

'It is.'

'Well, well. Did you come to see the party?'

'I did, yes.'

He came out into the moonlight; closer now, she could make him out better: he fumbled inside his breast-pocket, drew an object out and sloshed it at her; he smelt of strong drink.

'May I offer you some refreshment?'

She hesitated. What she really wanted was to be back in the kitchen at Longbourn, with a warm fire and a cup of tea.

'Hospitable place this, Netherfield.' His voice was over-careful, with a tendency to slur.

'I think I've probably—'

'Plenty more where that came from,' he said. 'Go on, just a taste.'

She took it from his hand.

''S rum,' he said. 'Bingley's finest, straight off the plantation.'

She uncorked the flask and lifted it to her lips. The burn of liquor caught at the back of the throat and flared up her nose.

'Good stuff, eh?'

A wave of laughter washed out of the bright rooms, and over them, the pair of them there together, in the shadows.

'They're having a high old time tonight,' he said.

He stumbled a little; she passed the flask back to him.

'You'd think, wouldn't you, that there was nothing to do in all the world, but to dance and drink and laugh and eat and wake up at midday tomorrow and open another bottle of wine and do it all over again.'

She peered up at him. Her legs were whipped around with petticoats, her feet were cold in their damp boots, the wind chilled her cheeks and teased her hair into tats and made her eyes wet and blurry. He seemed to be onto something here.

He dragged on his cigarillo, blew away smoke. 'Beasts, they are, the lot of them, don't you think? Just animals.'

She blinked. The blink seemed strangely slow, and when her eyes were closed, her head reeled, and her gorge rose. She swallowed the burn of it back down.

'To be milked and fleeced and made into bacon,' he said.

He tipped the flask towards her again. She shook her head to try to clear it: it was as if the lid had been lifted off an ordinary stone jar, and a cloud of flies had come seething out, and now were buzzing all around her.

'You and me, though, Sarah – you and me – we know what's what.'

His arm slid around her waist, and it tugged her to him, and crushed her up against him. He was going to kiss her. This was the moment when the world would change. Because Ptolemy Bingley was something. He was brilliantly something. He would move in a different world, a world of London streets and dancing and entertainments and tobacco and faraway places where the air was like a warm bath and you'd never catch a chill. And if she kissed him now, she'd go there with him; she could swim in that world too, like a fish swims in water.

He breathed smoke and liquor into her face, looming close. Then his mouth was on her mouth, wet, and there was the taste of smoke and liquor and teeth and onions, and the crush of his lips – how to breathe, while being kissed? – and there was the music and the clutter of voices from the big house, and the wind shoving and pulling at them, and she thought, I want this, I know I want this. This is how you get from one world to the next.

Chapter VIII

. . . if encouraged to read and improve himself by such an
example as her's, he might become a very agreeable companion.

THE FAMILY STUMBLED down to breakfast looking grey; even
Mr Collins, who, as a clergyman, might have been expected to
be moderate in his pleasures, was green about the gills. Sarah did not
feel entirely well herself: it seemed that somebody had jammed a knife
into her head, and every so often decided to flick its handle with a
finger.

Her stomach churned as she waited on table: the shovelling and
chewing and rolling of food down throats, and the grinding of jaws,
and the swilling of tea and coffee. His words came rearing back at her
through the fug and forgetfulness of drink: *beasts, they are; cows and
sheep and pigs, to be milked and fleeced and made into bacon. You and
me, though, Sarah – you and me.* It made literal sense to her now: the
way they peered and grabbed and snuffed at each new platter of toasted
muffins, bacon, buttered eggs.

She should not have made Sarah sit up late, Mrs Hill realized; the
girl needed a firm hand, no doubt, but she also needed her sleep. This
was a truth to which Sarah's debility today bore witness. Mrs Hill herself had had little benefit from her early night: she had lain awake for
hours, listening to the house sounds, to Sarah tidying around below
(she was a good girl, after all, when she wasn't being led astray), to the
mutter and thrash of Polly dreaming across the narrow landing, to

149

the scuttle of the mice in the wainscot, the wheeze of her husband's breath, to the wind pummelling the roof and howling in the chimneys. When she did finally sleep, she was still somehow aware of the wild night beyond; she dreamed that she was waiting up for the carriage, and that when it returned, and she opened the front door, a litter of piglets scurried in, dressed in muslin evening-gowns and dancing shoes.

In the grey light of day, Mrs Hill understood that she must find a way around this; a way of dealing with Sarah that was not head-on, but that slipped instead around the edge of her stubbornness and into the sweet and giving nature it defended. But even as Mrs Hill was thinking this, she was scolding the girl, saying that she'd better lift her chin up before she tripped on it. The only reply she got was a long look and a stiffening of the shoulders, and a clattering-down of dishes.

'I expect a civil answer when I speak to you.'

'Speak civilly to me, missus, and you shall get one.'

Mrs Hill's jaw dropped. She was about to step cleanly over the brink of her temper, but then James pushed in through the hall door, and she saw herself as she must appear to him – a bitter, frowning old scold – and she clamped her mouth shut. She would say something kind instead. Something soothing and considerate that would reconcile her with the girl, if she could but think what.

Her efforts to summon something up were broken by a flurry of activity overhead. They heard the breakfast-room door flung open and slammed, then a race of light footsteps down the hallway and up the stairs. One of the girls, running to her bedchamber. Then more footsteps, heavier, going the opposite way to the first: Mrs Bennet's. She was heading to the breakfast room.

In the kitchen, the four of them stood stone-still, heads cocked. James, on the threshold, pushed the door a little wider.

'What is it?' Polly asked. 'What's going on?'

'It'll be Mr Collins,' Sarah said. 'He'll have gone and proposed.'

Polly was agog. 'Who to?'

'Elizabeth.'

'Really?'

'Shhh.'

Mrs Hill and Sarah moved to stand by James; Polly crept up too, and then Mr Hill shambled over to join them in the doorway, shaking his head. They listened to the low burr of voices.

'What are they saying?'

Sarah put her finger to her lips.

They heard the breakfast-room door flung open again, and then Mrs Bennet's footsteps pounding down the hallway. She passed into their line of sight: they shrank, Polly ducking low, Mr Hill stepping back, Sarah squeezing in behind James, and Mrs Hill turning completely away, back into the kitchen.

'I never knew she could move so fast!' Polly said.

They saw her throw open the library door; Polly made big eyes at Sarah: she hadn't even knocked!

'Oh! Mr Bennet, you are wanted immediately—'

Mrs Bennet pulled the door shut behind her, cutting off the noise. James took his weight off their own door, and let it fall closed.

Sarah went back to the table, lifted the dishes. 'Poor fellow.'

'Poor fool,' James said.

Mrs Hill shook her head. 'What an awful shame.'

'Mary would have had him . . .' Sarah headed for the scullery.

Then the library bell jangled. They stopped, watched it dance there on its spring.

'I'll go,' said James.

'No,' said Mr Hill. 'They'll want Miss Lizzy fetching down, so—'

'I'll go,' Sarah said.

Mrs Hill stepped back to let her pass. This was a disaster, and it hit her like a horse's kick. Now he might marry *anybody*. Who knew what little ninny with a head full of fashionable nonsense he might pick up at Bath or Bristol or Canterbury, or wherever it was that clergymen went looking for their wives? But if – as Sarah had said – Mary might have him, could snag him, they would be so safe with her: Mary would not want novelty simply for novelty's sake. With Mary in charge, the world below stairs would be as secure as anything in this world could hope to be.

The two elder girls were sitting on their bed, heads together, hands clasped. They looked up in apprehension when Sarah knocked and poked her head round the door; they softened when they saw that it was just her.

'You are wanted in the library, Miss Lizzy.'

Elizabeth was not quite able to compose herself. She seemed to be on the verge of breaking into some outburst of emotion, though whether it would be laughter or fury or a wail of mortification, Sarah could not judge.

'The whole household knows, then, I take it?'

'Knows what, miss?'

Elizabeth lifted up her eyes. 'You little politician.'

Jane kissed her sister's cheek, and, when she got up to go, stayed her a moment with a hand.

'You must remember, Lizzy, that he is a respectable man, and in proposing, he meant to do what he thought proper, and right. So do be kind to him, my dear.'

'Not for all the world, Jane! We have come *this* far on the barest of civilities; I dare not think what might happen if I am kind!'

Jane shook her head and smiled. 'You do not mean it. You know you do not.'

Then she glanced up at Sarah, and seemed to notice her properly, running her eyes down the length of her and back up again, noticing the limp yellowish-green poplin.

'Do you not wear your new dress, Sarah?'

Sarah curtseyed. 'I am saving it, miss, for very best.'

Sarah accompanied Miss Elizabeth down to the library, knocked and opened the door for her, while Elizabeth stood back, steadying herself. Inside, Sarah spied Mrs B. standing by her husband's desk, arms folded, glowering, and Mr B. still seated there, in the act of removing his spectacles.

'Come here, child,' cried her father as she appeared. 'I have sent for you on an affair of importance. I understand that Collins has made you an offer of marriage. Is it true?'

Sarah closed the door on the three of them.

You saw it all the time, it not working out fair.

Mrs Hill carried coffee up to the breakfast room, where Mrs Bennet, furious with her second daughter, was attempting to enlist Charlotte Lucas's support in her cause, and where the other young ladies had gathered to gossip. It was like buying a pig-in-a-poke, marriage was; you just could not know what you were getting, and people were always trading badly. You saw beautiful young provincial girls on the arm of some elderly accountant. Still hale and handsome men in their middle years with a wife already fat and faded. Whether this was a tragedy or not depended on where you stood within or in relation to it: one party maybe had got sold a pup, but the other did get to enjoy a splendidly good deal.

Mrs Hill poured coffee and handed out the cups. Elizabeth took hers with a steady hand; she rewarded Mrs Hill with a smile.

Mrs Hill thought, What it is to be young and lovely and very well aware of it. What it is to know that you will only settle for the keenest love, the most perfect match.

The morrow brought no abatement in Mrs Bennet's ill temper or ill health; she complained of nerves, retired to her dressing room with Mrs Hill and took nearly half a bottle of Cordial Balm of Gilead; it made her at first irascible, and then it made her mumble, and then it made her fall asleep, her breath reeking of *Eau de Vie*. The sisters – all but Mary, who preferred to stay at home – departed for a morning walk to Meryton, to escape their mother's sufferings and Mr Collins's wounded pride, and to enquire after Mr Wickham, who had been unforgivably absent from the Netherfield ball.

Mrs Hill and Sarah had no such opportunity for escape. Mrs Hill spent more time than she considered healthy confined to Mrs Bennet's dressing room, adjusting stays and neckerchiefs and pillows. When she did escape, the first thing she did was knock on Mary's door, making the girl stumble to a halt in the middle of E major. Mrs Hill peered round the edge of the door, and Mary peered back at her, alarmed.

'What is it, Hill?'

'Excuse me, Miss Mary, but . . .' She came in. 'Mr Collins is all alone downstairs, and I thought maybe you should know.'

'I was practising—'

'Yes, but you did not know that he was quite by himself – you would not wish to be thought discourteous.'

'He has proposed to my sister, has he not?'

Mrs Hill could only nod.

Mary was silent for a long moment. Then, decided, she stood up and shook out her skirts. Mrs Hill saw now that her eyes were rimmed with red. She had been crying. This boded very well indeed. The girl sidled past Mrs Hill, and trudged towards the head of the stairs.

'Only because I would not want to be thought discourteous, you understand.'

Sarah, meanwhile, was kept running up and down stairs by Mr Collins's requests that she mend the fire, provide refreshments, and answer his enquiries as to the location of his copy of Fordyce's *Sermons*. He feared he might have left it in Mr Bennet's library, and he was not certain that he wished to disturb that gentleman, who had shown such singular lack of right feeling towards his suit. Might Sarah go and see about it for him?

She might, and did, Mr Bennet only glancing up from under his bushy eyebrows as she tapped and nudged open the door. He held up the small brown volume wordlessly; she took it off him and curtseyed.

Polly, however, was left more at her leisure, being unsupervised. She trundled around with her duster and a dreamy air, and then, a little before midday, she sloped off and could have been found – if anyone had gone out looking for her – playing at jacks by the stable wall with James. It pleased her so much when she won, that he became increasingly clumsy and cack-handed, the better to enjoy her crowing delight.

Sarah handed Mr Collins the little book.

'You are a good girl,' he said. 'I think you are good, you know, what-ever they say.'

'Thank you, sir.'

'One thing I have found here—' He dropped his voice: 'Rather puz-zlingly, I have found that my position is quite similar to your own.'

Sarah just looked at him. 'Really, sir?'

'I mean to say—' He glanced around him, as if afraid of being over-heard, though the breakfast room was desolate at that time of day, and the house itself almost deserted. 'One intends only what is right and good, one does what one sees to be one's duty. And for one's pains, one is rejected; one is found to be at fault. One is laughed to scorn.'

'I'm sorry you are unhappy, sir.'

'Thank you,' he said with genuine warmth. 'Thank you, my dear child.'

He was just a child himself, she saw. And lonely. He was the kind of man who probably always would be.

'Would you like some cake?' she tried.

His countenance brightened. He *would* like some cake, he realized. He would like some cake very much indeed; he would like it above anything.

When Sarah brought a slice of fruitcake up on a pretty blue-rimmed plate, she found that Mary was now also in the breakfast room, sitting stiffly on an upright chair near the young clergyman; she looked round, heavy-eyed, when Sarah came in. Sarah had the distinct im-pression that she had disturbed not a conversation but a silence. Mary must be struggling to converse with him – Sarah could sympathize – too much time spent with books had not fitted her to be easy with her-self, and other people. The young lady got up abruptly, and went to the window, and Mr Collins got up too, looking relieved. He took the plate from Sarah and was profuse in his thanks, but then, with Mary there, did not know what to do with the cake after all.

*

The girls were accompanied home from Meryton by two officers. Sarah, glancing out of an upstairs window, saw them coming down the footpath – the four young ladies, the two soldiers in red coats, all of them ambling easily along like old friends. They would reach Longbourn in moments, and would expect refreshments, and the house was all at sixes and sevens, and nothing ready or fit to be seen.

She rushed up to the dressing room to warn Mrs Hill, who closed her eyes, and set her jaw, and muttered something that was best not taken heed of. Then the housekeeper informed her mistress there were guests expected shortly, and plodded down to the kitchen. By the time the party was in the hall, Mrs Bennet was found to be quite in spirits again, and properly attired, and on her way down to greet them. Sarah gathered cloaks and hats and went to hang them; Mrs Bennet stayed Sarah with a hand.

'But where is James?'

'I do not know.'

'But I want James. I don't want you here. I do not see the point in us keeping a footman at all if we must have women waiting on us all the time.'

Sarah could only agree. The guests now settled in the parlour, she ran down to the kitchen. Mrs Hill set about the added inconvenience of tea; Sarah ghosted around her, trying to look helpful, since if she either did nothing, or got in the way, she'd get her head torn clean off.

And then the outer door opened, and there was Ptolemy Bingley, fresh as butter from the dairy and with a direct look at Sarah that made her turn her face away, and made Mrs Hill slap down the teapot on the tray, march over to him and demand, hands on hips, what it could possibly be that he wanted here this time.

Sarah was supposed to disappear; anyway, the longer she stayed, the greater the chance was that he would let slip some hint about the carriage ride, or their encounter in the Netherfield demesne. She backed away towards the hall door as he bowed to Mrs Hill and brought forth a note. He seemed deflated, somehow, Sarah noticed. Solemn.

'For Miss Bennet.'

Mrs Hill snatched the letter, slapped it down on the tea tray and strode over to Sarah with the lot. Sarah took the chinking tea things off her. The letter was sealed with a pretty yellow wafer, and looked innocent enough. She looked up from it to Ptolemy.

'Right, you,' said Mrs Hill. 'Get that lot upstairs.'

Sarah left. Mrs Hill turned her attention back to the mulatto. He lingered in the doorway, letting in the cold.

'You expecting a reply?'

He stepped across the threshold and shut the door behind him.

'You *are* expecting a reply, then?'

'I will take one certainly, if there is one.'

Polly ambled into the kitchen, and edged past Ptolemy, giving him one of her long stares. In reply, he gave her a bow. Then, as if to point out the incivility with which he was being met, he crossed over to a fireside chair and sat down – Mrs Hill would not mind it, he suggested, if he warmed himself a while.

She did mind it. She minded it very much indeed, and she was just about to give him a piece of her mind – coming round here with his good looks and his nice clothes and his London ways, turning her girls' heads – if Sarah had not clattered back into the kitchen just then, and seeing him there in the fireside chair, had pulled up short like a pony. Mrs Hill saw that their eyes met for just a moment; she did not like the way Sarah smiled to herself as she turned away. It was a far too private smile.

She'd found she was not welcome in the parlour, Sarah told Mrs Hill, for all she'd brought up the note from Netherfield. She'd been told to leave the tray and then run straight back down to the kitchen, and not return upstairs until the guests were gone.

'Mrs B. says we must send James up immediately to wait upon the officers.'

Mrs Hill flung out her hands. 'Do you see him here?'

Sarah looked around, shrugged.

'I am up to my eyes, Sarah. If you want him, you go and find him.'

'I don't want him. Mrs B. wants him. I just thought you might know where he is.'

'Well I don't.'

'Oh,' Polly said. 'That's easy. I know.'

Mrs Hill rounded on her, snappish: 'Well, where is he, then?'

'He's hiding.'

Mrs Hill and Sarah stared. Polly reached the jar down from the dresser and coolly helped herself to a piece of barley-sugar. She slumped into the other fireside chair, eyeing Ptolemy.

'He don't like soldiers,' she said, around the barley-sugar. 'We saw the soldiers coming, so we hid. But then I got bored, and I thought you'd probably be cross if I was gone much longer, so I left him to it and came to help you.'

Polly wriggled in her seat, self-satisfied: James was naughty; *she* had been good.

Mrs Hill waved all this away. 'Nonsense. Don't talk daft. Hiding!'

Polly began to protest: it wasn't nonsense, and it wasn't daft; they *were* hiding. And if it was nonsense, it wasn't her nonsense, it was James's, but she was briskly shushed. Sarah was very conscious of Ptolemy Bingley observing all this fluster and bad-humour from his seat, quiet though, his eyebrows raised. Sarah felt the urgent need to turn the conversation.

'So is this a dinner or another ball, or what is it, Mr Bingley?'

'Sorry?'

'The letter. An invitation, I expect?'

'No,' he said. 'It's not. It's . . . We're leaving.'

'Leaving?'

He nodded, his lips bitten tight between his teeth.

'Leaving?' Sarah reached for a chair, drew it out, and sat. 'Just like that?'

'Mr Bingley went up to London on business, and directly after, his sisters decided they would follow him . . . And Mr Darcy, his friend who has been staying . . .' He paused a moment, just looking at her. 'And so. We're leaving. The whole shooting match.'

'And you go too, to London.'

It was not a question, but he nodded anyway.

158

Sarah got up and moved across the kitchen. She opened a drawer, and stared down at its contents – jam-cloths, a scalding-dish, a few worn and fruit-stained wooden spoons. He was off to London, gone for ever, gone to see the plays and visit Astley's and wander up and down the beautiful arcades.

'And the house is to be quite shut up?' asked Mrs Hill, who had left off her squabble with Polly, and now seemed to have forgotten, or to consider redundant, her edict that Sarah must absent herself from the mulatto's company.

'It is indeed, ma'am. Most of the staff have gone on already. We few are left to settle some remaining business, and follow afterwards.'

'Of course, of course. And Mr and Mrs Nicholls will stay, to keep an eye on things.'

'When do you go?' Sarah could not look at him.

'Later today.'

'And when,' Sarah shifted the folded muslins into a corner, then lined up the wooden spoons so they now lay in a neat row, 'when will you return?'

'No more this winter, I believe.'

Mrs Hill nodded approvingly. To hear of domestic matters so well arranged – and so conveniently to her wishes – was very satisfying. But to Sarah this was desolation: a whole winter to wear out at Longbourn, without interest, or pleasure, or respite. She bit her lip. Spring was such a long while off. If he ever came back at all. If he did not stay in London, and open up his shop. Because who would come back here, if you had all of London at your doorstep?

'Well, we will all miss you here, I am sure,' said Mrs Hill. 'But don't let us detain you. You must have plenty still to do.'

He pushed down on the arms of the chair, getting up. 'And all this, just as I was getting accustomed to the mud.'

Sarah felt choked by sheer thwartedness. She shunted the drawer shut, making the spoons rattle out of order again, remembering the reeling sensation of that night, the kiss, the taste of smoke and onions, the press of his body against hers, which had seemed to promise

159

something. All of it over now, and there was no point to any of it at all.

'Look me up, eh, sweetheart,' he spoke low, when he passed by her, so that only she could hear. 'Whenever you're in town.'

The officers did not stay long after Miss Bennet's receipt of her letter. Jane slipped away as soon as she could, looking white and sick and making Sarah feel a lurch of sympathy for her. Jane had expected something of the other Mr Bingley – she had, at least, hoped.

Sarah brought the gentlemen's cloaks; while they swung them on and fastened them, Polly waited, balancing a cockaded hat on either hand, in awe of the moment and her participation in it. A handsome officer – who was, it turned out, the fabled Mr Wickham – gave her a small coin in exchange for his hat. She grinned and thanked him and pocketed it, and bobbed him a curtsey. Then he took off his glove, and touched her cheek. Struck, as people sometimes are, by a child's sheer loveliness.

Chapter IX

. . . she bewailed it as exceedingly unlucky that the ladies
should happen to go away, just as they were all
getting so intimate together.

JANE BORE IT well, considering that she would have to just sit and
wait. Sit and wait and be beautiful, and wan. Sit and wait and be in
love. Sit and wait until Mr Bingley shook off his sisters and returned
to claim her. That was how things worked for young ladies like Miss
Jane Bennet.

Sarah's position was quite different. She did not have Jane's loveliness, or her gentleness, or her one thousand pounds in the four per
cents. She did not have in her thoughts that one clear and certain word,
which seemed to be the answer to all questions and the end to all un-
certainties – even if it did not bring happiness, and remained for ever
unspoken – love. She had nothing, in short, that she could cling to;
nothing that she could rely upon to entice a man away from the
delights and opportunities that were offered elsewhere. But what she
did have was an invitation to go after him.

The Bennets were engaged to dine with the Lucases the very same
day that the news had been received, which provided some distraction
for the miserable, mortified and disgruntled amongst them, and a
respite from cooking for the others. James was occupied with ferrying
the family around; Polly swept and polished in her perfunctory way;
Mrs Hill contented herself with mending Mr Collins's trousers, the

buttonholes of which had become sorely stretched, the buttons hanging on by just a thread: too much, perhaps, in the way of cake. Sarah cleaned the girls' boots, muddied from the excursion into town; she scraped off crusts and clots of mud with her fingers, wiped the leather clean with damp rags, and then rubbed it with greasy dubbin.

Three miles away, in Netherfield's cold drawing room, Mrs Nicholls was wafting dustsheets over furniture, while downstairs Mr Nicholls locked the wine cellar, and then the gun room, and then the plate room, jingling the keys as he ambled off along the echoing corridor. And the Bingleys' remaining trunks, along with the few bits of furniture that were wanted in the Hursts' Grosvenor Street house, were creaking along on a canvas-covered wagon down the London road, and Tol Bingley was watching the wide wet muddy world go by from his seat beside the wagoner, and beginning to reconsider – vaguely yet, and still in a resistant way, surprised at the grey ache he felt on leaving this place, on leaving that girl, Sarah – what he wanted most in all the world.

That night, Sarah listened to the scratch and scrape of Mrs Hill locking the place tight, and watched in the moonlight as Polly twitched like a puppy in her sleep. When all was perfectly quiet, and Polly was snoring, Sarah drew her wooden box out from underneath the bed, and packed her comb and slippers and a chapbook in it. In there, always locked safe, was a worn old rag-doll with unmatched button eyes.

A fox barked somewhere out across the frosty countryside; downstairs, the clock struck one; she sat silent and listening, a blanket around her shoulders. The clock struck two, startling her out of a shallow sleep. She sat for a few minutes more. The house was now quite still.

She crept from her room, her boots in one hand, her box heavy under her other arm; she softly shut the door behind her. In the kitchen she laced up her boots, gave the cat a stroke. 'Bye-bye, Puss. Good luck.'

Tol Bingley had left for London; Sarah would not be far behind.

*

There had been a story in the newspaper about a young Spanish woman who dressed herself in britches and went off to be a soldier; even now she was leading skirmishes against Boney's troops in Spain. The paper also said – Sarah had been baffled by the circumlocutions for a time, but had then started to see through them and understand – that she had taken lovers; not from amongst her fellow soldiers, but women, from amongst the camp followers. And there were other stories too, of Mother Ross, who had gone for a soldier back in the olden days, and was fierce and foul-mouthed and who would never have been found out if she'd not got wounded in the thigh, so that when they stripped her to search and dress the wound, the surgeon's apprentice had seen her private parts and thought for a moment that it was another wound and a worse one; the boy had fainted: only on examination by a man who had seen what he was looking at before, was Ross understood to be a woman. And those Irish women who had long and profitable adventures as privateers, and dodged the noose – for a time, at least – by getting themselves in the breeding way.

It was a thought, that. Not to attach yourself to a man, but to confront instead the open world, the wide fields of France and Spain, the ocean, anything. Not just to hitch a lift with the first fellow who looked as though he knew where he was going, but just to *go*.

A seed of unease: as she walked on in the dark, it sprouted and grew.

The sheep shuffled themselves into a tighter pack in the field beyond. Her feet skidded on ice, scuffed on stones; trees stood bare against the starry sky, the pale shape of an owl swept overhead. She climbed up as high as the drovers' road; she stopped there, on the crossroads, on the edge of everything she had ever known. The hillside stood wide and empty, and it seemed that there was nothing but the stars and nightbirds.

But there was also, unknown to her, James. He followed her secretly, unnoticed, as he had learned to do.

There were nights when sleep was fitful for him; there were nights when sleep came not at all, when the old pain flared and shivered through him and would not let him rest. It seemed somehow to be attuned to the weather; the shift from clear skies to cloud and back again sent ripples of red flame through him, so that on some nights he gave up even the attempt to sleep and would distract himself instead with books, reading by a low light, hunched in blankets, grateful for the good fortune and generosity that bestowed a new candle on him every time the old one burnt itself to drips and puddles. Those nights, it was as though his flesh was dreaming; as though his body was remembering other times and other places. It made him vividly aware that nothing was for ever: that even pain had its tides, its pauses.

And it kept him alert to the world; he felt the scrape when the kitchen door was opened and then shut; her footfalls across the yard were like the pad of fingertips on his skin, and when she passed the end of the stable building, and was gone, he felt the tug of her away into the night. The lopsided drag of her gait suggested she was carrying a weight – the wooden, lockable box that all women and girls like her possessed; their only private space beyond their bodies in a life of shared bedchambers and scrutiny. And if Sarah had taken her box, she was not just sleepless, restless, wandering: she was gone.

His thoughts lit in turn on the immediate causes – Netherfield's being shut up, Ptolemy Bingley's departure for London – and then bundled into a downhill helter-skelter, through the chances of her happiness, fears for her safety, the dangers of the world beyond, her ignorance of them; and then on into an image of this place without her, without a glare or shrug or roll of her eyes, without a glimpse of her slim figure slipping round a corner; without her unyielding, breathing flesh beside him in the room – to arrive at the shock of a full stop: he loved her.

Oh.

It could have no effect on anything at all.

What he felt did not matter: it changed nothing.

But it interested him.

He held the phrase in his mind as a priest might hold a chalice, dazed by what it conveyed beyond its practical reality. If he loved Sarah, then it meant that he was, despite all that he had done, and all that he had failed to do, capable of feeling, and capable of good. Because he wanted nothing from her: this was a generous, expansive feeling, unattached to the possibility of gratification; it was a simple happiness that came from knowing that one particular person was alive in the world. He felt grateful for it; grateful that she had, however unwittingly, enabled him to feel like this.

And though love might not matter, gratitude did. It brought with it a sense of obligation.

He twisted himself up from his bed, pulled on his britches, stuffed his feet into his boots, and dragged his coat on over the snare of pain. Then he headed out into the night, scanning the grainy darkness for her moving shape. He caught it – a blue shadow amongst the wider blue – flitting across the paddock. He followed obliquely, slipping along the boundary wall, hanging back as she opened the little gate into the lane.

No difficulty in this. She did not expect to be followed; she was artless, and did nothing to disguise her progress. And she went slowly, so small in all this darkness, under the wide sky; she was sloped by the weight of her burden. She came up to the woods, and stepped out of sight into the deeper dark. He still followed, but with a more hesitant and uncertain tread now.

What, after all, was he hoping to achieve by this? That at a few choice words of his, she would see her mistake, understand the danger, and come back with him to a life of quiet drudgery at Longbourn? And even if she did, could he wish that for her? Could that really be a proper expression of his gratitude?

Who knew: she might be happy with Ptolemy.

She came out of the woods, onto the open hillside; the moon was bright. He paused at the tree-line; she climbed on doggedly towards the drovers' road. He watched, lips pressed tight; she was gone; she was her own woman, and who was he to stop her? He might have turned then, and gone back to his bed, and feigned surprise when, in the morning, she was found to have done a moonlight flit. He might have just jogged on through the days, and kept his head down, through weeks and months and years, and begun to forget about her, forget how she had made him feel – *that* she had made him feel – if she had not, at that moment, reached the junction with the drovers' road and stopped dead, and stood there silhouetted against the stars. Then she let the box fall to her feet, and rubbed at her forehead with the heel of her hand, looking out across the open silent country.

The way was clear; the night was calm: the only thing to stop her was her own uncertainty.

Sarah, though he could not know it, was thinking of sea-shells, and of his sleeves rolled back when he was drying dishes, and the taste of smoke and onions and a kiss that she wasn't sure that she had liked, but which had seemed at least to mean something, to suggest that there was a germ of possibility in a life that had hitherto seemed entirely barren of it. She was considering, too, the difference between hitching a lift for a lifetime, and not just for the journey home. And then she turned, and looked back, and her big eyes caught the starlight.

The word was out before he knew that he was going to speak: 'Stay.'

She stiffened, turning towards the sound of his voice. He came closer, scuffing his boots on the rocky track, so that she could hear him, and so locate him. He saw the moment that she recognized him – the softening of her body – but then she drew herself up again, and shifted her box to one side with a foot, as though she could hide it from his notice. As though that would make any difference now. But it made him smile.

'You had much better not go,' he said. 'You will be missed.'

'They will hardly notice. They will get another maid.'

She looked away. She seemed again resolved. From somewhere off to the north, a curlew called. When James went to speak again, he found his mouth had gone quite dry.

'Well then,' he said. 'If that is how it is, then bless you both.'

Silence still from her. She dug at the turf with a toe, staring away across the downs.

This was the chink, the uncertainty. She was not sure of Tol Bingley. He felt it.

'Or—'

'Or what?'

'I mean, I have no wish to interfere—'

'Then you go an odd way about it.'

'—but if you are not entirely sure, of your – of your feelings, or of his intentions, you might delay this, you might write . . .'

She tilted her head, still not looking at him.

'It would be a little less final than this.'

She did not speak.

'Or,' he said, 'perhaps you would like me to write for you?'

At that, she fixed her eyes on him. 'You are very certain of yourself, aren't you, Mr Smith?'

She came marching up towards him, pushed the hair back from her forehead.

'You think you are the only one in this place who has any intelligence at all, don't you? I may as well not be alive. I may as well be a puppet or a doll, for all you'd notice.'

'No, indeed, I do not for a moment—'

'Well, you clearly assume I cannot write.'

'Not everybody can.'

'Sunday-school taught, you think me – learned to read the Gospels and that's that? Well, in fact my father was a thinking man, and he taught me to write, when I was little. But it doesn't occur to you, not for a moment, that I might have that side to me, now does it? Of course not. Because you think me beneath your notice. You think me nothing at all.'

He found his sense of her was skewed again. There was an innocence about her, and an independence, but there was also this ferocious need for notice, an insistence that she be taken fully into account, and it made him feel so tenderly that it almost choked him. He wanted simply to tell her, It really does not matter what I think of you, it does not matter in the least.

'You think you're so clever because you have your books; because you've travelled and seen something of the world, and you have your fancy sea-shells to prove it, and now that I am trying to do something for myself—'

'My *shells?*'

She stood, open-mouthed, realizing what she had done. 'I was cleaning . . .'

It was as though a poultice had been torn off him, taking the skin with it. He let a breath go.

She shuffled.

'I haven't told anybody, if that's what you're so worried about.'

A thrill ran through him. The empty hillside, the sky infinite above them, and she speaking so freely to him, of things that came from a different life, from half a world away.

She wandered back to her wooden box, nudged it with a toe, as a distraction. 'I could be halfway to London by now.'

'I'm not stopping you.'

She folded her arms, looking across the open countryside. Her profile was precise against the paling sky. And then, suddenly, she ducked down, swept the box up into her arms and was off, striding along the high turf road.

'Sarah!'

He ran to catch her, grabbed her arm. She twisted, trying to shrug him off. He felt the slender strength of her, the shift of tendon and muscle.

'Sarah.'

She pulled away from him; he held on, not hard, but unyielding.

'Write to him. I'll beg a frank for you. I'll even take your letter to the post office. If he will come for you here, and marry you, and take you off to London, and if you think that that will make you happy—' The words were tumbling out of him now, unanticipated, surprising even him, making her eyes fix on his face, and widen. 'Of course I will not stand in your way. I couldn't. But I will *not* let you go tonight. Not like this. On my conscience, I cannot.'

A breath held, and then its uneasy release: still she pulled and twisted against his grip.

'Let go of me.'

'Sarah. This changes you for ever. Right now, you could still go back to Longbourn and no one else would ever know what happened here tonight. I can keep a secret, I really can, I promise you. But once they wake up and find you gone, there can be no return. You would be tainted by this.'

The words stumbled to a halt. He was afraid. And he had not been afraid for years.

'Please.'

She went still. He could feel her pulse throb in the crook of her arm.

'Come back with me,' he said. 'Tonight. Not for ever. But for tonight.'

And then she did something that he had not for a moment considered even possible. She let the box fall; it landed with a hollow thud on the frosty track. Then she stepped up to him, and slid her arm around his waist, stood on tiptoe, and kissed him.

Sarah, being in many ways a practical person, had known all along that she was working with insufficient information. That one kiss, deep in drink, with Ptolemy, was all she had to go on: it had not been very nice, but she simply could not know if that was what kisses were generally like, or if it was just that particular kiss, or that kisser. She could not know whether what she had felt – dizzy, her pride gratified, her body uncomfortable – about Tol Bingley amounted to love, or even anything very much at all. And here was James, now, with his hand wrapped around her arm, and his touch and his closeness and his voice pitched low and urgent, and it all seemed to matter, and it was all doing strange and pleasant things to her. She felt herself softening, and easing, like a cat luxuriating in a fire's glow. And there was just now, just this one moment, when she teetered on the brink between the world she'd always known and the world beyond, and if she did not act now, then she would never know.

She caught him, as it were, on the hop. Her lips colliding with his, surprising him; he swayed a little back, against the arm she'd reached around him. Her lips were soft and warm and clumsy, and her small body pressed hard against his. It was too much to resist. He slid his arms around her narrow waist, and pulled her to him, and let himself be kissed.

There was just the warmth of his mouth, and the warmth of his lean body against hers. Her breath grew quick; her body grew eager, wanting – then she dropped back to her heels, heart pounding; she leaned in against him, shaken by this.

'Oh,' she said.

She could feel his hand on the back of her neck, the other arm around her waist, holding her to him. Her head lay against his chest; she could hear his heart beat. She blinked in the darkness, her eyes wet. She had not been held, not by anyone, not since she was a little child.

'Will you go?' he asked, after a while, his hand on her nape, where her skin was warm, and her hair was cool.

For a long moment she didn't move or speak. Then he felt it against his chest: she shook her head.

*

They made their way back down to the house, he lugging her box on his shoulder, her hand in his hand. It was deeply dark, down off the hill and low between the hedges, now the moon had set. Stumbling, she felt the pressure of his palm and the pad of his thumb, the wrap of chill fingers across the back of her hand. She was more aware of that than the rocky track beneath her feet, the cold air, or any other thing around her.

Their feet crunched on stone; they slithered over ice, and, where it had thawed, into mud. She held up her skirts, and when a foot skidded out from underneath her, his hand tightened on hers, halting her fall. This made her glance round at him, think how strange, how good it was that he was there. She could feel the living certainty of his hand, but could only see a vague shape of him in the dark.

The house loomed out of the night, a dark hulking mass. They stopped at the corner of the stable, and peered round into the yard. She could see the glimmer of the kitchen window; other than that, the yard was a great pool of shadow.

It was impossible. She could not go to her room without Polly noticing she had been gone; she could not get her box back under her bed without somebody seeing it on its way there; her boots and petticoats must be filthy: everyone would know what she had done.

'It is too late. They will know. They will throw me off.'

'Here,' he said. 'Give me . . .'

And he knelt down at her feet, and cupped his hand around her ankle; she let him lift it, felt the movement of his hands as he scraped the mud off her boot. She could see just the dark shape of him, the curve of the back of his head. He let go of her ankle, and reached for the other, and she let him take it too, his hand warm.

He looked up at her. His face was now palely visible.

'Let down your skirts over your petticoat.'

She shook them out, to cover up the mud.

He got back to his feet.

'Just go and be,' he said softly, speaking close to her ear. 'Just be in the kitchen. Put your head on your arms and have a sleep if you can.'

She nodded, her hair brushing against his cheek, catching on stubble.

'When the household's stirring, just get up too and go about your business as though you slept your night in your bed just like anybody else.'

'What about you?'

He lifted the wooden box again onto his shoulder. 'I'll shift this later, when the coast is clear.' He touched her, just lightly, at the waist. 'Sarah,' he said.

'Yes?'

'Thank you.'

Then he was gone. He slipped round the corner, and into the deep shadow, skimming round the side of the stable. He must have ducked straight inside, because she heard the horses whinnying their greetings.

171

*

At half ten, when she handed him his cup of tea at breakfast, he smiled straight at her, and her heart did a little flip, and her own smile went all wonky.

Polly took two lumps of sugar from the bowl, and then, when no one seemed to notice, took a third and slipped it straight into her cheek. She shunted the sugar on to Mr Hill, who loaded up his tea with sugar crumbs. Polly, sucking her sugar lump, eyed James and Sarah, intrigued by their silence.

'I don't like this, sloping off without a word, without so much as a by-your-leave.'

Sarah and James both looked up, alarmed; but Mrs Hill was squinting peevishly out of the kitchen window.

James cleared his throat. 'What's that you say, Mrs Hill?'

Mrs Hill nodded to the window. 'Where is *he* off to now, I wonder?'

Sarah turned to follow her line of sight, and watched as Mr Collins, in his sober black, scurried across the yard like a lost mole. She let out a careful breath.

'Wherever it is, it can't be far,' James said, 'or he'd have called for the carriage.'

He lifted his cup and drank. Sarah got up and moved to the dresser, but then couldn't think what she might reasonably need there.

Mr Hill stirred his tea with much clinking of spoon and china, and Mrs Hill muttered on about their unpredictable guest. But Polly still just looked from James to Sarah, Sarah to James, and back again. She knew something was afoot. It had to do with the morning's cold bed, the dark circles beneath both pairs of eyes. They were twitchy as rabbits, the two of them. Something was up, and although she didn't know quite what, she was perfectly willing to speculate.

That night, when Sarah stumbled up the stairs to her attic room, she found her box was waiting underneath the bed, a little more scuffed than before, perhaps, and a bruise in the wood where she had dropped it; but it had been cleaned of mud, and there was nothing about it to suggest it had borne witness to any impropriety. She undressed and sank into bed, the boards creaking underneath her. Despite her deep fatigue, her mind was alight. She was very far from sleep.

This world was a maze. She'd turn this way and then that, race on a few steps, make her choice; but then she'd find herself turned quite around, and sliding back to the start, back into her place. To Longbourn.

But for now, that did not seem entirely bad.

CHAPTER X

Saturday . . . Sunday

Mr Collins departed early that Saturday morning, to be back in Hunsford in time for divine service the following day.

Despite the disappointments of his visit, the day of Mr Collins's departure brought a fresh hope to Mrs Hill's parched and anxious breast, in the unlikely form of Sir William Lucas, puffed up with pride and the news of his eldest daughter's engagement. He followed hard on Charlotte's heels, who had called in the morning, and sat awhile alone with Elizabeth, though this was such a common occurrence that Mrs Hill had not suspected anything of it at the time. Charlotte's main object had been to forewarn her friend: when Sir William made his announcement, while Mrs Hill served the tea, Lizzy looked uncomfortable, but she did not look surprised. Mary, though, looked miserable, and was obliged to leave the room soon after.

Poor Mary; she must take some blame for that. But – it was as though a sack of bricks had been lifted from Mrs Hill's back. The future was no longer such a terrifying place. Charlotte Lucas was a steady young woman, who knew the value of a good servant, and who had far too much sense to replace staff simply for the sake of appearance or fashion. Nothing was certain, of course – for nothing is certain in this life, except that we must leave it – but Charlotte had been in and out of Mrs Hill's kitchen since she was a little girl, asking for recipes, a loan of sugar or a jelly mould, and was known to be particularly partial to Mrs Hill's lemon tarts, and indeed had on several occasions been heard to say that nobody could make a lemon tart like Mrs Hill.

Back in the kitchen, Mrs Hill set about whipping up a batch of lemon tarts to send back with Sir William. These little attentions were more than worth the effort.

The next day was a blustery, blowy day, the first Sunday of Advent, and so the Advent candle burnt by the lectern and their breath smoked in the cold nave.

The Bennets sat together in the family box-pew, and the servants sat in the free seats at the back, James on one side of the solemn bulk of Mr and Mrs Hill, and Sarah and Polly on the other. Mr Hill sucked his few teeth, and Mrs Hill tucked her chin in, as she always did when she was feeling pleased. In the shuffle and creak of kneeling, the young ones managing it rather more quickly than the older pair, Sarah took the chance to glance past the Hills and catch James's eye. The aftermath of this made her feel quite distracted throughout the aptly named Mr Long's sermon.

The Bennets were slow to leave, as always, shaking hands and nodding and talking with their neighbours, and clogging up the porch, the two youngest ones linking arms and giggling with the farmers' daughters. Sarah, in the crush, was able to study Miss Lucas's face discreetly; she wondered what it was like to know that you were to be married, that you would have a home, an income, that you were set up for life. To have achieved all this simply by agreeing to put up with one particular man until he died.

Charlotte just looked awkward, and a little tired. Perhaps it was exhausting, to achieve so much at such a clip.

'How are you now?'

Sarah found herself, by accident, or by his design, near James. They passed together through the porch, and made their way to the edge of the crowd, and carried on a few paces side by side. He was a column of buff and grey in the corner of her eye. She held her bonnet to her head; the wind tugged at it: she saw the way the yews were combed by

175

the breeze, the green parting and re-parting and rippling like a sheep's fleece. She spoke low, looking dead ahead, so that it would not be obvious to Mrs Hill or Mrs B., or any other of the two-dozen or so matriarchs and busybodies assembled there, that she was actually conversing with him.

'I can't think,' she said, 'any more, what I was doing. I can't think who I was just then, at that moment. I no longer see how I could have thought it was a good idea, to go and do that, at all.'

'When you kissed me?'

She swung round, bright. 'No!'

His eyes creased, and she knew that he was smiling. He moved away, and was lost amongst the villagers, slipping between shabby farmgirls and broad labourers' shoulders in their straining Sunday best.

When she was a girl, and still growing, ravenous, whenever there had been a cake – a sponge cake, dusted with sugar, which Mrs Hill had conjured up out of eggs and flour and creamy butter – Sarah would never even let herself look at it, because she knew that it was not for her. Instead, she would carry it upstairs to be rendered into crumbs, and the crumbs lifted from the plate by a moistened Bennet finger, and the empty smeared plate carried back again. So Sarah would stare instead at the carpet underneath her feet, or at the painting of a horse with a strangely small head that hung at the end of the hall, or the rippled yellow curtains in the parlour, and would do her best not to breathe, not to inhale the scent of vanilla or lemon or almonds; even to *glance* at the cake was an impossible agony.

And for months, she realized, James had hardly looked at her at all.

It was a situation – though it occurred to neither of them to consider it this way – almost guaranteed to amplify desire. After that Sunday morning, there were no opportunities for properly private communication; barely a word could be exchanged unobserved. Those first few weeks of December were, therefore, marked by the catching of eyes, the exchange of smiles, by fingers brushing as burdens were exchanged.

At night, Sarah twisted in her bedsheets, hot despite the winter weather, while Polly snored beside her. Her lips were haunted by his lips; her body remembered the press of his: her second kiss had been nothing like the first. Her mind conjured, unbidden, the unbuttoning of his shirt, the peeling back of linen, the press of lips to collarbones, the taste of skin and salt. She curled up to the edge of the bed, bunched up her shift, and let her fingertips dip into the wet between her legs.

So daylight, and his presence, made her flush. The things that she had done with him, in the dark, when he was not there.

Mr Wickham, at this time, grew ever more present at Longbourn. He had, it seemed, a penchant for in-between places; for lobbies, vestibules, thresholds, from where he could observe both the gabble and swarm of company, and the bustle of the servantry; from where he could parcel out his Spanish money – his little bits of flattering nonsense – to each woman as she passed, no matter what her age, her marital status or her class.

On one occasion Sarah came upon him leaning in a doorway, when she was approaching it with a heavy tray. His foot was pressed back against the lower panel, so the door was pushed half open; his shoulder was against the doorjamb. He did not move out of her way. She did not like it, his lingering, assessing gaze; now that she had come to be a little more knowing herself, she knew knowingness when she saw it.

'Hard going, that,' he said, with a nod to the tray.

'May I pass, sir?'

He seemed not to hear. 'Heavy for you, slip of a girl that you are.'

She shifted her grip on the tray. 'Can I help you, sir? Is there something you need?'

'Oh no. You don't need to worry about me, I'm a steward's son, so . . .'

Sarah lifted her right foot, took her weight on the other, and so gained some relief for her tired ankles. So he was a steward's son – so what? He wasn't offering to carry her ton-weight tray down to the kitchen, was he?

'If you don't actually require anything, sir . . .'

He shook his head, lips pursed beneath his moustache. 'Nothing, no. I am admirably well provided for.'

She curtseyed carefully, so as not to shift the crocks, and moved towards him. He stepped back, to let the door open for her, but not quite wide enough, so that she must pass too close, her skirts brushing against his legs. She knew that he watched her go, too, but she would not give him the satisfaction of seeing her glance back.

*

Mr Collins soon returned to Longbourn House. This was a bother and a trouble to Mrs Hill: she still needed to secure him; she was as keen to please him as ever, but she now had much less time in which to do it, since he was engaged for a good part of every day in love-making at Lucas Lodge. And Mary was also a source of unease and guilt; Mrs Hill should not have encouraged her interest in him, as it had done nobody any good. But there was nothing to be done about that now, at least not by her. Mrs Hill contented herself with cramming as many good things as possible into the beginning and the end of Mr Collins's days. His washing water was fresh and hot every morning; his towels were the finest the linen closet could provide, and scented with lavender. He had the best ash logs for his fire, and warm sweet milk on his night-stand when he returned from wooing and went to bed. Whether he noted these little attentions, or attributed them to their proper source, Mrs Hill had no idea, and was given no indication: he said nothing about it, but then he said very little to anybody at all at Longbourn, so occupied was he with his wedding plans and his bride-to-be.

Then he was gone, called from Longbourn and his amiable Charlotte by the arrival of another Saturday. Mrs Hill was in a turmoil of frustrated intentions: if she could but get her hands on Charlotte Lucas, even for a little while; if she could but give her a good dinner, and another batch of lemon tarts, she'd feel that much easier for it. Charlotte Lucas knew the value of a good dinner; she would not resent being reminded of it.

But it was not to be hoped for: Charlotte, for obvious reasons, stayed away from Longbourn.

*

Two days after Mr Collins's latest visit, the Gardiners arrived. Mrs Bennet's brother, his wife and their young family had come to spend Christmas at Longbourn. They were to stay a week, and Mrs Bennet had so carefully provided for their entertainment that they did not once in all that time sit down to a quiet family dinner together: either the house was teeming with visitors, or its inhabitants were rushing to be ready for some public or private entertainment in the neighbourhood, or it stood empty of all but servantry.

Entertainments must be prepared for in the kitchen; it being the Christmas season, there was always some particular dainty to be constructed, some special meal to prepare and serve, some item of adornment to be laundered; the kitchen was cluttered and hazardous with additional servants: the Gardiners' maid, visitors' coachmen, a to-and-fro of neighbouring families' servants with invitations or replies. All of them with bodies to get between you and the thing required, legs and feet to trip over, and elbows to nudge precious things to the teetering brink of dressers and shelves. There was never a moment to be had alone, even when the house was quiet, for James and Sarah. She and Mrs Hill both went about soaked in sweat, teeth gritted, chilled to the bone the moment they stepped outdoors.

Mr Wickham seemed to get in everywhere, turning up in the most unexpected places, like spilt quicksilver. You'd round the stairs and he'd be there, on the half-landing, apparently studying a painting; you'd come into an otherwise deserted breakfast room, and find him lounging by the sideboard nibbling a bit of kipper and running a nail along the joins in the veneer. And, once, James caught the scent of a cigar, and looked up, the end of a girth in one hand, the buckle in the other, the horse's belly at his cheek, and saw the young officer there, standing silently in the doorway, watching, perfuming the winter air with his tobacco.

Wickham saluted.

James gave him a nod in reply, then continued with his work. He unfastened the buckle, then lifted the side-saddle away, the stirrup and girth dangling, and went to stow it with the others. He felt Wickham follow him with his eyes. James wedged the saddle down onto the saddle-rack, wiped it over with a cloth.

'What are you doing here?' Wickham said eventually.

The mare blew warm breath. 'Getting on,' James said, taking the spitty bit from between her teeth. Wickham pushed away from the doorway and wandered closer. James quietly continued removing and cleaning off the tack.

'All this' – Wickham gestured around with a trailing cigar: the clean cobbles, the heaped straw, the leather gear, the glossy horses' hides – 'this is all boys' stuff; it's for young lads and old codgers. It's not proper work for a man.'

'If you say so, sir.'

'And there's plenty of proper work to be had, isn't there, if you want it.'

James straightened up; he looped the tack together. Wickham was just a puppy, all unearned swagger and needle-teeth. Growling at nothing.

The young officer tilted his head now, making a show of deliberation. 'I mean, the old butler here's a bag of bones, he's no use to anyone, so he may as well be buried up to his neck in the country, doing nothing.' And then he jerked his cigar towards James. 'But you. Sirrah. You are a different matter.'

'Is that right, sir.'

Easing the mare's head collar on, James kept his eyes on his work, freeing the mane where it was caught under the strap.

'A man without dependants, and without other prospects—' Wickham drew on the last of his cigar, then spoke over the smoke. 'You should get yourself down to the recruiting officer. That's what you should do. That's what any able man, who cares about his country, should do, at times like these.'

'I am quite right here,' James said, hanging up the bridle, then brushing his palms together.

'Well, then. There we are.' Wickham dropped his cigar-end and ground it out with the toe of a gleaming boot. 'You are an inveterate coward, I see, and there is no help for it.'

'Is that so?'

'That is so.'

'Then tell me, sir,' James heard himself ask. 'If you would . . .'

Wickham, who had been turning to leave, now paused, and glanced back. 'What?'

'Just so I know.'

'Yes—'

'Where was it that you last saw action?'

Wickham went blank, half shook his head.

'Was it in Spain or Portugal?'

He frowned. 'What's your meaning, boy?'

'Perhaps you were there at the Siege of Roses? Or did you fight at the Battle of Vimeiro? Or did you stand against the French at La Coruña?'

Now the young officer's cheeks flushed red. 'How dare you—'

James just looked at him, all innocence. 'I only wished to know where you earned the right to call me a coward.'

'If I had had the good fortune – I would have served—'

James bowed. 'I do apologize, sir. I was forgetting you had just recently bought your commission.'

'I will undertake anything required of me—'

James took the mare by the halter; passing Wickham, he led her out into the yard.

'I dare say you will get your hands bloody soon enough. Situation's promising in the north. Slaughtering mill-hands: proper job for a man, that.'

'The Luddites are a menace—'

James turned to fetch the old piebald stallion, who stepped out proudly with his feathered hooves.

Wickham found his flow now: 'They're a threat, those croppers, Luddites, all of them, a threat to property, to their own kind, to the prosperity of the nation—'

'I bow to your better understanding, sir.'

And James did bow; then he led the two horses off across the yard and down to the low field, where they were wanted for the winter ploughing. They huffed steam in the cold air, their heads nodding along on either side of him, in a kind of tacit, companionable approval.

But James had been a fool, and he knew it. If he was lucky, Wickham would decide it not worth his trouble to pursue his grievance, a footman being by rights so far beneath his notice. Come the spring, the Militia would be billeted elsewhere; and so the spring, for James, could not come too soon.

Nor, for that matter, could the end of the Christmas festivities.

The four Gardiner children disported themselves about the house like a pack of puppies, wriggling in everywhere. Sarah and James could not pass each other in a hallway, or even on the servants' stairs, without a bundle of little ones clattering up or down, or shrieking past them, on some great adventure through the house. Either that, or Sarah had a little one dragging on her apron strings and whinging, while she smiled lopsidedly at James and continued on her hobbled way.

There was not a moment, and no peace to be had, not even at night. Sarah and Polly were obliged to share their room with the Gardiners' maid, Martha, who had ginger curls that she was very proud of, and a pallet on the floor, which, she complained, was stuffed with broken pots, and who talked about London, about dances and alehouses and beaux, Cock-and-Hen clubs and bullock-hunting on a Sunday. Polly sat bundled up in her shawls and blankets, looking like a caterpillar in its cocoon, her mouth hanging open at the girl's tall tales. Sarah propped her head on a hand, smiled stiffly, distracted, dreading that at any moment there would be mention of one Ptolemy Bingley, Esquire, former footman to the Bingley household, who had opened a new tobacco shop that was all the rage with the gentlemen-about-town; dreading too that she would blush and be noticed and be teased for it; regretting not him, but that she had once thought of him as a possibility.

The Gardiners' youngest was not yet breeched, and so a bucket of nappies soaked by the scullery door, the stink leaking out from underneath the lid. Someone had to scrape and rinse and then boil them every day – they simply could not be left longer, the smell was so terrible – and, if it was wet outdoors, they must be hung to drip-dry in the scullery. Some days the task fell to Polly, her face a picture of disgust – she was too young to have had the seasoning experience of cleansing the Bennet nappies – sometimes it was Sarah: the Gardiners' maid seemed to think this stay at Longbourn was her own holiday from scrubbing. And then one crisp still day, when Sarah went to lift the pail, she found that it was empty, and when she walked out down to the paddock she saw a row of nappies flapping white on the line, like a ship's signal flags, an unconditional surrender; James was pegging out the last of them, and when he saw that he was watched, and who watched him, he looked a little sheepish, but finished hanging out the linen squares.

'That's kind,' she said, coming close.

'Your hands looked sore.'

Sarah could not account for it herself, but her eyes welled up and her nose prickled, and she was obliged to turn away and pick up the basket. They walked side by side back up to the house, and she felt, for those brief moments, a lightness and an ease that she only realized afterwards was simply happiness.

Wickham was always the focus of much attention at the table; the ladies all seemed fascinated with the tragedy of him. Sarah overheard it in scraps as she brought forth the plates and platters. The church he should have preached at, the living that he should have had. The position he should occupy in the world, if it were not for the abominable pride of that great tall gentleman Mr Darcy. She tried to imagine Wickham in clerical black, like Mr Collins. Surveying his congregation from the pulpit with those knowing eyes. Eyes that seemed to see not just the surface of things, not just the clothes, the outward aspect, the veneer: eyes that saw through all of that, and knew everything that went on underneath.

When they had returned the guests' hats and cloaks to them in the vestibule that evening, Polly wandered down the hallway, jingling coins in her apron pocket. Once in the kitchen, she trickled farthings from one hand to the other.

'Where did you get all that, then?' Sarah asked.

Polly tossed her head. 'You all think that I am just a little scrub, fit for nothing but laying fires and emptying chamber pots. But I shall have you know that there are some as think me very fit indeed to serve on gentlefolk, and are very much appreciative of me, yes they are, for taking care of them, and giving them their dinner and their hats.'

The truth of Mr Wickham's predicament, Sarah was in no position to judge, but she was certain of one thing: she did not like him. She did not like the coins that chinked in Polly's pocket, nor, now that she came to think about it, the way that he had taken off his glove that time, to touch the girl's baked-custard cheek. But there was no danger in it, how could there be? Polly was just a scrap of a thing, a gangling foal; she had not even got her monthlies yet – she could not be an object of interest to him, surely? Not in that kind of a way.

James, for himself, watched the officers depart that evening with the relief a condemned man feels at a stay of execution. He stood back, in the shadows, once he had brought round the horses and hitched them by the front steps. The officers mounted up and trotted off, and were waved away: those pretty, smart young gentlemen with their shiny buttons and dressed hair and their cheerful noise that carried out of Longbourn with them, and followed them down the drive, and off into the night, and all the way down the dark road to Meryton.

They were just boys, he told himself; they were just playing at soldiering. And Wickham was perhaps indolent and cowardly enough to let this slide – he would soon find much more useful projects than harassing the Longbourn servantry. But whatever James told himself, he could not be consoled: things could not be the same at Longbourn now; he could no longer be at ease. He had let his mask slip; his other self had glimmered out, and he could not bear to let that creature loose, not here.

Chapter XI

*'But do you think she would be prevailed on to go back with us?
Change of scene might be of service – and perhaps a little relief
from home, may be as useful as anything.'*

JANE, OF COURSE, could go to London just like that, without it being
any great thing: she could go, and having gone, she could still come
back. She had a coach to take her there, her extended family to protect
her, the Gardiners' house in Gracechurch Street to accommodate her,
and her aunt to chaperone her as she went about town and enjoyed its
pleasures, and kept an eye and an ankle out for her Mr Bingley.

That last was uncharitable of her, Sarah knew. She should not
begrudge Jane her pleasures, simply because they were denied to her.
Jane was sweet and beautiful, and so deserving of sweet and beautiful
things. If you yourself were bitterish and scruffy – Sarah smiled as she
blackleaded the breakfast-room grate, on her knees, her fingers sooty
and her nose ticklish – then you got bitterish and scruffy in return:
maybe you got James.

Christmas over, the house emptied; the Gardiners, their troop of
little nuisances and Jane all departed. And Longbourn seemed to
expand, to breathe out in relief.

Mr Collins was returned to the vicinity, Mrs Hill soon learned,
though not to Longbourn. The wedding fast approaching, he took up
his abode at Lucas Lodge. Mrs Hill's feelings on the matter were mixed.
On the one hand, she was missing this opportunity to impress him; on

the other, she was already exhausted by her efforts to impress – and disheartened, somewhat, since she was uncertain as to the level of her success.

She consoled herself with the knowledge that at Lucas Lodge there was nothing particularly to delight, unless it was his own wife-to-be's mince pies, and Mrs Hill was not in competition with his wife. Instead, she set about fashioning a little reticule for Miss Lucas, in a dove-grey Norwich bombazine, which was, she thought, very suitable for that young lady's new position as a clergyman's wife. She presented it to the young bride-to-be at Charlotte's farewell visit to Longbourn that Wednesday. The young lady received it with her characteristic good grace, and what seemed like genuine pleasure. She was not above these little kindnesses, and there was likely to be but little pin-money in her settlement. The reticule would, it was to be hoped, see much use, and at every occasion cause her to think kindly of Mrs Hill and the good servants at Longbourn.

Miss Lucas was married on the Thursday, and the bride and bridegroom set off for Kent from the church door. Mrs Hill and Sarah and Polly stood in the road, just outside the lych-gate, to wave them off.

'Mrs Collins does look lovely,' Sarah said, when the couple had climbed into the chaise.

'All brides are beautiful,' said Mrs Hill. 'It is the one day when any woman is allowed to be so.'

'What was your wedding day like, Mrs Hill?'

'It was a cold day too,' she said. 'It was a long time ago.'

They were joined, when the well-wishers had cleared from the churchyard, by the Bennet family, and they all walked together back up to Longbourn House. All the way, Mrs Bennet kept saying that she *wished* they might be happy, though her tone made it clear to Mrs Hill that her thoughts were occupied with her own girls, and not really Mrs Collins, and that she was not at all sanguine in her hopes.

Mrs Hill, however, was warm enough in hers. Mrs Collins had held her new dove-grey reticule on her lap, in the hack-chaise: this augured well. The marriage of Mr Collins and Miss Lucas was not the worst possible outcome for the servantry, not by a long chalk. Though Mary, poor Mary, walked a little ahead of the others, and went straight upstairs to her piano, and played melancholy airs all afternoon.

'She is a good girl,' Mrs Hill said, nodding over her needlework later on. 'I always liked Miss Lucas, and I think we are a little more secure, because of this.'

But the whole thing left Sarah feeling very ill at ease. It was all as arbitrary and as far beyond their control as the weather. To live so entirely at the mercy of other people's whims and fancies was, she thought, no way to live at all.

That night, the branches cracked in the frost, and the ice deepened itself by inches, and the sheep huddled close together on the hillside and steamed. Sarah lay awake; the church clock had just struck midnight; her breath plumed and her nose was cold. All was quiet. Quiet, apart from Polly's breathing, and the bronchial wheeze from Mr Hill across the landing.

In the stable loft, ice climbed across the inside of the windows. The cold made James ache, and tightened the knots in his flesh, which made it impossible to sleep. His candle offered only an illusion of warmth, and but little light, along with the rank smell of old mutton fat. Faint body-heat rose from the horses below, which kept him from perishing entirely; with it came the stable smell; meadowy, dungy, with the warm musk of horse sweat.

He had become used to all of this. He had barely noticed it for weeks. Now, though, the scents of the place seemed to nudge their way back into his consciousness: they were so particular to this place, and his thoughts had been stretching far away from there.

He sat on his bed, still in shirtsleeves, with a blanket over his shoulders, and a book of Scottish maps on his lap. This way of rendering the hard facts of landscape was new to him: the little upward flicks of the pen for mountains, the tiny clustered trees for woodland, the blue patches of lochs. He wanted maps of other places, he wanted maps of places he had been, he wanted to follow routes across terrain that his feet had trodden. If he could show Sarah – but he must not think of Sarah. He could not let himself be drawn to her again; he could not let her risk herself like that. Every time Sarah stepped into his thoughts, he would lift her up and set her aside, and return to the happy details of the map. Oh look, a forest, he'd think. Oh look, those crags. And then there she'd be again, with hair escaping from her cap, stomping up towards him with a frown and a slopping bucket— No. He lifted her up, set her aside. He must not think of Sarah.

He smoothed the paper, settled his blanket around his shoulders again. Dumfries and Galloway. Fascinating.

Then he heard the kitchen door go; he stilled, listening. It was her; he knew her tread. What could she be up to, out at this time of night? He got up and crossed over to the window, pulled back the curtain just in time to see her ice-clouded shape pass below. She ducked in through the stable door beneath him.

He threw off the blanket, reached for his coat, started to pull it on, then slowed down, wincing, his muscles locked; he eased it on. The blanket was tumbled on the chair; he whisked it up and folded it and laid it on the foot of his bed. Then he sat down on the bed again and pretended to look at the map.

And she was there: there she was. True as life and twice as terrifying. Dark head and bird-shoulders and then body, all wrapped up in that ratty old blue coat they kept by the back door, the colour of it just so good against her skin. She hitched herself up to sit on the edge of the trapdoor, legs dangling down into the musk of the stables, and her face sweet and troubling in the candlelight.

'Good morning,' she said.

His mouth had gone dry. 'What?'

'Good morning.'

'Why—?'

She swung her legs round and got up. She wore no stockings; her bare feet were wedged into her boots.

'Sarah—'

She clomped right up to him. She looked down at the map. 'What's that?'

'Sarah—'

'Is that a picture?' She sat down beside him.

'It's a map.'

'Of where?'

'Scotland.'

'Scotland?' She leaned in to look at it. 'Oh, it's beautiful.'

A curl fell forward; he glimpsed a curve of skin as the blue coat fell open. Underneath it, she was just in her shift. He looked away, but she was so close that he could smell her; the day's work, hard soap, vanilla.

'Sarah.'

'Have you ever been there?' She sat down beside him now. 'To Scotland, I mean.'

'No, but – Sarah, please—'

Her clear eyes studied him. 'What is it?'

'Go back. Please. Go back to your bed.'

She was so close that her hip bone pressed against his. Linen, wool, velvet, linen. Either side, the warm pulse of their separate flesh. He got up, and moved away, putting space between them.

'I can't—' he began.

'I thought,' she spoke over him, 'that we got off to a bad start. So I thought, "Start again." So. Here I am, starting again. Good morning.'

'Sarah.'

'Yes.'

She still sat there, on his bed, looking up at him.

'Sarah, I don't know what you expect. From me. But this' – he gestured at the little room, the one candle, the borrowed map – 'this is not just everything I have. It's all I'm ever likely to have. It's the best that I can do.'

She shrugged. 'Doesn't matter.'

'I've nothing to offer you.'

'Why would you offer me something?'

'Sarah, please—' He turned away to the window, and peeled back the curtain, so as not to look at her; he blinked out into the dark beyond the frosted pane. There was a whole world out there, and so many people. Englishmen and Frenchmen and Turks and Indians and Americans. Millions and millions of men, and Sarah, she had met only the tiniest handful of them. He could not let her settle, not for him, not for this.

'Go back,' he said again, not looking round.

For a moment there was silence. Then he heard the thunk of dropped boots, and the pad of bare feet on the boards. Her hand, when she took his, was small and cold.

'Come away from the window,' she said.

The curtain fell back. He let her turn him away from the night.

She stood on tiptoe and touched her lips against his lips. And for a moment he just held her by the upper arms – so slight in his hands – keeping her still at this little distance. But it was too much to resist: he drew her to him, and let her body lean into his, the length of it, the bones and softnesses of her, and the warmth.

She felt the haze of his stubble against her skin, the curve of the back of his head in her hand, the snag of a broken tooth against her lip. She knew what the birds did, and the bees, and the cats and sheep and cattle, and no one blamed them for it. Girls like her, and men like him – nobody looked askance at a big belly at the altar, nobody cared so long as it was under plain calico or stuff, and not silk.

James pushed her away, but he did not quite let go of her.

'Sarah, you must not.'

She plucked open the top button of his shirt. 'You don't have to worry about me.'

'It is impossible, Sarah. You have to understand that it is impossible.'

She eased his coat off his shoulders, undid his tiny shirt buttons one by one, frowning and intent. He must stop her; he should take her by the wrists and stop her. But then she dipped forward, and her lips were on his collarbone, and her warm breath and her small icy hands were on his skin. He touched her hair, his lips parting to speak; now, while there was still time. But then her fingertips brushed across a scar

190

– he caught his breath; that blank feeling where the nerve was gone – and it was all too late. Her hand stopped, and slipped over the scar again, and followed the line of it over the cusp of his shoulder, and a little way down onto his back. She went still. Her palm lay softly on the real, terrible mess of his scars.

'It was a long time ago,' he said. He swallowed. 'It was another country.'

She pulled away, looking up at him, her forehead creased. Her expression, any moment now, would collapse into disgust. He would beg for her silence; she would be kind, no doubt, and she would leave. And he would have to see her every day. He would live on pins and broken glass. But her expression didn't change, and she didn't say a word. She just pushed his shirt back, so that it slid off his shoulders. He stood there in the candlelight, half naked, still, almost unable to breathe. Then, her hand running over his shoulder, she moved round him, till she was standing behind him, her touch never leaving him, her hand resting now where the skin had been unmade and had made itself again.

For him, it was a firing-off of sensation here, and there, a pause and blankness where the feeling was gone. It was a choked throat, and hobbled words.

He had to explain. About how he had come by it. He had to apologize; he had to beg to be forgiven. And then accept the silence, and the broken glass.

But her arms twined around him, slipping around his belly and his chest, and then she rested her hot cheek against his damaged back, and held him.

CHAPTER XII

She was then but fifteen, which must be her excuse . . .

THERE IS A certain kind of knowledge that has no words. A physical understanding can emerge out of propinquity, out of intimacy
sometimes, and also out of the uncountable repetitions of work and
play. One body can come to know another body, to anticipate its needs
and actions, without any recourse to conscious thought. For Sarah,
though, it was not formed through gradual accretion: she was whisked
up in this new understanding, released from herself, her body so suddenly in sympathy with James's; it had the overwhelming certainty of
a revelation.

Words had become overnight just little coins, insignificant and
unfreighted, to be exchanged for ribbons, buttons, for an apple or an
egg.

And over the weeks and months that followed – when she eased out
of her bed, leaving Polly asleep, flung starfish-like across the extra
space, and crept chilly and barefooted across the yard to his room; or
when she found him in the kitchen garden and surprised him with a
kiss; or when she simply glimpsed him at a distance, crossing the fields
with fallen timber to split for kindling – this understanding seemed
entirely and stunningly sufficient. She knew now, without any conscious thought at all, what it meant to be alive in the world, and why
their continuance in this sequestered place was entirely worth the while.

The turn of the year towards spring, with its lengthening of the days, the appearance of the first green points of snowdrops, and then their white heads lolling in the February wind, and then lambs staggering in the meadow: she knew all this too, had slipped into sympathy with the changing world, with what spring was for. Her body had hitherto been a carthorse, dragging her through the days: now she lived in it differently. It had become a thing of luxury and delight.

She did not ask about the scars. They belonged to this realm of congruence, of ineffable bodily logic: they were not to do with words. The soldier flogged to bloody submission in the rain, the wounded man warm in her arms: each explained and justified the other. They never spoke of this, either, but she knew that he was taking care not to burden her with pregnancy; she understood, and was grateful for it, and for the pleasure that he nonetheless afforded her.

But there must come a time when the insufficiency of this understanding is made all too obvious, when circumstances reveal the gulf between two people, the impossibility of its distance.

Sarah, having come lately to her knowledge, did not suspect any of this yet. She was dreamy with her new understanding, lulled with contentment, not thinking beyond the pads of her own fingers, the tip of her tongue.

James, though, knew better. His arms around her, her head on his chest, he felt the sleek length of her body against his, and the rise and fall of her breath, and the saltwater trickle down his temples, and raised a hand to wipe the wet away. She stirred. He smoothed her hair, kissed her forehead. This was a beautiful disaster, and it could not be undone.

And Polly, mumbling in the darkness, and surfacing to find the bed cold and empty beside her, sat up, blinking, and knew – through an immediate, physical understanding – exactly where Sarah had gone.

The days, the work: they were as they always had been. Mrs B. still nagged and fretted, and Mrs Hill still lost her temper, and Sarah still did the weekly wash with Polly's scant assistance, and steeped the monthly napkins, and Mr Hill still spat upon the forks to clean them, and across the yard the horses stamped and whinnied as James prepared them for the plough or, more usually, for the carriage to take the ladies out on morning calls or to drink tea in the afternoon. But it was good now. In substance it was changed not at all, but for Sarah it was nonetheless transformed.

Sarah took Elizabeth's letters to the post office at Meryton, addressed to Jane and Mrs Gardiner in London, and to Mrs Collins in Kent, with coins in her pocket to pay for any letters that were to be fetched back with her. These plump little packages folded tightly in upon their secrets: Sarah studied their covers as she walked back home through the new grass; she turned them over in her hands, lifting them to smell them, tracing the coloured wafers with a rough fingertip. They flitted wherever they liked, these letters. They darted back and forth across the countryside like birds.

'Do you ever feel,' Elizabeth asked Sarah, who was lacing up her short-stays for her one morning, 'that the days go by just like that' – she snapped her fingers – 'even though nothing ever really happens at all?'

Sarah smiled.

'It was Christmas only a moment ago, it seems, and now it's February, and before you know it, it'll be March, and where did January even go?'

What could she say? For Elizabeth the days had scudded by, but for Sarah they had expanded and swelled and grown beyond all possibility, so that every crease and dimple in them, the scent and silk and warmth of her hours, now absorbed her senses so completely that she was dazed by the world, soaked in it, more alive than she had ever been before.

'I shall be off to Kent in March,' Lizzy said.

Sarah nodded, teasing the laces straight; she gave a quick final tug, and tied a long loose bow. Then she lifted Elizabeth's petticoat and dropped it down over her head. The young lady's voice came muffled as she fumbled her way through the folds.

'Truth be told, Sarah, dear, I am not so certain about it.'

Sarah fastened the petticoat hooks-and-eyes, then took up the periwinkle morning-gown from the bed, and lifted it so that Elizabeth could slip her head and arms through; Sarah settled the neckline and shoulder seams while Elizabeth tugged the sleeves straight. When she was done here, Sarah might see James in the kitchen, or pass him in the hallway, as he took the family's breakfast up to them.

Elizabeth fastened the cuffs herself while Sarah did the bone buttons at the back.

'And of course it will be lovely to see Jane. But six weeks in Kent, with the Collinses—'

She glanced back at Sarah – Sarah nodded, she had finished; Elizabeth moved away, towards the window, leaving her nightgown in a heap upon the floor.

'I fear there cannot be much pleasure in that.'

Sarah retrieved the nightgown, then shook it out and folded it. She slipped it under the pillow. 'Is there anything else you need from me now?'

'Oh, thank you, Sarah, no,' Elizabeth said. 'That will be all for now.'

Sarah bobbed a curtsey, and left. The bedchamber door closed, she crossed the landing at a smart step, then slipped through the door into the servants' stairs. Then she thundered down the steps and out into the hallway, to see if she might find James.

It was a chill day when Mr Wickham actually ventured into the kitchen, bringing with him a sharp draught and the whiff of tobacco smoke. Hitherto he had lurked on thresholds; now he broke entirely through the caul between one world and the other, as if for him it simply did not matter.

'Ah, so here we are. The kitchen!'

Polly gaped, her whisk falling still in her drift of eggwhite. Mrs Hill turned from the range. Sarah straightened from her work, saw him, and her hands stilled too in the pestle. It was as though a peacock had flapped down to join the plain old gallinies, and started sauntering around the yard with them, pecking at their scraps.

195

'This is more like it. What are you making? Macaroons? How splendid.'

'I think you are lost, sir,' Sarah said.

He rubbed at his cropped head with a boyish air and grinned. Sarah thought, He knows exactly what he is doing; he knows exactly how to seem most charming. He turned from her, and addressed himself to Mrs Hill.

'I do so like a kitchen, you know,' he said. 'And so I thought I would come and see yours. And you have a delightful example of the species here.'

'You'd be more at home in the parlour, sir,' Sarah said.

'Appearances will deceive, my dear girl.'

He leaned in against the table, beside Sarah. He raised his eyebrows at her, but when he spoke, he addressed himself again to Mrs Hill.

'My father was a humble steward, you see, my dear madam, and I have been in and out of kitchens and offices and stillrooms all my life. A kitchen is the one place where I can feel quite at my ease.'

Polly, recovering herself a little, took up her whisk and began to beat the eggwhite again, her eyes like inkwells. Sarah, glancing from her to him, caught the moment when he winked, and then turned and caught Polly's delighted shy look in response. He must charm everybody, must this fellow – it seemed like a compulsion.

'You will be missed by the ladies,' Sarah said.

'Ah yes, the ladies.' He pursed his lips. 'The ladies.'

Polly's whisk kept up a slow and ineffectual clatter. He moved away from the table, and crossed to the fireside; he settled himself down in Mr Hill's empty chair, with the air of someone coming home.

'They are so exhausting, aren't they, the ladies? All that *chatter*.'

Polly covered her mouth with a hand, and giggled.

He smiled at her, his mustachios lifting up at the corners. 'I would so much rather be cosy down here with you lovely girls.'

'We are a working kitchen here, sir—' Sarah tried.

'Oh, that's the charm of it, don't you know. That's what I love, that's what I am used to.'

'Perhaps you would oblige us, then, sir, by joining in. If you are to be here, you may as well be useful.'

Mrs Hill, who had thus far been struggling with a shock so profound – a guest in the house had actually trespassed into her kitchen, was even now sitting by her kitchen fire – that she had been entirely unable to speak, now cleared her throat.

'I'll fetch them turnips. They's muddy as anything, and need a good scrubbing before they're peeled.'

He looked from Mrs Hill to Sarah to Polly and back again. A slick smile at their little joke.

'But where are my manners? Thinking only of myself, and not of my hosts; they will wonder where I am.' He pushed himself up from the chair, turned to Polly. 'Might I have a guide back to the company, Little Miss? You will spare me a moment's favour, I hope.'

Sarah hesitated. But Mrs Hill jerked her head to Polly, keen to be rid of him: the world must be restored to its proper order.

'If you please, Polly.'

Polly dropped her whisk, wiped off her hands and darted for the door. She did please: Mr Wickham was, after all, an excellent tipper.

'It's this way, sir, back to the company.'

James had seen Mr Wickham cross the yard some moments earlier, his red coat almost glowing in the grey day. He obeyed his first impulse, and stepped back, into the stable doorway, to observe the officer unseen. From there, he watched as Wickham ground out his cigar against the wall, smoothed his moustache and his hair, tugged his scarlet coat straight, and then pushed open the kitchen door.

James swallowed back the sickness. It was as if there was something spoiling in his belly. Wickham was seeping in everywhere, slipping through the cracks and oozing across the floor, and starting to look as though he'd always be there, and would be got used to, like rising groundwater.

He slid out of his hiding place and skirted round the edges of the yard, keeping out of sight of the window till he came right up beside it. There was a haze of scarlet in the fireside chair. He saw the young officer ease himself to his feet. He saw Polly scamper across the kitchen and hold the hall door open for him, saw the officer breeze across the room, and pass her. He watched the girl, grinning, follow after him, and the door fall shut upon them.

James slammed in through the kitchen door, making Mrs Hill start, making Sarah turn and smile, and then her smile faded and was gone.

'What is it?'

'What did he say?'

'Nothing—'

'What did he do?'

'Well, he came into my kitchen—' This from Mrs Hill; but from Sarah, a half-shake of the head – nothing – but then a glance after Polly.

He took in the lay of the land; the women stalled in their work by his sudden entrance, staring at him blankly. But Polly – where was she? He crossed the room in three strides, leaned through the hall doorway, and looked out.

'What is it?' Sarah came over, wiping her hands, and peering out beside him.

They watched as Mr Wickham, in his pristine scarlet coat, walked side by side with Polly down the hallway. Polly, half-skipping to keep up with his stride, kept glancing up at the impressive figure now in her charge. She rubbed her nose with the back of her hand.

Sarah and James watched together, as Polly heaved open the door into the parlour; together they heard the peal of silver bells as the ladies exclaimed at Wickham's shockingly long absence, and demanded he account for it; as though they were, in that moment, all Penelopes, and he Odysseus returned.

Struggling with the heavy door, Polly bobbed Wickham a little curtsey as he went past her. His hand rested a moment on her slender arm.

'Thank you, Little Miss.'

Then he was gone, and Polly clapped the door shut. Smirking, she flounced back down the hall towards the kitchen. James and Sarah parted to let her past. The door fell closed, cutting them off from the rest of the house.

Sarah saw that the blood had drained entirely from his face.

'What is it?' Sarah asked him. 'What's wrong?'

He watched Polly, who had picked up her whisk and was poking at the eggwhite with it, a dimple in her cheek.

'Is it Wickham? James, what is it? What do you suspect?'

He shook his head, and then just turned away. He darted round the end of the kitchen table, and out into the scullery. Sarah, leaving the almonds unfinished, followed him into the cold damp of the outer room. He had gone straight to the window, and stopped there, looking out. He looked so stricken. She glanced along his line of sight. Outside, chickens scratched at the moss between the flagstones, and nothing was happening at all.

'James?'

A jaw muscle worked, but still he did not speak.

'James. What is it?'

She touched his arm. He looked down at her hand, and then he looked up, and met her eyes. She could not read his expression at all.

'The officer is gone,' she tried.

He blinked at her.

'We are all quite well.'

Then, after a moment, he nodded.

'Are you all right?'

He took in a big shaking breath, and let it go again. He leaned to look past her then, back to the warm light of the kitchen: she followed his line of sight. Polly crossed the doorway with her basin of whipped eggwhite, both arms wrapped around its girth.

Then James just pushed away from the window, and gave Sarah a thin smile, and went back to his work.

CHAPTER XIII

. . . a little change was not unwelcome for its own sake.

MARCH CAME – WITH a gentle hint of spring in the breeze, thick mud in the lane-ways, and a royal rash of purple and gold crocuses across the orchard floor, planted when Mrs Bennet was a young bride, confident of her future happiness – and Elizabeth was to leave.

She was to go to Kent, where she had never been before, and to London on the way, where she had already been many times to stay with her uncle and aunt Gardiner, and where, now, Elizabeth finally offered to take Sarah.

'I have spoken to Sir William, and mentioned it in a letter to Mrs Collins, and since neither of them has any objection to the scheme, and indeed Mrs Collins is quite relieved, since she only has, beyond her housekeeper and a manservant, one little girl to scrub, and indeed says in her letter that she had been concerned how they were to manage, particularly when it came to laundry, if we did not bring our own maid with us, but did not wish to deprive my mother of her help – and everyone knows that the Lucases really cannot spare another body, not since they lost Charlotte's assistance in the kitchen.'

Sarah set the trunk down on the floor, and wiped her dusty hands on her apron, and waited, since she had not yet the pleasure of fully understanding her young mistress.

'But as we are to travel there in the Lucases' chaise,' Elizabeth continued, turning a book round to examine the spine, then offering it to

Sarah, who took it mutely and without looking, and slipped it into her own apron pocket. 'We shall be crammed in quite tight, so mind you pack lightly for yourself, just a small bag, or that old box of yours, if you prefer. Though I suppose if you had some other little items they could go in a corner of my trunk, which is to follow by stagecoach.'

'I am coming with you?'

Elizabeth lit up. 'Oh, did I not say? It is not quite the wide world, Sarah, dear, but it is the best that I can do for you for the time being. We shall pass through London, and stop there one night on the way, and we shall stay there again on the return, and that should be of interest, and if nothing else it will be a change of scene.'

Sarah sank down on the trunk, and then was obliged to remove the book from her pocket, as it dug into her thigh. London. Kent. That this should happen now, when it was not simply a delight. It was as though Elizabeth had said, We are off on our travels, and you may come, but you must leave your leg behind.

'Are they near the sea, the Collinses?'

'No. I suppose they are somewhat nearer than we are here. You shall have to travel on the rumble-seat, so you must wrap up well and pray for good weather.'

Sarah nodded. She looked down at the book in her hands. It was *Pamela*, Volume II.

'Do you not like my little scheme?'

She glanced up. Elizabeth looked puzzled, and a little hurt. 'Oh, I do, miss, I really do. It's just a surprise, coming now, all of a sudden like this.'

'I was not sure of it, till I heard from Mrs Collins. I thought that you would be pleased.'

'I am, miss. I am. Thank you.'

Elizabeth nodded, and murmured her acceptance, and returned to her books. Sarah watched her for a moment, her head bent, her gaze thoughtful, as she considered which volumes to take with her and which must be left behind. Sarah wondered what it could be like, to live like this – life as a country dance, where everything is lovely, and graceful, and ordered, and every single turn is preordained, and not a foot may be set outside the measure. Not like Sarah's own out-in-all-weathers haul and trudge, the wind howling and blustery, the creeping flowers in the hedgerows, the sudden sunshine.

March is a terrible time for the cleaning of boots; worse even than the depths of winter. In March, gentlemen and ladies start to sniff the air like rabbits, and decide it is fine enough to risk a morning walk. A turn about the park might even be taken after dinner; nicely shod feet slither oblivious in mud and mire, while their owners try to get a closer look at a clump of pale wild daffodils, marsh marigolds, or violets turning their tiny perfect faces up towards the spring sun.

James had the Bennets' boots lined up in a row, the seven pairs in diminishing order of size. He had brushed the dried mud off one small pair, and was now rubbing down the leather, scooping a rag into the greasy dubbin-pot and smearing it onto the instep, the toe, the cuff, then buffing it hard with another rag. He whistled under his breath, beautifully absorbed. She sat down beside him, and he noticed her. He did not look round, but his eyes creased, and she had come to know that this was how he sometimes smiled.

'You're almost out of dubbin,' she observed.

He nodded.

'I'll make you some more when I get the chance. There's that old ewe that died yesterday, she's to be boiled down for tallow.'

She picked up a boot – one of Elizabeth's, delicate and prettily made, but all stuck and clabbered with mud. Elizabeth's were always the worst. Sarah pushed off clots with a thumb, peeled away flakes of dried mud, turning the boot round in her hands.

'You don't have to do that.'

'I used to have to do all of them, before you came.'

His eyes creased again, and he started up his whistling once more, low, and breathy, and familiar.

'You know she's off?' Sarah asked.

'Miss Elizabeth? Yes.'

'She said I could go with her.'

'Oh yes?'

'She said, London, and then Kent.'

He paused, and then nodded. 'You'll like that, I should say. You'd like to stretch your wings a little. Do you good.'

He tilted the little boot in his hand, examining the toecap, the little buttons, the delicate curve of the instep. The brown leather had a dull sheen to it now, like an old conker.

'But,' she said, 'six weeks, it is to be. More or less.'

He turned to her, and simply smiled. 'I shall still be here when you get back.'

They were collected, early on the day appointed – so early that the cockerel was still doing his pieces from the pitched roof of the hen-house – by Sir William and Maria Lucas in their chaise. The party was to journey the twenty-four miles to Gracechurch Street that morning, stay there overnight, and be with the Collinses the following day.

Screened from view by the blue leather calash, James hitched Sarah up onto the rumble-seat on the back of the chaise, his hands gripping her waist. It was not really a seat as such, but the platform where a groom might stand and to which, now, beside her, the overnight bags of the travellers were lashed. Her feet dangled. She touched her bonnet into place, and then tucked the skirts of her pelisse in under her thighs, so that the hem might not trail and catch. James cast an eye towards the heavens.

'I think it will stay fair.'

'Yes.'

'And the worst of the mud will miss you.'

'I shall be quite all right.'

James passed a baggage-strap behind the post, and fastened it around Sarah's waist, buckling her safely in. He had to lean close in to do this. The scent of him – leather, horse, hay – the angle of his cheekbone – she would keep the memory with her.

'It's not far, London,' he said.

'I know. You told me.'

'Sorry. I'm insufferable.'

She shook her head. Then tilted it, smiled. Maybe. A little bit.

'You'll be there by midday.'

He touched her cheek with a rough fingertip. Then he stepped away, his face gone blank, avoiding Mrs Bennet who was bustling around the carriage, calling out superfluous instructions, making her second daughter, waiting to be handed in, flush with irritation.

Mrs Bennet was, she'd informed Mrs Hill, entirely resigned to the marriage of Mr Collins to Charlotte Lucas, but the picture she was now confronted with – proud father and excited younger sister off to visit the newlyweds, with one of her own daughters cast in the role of the spinster friend – was simply too much to bear. Sir William's affable demeanour she found particularly provoking. When he bowed to her from inside the chaise, and commented favourably on the day, she would not hear of it being pleasant at all.

'I am afraid the London road will be terribly dirty after all this rain.'

'What trouble is a little mud when we have a nice cosy little chaise, and good friends waiting at the end of the journey?' He waved her concerns away. 'We'll take good care of your dear Lizzy, don't you worry.'

Mrs Bennet could only nod, and thank him, and go to join her remaining family on the steps.

'If you had but insisted on Lizzy marrying Mr Collins,' Mrs Bennet hissed to her husband, 'it would have been *me* off in that chaise, going to visit *her*.'

'If Lizzy had married Mr Collins, I very much doubt Sir William would be driving you to Kent, good neighbour though he is.'

'You take pleasure in deliberately misunderstanding me.'

The tendon flickered in Mr Bennet's temple: he set his jaw. Mrs Hill knew what was coming before it was said. The words were hard, and fell like marbles.

'Believe me, my dear, there is precious little pleasure to be taken in it.'

Mrs Bennet coloured, and began to protest at his unkindness; her noise was as inevitable as the unkindness itself.

Mrs Hill moved in beside her, and offered her arm. 'Madam.'

Mrs Bennet looked at her housekeeper, blinking, her chin crumpled. She took her arm. 'Thank you, Mrs Hill.'

Mrs Hill nodded. She kept her gaze fixed on the chaise, and would not look at Mr Bennet.

'There she goes, then,' Mrs Bennet said to her companion. 'My little girl. Well, I hope that she is happy.'

And then she turned away. Together they climbed the steps towards the house, Mrs Bennet continuing her soft complaining, and Mrs Hill doing her best to soothe her with bland consoling nonsense, though all the while inwardly seconding her sentiments: Elizabeth had better be happy. If Elizabeth was not going to be happy, she may as well have married Mr Collins, and been safe.

Sarah now got to see something of the wide world. She saw it backwards, reeling away from where she sat, feet dangling, jolted by every rut and pothole.

Longbourn shrank; the house was soon screened by shrubs and trees, and then, at the bend of the drive, was gone. Then they were at the crossroads; they turned, rattled on, and then the crossroads too was lost to sight as the road fell away; then the stump-limbed tree was there, and passed, and was shrinking, shrinking, gone. They rumbled on to Meryton along the turnpike, and then clattered through the town, past the pastry-cook's and the Assembly Rooms and the haberdasher's and the inn on the corner; the grocer's daughter was out with a basket, making her deliveries; seeing Sarah on her perch, she waved and smiled and Sarah waved back at her excitedly; then they were out beyond the little town, clattering past a drill-ground where the soldiers, scarlet against the green, marched, halted, span round and stood stiff as pegs, while an officer barked out orders at them. Onto the new toll-road there, a coin tossed to the keeper and the creak of the pike, and then they were bowling along, the chaise springs complaining. Swaying on the back perch, Sarah was soon out beyond anything she knew.

The ground blurred between the humming wheels, and the sky was pale blue and clear above her, and from the other side of the calash she could hear the voices of the more comfortably situated passengers, and Sir William, who cried out, when they crossed a simple sluggish river choked with reeds, 'The mighty Thames!'

They skimmed along past high hedges, through villages strung along the road like beads upon a thread. They passed between deep fields of watercress, trickling with rills of chalk-clean water, smelling sharp and peppery and green. They passed through market gardens, the raised beds thick with growth, mulchy and warm. The fields grew smaller, subdivided, the market gardens more closely packed, with sheds and lean-tos built of clapboard and rough timber. They slowed at a flock of geese that flapped and honked onto the broad grassy verge, chivvied there by a girl in a broad-brimmed hat who hissed back at them and swiped at them with a stick, and, after the chaise had passed, stared frankly back at Sarah, her face red and scrofulous. They clattered through a ford and water heaved up on either side in fountains. There was a smell of shit from the brown-skimmed fields, and the cattle stood thin and unmoving as though cut from painted tin. And then the road was sloping down, and there was more traffic, trailing long-wagons, painfully slow, bouncing gigs and carts, and post-chaises, and then a mail-coach thundering past; and then there were houses, and there was smoky, dirty air; and then they were rattling over cobbles and deep into town, Sarah's head tilting back and her mouth falling open as she looked up at the buildings rearing above her like cliffs that stared at each other across a stream; and the stream was the traffic, and she herself was part of the traffic, this great ebbing surging traffic of London, the cabs and barrows and drays and carts and the people, just the endless variousness of the people: fishwives in raucous stinking gangs; barrow-boys with their jaunty caps and their bold eyes; a beggar in a filthy rag of a red coat who scooted along on stumps then fists, stumps then fists; a milkmaid with pails swinging from a yoke, whose milk looked bluish grey, and slopped queasily, and left bits on the insides of the buckets, and did not look like the milk at home at all. The streets were slick with dung, and there was a taste of soot in the air, and the smell of cesspits, and bad vegetables, and fish. And the noise – iron-clad wheels, iron-shod hooves, the cries of costermongers and dockers, muffin-sellers and cabbies, and the crowds, and the jostling and pressing up close, and the horses of the coach behind nodding in tandem at her. Then a dirty-looking youth slipped between the carriages; he dodged up to her, and she thought he was going to say something, but he just made a grab for her skirts, ruffling them back: he slid his hand over the top of her stocking, and then in between her thighs. She pulled away, kicking out at him, fumbling her skirts down; he retreated, grinning, showing a black gap where his front teeth should have been. He was gone before he'd even really been there, and left her shaking.

And to think it had once seemed a good idea to come here alone.

They turned into Gracechurch Street, and after a hundred yards or so of cobbles, Sir William pulled up the horses. Sarah looked up at a fine, tall, flat-fronted townhouse. The steps were scrubbed quite white, and she felt a new sympathy for Martha, the red-haired Gardiner housemaid, who had seemed so wilfully idle at Christmas. How her hands would smart from the soap, how her shoulders would ache with all the scrubbing, to get the stone that white in all this dirt. Sarah undid the buckle, loosened the strap, and slid down from her perch; she stood unsteadily at the back of the chaise, her legs quite numb beneath her.

Up above, Jane stood at a window. She looked pale and ghostly behind the watery pane: Sarah raised a hand in greeting, but Jane just turned away into the shadows, and a moment later she and Mrs Gardiner, and the children, were trotting down the pristine steps, to meet the carriage.

Sir William, Maria and Elizabeth got out of the chaise, stiff from their journey. Sarah, pins-and-needles in her thighs, set about un-buckling the small baggages. She handed them to a waiting footman, who carried them indoors. The chaise and horse were left in the care of another footman, who walked the horse round through an archway into the mews beyond. Sarah climbed the scrubbed steps, now marked with footprints, and stood in the gloomy hallway, waiting to be noticed, and told what to do.

The house was all up and down and front and back, and nothing sideways to it at all. The windows were large-paned and lustrous, and looked out onto blank brickwork at the back, and at the front, stared across at the house on the far side of the street. Sarah, instructed by Martha, who seemed pleased to see her, climbed up and up and up to the servants' attic, and set her wooden box on the floor there, beside the pallet that had been rolled out for her. She looked out of the window, across smoky rooftops; a few young trees were huddled shyly in a square. Further off, she saw the masts and bare rigging of ships at the quay. And then she had to scurry all the way back down again: they were going out.

Elizabeth was to go shopping with her aunt, and had told Sarah she could come with them; there was nothing immediate for her to do in the way of unpacking, et cetera, as they were off again on the morrow. Sarah rode up front with the coachman, an incomprehensible cockney, who persisted in pointing things out to her – landmarks, she supposed, and points of particular interest; she obliged him by staring off in the direction that he pointed, and nodding at whatever he said.

They crept in thick traffic along the mercantile roads, and then, when they were in the calmer parts of town, they picked up the pace, clipping along the streets, round two sides of a square that had been laid out like a formal garden, and then looping into a crescent, where white-fronted townhouses stood like a row of fine white teeth. At the end, the work was unfinished and instead of a house there was an empty lot, raw, the foundation-troughs and cesspit already dug.

They turned onto a broad avenue, and the driver pulled up the horses. The carriage waited for them while they went into the shops.

Sarah followed Elizabeth and her aunt down one arcade, and then up another, and in and out of stores stacked high with bolts of coloured cloth and patterned paper and rolled carpets – Mrs Gardiner was soon to redecorate a sitting room, and had solicited Elizabeth's opinion in the selection of patterns and colours. Sarah was soon lugging paste-board boxes, paper packages and rolled samples of wallpaper. She had seen all of this before; she had daydreamed it. It was all very fine, but it was not as lovely as the daydream, and the packages slithered and slipped from her grip, and a box dug into her side, and how could it be that a person needed so much of all of this, and how could it be that one printed paper was so vitally, importantly lovely and another was entirely dismissable, or that any of it really mattered so very much, or indeed at all?

Then they returned to the carriage, and drove a little further, to another terrace of white houses, where Mrs Gardiner then went to get her teeth filed – she had had it done once before, and now must have it done again. Elizabeth declined the offer to have hers looked at too. She sat in the carriage outside Mr Spence's establishment, and waited with Sarah and the coachman, and asked what Sarah thought of London.

'It is not what I imagined, miss.'

'How did you imagine it?'

Sarah shook her head. The real now overlaid the daydream, clouding it. 'I cannot rightly say, now, miss.'

They watched as the fashionable folk clipped smartly up the bright steps, past the polished brass plaques, and in through the smart blue door; they watched them stumble back out with bloodied hand-kerchiefs to their faces.

'I think I made the better choice,' Elizabeth said.

'Indeed so, miss.'

Elizabeth's decision was further vindicated by the uncomfortable aspect of her aunt, who emerged from Mr Spence's offices rather swollen about the lips, having had to have all her lower front teeth rasped away considerably.

Then there was dinner, which Mrs Gardiner could not eat at all, and Jane only picked at, and which Sarah partook of with strangers in the tiny servants' hall, struggling not to yawn. Then the family went out to the theatre in the Gardiners' coach, and Martha packed the children off to bed, and the household loosened its collective collar, and collapsed into fatigue.

London. The crowded heart of the city. Where there should be dancing bears and frolicking beggars and fireworks fit to scare a soldier. Sarah lay down on the pallet, and drew the blankets up to her chin. Martha blew out the candle, and it was dark.

Sarah curled onto her side. The mattress was thin, stuffed with old hair, and her hip and shoulder pressed against the wooden boards beneath. Despite her tiredness, she could not sleep: the noise – the sheer depth of it, layer after layer of sound – cabs rattling along the street in front, drays rumbling down to the docks, cats fighting or mating in the alleyways, the creak of rope from the wharves, a dog barking, a clock, and another clock, and another still more distant clock chiming out hour after hour of the night, into the darkness, as the Gardiners' housemaid snored oblivious in her bed, and Sarah twisted and turned and tangled herself up in blankets that smelt of someone else.

Kent was wide and green; those were hop-vines planted, and over there was lavender, which looked grey now, but later in the year would make the fields quite purple. The barns stood on those stone footings, Sir William said, to keep out the rats: he was a fount of information, and supplied it freely to his two young charges within the chaise; Sarah overheard everything through the umbrella-skin of the calash.

At a toll-house, the keeper's accent was so strange that Sir William could make himself understood only by speaking loudly and slowly, and with grand gestures, which rocked the chaise on its springs. The transaction complete, Sir William drove away saying that it was a mark of true breeding to be able to make oneself understood by the lower orders wherever they were to be found, and that he himself was particularly fortunate to have the happy knack of it. Sarah, seeing, as it were, the aftermath of everything, watched the keeper spit on the ground and say something that she could not hear, but the meaning of which was perfectly clear to her, though she had no claim to any breeding whatsoever.

210

And then there were the palings of a park rippling by, and she watched a fieldfare call from its perch on the fence, its beak open like a jug, pouring out song; and then they descended into the village, past cosy low-eaved cottages, and beds dug for spring planting. Sir William pulled up in front of a pleasant, decent house, perhaps a third the size of Longbourn, with green fencing, and laurels, and the garden sloping down towards the village street, and then Mr and Mrs Collins were coming out of the front door to greet them.

When the little group had gone in through the gate, she followed after with the bags. At the front door, Mr Collins stood aside to let her pass.

'Well, well—' He searched, but could not find her name. 'My child.'

The housekeeper at Hunsford Parsonage was like a horsefly at Sarah's ear, buzzing, always threatening to bite. Every scrap of work must be observed and its results scrutinized; everything must be done to perfection and beyond. She would drop to her hunkers to look along the length of a polished tabletop; she would peer, head cocked like a hen, into scoured pans; she held up drinking glasses to the light. The Collinses' housemaid was consequently a timid, rabbity thing, always on the hop. Sarah tried conversing with her that first afternoon, in the scullery, where they had been set to clean the brass and copper together. The girl just stared at Sarah, her mouth falling slowly open, rag in one hand, and a cup of salt-and-flour-and-vinegar paste in the other. Then, realizing she had stopped working, she shuddered back into life, rubbing at the samovar as if she was trying to wear a hole in it. Sarah, eyebrows raised, scooped up some paste, and continued with her own work, and did not trouble the girl again. But she could not make sense of all this agitation: Mrs Collins was sensible, and Mr Collins very easily pleased, so why should it be that the Hunsford servantry lived on hot coals like this; you would think they suffered the most exacting of employers.

And then, one morning, Lady Catherine de Bourgh came to call. *The master's patroness*, the housemaid whispered, eyes goggling; she

211

curtseyed deeply. Sarah dipped a curtsey herself, and observed from under her eyelashes as the grand lady trod slowly past, her eyes assessing each girl in turn from cap to boots.

Lady Catherine roamed the parsonage. She climbed stairs and opened cupboards. She lifted a vase from the mantel to see that it did not leave a footprint in an otherwise too-faint-to-notice fall of dust. She peered and picked at Mrs Collins's embroidery and said that really she should be concentrating on her needlepoint, and not wasting her time on this wild satin-stitch stuff. Then she deigned to accept the offer of refreshment, and all was thrown into frenzy in the kitchen; the tea had been considered far too strong on the last occasion that Lady Catherine partook of it, and the servants had been accused of profligacy with the leaves.

This time, the brew passed Lady Catherine's lips without comment, which caused the poised and anxious housekeeper actually to sigh, and then blush at having sighed. Lady Catherine's opinions on the state of the tray-cloth were, however, heard by all; they caused the housemaid to shrink still further, and scurry off to be busy elsewhere, so that she might not be found till some of the immediate burn of shame and fury had subsided: 'If your housemaid cannot remove a simple stain like that, you really must replace her.'

About a fortnight later, not long after Sir William's return home to Lucas Lodge, they killed a sow. Mr Collins looked on, arms folded as it struggled and squealed, then bled out, twitching, and then went silent and still.

'Fine pig, that Berkshire is. Was. Finest in the county, I should say. Good and fat.'

Sarah carried the bucket of blood back to the kitchen, where the sow was also carried, trotters in the air, for butchering. It being heavy work, the manservant jointed the beast; the housekeeper stripped off fat and dropped it into a tub. She nudged at it with a toe.

'You get that sorted for us, eh, Miss Sarah?'

Sarah blinked at her.

'You do know how to make soap, I suppose? You do have soap in Hertfordshire?'

'Where's the lye?'

'Where you'd expect it to be.'

In the parsonage scullery, Sarah measured the lye into the water with an old cracked cup. She lit the fire beneath the copper, and set the fat to melt. The porkiness of it bubbled off a little bit, or she just got used to it, for it did not seem to smell quite so like Sunday dinner after a while. She poured out the liquid fat, then lifted down a bunch of lavender, and tucked it into her apron pocket. It had never failed to astonish her, down the years of helping Mrs Hill, how soap that made things clean was such a foul thing in its own making. She stripped the pale dried lavender, and dropped the buds into the curdling porridge.

The soap was poured into the mould, the mould wrapped around with cloths, and the bundle hidden in a cupboard to continue cooking on its own. Sarah stepped out blinking into the yard. A bay horse scratched its neck against the top of the stable door. Above the tiled roof she could see the tops of plane trees, and a white bird soaring up into the blue. She watched it skim away, over the wide patchwork of fields, copses and forests – and beyond all that, the sea.

The sea. Elizabeth had said that they were closer – might she catch a glimpse of it from here? What was the point of her being in Kent at all, if all she got to see was the innards of a pig, and of the parsonage?

She pulled her apron off and slipped out of the back gate. Breathless down the village street, she strode past bantams scratching in the grit, and bare-twigged rose bushes in a garden, and a woman who came out of a cottage and folded her arms beneath her bosom and stared at her.

Beyond the dwellings, the hedges were high and budded with green; she climbed up onto the cross-tread of a stile, to see beyond. There was a clayey ploughed field, sprigged with early growth. Here and there, across the weald, she could see smoke twining into the air, church spires, barn rooves with baked-clay tiles, and layer after layer of green, until it melted into the distance. But she could not see the sea.

And it was all so very like Hertfordshire. Here, though, there was no trace of the associations that had made Hertfordshire the centre of the world.

At the parsonage, the housekeeper was standing at the back door with her fists jammed into her scrawny waist.

'The soap was done, so—' Sarah began.

She was silenced by a cuff round the head, and was shoved indoors.

This was a respectable household! What would people think! More importantly, what would people say! More importantly still, what would Lady Catherine think and say, when she found out? Gadding about the countryside like a proper dollymop.

Sarah smarted with outrage – the housekeeper couldn't hit her: Sarah wasn't hers to hit; and how dare she call her names? But the woman was not to be argued with; she marched Sarah down to the kitchen, still scolding, because Lady Catherine was *bound* to find out, and Sarah need not think that anybody would stand between Sarah and the full force of Lady Catherine's disapproval.

The doorbell rang. It made her jump. As instructed by the house-keeper, Sarah had scattered tea leaves and was sweeping them, and the dust that they had laid, up into a pile. But she had no instructions regarding the parsonage door; back at Longbourn it would be James's or Mr Hill's job. So she waited, with her broom, for the thud of the manservant's feet. But he did not come.

She chewed a snag of skin by her thumbnail. Whatever she did, she was bound to be in the wrong. Run for assistance, and leave the visitors waiting; open the door, and be found to have overstepped herself. And what if it was Lady Catherine, looming on the threshold, come to admonish the Collinses for keeping an unruly household; what would she say on finding the door opened by the miscreant herself?

Sarah glanced down the empty hallway. Not a footfall, not a creaking door. She could hear Mr Collins's voice from outside, and brief, lower-pitched replies. Mr Collins must have gone out earlier by a side door, and now was returning with visitors. They must be people of some standing, since they must wait at a locked main entrance, rather than be brought in some other way.

Every ticking moment made it worse.

She leaned her broom in the corner. Then she drew the bolt, and opened the door.

In the event, it did not matter whether or not she had overstepped herself, because in the instant the door was opened, she ceased to exist. One moment she was there, creaking the door back on the bright morning, and the next she was gone; the two grand gentlemen filled the doorway, and stepped through it, and moved past her, and did not so much as glance her way — for them the door had simply opened itself. Mr Collins bustled through behind them.

'Just through there, Mr Darcy, Colonel Fitzwilliam, if you would be so kind, the second door on the left.'

A blur of rich colours — one green velvet coat, one blue — and the soft creak of good leather, and a scent off them like pine sap and fine candlewax and wool. She watched their glossy boots scatter her tea leaves across the wooden floor. The two gentlemen were so smooth, and so big, and of such substance: it was as though they belonged to a different order of creation entirely, and moved in a separate element, and were as different as angels.

Mr Collins, in his clerical black, closed the door behind them, and all was dim indoors. And she was there again, returning to her own flesh: he turned to Sarah with a terrified smile.

'To think, I was out for my walk, and came upon Colonel Fitzwilliam, and Mr Darcy! And they would come here, my dear, back to my humble abode!'

She smiled encouragingly for him.

He went after them, rubbing his hands and muttering, baffled as to why such happiness should make him feel so distressed. He disappeared into the parlour; she could hear him offering seats, refreshments, jangling the bell. Summoned, the housekeeper came striding past, casting an accusatory glance at Sarah.

Sarah retrieved her broom and began, again, to chase the damp leaves around the floor.

'Clearly,' Elizabeth said, struggling out of her petticoat, 'he takes after his aunt, Lady Catherine. He must be trying to find fault with me.'

'He will have his work cut out for him.'

Sarah set Elizabeth's hot water down on the washstand, and unfurled a slice of soap from its muslin wrapper, while Elizabeth wafted the compliment away.

'Oh, I am not his idea of what a woman should be, not at all. I heard him once, you know, listing his requirements; a woman would need to combine all the Three Graces in one person, to stand any chance of charming him at all.'

'But he cannot be a reasonable man, miss, if he seeks you out simply to find fault with you.'

'Well, there we are, then. He is not reasonable.'

This soap was scented with rose petals, which had turned with age as brown and crumbly as tea. Her own lavender-scented batch had been drying now for a fortnight; it would be another month before it was safe to use on a lady's skin. And by then they would be home! The thought was like a cool breeze to Sarah, as she laid out the towels, one on the marble top, another down on the floor for Elizabeth to stand on.

'And yet I cannot for the life of me understand why he keeps on coming here, with the colonel and without, or lurking around at Rosings, and just, well, *looking*.'

Sarah peered closer at the soap – a small fly was stuck there; it had seemed, for a moment, to be a scrap of petal. She picked it swiftly out, flicked it away; the young lady was too busy with her thoughts, and her undressing, to notice what her maid had just done.

'It cannot be for the society, since he sits ten minutes together without opening his lips. And it cannot be for the cakes, because they really are nothing very remarkable at all, for all Mr Collins does go on about them – oh, these laces!'

She threw up her hands in frustration. Sarah came close and unknotted the cord, then teased it out through the eyelets of Elizabeth's short-stays. Once they were loosened, Sarah slid the stays down; Elizabeth put a hand on Sarah's shoulder and stepped out of them.

'You have no notion at all, then, miss, why he might be looking at you so much?'

'Perhaps he is thinking about his dinner. I don't know. I have no idea at all.'

Sarah laid the stays down on the bed; Elizabeth slipped her shift off her shoulders, let it fall to the ground too. She stepped out of it. Feet bare on the towel that Sarah had placed for her, Elizabeth wrung out a cloth, and washed her face, and then her neck and ears.

Sarah wafted the young lady's gown out on the bed; perhaps Elizabeth was right, in a way; perhaps he did look at her hungrily; she just did not yet know the nature of the hunger. Elizabeth rinsed out her cloth, and rolled the soap in it; she lifted it, dripping, and washed her underarms. The greyed water beaded on her ribs, and ran down her; the towel darkened beneath her slender feet.

Sarah said, 'You do not suppose he could be partial to you at all, do you, miss?'

'Oh, goodness me!' Elizabeth laughed, and sloshed her cloth back into the bowl again. 'Don't be such a silly, Sarah.'

Elizabeth had a headache. It was the second headache of the day. She had been rereading her letters from Jane, and they had made her tearful, and the tearfulness had brought on these headaches and there was no way that she was going to Rosings now, not since she had such an excellent reason to be excused.

Sarah would have loved to have a letter to look at herself; she would have loved to have the luxury of tears and headaches: the darkened parlour, a cool cloth for the forehead, and the peace that came with the family gone out to drink their tea.

This time, when the doorbell rang, Sarah ran for it, to caution any visitor – she anticipated a poor parishioner with an elderly or ill relative – that the family was not at home. But it was Mr Darcy again, his big glossy self; then he was past her, and heading down the corridor, and opening the parlour door. She heard Elizabeth's exclamation, imagined the spiriting away of the damp cloth, the swift drawing open of the blinds. But Sarah could not have even slowed his progress, no more than one of the evening shadows could trip him up. She stood there on the threshold, feeling quite transparent: the brassy polish of the doorknob seemed to shine through her hand; the evening blue leached right through her.

Sarah sat down on the front step, the door ajar behind her. There were just days now to be counted – nine days, and this one blessedly nearly over – until they began their journey back to Longbourn. Her face lifted towards the cool evening air, breathing in the sappy scent of laurels, she rested her head back against the doorjamb. A nightingale sang in the nearby trees.

I would write you a letter, James. If I had paper. If I had ink. If I had a frank to send it by. I would ask you how things are now, at Longbourn; how Polly gets on without me there to soften the edges for her. Whether Mr Hill has got round to making the dubbin yet, since I had not before I left. I would write to you about the bay horse scratching her neck, and the nightingale that's singing, and the sow with her black fuzz and her white trotters and her snuffly pink nose, who is now rendered into soap that's drying in the closet, and that Miss Elizabeth just washed herself with soap that had a fly in it, and the fields that were just green shoots when we arrived and are now tall spears, and about Mr Fitzwilliam Darcy, who is such a polished meaty thing that he makes me slip, for a moment, out of this world entirely, and I become a ghost-girl who can make things move but cannot her-self be seen. I would write about how you make me be entirely in myself, and more real than I had ever thought was possible. I would ask if you miss me like I miss you, so that there is not another spot in all the world that seems to mean anything at all, but where you are. That the days until I see you again are just to be got through, like cold souse, or plain work, and that nothing good is to be expected of them at all, but that they will eventually be over, and I will be on my way back home to you.

She heard a door shut within the house. There were quick footfalls coming down the hall. She got up off the step and stood aside just in time, or he would have walked straight through her: the front door was whisked wide, and Mr Darcy strode past her shadow, and marched down the path. He left the gate swinging. When he was out of sight, she slipped down the path after him, and latched the gate shut.

Back in the house, she crept down the hall and cocked an ear outside the parlour door. She could hear the quiet sounds of Elizabeth crying. Sarah's hand rested a moment on the doorknob, but then she turned and crept away. Sometimes, she thought, it might be better just to disappear from notice, than to attract a gentleman's particular attention like that.

For James, all this time, Longbourn was not so much quiet as sharp-edged: all softness gone from it, the household jarred and jangled. Though fewer in number without their elder sisters, the young ladies generated considerably more noise. When it was not Mary's scales and arpeggios, or the same Italian air begun over and over till the same tricky moment broke her off, it was Kitty and Lydia squabbling about the ownership of an item of clothing, or shrieking over the gossip. More often it was both faltering piano and screeching girls, while Mr Bennet shut himself in his library and only emerged at the sound of the dinner bell, and Mrs Bennet complained to no one's hearing of headaches, and Polly carried heavy ewers up the stairs and stinking chamber pots back down, and Mrs Hill, moist-eyed, chopped onions, and Mr Hill, having sipped sherry in the cellar, slipped discreetly out of the house to meet a friend. James drove out when required, and waited on table, and sponged the mud off coat-tails, and dabbed the grass stains off pelisses, and teased the candle grease out of shirt-fronts, and lugged water and wood, and sometimes even enjoyed going about with little Polly to collect the eggs or herbs or salad leaves, but felt, all the time, suspended, like a piece of music broken abruptly off, a note left hanging in the air.

The younger girls walked into Meryton most mornings. They went to make purchases of ribbon or pink Persian or stockings or tooth-powder, or to call upon their dear aunt Philips. They made their way on foot, and so James did not see it for himself, but from their chatter on return it was clear to him that a brace or two of officers could be conjured up quite readily; all a young lady had to do was wander up and down Market Street a while.

Then there were parties and suppers-and-cards at their aunt Philips's, and balls at the Assembly Rooms during the fullness of the moon, which did require James's assistance with the carriage, and once there was a large party gathered for the evening at Colonel Forster's lodgings, and James drove the younger girls there too.

James waited outside the lit and noisy townhouse, having assumed his usual attitude: shoulders rounded, hat low, gaze averted.

The uproar built and grew all evening, until it sounded as though it was perfect Bedlam in the colonel's rooms. Someone should call the constable, or rustle up a magistrate to read the riot act. It grew very late – the town clock chimed one, and then the quarter hour, and then the half. And then, when the party finally broke up just after two, a young man came sauntering forth, tricked out in a lady's gown and cap, with rouged lips and cheeks, and with uniformed officers draped on either arm. The boy flounced off down the street to catcalls, batting off the straying hands of his fellow officers. Lydia and Kitty watched this little show, hands pressed to their sides, helpless with laughter.

'Did you see?' Lydia was still breathless as she flumped down onto the upholstery. 'Did you see Chamberlayne, James? Only think what fun! We dressed him up to pass as a lady, and nobody knew him at all! Not till we started laughing, anyway.'

James bowed, and clapped the door shut on their noise. He climbed up to the carriage box. The night cool in his eyes, he drove them home; there was constant gabbling below, like a crate of turkeys. It had left him feeling deeply ill at ease. There might be no harm in making free with a boy like that, but in the end the girls would meet with something dangerous, and then this cast-iron sense of their own importance would be no good to them at all.

CHAPTER XIV

Wickham will soon be gone; and therefore it will not signify to anybody here, what he really is.

THE LANE-WAYS were thick with May blossom when James drove Kitty and Lydia to meet their elder sisters and Maria Lucas at the posting-inn.

Sarah had travelled inside the post-chaise on the return journey, on the fold-out seat to one side. She had kept her feet tucked under her, so that her boots were out of the way of the ladies' pretty shoes. She had been cramped and uncomfortable, watching the world streaming sideways past her, swaying nauseously all the way from London.

All stuffiness and sickness were quite forgotten as they drew up at the inn, and she glimpsed James.

He opened the post-chaise door, and helped her down. His hands were on her waist, and his eyes were on her eyes. And then he turned to offer his hand to Miss Jane, and then Miss Elizabeth, and then Maria Lucas descending behind them. Sarah, too happy to smile, the ground now betraying her and swaying under her feet, followed the ladies into the inn, and waited outside the privy door for them, so that they would not be disturbed.

While the ladies took some refreshment in a private room all together, and after Sarah had relieved herself, she returned to James, and sat on a mounting block and watched as he put the lovely old Longbourn horses into harness after their rest. She took off her bonnet, and raised her face to the warm Hertfordshire sun. She thought, There is no happiness in all the world so perfect as this: James here, and the noise and bustle of the posting-inn, and a mug of small beer that he brought for her, and put in her hand, and a slice of pie. He sat down beside her, and she handed her cup to him, and he took a little sip, and handed it back.

'That is a pretty dress on you.'

She ran a coarse palm over the sprigged poplin; it was the day-dress that Jane had given her, which she kept for very best.

'Thank you.'

They both watched, out of the tail of their sight, the sentinel as he marched pointlessly up and down, on guard at the town gates. There were troops everywhere these days. It made you twitchy; you could not turn round without seeing a red coat and a Brown Bess.

'We were two weeks in London.'

He nodded.

'I would not have minded quite so much,' she said, 'but, two whole *weeks*.'

He laid his hand on her arm, and she leaned against him, and her eyes swam. He reached round and wiped a tear away with a rough thumb. She rested her head on his shoulder.

When the ladies finally emerged from their luncheon, Sarah and James were waiting separately. James handed the young ladies in, and then passed them their purchases and more tender items of baggage. When the ladies were packed tight, he helped Sarah up onto the box, and then got up beside her. He conveyed them all, at a steady pace, back to Longbourn House. On the box, Sarah and James could lean and sway side by side, together, and nobody would think it strange, or remark upon it.

Mrs Hill squeezed her hand and kissed her cheek, and said, 'I am glad you are back,' and turned away so as not to show her face. Polly crushed the breath out of her, and then, when she had released her, made little excited jumps on the spot, asking questions, and not waiting for her to answer. Mr Hill bowed, and then quietly patted her hand.

The kitchen seemed very dark, and cool, and lovely, and had shrunk.

When they had all just begun to settle back into themselves, Miss Lyddie sauntered in through the kitchen door, and went to help herself to barley-sugar. Seeing Sarah, she stopped, and offered her the open jar.

'It is good to have you back, Sarah. We have missed you here.'

'Thank you, miss.' Sarah took a piece of barley-sugar.

'There's no one here can get out a wine stain like you do. I want you to have a look at my good muslin later, and see what you can do. Not that it matters much now, any more.' Lydia sucked her barley-sugar, pensive. 'I don't suppose you have even heard, though, have you? It's such terrible news I dare say folk have kept it from you, and I don't know how we shall bear it at all.'

Sarah stuffed her sweet into her cheek. 'Oh goodness, no, what is it?' She assumed a disaster, sickness, death.

'It's the Militia, Sarah. They're leaving.'

Sarah presumed to take Lydia's hand, and press it.

'It is a shame, but we always knew that they would go.'

Lydia nodded, unconsoled. Sarah felt for her. The days would be interminable, and the evenings dull, and even the Meryton balls would be miserable affairs, with only the same attorneys and aldermen's sons and curates to dance with, and the best hope of the season now that someone's grown-up nephew might come to visit. The utter tedium of a summer spent at home in the country, for a fifteen-year-old girl with no taste for landscape, or reading, or reflection: it was a dreadful shame indeed.

When the Militia left at the end of the month, James would be happy; Polly knew this, and she was glad, because she liked James. James was her friend and played jacks and came with her on her errands, and gave her bits of chalk to draw with in the stable yard. But when the Militia left, Mr Wickham would go with them. And Mr Wickham gave her money. He handed over pennies and halfpennies and farthings as if they were trash for which he could have no possible use himself. She liked to trickle these coins from hand to hand; she liked to build them up in columns and colonnades on the floorboard beside her bed, and imagine what she would buy with them when a scotchman came, or when she next went to Meryton on an errand. He called her Little Miss, and that was nice. He gave her smiles, too, and asked her questions, and sometimes he touched her cheek. She was not sure that she quite liked that, but she did know that it mattered.

'If he gives you any trouble,' James said to her one time, 'you come and tell me, and I'll sort him out for you.'

James was a good fellow, always ready to play at five stones or shove-halfpenny, but when it came down to it, he knew nothing about anything. What would *he* do to a man like Mr Wickham, an *officer*, who had pistols and a sword? And, anyway, it didn't signify, because Mr Wickham didn't give her any trouble. He was the only person – James, perhaps, excluded – who never did. She got no chores, no scolding, no nagging off him. Instead, he gave her coins and smiles and a kind word from time to time.

And then they heard that Lydia was to go to Brighton with Mrs Forster, the colonel's new wife. This was good news for Lydia, but it had the elder sisters muttering, and it threw Sarah and Polly into a frenzy to get linen clean and dresses pressed and folded and packed in good time for departure, so that Polly, having at first been sad to think of Wickham going, now could not wait for him to be gone, since it would at least mean that all the laundering would be over for a while.

Sarah was imprisoned for much of this time in Kitty and Lydia's shared room, engaged in a Sisyphean task. As soon as a trunk was packed, Kitty would re-open it, plunge elbow-deep in, in ferocious tears, and rummage for her own things that had been sequestered there at Lydia's insistence. Kitty would fling out an evening-gown, her new gloves, snarl at the discovery of her best petticoat. While Kitty was convulsed with outrage, Lydia quite calmly gathered everything up and folded it again, preparatory to putting it back: Kitty must be reason-able, and see sense; if *she* was going to Brighton and not Lydia, Lydia would certainly let her have all her best things, and welcome, without putting up anything of a fight, without thinking twice about it, for what was the point of having pretty things at all, if no one was around to see you wearing them?

In her own room, Mary closed her eyes and rested her fingers on the piano keys, and took a breath and let it go, and, trying to ignore the shrieks and clattering and squabbles from next door, began again her Irish air. One day, she knew, her fingers would fly about the keyboard with the facility and delicacy of tiny birds. One day. But until then, there was just the lumbering work of practice, practice, practice, and the distraction of those silly sisters, whose immoderacy of behaviour was now manifested by a series of high-pitched squeals that suggested that Kitty had lost her temper entirely, and was now pulling Lyddie's hair. If they could but think of higher things, of music, religion, good works, instead of officers – her fingers plodded up and down the keyboard, picking out the sweet opening notes of Haydn's *Love Dialogue* – then they would, no doubt, be happier creatures for it. Her thoughts drifted unwittingly to that courteous, gentle Mr Collins, who, she was certain, she could have made quite happy. She had no such confidence in Charlotte Lucas, who might come one day to deserve him, but who certainly did not love him, not like Mary did; and who must never be allowed to suspect what turmoil she had, with her rank opportunism, engendered in Mary's tender breast. Because Mary had allowed herself to daydream, and she should have never allowed herself that. She had let herself think of the possibility of reciprocated love, of marriage, of the new importance that it would bring to her; of how, on becoming Mr Collins's bride, she would have also become the means of her family's salvation, and no longer just the plain, awkward, overlooked middle child.

On the very last day of the regiment's remaining in Meryton, Mr Wickham was to dine with others of the officers at Longbourn. Just this one evening to be safely navigated, and then they were out into clear water. The neighbourhood would be free of Militia. And it would no longer matter what Wickham's intentions might have been regarding Polly, or James, once he was seventy-odd miles away at Brighton.

James served silently at table, ghosting in between the officers and the ladies, keeping his eyes low, his shoulders rounded, treading the thin line between conspicuous efficiency and equally conspicuous lassitude.

I will be, he thought, what they think me, which is nothing much at all.

But, as he filled Wickham's glass, the young officer turned his head and looked at him. A long steady look, which James was determined not to meet. Instead he watched the wine tumble into the glass, and the glint of the carafe as he turned it to catch the drips, and the purple stain on the napkin with which he touched the crystal lip. Then he stepped away, and went to fill Elizabeth's glass. Elizabeth, comfortably, did not acknowledge him at all. Whereas that look, from Wickham, a bright tiger's eyes: it left him shaken.

Wickham now deliberately engrossed himself in Miss Elizabeth; his notice strayed only once to the young maid, clearing dishes, but then was swiftly dragged back to his silverware, his cuffs, his companion. He seemed particularly intent on being charming, as if, James thought, he knew that he was suspected of something, and was attempting to forestall criticism.

If only Wickham was in the regulars, James thought, as he descended the cellar steps with a candle to fetch up more wine, he could allow himself the pleasure of imagining the pretty young fellow sent off to fight in Spain. He could imagine him caught by the *guerrillas* and strung up from a tree, his cock cut off and stuffed in his own mouth, left bleeding and to the mercy of the wolves. That'd take the shine off him a bit.

Both guests and family drank too much that night. James and Mr Hill had to run down to the cellar more than once for further bottles. The large party, gathered in the drawing room, was noisy with wine and the deep feeling it engendered, and kept at their conviviality for long and footsore hours; there is nothing like the imminence of parting to make people unduly fond of each other.

Mr Hill, old and exhausted, sloped off to bed at eleven, with a wink to James.

'You'll manage without me, eh? All these young fellows; it's all a bit too much for me.'

Polly collected up the smeared and sticky glasses in the now empty dining room while the party rumbled on elsewhere. She turned with a tray of rummers, and found Wickham lounging silently in the doorway. She came towards him, tired but easy, attempting a smile; he swirled a glass of blood-dark port in his hand.

'Are you going to congratulate me on my escape, Little Miss?'

It was his way of coping with society: he had to have these little releases, time with people who were like him, who understood him.

'Well done, Mr Wickham, sir.'

He meandered further into the empty dining room, coming closer, still between her and the door. When he smiled, his teeth and lips were stained with drink.

'And how are you, Little Miss, tonight?'

Tired, footsore, wanting her bed. 'Sorry that you're going, sir.'

He nodded, woebegone. 'It is very sad,' he said. 'But I was thinking—'

'What, sir?'

'You know that we are off to Brighton?'

She shifted her weight, dropping a hip; her feet throbbed. If she was nice to him, one last time, chances were she'd get a penny off him before he went.

'Yes, sir.'

She glanced down at his waistcoat, the usual source of coin. He just swirled his port around, lips pursed. His hand still didn't move towards his pocket.

'I'll bet you don't get as many sweet things as you'd like.'

She looked up at this, attention really caught now: she shook her head.

'D'you know, there's a sweetshop in Brighton, where there are jars and jars of bonbons and comfits and rock, all the colours of the rainbow, any flavour you can think of.'

'Is there pineapple?'

She had heard of pineapples; she had heard they had them in some grand houses, though she had never seen one herself. She imagined them to be a bit like russets, compact and very sweet, but with a skin covered with the sharp green needles of a Scots pine.

He nodded, smiled slightly, added his glass to her tray, and pocketed his hands. Britches pockets, though, not waistcoat.

'Really? Even *pineapple?*'

'And many more besides.'

She swallowed, dreamy and acquisitive. He leaned back a little, watching her, his eyes half closed.

'How old are you, Little Miss?'

'Don't know quite. Twelve, thirteen, maybe. Why?'

'Shall I buy you some pineapple bonbons, then, and send them back to you?'

Polly stared up at his big face, which everybody said was handsome; the sprouting moustache, the open pores between his eyebrows, the broken veins on his nose. Grown-ups could be so very unpleasant to look at, if you got too close.

'Oh, would you, though? Would you really?'

She wanted to ask what the other flavours were, before she committed herself to pineapple; whether there would be lemon drops and cough candy, coltsfoot rock and aniseed.

'I would. I will. If you'll be sweet to me now.'

He moved towards her, a little unsteady on his feet. She stepped back as he came closer, thinking he meant to go past her. But he leaned in, and very carefully and deliberately, took the tray out of her hands, and set it down on the tabletop. The goblets chinked against each other in his clumsy grip.

'You will be, won't you? Sweet.'

'Sir?'

'The way you look at me, like butter wouldn't melt—'

The table edge pressed into the small of her back; he leaned closer; his breath thick with wine and tobacco. She turned her face away, nose wrinkling. Then his hand came up and touched her cheek, and then ran down her throat. It stopped at the collar of her dress. Her heart was beating like a bird, and she felt gooseflesh rise on her arms, and she did not know what she was supposed to do.

'Polly?'

It was James's voice. Wickham went still and cold. Then he took a step back from her, and turned towards the newcomer. James had an empty decanter in his hand, and a deep line between his brows. Polly took a sidelong step away from Wickham, who adjusted his coat-front, tugging it down.

James did not so much as glance at Mr Wickham. 'Mrs Hill wants you in the kitchen.'

'In a minute.'

For all that this was strange, and not particularly pleasant, Mr Wickham had always been kind to her before.

'You do not seem to understand. You are wanted *now*.'

Polly raised up her eyes to heaven, but complied. Lifting her tray, she walked out of the room with the posture of a queen. Though she scowled, in passing, at James. He turned to follow, but then Wickham called out after him.

'A moment, Smith.'

He paused, turned. Wickham turned to the sideboard, lifted the decanters one after the other, and examined them, plucking out the stoppers, sniffing.

'You'll excuse me, sir, I—'

'No, I won't excuse you. Damn you.' He held a decanter up to the light. 'D'you know, I was just going to leave it—'

He found a glass, slopped in an inch of whisky. Despite everything, James winced for him: he would feel like death itself tomorrow.

When Wickham spoke again, over his shoulder, the words were blurry with drink: 'Because I thought, what's the point, really? We're

230

leaving, and I thought, why bother myself with that? Why not just let a man go about his business, live and let live? Why not? Too much trouble to do otherwise.'

James felt a prickle of unease.

Wickham turned back to face him, rather unsteadily, reaching out a hand to lean on the sideboard. He missed, but he recovered and steadied himself, though he listed now a little to the left.

'See, a man like me,' he said carefully, ''s not so easy for me to get along. Neither fish nor fowl, me. Frog, really; or a toad. No place in the world for me but in the mud. You, you've got yourself nicely set up here. Cosy little billet. Well supplied with comforts. But you're a dog-in-the-manger, and you begrudge me mine.'

James went to speak, but found that words escaped him.

'Can't see how you get away with it, truth be told. Anyone can see that little doxy's getting a good going-over; she's just oozing with it—'

Afterwards, the only way that James could think of it was that he had taken, somehow, a step away from himself. He knew what he was doing, and knew what would come of it, and yet he did it anyway. He watched his hand set the decanter down on the dining table, and it all looked perfectly steady and cool. He took two brisk steps up to the sloping officer. The loss of his temper was an active thing; like shedding a heavy coat on a hot day, it was a relief to shrug it off.

His fist landed on Wickham's temple. A nice sharp crack that the officer did not attempt to deflect, or even flinch away from, because he simply didn't see it coming. Wickham staggered back against the sideboard. He fumbled at it for support, making the decanters shake and jingle.

And there, James thought, as he shook the sting out of his knuckles, shifting his balance and then bringing both hands up to ward off any retaliatory blow, that was the line that I must not cross, and I have just gone and vaulted right over it.

'You can't touch me.' Wickham sounded more puzzled than angry. He struggled upright, touched his fingertips to his temple, then looked at them. The skin was not broken. There was no blood. 'There are rules, dammit. Don't you know the blasted rules?'

He touched his temple again, and then, to James's astonishment, he began to laugh. He patted down his pockets, and drew out a case of cigarillos, and lit one from a candle.

'See, thing is,' he said, 'I had my suspicions, but it had just seemed like too much trouble before. But then you go and cross me, and now you go and hit me, and it just seems like no trouble at all.'

'You're a green boy,' James said. 'Your boots aren't even broken in yet. I'm not afraid of you.'

Wickham tucked his chin in, raised his eyebrows: Really? He turned to the drinks tray, topped up his glass, and then poured another, and sloshed it towards James. James just looked at it.

'Go on. One soldier to another.'

James saw his hand reach out, felt his raw knuckles sting as his fingers wrapped around the tumbler, saw the glass brought to his lips. He sipped. The whisky burnt. He set the drink down on the table, beside the decanter. This time, his hand was unsteady, and the glass rattled on the tabletop. There was no going back from this.

'It is just your word,' he tried. 'You have no proof.'

Wickham shrugged. 'I could find your attestation; I could hunt down the Justice of the Peace who witnessed it. Though I'll bet there's no legal discharge to be found, is there? If I could take the trouble to go looking for it. But I am by nature one of life's lilies, I'm not keen on either toiling or spinning, so all I can really think I'll bother with is this: I'll just mention it, to Mr Bennet, and then to my colonel. This little exchange of ours. My suspicions, and then what transpired here. That's the jam on this, you see: I wouldn't even have to do a hand's turn.'

The old man must be spared this. 'Mr Bennet—'

'Mr Bennet needs to know, don't ya think? Man like you. Put his trust in you. Needs to know what you've been up to. Despoiled the housemaid, struck a gentleman—' Wickham tilted the whisky in his glass, watching the slide of the meniscus. Then he looked up, and fixed

James with his pale eyes. 'Deserted the Army. And that's a capital offence. This is a time of war.'

This had always been coming; it had always been sniffing along after him. He had got soft, he had got comfortable, and he'd got careless, and this had crept right up to him and sunk its teeth into his neck.

'So I think it would be best for everyone if you'd just scarper.'

Noise swelled from the drawing room; a roar of laughter; candlelight flared and the shadows shrank. But Sarah. He turned and stumbled for the door.

''Cos they'll string you up, you know, if they get their hands on you. They'll thrash you raw.'

In the hallway, candles burnt steadily in their sconces: just angled shadows, emptiness. Where was she?

Wickham called out after him, 'They will break you on the wheel, my friend. On the fucking wheel.'

James blundered down the hallway, a hand skimming the wainscot. He stumbled down to the kitchen: the fire had burnt to ashes, a stranger servant slumbered by the hearth.

Oh God, Sarah. Where was she?

He slipped out across the stable yard. In the loft, he shoved his few things – books, linen, a bundled blanket – into his old canvas knapsack, on top of the rattling shells. He slung on the coat that Mrs Hill had given him, pulled the bag onto his shoulder, and ducked out into the darkness; he ghosted back round the side of the house.

At the parlour window he saw her, and it stopped him dead in his tracks. Inside, Sarah slid through the crowds and clustered furniture like a mouse making its way through a drawer. He watched her slim frame wind between the rich gowns and red coats, past the bosomy girls and stout dames and egg-bellied gents. He watched her fill a glass, then offer to fill another, and a fat hand flop over the top of the crystal and a ringleted head shake. He watched her turn away, and come towards the window. She was pale and tired, her eyes glittering; he ached to touch her.

She paused to set down the decanter on a side-table and then stepped right up to the sash.

She was so close.

If she sees me, he thought, I will beckon to her; she will slip out and join me here. I will tell her everything. I will beg her forgiveness and her understanding. I will say goodbye. And that will make leaving her just a little easier to bear.

But Sarah, inside the stuffy parlour, saw only the mirror of the room: the press of company, the crush of clothes and bodies, the wine-stained teeth and clammy-white skin, a clutter of furniture. So she reached up, and took hold of the curtains, and drew them closed.

And was gone.

He stood there in the sudden dark. He let a breath go. Then he dragged his bag up his shoulder, and walked on.

Lydia was to return with Mrs Forster in their carriage to Meryton; they were to set out from there with the regiment early the next morning. When the party finally broke up, her departure from home was more noisy than affecting, and James's absence was inconspicuous in all the fluster of leavetaking. The Forsters' manservant brought their carriage round. Mrs Hill and Sarah conveyed cloaks and hats to the flagging guests, then stood to watch from the front steps as they trailed away, the pack of officers on horseback, and the Forsters' carriage rumbling off into the dark. Sarah pressed the heels of her hands into her eyes, and rubbed. And that was that, she thought: they were gone, and James was safe, and Polly was safe, and now they would be left alone.

'Where is James?' Mrs Hill wondered out loud, as they returned to the empty kitchen.

Sarah yawned luxuriously. 'Gone to bed, I expect, missus. It's well past midnight.'

Sarah was woken by the cockerel. She lay, relishing the warmth and ease of bed, the reassurance of Polly's untroubled breathing beside her.

She swung her feet out from under the covers, pulled on her stockings, and splashed her face.

Pattering down the stairs, she tucked her hair into her cap, calling back up to Mrs Hill who was following cheerfully down behind her, both possessed of that particular kind of pleasure that comes with the prospect of a day's fine weather, and of a core of hard-won, secret happiness: the expectation that things, after all, were turning out for the best.

The kitchen was quiet. The fire, Sarah noticed, was dead. She unhooked her apron from the peg, slipped it on. Walking through to the scullery, she passed the strings around her waist and then knotted them in front. The water-tank, she knew just by the look of it – dull, unmisted – was empty, but she rested a hand on it anyway, and tapped its hollowness with her fingertips. She stood still. She listened. Silence but for a wood pigeon's call, and Mrs Hill rummaging in the kitchen.

No.

She went straight back through into the kitchen, and opened the door onto the yard. The morning was cool and golden, and there was the wood pigeon again, and a blackbird singing. She heard the clunk of hoof against the stable door. A scrape. No human sounds at all.

She ran, her boots clattering across the flagstones.

Mrs Hill peered through the open doorway, and across the yard; she saw the girl's streaming tangling skirts, and her cap as it fell, and landed on the flags, and lay there white as a mushroom in the fields. Polly came thumping down the back stairs, singing softly to herself. She fell silent, seeing Mrs Hill standing there, staring, and the door flung wide open on the morning.

At the stables, Sarah swung round the doorjamb, into darkness. The horses whinnied, scraped, anxious.

Mrs Hill came out blinking into the yard. Polly followed her.

'What is it?'

'I don't know.'

They crossed the yard, approaching the stable door. They could hear

235

the sounds of Sarah's movements inside, scrambling feet on the ladder, stumbling footfalls across the loft room above.

'What's happening?'

Mrs Hill shook her head, not because she did not know, but because she was afraid to think. The knowledge was shoving and elbowing its way in, unbidden, but she would not let it through.

There was a pale shape through the inner darkness: Sarah slithered down the ladder, and came out from the back of the stables towards them. She swayed there, clutched at the doorjamb. And Mrs Hill knew – deep inside her, in the hollow beneath her ribcage, where her baby had curled, his little feet pressed against her inner flesh, had slept and stretched and heaved himself about – what Sarah knew already, but could not yet find the words to say.

That he was gone. That James had gone. That he was lost to her again.

End of Volume Two

VOLUME THREE

CHAPTER I

1788

WHEN HER BELLY grew too big to go unnoticed, even with her corsets pulled tight, she packed a bag and said goodbye to him, and walked out along the drovers' road to the distant farmhouse where they expected her. Though her body was a hard discomfort to her, and the season was bitter, she went on foot, because if she went with the carter or was took in the carriage, then someone was bound to observe it, and there would be talk, and they would be discovered.

The shame of it. It was more than anyone could be expected to bear. She must be reasonable.

At the strange house she kept to her room. Mrs Smith, the farmer's wife, attended to her, and that was all. The weather was savage cold. She had a fire and a shawl and was allowed a Bible, which she scratched her way through, line by difficult line, searching for consolation, wishing she had had more schooling when she was a girl.

Mrs Smith was a lean woman of middle years, and the land they farmed was hard and dry. She had a baby half-weaned, a big stumbling brute of a girl with twin trails of snot between nose and lip. The woman was silent, her attentions purely practical. It did not matter: Margaret did not expect to make a friend of her.

*

In the witching hour of a winter night, she brought forth a tiny scrap of a boy, who opened blue-black eyes and studied her with a sleepy wisdom, and whose suckling was a dragging ache in her breast, and whose tiny ruddy fists kneaded at her as though he was quite deliberately reshaping her and making her into someone altogether new. What had hitherto seemed a problem to be solved was now revealed to be the answer: the very fact of the child made everything that had gone before shift and ripple and settle differently, because it all now led to this, and him. And he was as perfect as a syllabub, or a pillowcase straight off the line.

This could not be dealt with reasonably. Reason had nothing to do with it.

Still, she watched herself hand him over to the woman of the house, to wet-nurse, and she knew as she passed him from her arms that she would not hold him again, but also that he would be fed and kept warm and safe and brought up in the fear and love of God, and taken to Church and Sunday school, and given work when he was old enough to work, and would die, God willing, an old man by a fire; that he would, in short, have as decent a life as she could hope for, and that was so much more than she could do for him by herself alone. It still seemed a fair kind of deal: she would pay for the baby's safety with her broken heart, and Mr Bennet would pay for it with his money, so that he need not pay for it with his name.

When she was strong enough, she walked the twelve miles back to Longbourn. Her tears had stopped by the time she saw the chimneys from the lane, and the smoke rising.

Her milk still came, though. It welled out of her; it stained her shifts and blotched her stays. She folded rags and laid them between her skin and her clothes, until the flow of it diminished, and then was gone; then she missed it, and mourned its passing, because it had been for him. The blood dwindled, too, though sometimes, even months afterwards, when she lifted something that was beyond her strength, it would seep anew, bright red, and mark her clothes.

Her grief, though: the flow of that never dwindled, never ceased, though it could not be allowed to seep out into the light. She forced it down inside herself; it became a hidden pool, swelling, ebbing, full of sudden twists and undertows. She wanted the baby so badly; it would sometimes knock her breathless, and she would stand, silenced by pain, a hand out to support herself on mantelpiece or table. She shrugged off Mr Bennet's attempts at comfort; when he spoke to her she could not hear the words; she would not be touched. All that mattered was her little boy, out there in the world.

Miss Gardiner was a pretty girl; she was sweet and full of laughter. Her attorney father just happened to have her accompany him – she did so like to walk to Longbourn and take the air – almost every time he called on business. Margaret, hard-handed, hair under a cap, watched the girl's curl-tossing, her coquettish glances; she saw through the lickspittle father in an instant. She watched Mr Bennet, blind to stratagem, make a pet of the girl, and a fool of himself, and she felt numb.

Then they were married. She just thought, Well, at least that is over now.

The girl had Mr Hill dig little holes for crocus-corms in the orchard. The flowers came up the next spring, and seemed magical things, and far too soft and pretty to endure the February chill. The young mistress's belly was already big by then.

Mr Hill, the butler, having some notion of Margaret's distress, and not feeling any need to enquire further into it, asked if she could bear at all to marry him. He would expect nothing of her, he said, his strange rook-like head tilted to one side; he certainly would not expect the kinds of things a husband usually expected from a wife, by way of bed and babies. But between them, they might botch together some sort of a life; they might make a good name for the two of them, if they would both share his.

So she married him, with his thin arms and his long hands and his uneasy eyes, that cold day in February; that night they lay side by side in their shared bed as still as carvings on a tomb. All down the years since, he had talked decently to her, and he had been mostly kind, though sometimes careless, and he had never struck her, not once in all those years. Which was more than many wives could say, of husbands they had married for love.

He had his own arrangements, did Mr Hill. She met them from time to time. A man that Mr Bennet employed one autumn on the farm; another who'd been labouring just across the valley. They came and went with the seasons; sometimes she would see he was heart-broken, and she would comfort him with sweetmeats or other small kindnesses.

So Mrs Hill knew that she would never have another child. Mrs Bennet, though, it seemed, simply could not stop having them.

Her first pregnancy was interminable; she was heavy and clumsy and did not like it. She, who was used to being lively and sociable, spent whole days on the sofa in her dressing room. She would drift off to sleep of an evening by the fire, Mr Bennet looking on with fond concern, and sometimes shifting a cushion to support her pretty drooping head.

The confinement was a bloody battle. It exhausted everyone.

The midwife cleaned the child and wrapped it and put it in the cradle, and Mrs Hill was set to rock it until the wet-nurse arrived from the village. The afterbirth lay in a washbasin by the bed, dark and thick as liver; Mrs Bennet was white; she whimpered as the midwife cleaned and wadded her. Mrs Hill had never seen a woman so shocked. It was as though she could not accept what her body had just done to her, its callous betrayal of her best interests.

The baby, though, seemed quite content. Mrs Hill stared at her, entranced. She was a plump, curled bean of a girl, with soft gold-red hair, and tiny ridged fingernails like freshwater pearls. Then the woman from the village came in, gabbling at the midwife, loosening her bodice, scooping the baby up in one arm. She slumped down on a low chair, lifted her fichu, and slid the baby in there to suck.

The midwife covered the washbasin with a napkin, and took it away. Mrs Hill straightened the sheets, leaning over Mrs Bennet to tuck them in.

Mrs Bennet, her throat dry, whispered, 'Is it always like that?'

Mrs Hill hesitated. 'I don't know—'

The young woman shook her head, rolling it on the pillow.

'Never again. He can beg, and I won't do it, not again. Not for diamonds.'

But three months later, with the baby at wet-nurse in the village, Mrs Bennet threw up her morning tea at the washstand, and Mrs Hill held her hair for her, then cleaned up the spittle-thick streaks from the marble top.

If Mrs Bennet had had her boy, he would have been Jane's little brother, and elder brother to the rest of them. If the rest of them had been bothered with at all, since one sturdy male was all that was required.

That child would have been a perfect baby, a strapping toddler, a wilful lad; he would have been bundled off to school while his sisters stayed at home and sewed him shirts; he'd have been back for Christmas and Easter and the summer, running riot and getting into scrapes and being adored and spoilt rotten. Then he'd have been foisted off on one of the Universities, and there he'd have indulged in all the japes, jollies and misdemeanours considered a necessary part of a gentleman's education; he'd have acquired some useful acquaintance, no doubt, and, almost incidentally, a degree. Then he would have lived at leisure, accruing debt, and waiting to inherit.

But Mrs Bennet did not have her boy; she had, instead, her mishap.

It was a mishap with ten toes and ten fingers and perfect dark eye-lashes, though the eyes never opened. A mishap who had seemed in every way correct and in good order, apart from being so very small, and so still, and so blue, and cooling so quickly, having only his mother's heat in him. He never took a breath.

Mrs Hill, surprised by a sudden gasp, and a fall of blood, delivered her mistress of the tiny scrap herself, and knew before she held him, light as a kitten, skin thin as the skin on milk, that there could be no chance for him: he had come far too soon.

She wrapped him, and laid him aside, on the coverlet. Her mistress still crouched beside the bed, head buried in her arms. Mrs Hill held Mrs Bennet through her sobs, and, when he was fetched, through the agony of the surgeon's rummaging and scraping. She tended her through the lassitude and low spirits that followed. She administered those first three drops of laudanum, that first half-glass of Cordial Balm of Gilead. And she held her mistress's head for her when, three months later, Mrs Bennet started retching up her own night-time swallowed spit at the washstand. The sickness was, for her, so much worse each time.

'I do not know how I shall bear it, Hill. I really do not know at all.'

From time to time there was news of her boy. They called him James Smith; the farmer and his wife had put it about that he was a cousin's child, orphaned; everything was taken care of, Mr Bennet assured her. Mr Bennet would ride over from time to time, to pay the farmer for his services, and see how the boy got on. It was all very discreet. But the farmer's wife would have nicer things than other farmers' wives; there would be more sugar, a better quality of tea; neighbours would notice, Mrs Hill knew; it was the kind of thing neighbours always noticed. They would notice and they would talk.

On his return from his jaunts, Mr Bennet would ring the bell for Mrs Hill and she would go up to the library and listen to her employer's report on the boy's health and increasing height and under-standing, and she would nod, and would not cry, but the dark pool inside her would swell, and tug at her. It was better this way, she'd tell herself, as she let herself out of the library and went back down to the kitchen. It was better that he have fresh air and milk and Sunday school than a place in the poorhouse, or a life on the roads, which was all that she would have been able to give him on her own. And whatever she might have done or said or threatened to do, Mr Bennet was never going to have offered her better than this. He had never even once, during her time of difficulty, so much as mentioned the possibility of their marrying.

The household continued to expand, girl upon girl, and each more trouble than the last. Lydia at a year old was already a tumbling ball of mischief, and her elder sister Kitty was still not reliably clean and dry. Worn to a shadow, Mrs Hill was told she might have a child from the parish, to train up as a housemaid. It would, after all, save the trouble and expense of getting the woman in from the village to help on wash-days. So Mrs Hill got herself an orphan, a bird-boned girl of six years or so, who said her name was Sarah, and who had survived six months in the poorhouse, and therefore could be confidently said to be free of the typhus that had done for her parents and her brother. The little thing was all eyes; Mrs Hill ached with sympathy, more for the parents than the child herself: how terrified they must have been to leave her all alone. For their sake, as well as the girl's, Mrs Hill determined that she would love her. And she did, as much as it was possible for her to love.

And then, one day, when Mr Bennet called Mrs Hill into the library, he did not wear his usual expression of practical, straightforward calm. He would not even look at her; his face was set.

The boy had run off, he announced. It was to be presumed that he had joined the Army.

'And he is being looked for – what is being done to recover him?'

Mr Bennet played with his paper-knife, then set it down and picked up some documents; he pretended to look at them.

'He is twenty, Mrs Hill. He is grown. He makes his own choices now.'

'But why – why would he choose that? It makes no sense; he must be found, you must buy him out.'

Eyes closed, a shake of the head. 'It is not to be contemplated, Mrs Hill.'

People would talk.

The scandal. Of course. He could not bear the scandal.

It had been a dreadful miscalculation, she saw that now: that all of them should be unhappy, so that he should not be disgraced.

Chapter II

1808

JAMES HAD NEVER even seen the sea before the day they trooped, a bunch of raw recruits, of ploughboys and runaway apprentices marching clumsily, unaccustomed to shoes, into Portsmouth to take ship. Glimpsing it for the first time, he was astonished by the silver brilliance of the sea, the way it just kept moving, but never shifting from its place. It seemed at once beautiful and monstrous.

He lost sight of it in the heaving streets, and was dazed by the crush and noise. They knew they were heroes because the crowds cheered them and the girls threw flowers. They were heroes because they were going to ship off to Portugal, and from there they'd fight their way to Spain, restoring rightful monarchs, and freeing the people from tyranny. If the Corsican Ogre was not stopped – well, it must not be thought of – he would be stopped, and before he could muster men and ships for England again.

Heroism had been prepared for by hours of drilling, of learning the Bess and the bayonet and the workings of the field gun, of fettling horses, of being shouted at by men whose accents he could barely understand, but who expected immediate compliance with their orders. New skills were bedded down by repetition; James became a gunner: the No. 2, the spongeman. He liked the sound of that. He liked having a name and title and designated role. Before this, he'd been nobody; that's what Old Misery had always told him.

Sergeant Pye was in charge of their detachment. He was from Ratcliffe. James really had to stare at him to understand what he was saying, and Sergeant Pye was averse to being stared at. James himself soon learned to avoid catching an eye, and barely opened his mouth in his company: when he spoke, the words came out all soft and country. People laughed.

The gunners wore dark blue, not red like the ordinary soldiers. They wore shakos on their heads. It made you stand up tall. It made you somebody.

They landed in a wide bay, stumbling from the boats on to the drifting sands. A day's dry hot march later, eyes narrowed in the glare, a halt was called at a deserted house, and they made camp. It was a grand place with wide cool rooms and high ceilings. The war had already swept through there.

James led his pair of horses through marble halls, following the whisper of water, shocked at the charcoal scrawlings – incomprehensible phrases, perfectly comprehensible images. The banisters had been pulled down and a fire made of them; the floor was scorched and soot patched the vaulted ceiling above. A human shit lay on a marble hearth. He found the doors out into the courtyard, led the horses up to the fountain and let them dip their heads and drink.

They were villainous, the French: he had heard it many times, but he saw it now, he felt it. They were corrupting. They had no respect for their superiors, for property, for anything at all.

Later, when they came upon another house, he saw the curtains heaped as bedding on the floor, the campfires made of splintered furniture; he smelt the latrine stench, and his opinions of the enemy were confirmed. Until he noticed that the obscenities scrawled there were in a language that he understood. This was the work of English soldiery, a troop that had gone through there before them.

At Vimeiro, they were posted on the hills, amongst the holm oak and olive groves. Sergeant Pye's orders skimmed over him; James's training took over, shifting and clicking him into place through all the necessary sequences of the gun. And his concentration was absolute – carelessness could lose him his hands; he had not seen it happen yet, but he had been told: you got your hands blown off, and you bled out at the stumps. It could lose him his feet, too, as the gun leapt back on her wheels with the force of the charge. He was not going to be careless.

By the time a barrage had been fired, and the infantry were stumbling forward through the rocks and scrub, James's throat was raw and his ears rang; the taste of black powder was in his mouth and nose. His hands were burnt and stained. They shook. He flexed them, rippled his fingers. Still there.

Lisbon stank. It was a blundering muddle of nastiness, of ragged paupers and processions of papish mummery, the streets so filthy that the priests carried their skirts held up like ladies and showed their pale hairy ankles. The blue-coated boys streamed through the foul streets, they drank and sang, their sense of superiority confirmed: they had their shiny buttons, and their good strong shoes and black gaiters, and their bread and beer and their sense of purpose, and they had seen off the French. This was something of which they could be proud.

Then the order came to march to Salamanca. The infantry could go as the crow flew; the cavalry and gunners would have to take the long way round, by the better roads.

The five men of their detachment travelled together: Pye, who was their sergeant, and in command; the spongeman who was James, and still considered green; the loader, who was an old hand called Stephenson; the ventsman, who had a broad scar on one cheek and his side teeth missing; last was a taciturn fellow with a broken nose: he kept the portfire, and lit the charge. Flanking their spans of horses and the gun, they trailed the red flow of cavalry, were followed only by the ammunition and supply wagons. At midday they lay in the gun's shade and she shielded them from the glare.

It was indeed the long way round. They marched east, along a lush, marshy valley, the roads rutted and wet and screened by reeds that hissed in the wind, and rattled. They turned north. The terrain became mountainous and hard. And the war became, for James, the shifting of an awkward object over difficult terrain in impossible weather. The Army was a vast segmented creature, forever lengthening and compacting, breaking into sections and re-forming.

By October, the five of them, and the four horses, were still dragging the nine-pounder across the wide land, dust rising from the wheels and worn shoes. They dug in on downhills, weight pitted against the pull of the gun; they clattered it across streams, the limber piled with the attendant kit. The rocky ground was cruel. They stumbled, shoved and cursed.

The horses grew thin; one of them died, and the No. 3, who had been a slaughterman in his old life, butchered her, and they ate well, and rolled and packed strips of horse meat to take with them. She was replaced with a Spanish horse, taken from a farmer who had protested, and then threatened them with a sickle, and when they had pushed him away he'd come back at them screaming, and thrashed around when he was held down, and then was silenced by a bayonet.

'I did warn him,' Pye said, wiping the blade on the grass.

Nobody could afford to lose a horse. Not a dirt farmer like him, anyway. A horse's labour made the difference between a decent harvest, and the slide towards starvation. Without it, the farmer and his family were already heading for death's door; Pye had just opened it for him, and ushered him through.

James tried his few words of Spanish out on the mare. Nonsense – obscenities and requests for beer and cake – though the sounds of it seemed to soothe her. She blinked at him with her sloe-eyes, and buffeted him with her muzzle. Her face was like old velvet stretched over wicker.

His sleep thin in the chill of an autumn night in Extremadura, curled under the nine-pounder, James would dream that the gun was his mother and he was her whelp; the other four, Sergeant Pye and all, were the rest of her stinking litter.

He plugged his ears with moss, against the sounds of the town and of the camp; of music, sex and fighting.

It was full winter and still the company had not reached Salamander, the lizard-city. Now they seemed to be wheeling east again across the arid scrub. James could not make sense of these twists and turns, unless the city itself was scuttling off as they approached.

The locals hid their livestock and their food: it was the only explanation for the empty stockades and shambles and barns and smallholdings. The soldiers stole and scavenged what they could, and still they were always hungry.

Late one afternoon, James's detachment scraped through a little oak wood, in the hopes of finding hidden sheep or cattle or, failing that, wildfowl. It did not look promising, but hunger kept them going. The wood was thin and dry, and silent even of birds. A picked-clean place, not even a pigeon left to coo. They walked on in bitter silence, cold, their breath misting, their feet shushing through the dry fallen leaves at the bottom of a gully. Pye was just turning to speak, no doubt to give it all up for a bad job, when there was a thunder of footfalls and a grunting, wheezing earthy sound; James spun round to see a wild pig bundling down at them from the top of the slope. Pye turned aside and swiftly loaded his pistol. He hit the beast square in its bristly muzzle, rendering it a mess of blood and brain, and still it kept bowling on down at them, under its own dead weight; James dodged, Pye leapt aside, the others scattered. The beast, being four-fifths dead already, hit the bottom of the gully, and stopped there, its front legs crumpling. They just stood looking at it. Then, with a wheezing, snortling noise, it keeled over on one side, bubbling with blood. A moment's silence, then James laughed: the relief. For the first time in a long time, the spun-tight knot inside him slipped loose. They would eat well that night.

251

'Anyone got any apples on 'em?' Sergeant Pye said.

'Eggs,' James said. 'Ham and eggs.'

He crouched by the fallen creature, and saw her swollen, reddened dugs.

'It's a sow. There's a litter nearby.' James got back to his feet. 'Listen.'

It was very cold. The light was failing. They stood in silence. The sound was almost too high-pitched to hear: a faint, almost bat-like squeaking. He raised a hand and beckoned for the others to follow. Halfway up the slope, they came upon a den dug into the bank between tree roots; a clutch of half-a-dozen piglets stared back at them with their small eyes. They were sturdy, milk-and-acorn-fed; they blinked pale lashes at the men. Then James reached in to take one, and the lot of them scattered squealing. The men scrambled after them, skidded down the banks; laughing, cursing, calling out to one another, all lost to the chase, as if this was home, and they were chasing greased piglets through the fair.

James caught one by its scruff and rammed it between his knees. He stuck its throat with his bayonet. It twitched and bled. Back at the farm Old Misery would have caught the blood in a bucket to make blood-puddings. He would never have believed he could have come to miss the old bitch and her cooking.

They strolled along with their muskets slung on their shoulders and the sow swinging from a pole they'd cut and now carried between two of them, her young hanging like moles from another. It was night now, but the moon had risen, and it gave a reassuring light to their hike back to camp.

There was just a second between James noticing that he was happy, and then realizing that he was afraid. He glanced around him – they were tracking along the bottom of a dry gully, between rocks and low-growing juniper; parched winter grasses brushed against his gaiters. All was blue and white in the moonlight, and nothing had changed, but they were in danger. He knew it in his creeping flesh. No obvious, immediate threat, not like a musket in your face, or a full-grown hog

252

charging at you: the kind of danger you wander into oblivious, and whistling.

He slipped his musket off his shoulder. 'Sir?'

Rock and grass, and higher up, a screen of goat-willow, and an outcrop of stone. All was still. But it was a shallow kind of stillness, like a breath held.

'Sergeant Pye, sir?'

Pye glanced towards him, and his smile collapsed. He raised a hand to quell the noise. His own voice was a whisper.

'You see something, country-boy?'

The men were all silent now, scanning the gully, reaching for their muskets. A shift in temperature: they had been careless; Pye had let them.

'Well, well, my lovelies,' Pye breathed. 'Pick up your petticoats, let's be getting back.'

No more talk, just the thud of boots on the dry ground, and the rasp of breath in dry throats. Once they'd cleared the gully, there was about a mile down the hillside to the camp. Past that scrubby twisted pine there, and they'd be out into open terrain, and the worst of it would be over.

A hundred yards. Seventy. Fifty still to go. They would get away with it. It looked as if they had got away with it.

Pye must have thought the same, because he turned to speak over his shoulder: 'You had me spooked, there, Jimmy-boy—'

And that was when the shot cracked out.

The men ducked, fumbling their muskets. James was on one knee, then on his belly, Brown Bess wedged to his shoulder, scanning: everything was silver, shadows, grainy in the moonlight. Beside him, Sergeant Pye hissed out orders. The gunshot echoed down the gully, a messy sound, bouncing off the rock. James searched the skyline, the scrubby trees, the outcrops. Silence.

'*Deje las armas!*'

Scrambling, twisting on the ground, James scanned around for the speaker. No sign of movement, no shifting or rustling.

'*O matamos a todos ahora.*'

'Put them down,' Pye said. 'Put down your muskets.'

The men looked to him, pale faces in the night. The sergeant jerked his head: get on with it. They were in the open: they could not fight an enemy that they could not see. Pye, the sweat on his forehead catching the light, set the example and laid down his Brown Bess; James complied reluctantly, laying the cool weight of her down upon the scrubby grass. The others followed suit, the gunmetal making dull clinks as the barrels slid together.

Then they drew close, back to back. James felt his shoulder brushed by Pye's, his arm jostled by Stephenson's. He could hear their breaths, coming fast and harsh. He still searched around him. The pigs lay trussed and abandoned in the dust.

Then there was movement, up on the hillside. James nudged Pye, jutted his chin: the bandits appeared from amongst the rocks. They came slithering down, scuffing through the dirt, and gathered around the soldiers. James saw the whiteness of a young boy's teeth as he grinned. The men had an outdoor smell about them, musky, like deer; an old man bent and scooped up the rifles and held them under his arm like a bunch of firewood. And their leader, face as craggy as the land, said something in Spanish, of which James recognized a few words: *ingleses, idiotas* and *hijos de puta.* They were all as thin as grass.

The sow and piglets were lifted and carried away, swinging from their poles, up some path through the rocks that you wouldn't know was there unless you actually saw those men walking on it. Then the troop of them just melted into the dark, and disappeared. James was left with an impression of a broad white-toothed grin, lingering in the air when the men themselves were gone.

Someone let out a low whistle.

Someone else said, 'Bastards.'

Pye wiped his forehead with a sleeve. 'We were lucky.'

'That was lucky?'

'That's just our dinner gone. It could have been worse. They could have gutted us. If we were French, they would've cut off our cocks and made us eat 'em.'

And then Pye turned and trudged on, towards the end of the gully, under the scrubby twisted pine.

At a crossroads outside Alba de Tormes, where they paused to water the horses one bitter winter morning, James read the milestone: *Salamanca 15 Millas*.

James said, 'We could be there by nightfall.'

Sergeant Pye grinned. 'We'll all be having Salamancan buttered buns tonight!'

Then the order came down the column, with a rippled sigh like wind through barley: they were to return to Portugal. James stopped in his tracks, just watching as the men wheeled the horses round, slipping and clattering on the mud and stones, and the gun carriage drew off, heading west again. Then he stirred himself and ran to catch up. He put his shoulder to the carriage, too, and they heaved the gun away. Away from Salamanca. Away from where they had been struggling towards all this time.

It was December. The skies were bare and white; snow swirled across the fields.

At Sahagún de Campos, James came to know that the hunger he had felt before was nothing. This was a new creature, and it was tighter, stronger, fiercer than he had ever known: it gnawed at his gut, crazed his teeth, squeezed his temples, made him sharp-eyed, twitchy and quick to anger.

When they came upon the town it was thronged with soldiers; the French had just been driven out. A great victory, the officers were saying, and against overwhelming odds. It would go down in history, like Crécy or Agincourt. Whenever Englishmen spoke of glories, and the French of humiliation and disgrace, they would talk of Sahagún de Campos, and shake their heads in awe.

The town was uncouth, filthy, violent. In the dark streets behind the

San Tirso church, under its archways, the wraiths gathered. They washed up in a tide-line, huge eyes catching the light, bones bulging at knee and elbow.

The redcoats and the gunners would go there; soldiers will take their comforts where they can. And God knows, the women, and the children, they sold themselves willingly enough. If will could be said to come into it, at times like that.

But the thing was – Pye laughed and swigged his tumbler of rough wine, a one-too-many tumbler that was tipping him over the edge of leery cheerfulness into queasy confidences – a fresh bit of flesh, insofar as anything in this godforsaken cesspit was fresh, it was stupidly easy to get; these youngsters were all so ready to be duped. You didn't even have to give them anything – just the promise was enough; they wanted to trust you. They were just so callow, so stupidly young. And when you'd done what you liked, and you didn't hand over your biscuit or your bit of bread, what would a girl like that be able to do about it? Fight you for it? Ha! Pull a *knife* on you?

James, sick, swilled down his wine, and did not look at Pye.

He took to ghosting through the narrow streets himself. He didn't desire those little bags of bones; he couldn't fathom how anybody could – they fostered in him instead an aching sympathy, and a sharper outrage. He understood now the joy of everything that he had been so desperate to shrug off: a warm bed, a cup of milk, the next day unspooling just the same as the day before, and the only pressing need being for a good smooth stone to throw at the thieving crows.

He came upon a ragged girl, lugging a smaller boy on her hip. James had a bit of bread about him – he fumbled it out, offered it to her. She looked at it, and then at him. Then, with a slow blink, she put the boy down, and murmured something in the child's ear that made him sit and stick his thumb in his mouth. She came up to James, hang-dog, unbuttoning.

James fumbled the crust into her hands; he held up his own and stepped back, shaking his head. 'No. No.'

He turned and strode away, leaving her there, bread clutched tight in dirty fingers, not knowing what to do. When he glanced back from the corner of the alleyway, he saw her crouching by the little boy; she had broken the crust in half, and was watching the little one gum at the hard stuff while she chewed her own.

He walked away, guilty and ill-at-ease. It would delay an end, perhaps. He was not even certain that was to the good.

He saw Pye there, walking the cloisters of San Tirso. His distinctive laugh, a dark coat flitting through the shadows.

He saw Pye lifting something bone-thin and tiny up against a wall, and fumbling with his britches buttons.

He saw Pye sauntering along with a ration pack, a flock of children following him, silent and wide-eyed.

James clenched and unclenched his fists. To witness this, and do nothing: it was a stain on him.

Hunger made his sleep thin and ragged: famine figures clutched at him, their cracked lips sucked at his. He woke shivering; there were crows circling above.

Two nights before Christmas, the order came to move off. The night was raw. There was snow threatening, but no frost, so that all was bitter cold and wet as they struck camp and harnessed the horses to the gun carriage.

The horses were in their traces, the guns under canvas to keep off the sleet, and Sergeant Pye had not turned up. James was dispatched to find him; he knew where to look. Round the back of San Tirso, he came upon him in a sidestreet, his cock in his hand, trying to piss. Pye looked up, feverish and pained. He saw James, and tucked his prick away.

'Had a bit of bad luck there,' he said.

'Sir.'

'You won't say a word, eh, Jimmy-boy.' He pulled at his britches, easing the fabric away from a sore.

'Sir.'

He tugged his coat straight. 'Well?'

257

'We're under marching orders, sir.'

'Well, hop to it, then. Get a bloody move on.'

The troops stumbled away from Sahagún in the spitting snow. Feet blistered and chilblained, they picked their way along to find the French, and fight them. The roads deep in slush, rutted and slithery, they had gone maybe three shivering impossible miles, when a dispatch rider sped along the creeping column, spattering mud, flying like the devil himself. James lifted his head, wiped his eyes, wondered for a moment, and then just trudged on. Half a mile later, the order tumbled back along the line: turn about. A massive movement of French troops had been spotted to the south. Napoleon was coming, and was moving to outflank them. Now they had to run.

They could not run. Not with a nine-pounder and horses thin as famine. They dragged themselves along.

They were to march now for La Coruña; the entire force was racing for the sea. The town was still in British hands and readily defensible; they would hole up there until the Navy could evacuate them all. This was not a defeat! Just as you swung back an arm to throw a punch, so an army must draw away, the better to strike again. They would sail for home, and they would regroup, and then they'd be back; they'd show that little Corsican cunt, Pye went on, his venom building, spit gathering at the corners of his mouth, stirring the other men to something almost like warmth, so that their eyes grew less dull, and their shoulders a little less slumped, and they began to recall what it was to be soldiers, and Englishmen, and hold their heads up high. But all James could think was to be back in England. Hedgerows full of birds and berries. Milk. A mild sun. An old fellow who'd nod to you in passing. Who did not expect you to beat him to a bloody mess, steal his dinner, rape his wife, and burn his house down around his ears.

Passing through a village at the tail-end of the company, in the dark fifteenth hour of a thirty-six-hour march, James tripped over something soft and solid. He landed, hands and knees, across it. His fingers were in mud, his shins wet; the road was sodden, and stank of wine and blood, and small things scuttled away in the darkness. He gagged: it was a body; he knew from the smell – blood, urine, and a trace of sweetness – and it was so slight it must be a child. He staggered back to his feet. He shambled on.

Up at the forward pair of horses, he took hold of a bridle, and laid a palm on a velvet neck. He whispered Spanish nonsense, and he kept on marching, one hand on the reassuring endurance of the horse. James's shoes were sodden tatters, his gaiters rags. His legs were weak, and his stomach sick with famine.

And he was afraid. This was true fear now, not just a battle's fleeting consciousness of mortality. This was a constant hum that built and grew until nothing else could be thought of, not at all.

When, in the dawn chill, a halt was called, they were out in open cold, the sky pale with high thin cloud. Smoke trailed from low tumbledown buildings a mile or so from the side of the road. James unhitched the forward pair from the gun carriage, and led them towards the dwelling. He was thinking simply: shelter, fodder, sleep. And then, as soon as he surfaced, he'd be up and off again. The fear was too sharp to let him rest for long.

The horses stumbled across the rutted field, their heads hanging low. When James heaved open the slumped door, a handful of redcoats looked up from their smoking fire; a couple of them reached for their Brown Besses.

'Gunner,' he said, to explain the blue.

Then they slumped, seeing he was one of theirs. One of them waved him in.

'C'mon, then, if you're coming. Join the party.'

The place was a shell; the roof was half collapsed. It was a barn, or stable, divided into precarious, worm-holed stalls; there was a little wispy old hay; he led the horses to it, and they lifted mouthfuls and slowly chewed.

The redcoats had built a fire of timber they had scavenged from the building: bits of rafter and board and a fallen roof beam were heaped on the bare flags. The old wood burnt smartly.

'It's perishing.'

James slumped down and watched the flickering flames. Fear faded to a murmur: the men talked, but he could not follow what they were saying, could not care enough to try, could not even speak, not any more. He leaned back, feet to the fire. He blinked.

When he woke up, the redcoats were gone. So were the horses. When he stumbled out into the daylight, the column was gone too.

Fear now was a creature; it slithered around him, covered his face and got in amongst his hair and he could not breathe and he could not think, and he just stared across the wide poor land, and along the empty road, then spun to look back off the way they'd come from.

He was alone.

Why had the other men not woken him?

That was a thought.

Because they stole the horses.

That was another thought.

It was a faint reassurance, that these thoughts still came.

He shivered, rubbing at his arms.

He looked up at the high pale sun. Mid afternoon.

But was it the same day, or was it the next?

Alone now, he found the road paralysing. It sliced across the open land, the fields stubbled or bare with winter; he felt as exposed as a louse on a shaven scalp.

The company's progress was easy to mark, and so to follow: the frost-scuffed tracks, lost bootsoles, a broken-axled wagon, dung, patches of yellow piss on the snow. He could not bring himself to walk the road itself, so he followed alongside it, on the far side of the ditch, stumbling over rocks and tearing through scrub. He kept glancing over his shoulder, scanning the horizon behind him, his neck prickling.

In the evening, he came upon a fallen horse; packs of flesh had already been stripped from the haunches. He hacked off a strip of flesh himself and chewed on it as he went; it was dry and crusted with blood and deeply satisfying.

He walked on as the light faded, and it grew dark; he stumbled through the shadows. He was nothing again: animate mud, crawling along the surface of the land. He would slither back to the company. He would be safe there, in the mire. Safe as far as La Coruña, where the Navy would come to dig them out and cart them off, like night-soil from an outhouse.

He met the first stragglers the following day; they formed themselves out of the dust-haze and the distance: a roadside shrine, two men sitting at its foot. The painted wooden Madonna had had her eyes gouged out, and the leaves and berries around her bare toes were frost-bitten and stark. A spring bubbled below, forming a basin in the stone; clean water welled there like in a boiling pan and a faint steam rose from it. The soldiers had drunk, and were resting; they looked un-commonly clean; one was still wiping his neck with a dampened kerchief. James stumbled up to them.

'English!' he said, waving.

The men looked at each other. One nodded. They didn't say a word.

'Thank God I've found you!'

He fell to his knees at the little pool, and cupped his hand and drank. He tasted the sulphurous warm water and the sweat and filth of his own hand. Chin dripping, he unknotted his own neckerchief to wipe the wet and dirt away.

'Are we far behind the main body here?'

The two men looked at each other.

'I was lost, I was left behind. I've been racing to catch up for – days—' He shook his head, defeated by the stretch of undifferentiated time.

One of them laughed; it had no mirth in it.

'What? What's happened?'

The soldier shook his head.

'Are the French come? Are we defeated? Is it a rout?'

Then one spoke. He was Welsh, and his accent so strong that for a moment James was not sure of what he was telling him, and it was only after the words were over, and the men were already scrambling to their feet and picking up their knapsacks, and heading away, that James quite realized what had been said.

'We are doing our very best, my friend, to lose ourselves for good.'

He came upon the tail-end of the Army three days later, on the edge of a small market town. The relief was so great it was as though his pack had lifted off his shoulders and he was going to rise up into the sky like a kite. The noise, the voices, the familiar chaos and stink: it disgusted him, and it felt safe.

A hundred yards into the rank mess of the Army, he found an officer, saluted and made himself known. The officer nodded, gestured him along, sending him to a big house on the main square, all fancy stonework and balconies, commandeered for the officers' accommodation.

He gave his name and rank to the clerk there. In the dim anteroom, the young man scanned through his lists, frowning; he had a boil on his neck. After a moment, he got up from his desk, opened the door and stepped out into the lobby. When he came back, it was with two armed guards.

'There he is. Do your work.'

The guards took hold of James's arms, and twisted them up behind his back. James tried to shrug them off.

'I don't— Why?'

'You are a deserter.'

'No—'

'Your sergeant reported you.'

'If I was, why would I come back?'

The clerk shrugged. 'Deserters do. They find out what it's like. They come back.'

James, his hands clamped in manacles, was dragged down into a cellar, which smelt of wine and mice and was lit by a narrow grille high up in the wall. Someone threw a blanket at him; he shuffled it around his shoulders, sank down against the cold stone, and closed his eyes. Fear loosened its teeth and slithered away and coiled up in a corner. They could not keep him locked up for long; with the retreat in full flood they simply could not manage it. They would have to haul him out to explain himself, and all would come clear, and he would not hesitate to point the finger. Those soldiers who had let him sleep on, while the Army moved off, who'd stolen his horses – it was a long shot that they would ever be found; indeed, they might well have deserted themselves, and taken the horses to ride rather than eat. But the thing was – and this was a thing of clear certainty and faith for him – it was all just a mistake: he had not deserted, and he would not be punished for something that he had not done.

The hours crept by; the light from the grille slid across the wall. He dozed, head drooping, and dreamed of the farm. Of meadow grass and cool skies and wild strawberries. Of the gentleman who had ruffled his curls, and said that he was as fine a chap as he had seen, and asked if he was happy.

James, waking now to clarity, felt homesick for a home that he had never really had. If he lived through this, through the retreat and any skirmishes that they might fall into on the way, if he made it as far as La Coruña and the sea, if he took ship for England – if he could just survive this disaster, and all the disasters yet to come in his eleven remaining years of service – he would one day return to Hertfordshire. It was something to promise himself, waiting for him at the end of everything: the paradise to come. If the old man was still alive, James would find him: Mr Bennet, who had, all those years ago, cared enough to ask whether James was happy. Mr Bennet was a good man, an important man, the most important in that village near Meryton; and if Mr Bennet would have him, James would be his man.

He was brought out blinking into cold light; the ground swooped underfoot. Voices lurched out at him. He was yanked along, stumbling, through blurred red and blue. A thin sleet fell, pricking his face.

He had his irons unfastened from one wrist, and then fastened again; his arms were looped around a rough wooden post. It seemed unnecessary. He tried to say, I won't, I wouldn't – but his mouth was dry and his words came out thin, and the guard did not listen or did not hear. But James would get his chance to speak, to explain, and then all would be understood.

The gunners assembled there were a stinking jostle of sodden, faded blue. Sergeant Pye swam into focus, feverish and glittery. He read the charge: James watched the mouth moving, and struggled to put the words together; then he began to understand, and felt the terror rise in him like floodwater, creeping up his ankles to his thighs, up his body to his mouth and nose. He heaved against his shackles; he shook his head. His parched lips unstuck:

'No—'

'Dereliction of duty, loss of vital *matériel*, desertion—'

'No!'

'Desertion in the face of the enemy—'

'I did not desert—'

Sergeant Pye cuffed him round the back of his head. His cheekbone slammed into the post.

James was not to speak.

The facts spoke for themselves.

James spat blood. His tongue touched a broken tooth. His vision blurred.

Pye continued with the charge.

Desertion in the face of the enemy. Amongst crimes a soldier might commit, the very rankest.

James's vision swelled and shrank. His head pounded. He blinked away blood.

Since it put his companions in danger. Since it left his friends to face without him what he himself would not.

And so the penalty for desertion in a time of war was death.

In the smear of light, through the sting of blood, on the far side of the market square, a skinny child stared out at James, and hitched a smaller child up her hip.

His skin bristled. His hands jerked uselessly in the manacles, itching to wipe his eyes clear – was it the girl he had shared his bread with at St Tirso? But his vision blurred, he could not see: he pressed his eyes shut, and breathed. Then opened them again, and he stared across the market square.

Leniency would be shown, since he had repented and returned.

'Fifty lashes.'

And this, then, as they stripped his coat and shirt away, was at last the full shivering realization of what must come, and that there was nothing to be done, but to go through it, and endure. Fear would have finally claimed him then, poisoned his blood and left him raving, but as the first lash tore into his skin, he closed his eyes, and bit hard into his lip, and pushed his forehead into the rough wood post. He breathed. This is not for ever, he told himself. There will be a time after this.

The pain was astonishing. The first blow was a flare of silver; it darkened to red and just kept burning. And as the lash hissed and licked, and hissed and licked again, peeling away his skin, it also ripped away his fear; it tore the fear up into bloody twitching shreds; as James fell out of consciousness, fear fell away from him stone dead. There was nothing for James to be afraid of, not after this.

When they were done, and he was bloody slumping meat, hanging from his manacled hands, they slung him face down on a limber, and shackled him to it by the right wrist. As if he would run. As if he *could* run. As if there was anywhere to run to, other than La Coruña and the sea.

He swung and jolted, raw, all the way to the coast.

He was released for the defence of the town.

Every last man, even the criminals and cowards were needed. He was still weak and feverish and his back burnt with scabs, and the scabs cracked, and wept.

Before the attack, the sappers blew up the powder stores, to deny them to the French invaders. The town walls shook; sparks flew up into the sky like fireworks.

They lugged the nine-pounder out along the ridge. Only he and Sergeant Pye now were left of the five members of the detachment who had started out. A red-headed boy had joined them, and a big bald silent fellow; a lithe man of middle years was the new ventsman. The boy, who was a loader, was missing two fingers on his left hand, but it didn't matter, he said, laughing, showing his empty mouth, 'cos he used the other hand to wank. New horses, too: a ragged Spanish bay, calm and stoical, who blew through her nose at James; he rested his forehead on her cheek. He said, '*Mi querida, mi querida, mi querida.*'

Scrubland fell away below them; the plain stretched beyond, rocky and bitter. The French were a line of blue coats, gunmetal, glinting steel. His dirty old shirt stuck to his scabs. He followed Pye's orders silently.

Behind them, ships rode in the bay, all beautiful and clean, and it was January the 16th, someone had said, and it was a whole new year, and he had not noticed that, no more than he had noticed Christmas.

He was not afraid. He was weak and faltering, his hands trembled, and a careless movement sent ripples of flame up his back again; his body shied away from this instinctively, but he was not afraid. He reckoned: I am sore, I am clumsy, I am weak, and so chances are I will get my hands blown off, and bleed out into the Spanish dirt. He reckoned: I would hardly feel it – the pain, the horror – before I was empty and gone. It did not seem a particularly terrible thing, not any more.

He nodded to the ventsman, whose face was lined and lean. His hands looked shaky.

James proffered his own hand to shake. 'James Smith.'

'Bill Hastings,' said the ventsman, his Adam's apple rolling down then back up his narrow throat. He pumped James's hand, nodding, too nervous for further talk.

The artillery wagon pulled up behind them with their ammunition; the lads there looked grey. The infantry were ranked to left and right, a handful of guns gathered on the other escarpment; behind their lines, in the harbour, the bumboats were already ferrying soldiers out to the waiting ships.

Us lot, James thought, the ones left holding the fort: we are here to die.

Roundshot screamed overhead, flew long, landing near where the horses were tethered, making them buck and whinny and pull. A shot crumped into the dirt in front of them; the men scattered and flung themselves to the ground. Pye was yelling all the time; James wiped the grit from his face, got back to his feet, back to his work.

Below, the infantry slogged it out; muskets and bayonets and scuffling and skidding and screaming in the rocky patchwork countryside.

'Frogs can't get to us.' Pye grinned. 'Their cavalry can't charge us here. Position is too strong.'

And it was true. The fighting continued, but no progress was made on either side. Stalemate. At dusk, the French retreated back behind their lines. This battle was unwinnable, but the result of the campaign was clear. However they might describe it to themselves, the English were already defeated; they might not have been massacred, but they were humiliated.

James watched as Pye spiked the gun. The clanging of the iron was muted, jarring; James's ears still hummed and buzzed from battle. He had dragged that gun halfway across Spain and back again, and now Pye was hammering an iron spike into its innards, and they would leave it behind here amongst the rocks.

Beside him, the ventsman glugged water, wiped the bottleneck with a filthy palm, all black powder and dust, and offered it to James. His hand trembled violently now, making the water slosh; the ventsman laughed.

'Fuck!' He shook his head, and didn't say anything more.

James took the bottle. His hand was still. 'Where you from, then?'

'Kent.'

'You miss it?'

'Oh, by God, Kent is lovely. And I got a lovely wife, Mary. Got a coupla boys.'

James nodded. He drank, and the water was sweet. He understood fear now; he knew its birth, its breeding.

What was left of the infantry, under cover of darkness, crept down towards the shore; the men were ferried out in little boats to the waiting ships. The gunners were to follow. The rest of the detachment were already scuffing and scrabbling down the slope; he found himself suddenly alone with Pye on the top of the escarpment. Pye waved him over to where the horses were hitched.

'Sort them ones out.'

James slipped in between their ridged ribcages as the horses stepped and swished. He talked to them, running his hands along their flanks, to let them know where he was, and keep them calm. He set about unbuckling the mare's gun-carriage tack. They'd forage for themselves, and roam a while unburdened, until someone claimed them.

'Don't waste your time.'

'Sir?' James looked to Pye. Blood on his neck-cloth, soot on his face. There was a sore on the wing of his nose; he scratched at it.

'Use your blade, Gunner. Don't waste your shot, either.'

James just looked at him.

Pye jerked a blackened hand, impatient, at the horses. 'Get a fucking move on.'

James could not move at all; he swallowed.

'Do I have to do everything round here?'

Sergeant Pye drew his own bayonet, and strode over, and stuck the mare in the throat, the Spanish bay. The other horses pulled away, shying, whinnying. The bay mare sank to her knees, her jaw still jutting upwards, held there by her halter; blood gushed from her wound and wet the dirt. The leather creaked, a strap snapped; she keeled over sideways; her head cracked to the ground. She lay, her big eyes blind, blood bubbling from her nostrils.

'Right. Get on with it.'

James felt his hands curl into fists, then flex.

'Are you squeamish?' Pye said. 'I thought you might be squeamish.'

'Sir.'

James drew his bayonet. Pye turned away, heading over towards a bony skewbald gelding.

When it came to it, it was as easy as falling. It was easier, since his body put up no fight against it, as it would have with a fall. He stepped over the bay mare's head.

'Sir.'

Pye turned towards him, lips twisted, ready to speak, but James just took him by the shoulder, and pushed his blade into him. There was resistance first, of layered wool and linen, skin, muscle. And then there was softness inside. The man's mouth opened. James felt the steel grate against the deep-buried spine. He saw black-pitted molars, the red flesh at the back of Pye's mouth. He jerked the bayonet upwards, twisted it. Pye's eyes widened, the whites yellow and veined, the pupils flaring huge.

James had killed before, he must have, he knew he had; but he had never killed a man so close to, not like this, not with blood warm on his hands, and the stink of breath in his face. The sergeant sank to his knees, the bayonet slicking out of him. James stepped back; Pye slumped forward and hit the ground, his eyes and mouth open in the dust.

James walked away. He did not follow the others straight down to the strand, but took a sloping angle, oblique, across the shambling drop. He let go of the bayonet; it clattered and pinged, bouncing down from rock to rock. When he reached the sand, he ripped away what was left of his shoes and let his gaiters uncurl themselves and fall away. He walked barefoot, away from La Coruña, away from the Army, away from blood and any thought of home. How could he go home now? How could he take all of this back there? He kept the lapping waves to his left, and the dark land to his right, till the ships' lights were out of sight, and he could no longer hear voices. Night sounds of birds, the shush of the waves: he peeled off his clothes – the faded stained coat, the filthy britches, the shirt that stank and stuck to him and shivered with lice. He walked out into the glimmering water.

He did not expect to live. He did not even think about it. He was not afraid. He wished only to be clean.

Chapter III

1809

A GLIMPSE OF a woman in black. Something trickling between his lips; thin goaty milk; he swallowed.

Then later, there was a narrow cot that smelt of canvas, the thin sunlight sheering through closed shutters. The sound of voices carrying up through the floorboards, the old woman's, and a younger woman's, and a child's.

There was a first stiff attempt to get up, and see where he was, and who was there, and what was going on; and then there was his collapse, shaking, back onto the canvas, and the shock at his weakness. When he did, finally, make it to his feet, a sheet wrapped around his naked body, he crossed the bare boards to the window, and pushed back the shutters on a dim evening, and a small village that straggled down a slope towards the sea. He could hear the women jabbering anxiously below, alerted by his heavy tread across their ceiling. One of them climbed up the stairs to him, peering up through the hatch in the floor. Her face was parched, her lips fallen in on a toothless mouth. He let himself be put back to bed. She muttered over him.

'*Señora*,' he tried, patching together his bits of Spanish. '*Dónde – los ingleses?*'

The old woman shushed him with her old woman's breath. She shook her head.

'*No sé. Los ingleses se han ido.*'

They were gone. He slumped back onto his bed, lay with his cheek on the canvas.

When he was able to move a little better, he cast around for his clothes. His coat and kit were nowhere to be seen – he remembered peeling them off, swimming out from the beach – but a black canvas pack hung over the back of a chair, along with unfamiliar clothes that seemed to have been left out for him. He lifted up a fisherman's blue smock and wide-legged trousers. As he moved, his skin felt tight across his back: he could see the edge of the scabbing when he turned his head, and when he touched it, it felt dry, and he had the notion that he was healing. Dressed, he sat to recover his breath.

He eased his way down a broad-runged ladder. Below, there was daylight, and the red glow of a fire, and a smell of cooking that made his head reel. And a child. One of those bone-thin big-eyed children who seemed to be haunting him all over Spain. She spoke in rapid Spanish, turning towards the open doorway, and he knew it wasn't her, not the girl from St Tirso or – afterwards. They would be bones now, those children; along with so many others: tattered cloth and greenstick bones in a pit in Sahagún.

And Pye. Rotting in a pit. Half-rotten when he died. Wide yellow eyes and open mouth.

Outside, a dark-clothed woman was sheafing through fishing-nets; the girl joined her, talking, tugging at her arm. The woman turned her head to regard him with the calm gaze of a painted saint. Her hair was covered with a red headscarf; she was starkly beautiful.

Then from beyond her, the old woman creaked up from her seat, and passed by him and went indoors to the fire. She came back with a cup of broth and motioned for him to sit. He eased himself down on a stone bench, and took the cup, warm in his hand. The younger woman got on with sorting through the nets, and the girl leaned in the doorway and watched him.

It was so still, just the shushing of the waves up onto the sand. Not even a gull's cry. He tried to follow what the old woman was saying.

There had been a man, her son, the young woman's husband; she was telling James about him. Though giving no other sign that they were listening, the young woman seemed to go still, the girl to straighten up. James understood that the man was gone – had died? It would be the French, or famine, or the sea.

He said, '*Es triste—*'

She brushed her hand through the air, as if wafting sadness, and thoughts of her lost son, aside – though her old pinched eyes suggested that the grief had not faded. She gestured down to the village below, and kept on talking.

He made out bits of what she said. He saw where a shutter had slumped on its hinges and hung like a broken wing, where mortar had crumbled away, where gardens grew scrubby and tangled with weeds. The boats pulled up onto the sand. The stillness. Not a movement. Not even a gull to wheel and scream. No sound but the hush of the waves. Not a soul beyond the women and him, the four of them gathered there.

They were a secret, he thought. God had forgotten them entirely.

'*Y usted,*' she said, drawing his attention back to himself, with a tap of her knuckly finger on the wood of her chair, and then pointing at his chest. '*Y usted, también.*'

'*Qué? Yo?*'

'You are departed. You are of the dead.'

At this, the younger woman looked up at him. He caught her eye but she just dropped her gaze back to her nets, and continued working without a word.

I am departed, he thought.

He had come through death and out the other side. The soldier that he had been – all that he had done and seen since he'd enlisted, since he'd sailed to Portugal and tramped through Spain, the filth, the bloody mayhem he had delivered there, the man that he had murdered – had been stripped away.

'*Puedo,*' he tried, making the women all look at him, making even the young woman smile. '*Puedo trabajar?*'

The old woman laughed. The girl looked from her mother to her grandmother and back to him again, eyes wide and teeth white against her olive skin.

'*Trabajar!* But what can he do? He is as weak as a little baby!' the girl said.

'*Si trabajo*,' he said. 'I will get stronger.'

*

The light little skiff was laid up like a turtle on the shore. James heaved it over, rolling it onto its keel. His back was tight, and fired off with sudden shocks of pain.

The old woman watched. She talked all the time, and from what he could make out, it seemed to be to do with her son, who would row with the fleet in the evening, and come back at dawn with a boat loaded with fish. He could see it as she spoke, the images unfurling: the boats creeping back in the silvery morning, the gluttonous drag of their laden keels. The women and girls crowding on the foreshore to welcome them home. Life must have been good enough here, once.

He rolled his trousers to the knee, and between them they pushed the skiff down the beach; the old woman stood back at the water's edge, keeping her skirts dry. The boat bobbed on the first waves, and he felt the wash and pull of the tide around his calves, and then suddenly there were gulls, a flock of them wheeling excitedly overhead with some bird-memory of the promise of a catch, and he glanced back and saw, on the breakwater, the young woman and the girl, side by side, watching. The young woman's head was uncovered, and her hair caught the light, and was dark as ink.

He thought, Perhaps I am doing this for her. Perhaps I am back from the dead to make things better here for her.

Then the water began to bubble and lick up between the boards, and the old woman exclaimed and flapped her hands, and he felt the tug and drift of the boat change, threatening to sink, and he heaved it back up onto the sand, the water sloshing inside and pouring out of it, his back an agony of flame. The old woman helped him haul it back up out of the reach of the waves.

'It wants caulking,' he said, in English.

When he looked back up the strand, the young woman and the girl had both turned and were walking away, their baskets on their hips, going to gather whatever it was they still found to gather in this starvling land.

After just the brief effort of shifting the boat, he was fit for nothing. He crept his way back up to the cottage, the scabs cracked and weeping across his back, feeling as weak as a baby, just as the little girl had said. He sank down on the bench and closed his eyes in the sun.

The young woman sat beside him.

'*Me llamo Maria*,' she said.

'*Me llamo James*,' he said.

Later, the girl upended a bag of marbles on the ground, and he watched her arrange them – beads, lost lead-shot, an old stone fishing weight – but she did not actually play. He asked if he might have a knife, and the old woman hunted him out a bone-hafted blade worn thin with sharpening. He worked on a fragment of silver driftwood, hard as limestone; he sawed off an inch of wood, then chopped away the edges, shaping it into a ball. All the time he sat sharp upright on the stone bench outside the front door; it was an agony to lean or slump. Later, they drank a broth of seakale and shellfish, and then he crept up to his cot above, and laid himself face down, and as he drifted in the shallows of sleep he thought of the three of them downstairs, bundled up together like puppies on the floor before the fire, since there was nowhere else for them to lie.

He had thought that the pain would keep him from rest, but his sleep was deep and dark as the sea, and as all-consuming.

He passed the chapel on his way down to the beach, tools and dry pitch-pot packed into a knapsack. The chapel doors stood open on the dim interior, and he saw the three figures of the women and the child, a few candles, but there was no sign of any priest.

On the foreshore, he built a little fire out of driftwood, to soften the pitch; its flames were almost invisible in the spring sun. He stirred as it softened, the heat and the tarry smell in his face. Each tool he handled – knife, and awl, and hammer – was worn smooth as pewter by use, by the sweat of those other hands. It felt uneasy. James slapped and scrubbed the tar into the thirsty wood, a shiver gathering in the back of his neck. But the breeze was warm, and brought with it the stirring, unsettling promise of the summer.

From time to time he had to stop, and close his eyes, and just breathe until the pain had eased a little, and he could go on.

Once, he felt himself watched, but when he looked up and round, there was no sign of the women or the girl.

He scuffed sand over the fire to put it out, and left the pitch to harden.

In the evening, the old woman patched red canvas sails. The young woman sometimes sang with her daughter. They had sweet, dusty voices. Princesses and knights and donkeys and stepmothers and houses made out of sugar and magic spells.

The skiff, pushed out onto the water, bobbed cockily there like a yearling colt. He dived down deep, and came up breathless; his skin was becoming sound, his body strong. He hauled himself back up over the side. The war was fading off into the distance; in his mouth Spanish had become as familiar as his broken tooth. The days lengthened and it was midsummer. When he climbed up to bed, the two women murmured on, talking long into the night.

One evening, the younger woman touched his arm when she handed him his broth.

That night, he lay awake, aware of the women's voices below him, speaking in their quiet Spanish, and it sounded like a prayer. He eased out of his cot, and went to the window, and opened the shutters. The night was brilliant with stars.

*

The old woman carried the sails and coils of rope down towards the shore; the girl dragged after them, lugging the folded nets. He set the slim mast, then watched and helped as she rigged the sail. The young woman stowed the nets, then between the two of them they shoved the boat out onto the breaking waves. Knee-deep in water, she stepped into the little skiff, skirts dripping; he hauled himself in beside her, making it rock. She unfurled the sail, and it caught the wind and billowed, and they were scudding off into the setting sun.

She showed him how to fling the nets out across the water. One net split, and came back slack and empty. The other heaved with fish, was so heavy that it took both their strength to haul it up, the skiff leaning dangerously; they spilt its flapping silvery contents into the keel. Untroubled for so long, the fish had flourished, their shoals grown fat with war.

There was a little fire burning on the beach that morning, when they returned. The old woman and the girl, who had watched them out, were watching them back in again.

They gutted the fish and dried them in the summer sun, hanging them out like washing on a line.

Then it was autumn, and the days grew shorter. The old woman said that they would go and pray to St Michael, to thank God for their continued safety, their deliverance, for the gift that He had sent.

James nodded his understanding. He watched the dark progress of them down to the tiny chapel. When he was certain they were settled in their devotions, he slipped away to the shore, and walked across the low headland; it fell away into a spit of sand, the grasses thin and fine as old men's hair, the sand drifting and scattering and settling; and white shells and then bleached bones, and then a sheep's skull, picked white, which made him catch his step a moment, not at what it was but at what he'd thought that it might have been. Then skipping sand-fleas, and trails of dried seaweed, and he was out to the edge of the world.

He walked into the shallows. The water crept up quietly and

brushed his feet and ankles. He shaded his eyes with a hand, and peered out across the sea. He waded out further; the waves crashed in, soaking the rolled legs of his trousers. He blinked in the low sun, his eyes scalded. He thought, I don't even know what I am looking for. I don't even know what sea this is; if this is the sea that I sailed across to get here, or another one. I don't even know what I would find back in England, if I did ever return.

When he came back to the cottage, the place had changed. There was an end-of-summer cool, a stretch in the shadows; a chill seemed to gather about the house, rising in puddles, and then pools, and then slinking together, and suddenly everywhere. Perhaps it was just the turn of the season; perhaps it was the holiness of the day, but something made the air seem dim, and liquid, and far too full.

They collected inside the downstairs room. The girl slipped in, and a cat that had taken to hanging around the place, crept in with her. The child sat down cross-legged on the floor and proceeded to arrange her marbles, sorting them by size and material. The cat stretched itself out and watched the girl's movements, and the marbles as they wobbled into stillness. The creature was in whelp. It had made prey, no doubt, of gulls and rats once all the better pickings were gone. Its skin and bones, its shoulders and hips seemed just a sling for its barrel belly.

The women were so conspicuously not watching him that it was impossible not to feel he was being very closely observed. Had they seen him walk out onto the headland, and wade into the water? Was that somehow not allowed? He'd known that it would not be approved of; after all, he'd waited until he was sure he was alone.

When the day's meal was served, the cat got to her feet and padded between them, and mewed. He gave her one of the gristly bits, which might have been winkles, or something similar from the sea, or might have been snails. She settled happily with it, chewing at it with needle teeth.

The girl watched this a while, then glanced up at him. He set his cup aside, and reached out two closed hands to her, knuckles upward. She tapped the left hand. He opened it, and on his rough palm rested a new

278

marble, carved out of bone-pale driftwood, as smooth as he could make it, and with a ripple around its middle, meant to look like the rim of foam on a wave, or like the twist of colour there'd sometimes been in glass marbles, back at home, back when he was a boy. Where now, at Michaelmas, there'd be hips and haws red as blood, and black-berries hanging like lanterns, and the birds making a feast of them, as he had too, when he was young; he had chewed the flesh off haws with the fluffy sweetness of year-old apples, he had scraped the seeds out of hips to eat the peel, he had stained his fingernails purple with black-berry juice.

The cat curled and bumped around his legs, then gathered herself and leapt into his lap, and lay there. He felt the uneasy shift of the young inside her belly, their squirming immanence, and sat perfectly still.

The women said nothing.

What did they suspect? And what did they want? Had they sensed that he was dreaming now of home?

He was woken by her body. The bones of her hip and shoulder, the cool silk of her skin. Thin as a whippet, and sweetly warm. He had not known that he wanted, had not really known what it was to want, until she coiled herself, bone and sinew and softnesses, around him, and for a while he lost himself entirely in the comfort of her body. Maria. The first woman that he had ever known.

He did not know why it had not occurred to him before, that he was necessary to them. That he could make the difference between a good haul and the slip towards starvation. He had worked because work was what you did. He had worked because they had been kind to him. He had worked because if he helped someone then he was perhaps a better man for it.

The old woman eyed him as he came down from his bed. Maria had gone in the night, like a mosquito. The child arranged her marbles on the floor, but did not look at him at all, as if she knew perfectly well what had taken place, and considered it a betrayal.

279

He went down to the beach, and worked on the boat, and in the middle of the day, Maria brought him a cup of broth and sat beside him as he drank it. She was stiff, her face turned aside, as if seeing him just in the corner of her eye she could believe him to be someone he was not. He dug into the sand beside him, shoving his fingers down in the grit, rubbing his knuckles against it.

'*Espero*,' he said, 'I hope . . .'

But the words would not come in either language. He hoped. What did he hope? That she lived to be old, that she had an easy death, and did not suffer too badly along the way. He hoped that someone might wash up here one day who could make her happy. He hoped that her daughter's life would be better than her own. That they would forgive him.

And when she was gone, back to the cottage and her scrubby patch of vegetables and sand, he tugged his hat down low over his eyes, and turned up the collar of his smock to keep the sun off the back of his neck, and walked along the beach and crossed the far headland, dry drifting sand in his rope-soled shoes, and the sun overhead and then descending in front of him, and he walked in the dead man's clothes, leaving behind him the dead man's mother, widow, daughter, the dead man's life.

He gathered sea-shells. Pale pink fans, bluish mule-ears, twirls of chalky white. He dropped them into his backpack, one by one.

CHAPTER IV

1810

IN LISBON, THE captain of the *Snapdragon* took him for a Spaniard: James was burnt brown with the Spanish sun, and found English words now hard as pebbles in his mouth. The captain signed him, and was glad to get him – crew being crew, and hard to come by, what with the Navy pressing every man that they could get their hands on, and the Army organizing the wholesale slaughter of the rest. This fellow seemed sane and sharp and biddable, and, though silent, could follow English when it was spoken to him, and he seemed ready enough to work.

James kept his counsel, and himself to himself. He kept his shirt on, too, though no doubt there would be those amongst his crewmates who had scars like his. It was better to avoid the question, to be unremarkable, to leave as light an impression as he could upon the world.

They sailed from Lisbon to Rio, with the mail and a cargo of linen cloth. He was too busy to feel sick, too exhausted not to snatch whatever sleep he could in his swaying hammock. They returned from Brazil to Portugal with coffee; the whole ship was heady and fragrant with it.

Back in the familiar port, James kept quiet, and pocketed his pay, and closed his eyes tight to the sights of the land beyond, the memories it conjured. They loaded the *Snapdragon*'s hold with casks of port wine, and barrels packed with blue-painted china. They sailed next for Antigua.

At English Harbour, the air was thick and warm and smelt of vegetation and rot. Slaves never crossed the gunwales nowadays, not since the new law, but they were still traded, they were still worked: slaves farmed the sugar and cut it and refined it; slaves carted it to market. Slaves made the carts that it was carted on, they iron-rimmed the wheels, they shod the horses, mortared the bricks, and shingled and thatched and cooked and stoked the fires and treated the sick and sweated.

James, rolling barrels by their bases, wiped the sweat from his own forehead and watched, as off the ships, and down the quays, the new captives trickled past from the foreign ships, their chains clinking; they were filthy, sick, half-starved, but he could see — in the way they held their heads, the looks they gave the place — what they were thinking: This cannot be real, I do not accept this.

The slaves that came down from the plantations looked differently, withdrawn; you could not see what they were thinking at all.

An English voice, harsh above the susurration of the footfalls, made James start and look round. Amongst those dark skins, a white man's face — though not white, but pink and puffy with heat and drink — was unnatural and gross. An English agent or a steward; he moved through the crowded market with a riding crop and high boots, assessing the flesh, saying a word here or there, striking a bargain, gathering up the goods. Looking out for the interests of an English gentleman who would rather stay at home, and spend the money there.

When James hung in his hammock, eyes closed, he could still see it all again: the black shuttered eyes; the pink man's sausage-skin sweat; the column shambling off to the inner dark of the island. If it were not for the rifle and the lash, someone could just lift their chains and wrap them around the nearest sweaty pink throat, and squeeze.

Loaded with sealed casks of sugar, the *Snapdragon* sailed for the port-town of Lancaster, in the far north of England. One night, out on the cold Atlantic, James dreamed of an endless march in the mud and snow; from a vulture's circling flight he saw himself, his detachment, the thousands of men in a shambling trail across the land. He woke

282

shivering and sick, and with a new, instinctive understanding of the mathematics of the world.

I handed my freedom right over. I signed it clean away. I sold myself.

It had seemed like such a small thing at the time; it had seemed to be no use to him at all.

They were chased home by the trade-winds, and docked at Lancaster, at St George's Quay, in August 1811. By then, James had been with the *Snapdragon* for nearly two years. The war seemed like a lifetime ago; those dark memories could not really be his.

He stared out at this busy city from the deck. The nearby warehouses were six storeys high, spanking-new; their fronts were slung with winches; creaking ropes hoisted crates up to their stores. The quayside bustled with dockers – men, and women too, with their skirts hitched and sleeves rolled on knotted muscle, matching the men for work and noise, matching them obscenity for obscenity. Above this clamour the city rose, built out of golden stone; the castle was lowering and ancient, but below that, on the hillside, everything seemed elegant and new. There were bright church spires and grand flat-fronted houses with big glazed sashes; the African Trade had been profitable for this place.

But, if he just turned and looked a little to the left, on the far side of the river, the rye fields stretched flat and silky, and further off, the hills swelled blue and purple like the backs of rising whales, and if you could get out there, beyond these bustling mercantile streets, and walk out through those fields, and up to those hills, and climb up through their heath and heather – the peace of that would be so deep, and so clean. He felt again that impulse that had come upon him in Spain, which had been lying suspended in him all this time at sea: to be in England, and in the service of a good man. To be at home.

He asked for shore leave, and having never yet caused one bit of bother, it was readily granted. After all, what harm could he get up to in a place like this? Why would a Spaniard go and slip his traces in a place like Lancaster?

His pay in his pocket, his bag on his shoulder, he had one drink with his shipmates in the Three Mariners, an ancient ramshackle building on the quayside, easing itself down into the mud on which it had been built. He drank a pint pot of beer while they toasted their safe return to England, and the restoration of health to the poorly king whose piss had apparently turned quite purple, and whose fat-arsed son had – it now transpired – been in charge since February; then they drank to the health of the milk-complexioned girl behind the bar, who smiled at James, and had pretty dimples. He looked away.

When they were ordering a second round of beer, he got up and said he was going for a piss. He walked out of the side door of the inn, and took his piss in the stinking privy, and then he buttoned himself up and walked away, and just kept on walking, crossing Cable Street, and then New Street under the shoemakers' signs, passing the tea-merchants' offices, and a rocking horse that hung creaking above a toyshop, its spots quite faded, its mane and tail worn scrubby by the weather. On Market Street, James stopped a young gentleman of Indian complexion to ask the way, but found that he could put the words together only with some difficulty. The young man tamped his pipe, and listened kindly, and then answered him precisely with directions out of town. James was soon striding out along South Road, the carriages bowling by, and ladies with parasols out taking the air, and chattering away to each other in their muddy dialect.

It took him a month to reach Hertfordshire. When his shoes fell apart he haggled over a scuffed old pair of English boots with a tooth-less woman in Bolton who reeked of gin. When his shirt fell to rags he bought another in a vile shop in Digbeth, and English britches too, so that he might no longer be taken for a foreigner. He scorched the seams with a candle stub, to rid the cloth of lice.

He walked the lane-ways dressed in strangers' clothes, his black canvas pack fading now to grey. He slept in shepherds' bothies, hedgerows and church porches; while his pay held out, and it was still summer, none of this was a hardship to him. He spoke to very few – a labourer in a field to check his road, a yeoman to beg a day's work from him, a farmer's wife to buy a sup of milk. Silence became habitual, and when he was called upon to speak, the confluence of languages in his thoughts made him pause and struggle for words.

He thought differently now; he no longer thought in houses, farms and fields, in enclosed spaces; now it was all distances and trajectories. He daydreamed of the lines that he had traced across the land, the threads that drifted off over the seas.

'Fine-looking fellow, that one,' he overheard a dairymaid telling her companion.

'Shame that he's a simpleton. Can hardly talk.'

'Don't mean you can't have him, though, do it?'

They cackled together; he walked on.

As the autumn came down upon him, he returned to familiar territory, to the landscape of his childhood. He followed the drovers' road past Old Misery's farm, and there was the spreading sycamore that he had used to climb, and the farmhouse still peering out suspiciously from under low eaves. He didn't stop. He picked blackberries, hips and haws, and ate them as he went, staining his fingers and his lips with juice.

He asked at the inn in Meryton if Mr Bennet still lived thereabouts; he muttered something about work, about hearing something from another fellow on the road – but the landlord was a ready talker, and no explanation was required: indeed, the Bennets did still dwell in the neighbourhood, he was happy to inform him – the Bennets' home was but a mile away, at the village of Longbourn. Theirs was the principal household. Mr Bennet, and his wife, and their five fine daughters were currently in residence.

James watched from the lane, hidden by a patch of holly hedge. A stream of young ladies flowed out of the house and across the paddock; they foamed over a stile, and flurried off like sparrows along the field path and out of sight. He watched as Mr Bennet himself – older, stooping – came out of the house, and strolled aimlessly in the shrubbery, hands clasped behind his back. James must pick his moment, choose his words; he made his way down the lane cautiously. As he passed a bare patch of the hedge, he saw two figures in the paddock down below. One was a child, the other a young woman, who was hanging white linen on a line. She paused in her work, and shielded her eyes, and stared across the space between them.

He had come halfway across the world for this. This was home.

CHAPTER V

But it is all, all too late now.

Mr Hill, when he was roused and consulted, sat up in bed and pulled the blankets up to his chest. He readily confirmed that he had not sent the manservant on any errand, nor had James previously informed him of an intended departure for Meryton, or anywhere else, that morning.

'It doesn't mean he didn't go, though.' Mr Hill wiped his crusted eyes, and then his spit-gummed lips. 'There might have been a mend to be made at the blacksmith's, or he might have gone on to the coachmaker's in Harlow, for new gear.'

His nightshirt was old and thin and he felt exposed under all this female scrutiny. He peered at his wife and the two girls, blurred in the shaft of early-summer sun from the casement. They could at least have let him get his britches on before they started all this.

Mrs Hill sank down on the bed beside him, tightening the blankets over his lap, making the boards creak underneath.

'He didn't mention anything. He didn't say a word.'

'They're not wanting the carriage at this hour, are they? I'll do it. You lot clear off while I get dressed.'

'He would never leave the horses,' Sarah said.

'Eh?'

'The horses,' Sarah said. 'No fodder, no water. He just – left.'

Mr Hill felt for his wife's hand, lying by him on the covers. He took

287

it, held it. She looked down at his old paw, wrapped around hers.

'He can't have just gone,' he said.

Mrs Hill nodded. His hand tightened around hers; her eyes welled.

'I'm so sorry,' the old man said.

Polly, hovering in the doorway, bit her finger and looked from one of them to the other, baffled and upset. Sarah just swayed there, in a patch of sunshine, looking as though a breeze would knock her over. Mrs Hill had gone grey, and Mr Hill was suddenly all soft and concerned. All was out of order. Polly didn't like it, not one little bit.

'Will you speak to Mr Bennet?' he asked.

Mrs Hill shook her head: she did not know.

'What will you do?'

She squeezed his hand, then let it go, and heaved herself up from the bed. She passed Sarah, then Polly, and set off with a heavy tread down the stairs. Sarah followed her; Polly took hold of Sarah's arm as she passed by.

'Why would she do anything?' Polly hissed. 'What has it to do with Mrs Hill anyway, whatever James is up to?'

'Not now.'

Sarah gently pushed Polly aside.

'Mrs Hill—' Sarah called.

The older woman paused on the turn of the stairs. Sarah clattered down the treads between them.

'Missus—'

Mrs Hill looked up, waited.

Sarah had no words to hand, but the logic of it, however inarticulable, was strong: the soldier flogged in the rain and the scarred man that she loved; the departure of the Militia and James's disappearance – each explained and substantiated the other, and made a kind of intuitive sense.

'Missus, the Militia, they left last night too.'

Mrs Hill swallowed, nodded. 'Go on.'

'I do not know what he had done—'

'What he had done?' The older woman's brow crumpled.

'James. Mr Smith. You would think once he had been punished—'

'I don't follow you.'

Sarah's lips were dry. 'I am sure, I know, that he is good; he has always been—'

Mrs Hill grabbed her shoulder, and shook her. 'Spit it out, for God's sake.'

'He had been flogged.'

Mrs Hill turned away. She pressed her forehead to the cool distempered wall.

'Mrs Hill—'

She shook her head, rolling her brow against the plaster. This was not the deal. This was not what she had paid so dearly for.

What did she expect him to do, Mr Bennet wanted to know. What exactly did she expect him to do about it, after all?

Mrs Hill chewed at the inside of her cheek: how could she know? She was not an educated man, a gentleman, with time on his hands and a network of useful and eminent acquaintances about the neighbourhood. She did not even know what might be done; what enquiries could be made, which individuals consulted. But something must be done. Surely something must be done this time.

Mr Bennet just played with his coffee cup and did not meet her eye. His hand, as it turned the cup in the saucer, shook a little.

'I suppose you want me to send out search parties? Scour the countryside?' He pursed his lips. 'The young man has broken his engagement here, which he had signed up for until the quarter day at Midsummer at least. It is quite inconvenient and wrong of him: we can assume he does not wish to be found, or he would not have left the way he did.'

'The Militia—'

Mr Bennet dropped his voice; he looked up at her now. 'What would they want with him? He served his time honourably, did he not?'

'He was not gone long enough.'

He went still, staring at her.

'Not to have been discharged,' she said. 'Not unless he was crippled beyond use.'

'A deserter, then—'

They just looked at each other, in silence.

'You could write,' she said. 'You could write to Colonel Forster—'

'And what would that achieve?'

'Just to know. Whether he has been – taken.'

He lifted a paper from his desk, adjusted his pince-nez. 'You wish me to write to that gentleman, and ask if they happen to have my bastard in their custody?'

'Your manservant.'

'What would people think if I did even that? What would people say? Mr Smith makes his own decisions, and his own mistakes. He is a grown man, after all; who am I to interfere?'

He is a grown man now, Mrs Hill thought; he has not always been. But there was no point opening all that up and picking through it again, so she just curtseyed, as she always did, and turned away. She went out of the library, and left the door standing wide.

Mr Bennet called out after her: 'Close the door, Mrs Hill—'

But she carried on down the vestibule, and out of the front door and left it wide too, and down the steps and crunched over the drive and through the gates, and was out walking along the main road of Longbourn village, where she began to be aware of herself, and that someone might notice her, walking out without a shawl or bonnet or apparent purpose. She climbed a stile, and sank down in the lee of a hedge. There was wood sorrel growing on the bank, and harebells, and there were cowslips nodding in the meadow grass at her feet, and a young cow ambled over, head swinging low, considering her with a bulging eye. It blinked its long lashes, and licked its nose with a rasping sticky tongue.

Wherever you are, Mrs Hill thought, God watches over you. He just looks on at you, with a strange eye and an uncaring heart.

CHAPTER VI

. . . her letters were always long expected, and
always very short.

THERE WAS A packet, addressed to Mrs Bennet in Lydia's careless, blotty hand. Inside would be a fat, thickly sealed letter for Kitty and a thin, more carelessly sealed one for Mrs Bennet: there always was. There was also a separate, neatly folded envelope with perhaps one extra sheet inside, which had come all the way from London to sit in Sarah's dry little hand and be regarded with bitter disappointment. From Mrs Gardiner to Elizabeth.

Sarah did not know what she had expected, but clearly she had expected something, or her chest would not feel as hollow and grey as it now did. She did not believe that he would have left her, without a word of warning or a promise of return, and no word from him since – not unless he entirely could not help it. And this chilled her, despite the sun on her face and the warmth of the day that made her sweat through her old yellow-green poplin. It was ice in her heart, to think that something dreadful had befallen him, and that he might even now be suffering terribly, and all alone, and that she could not go to him.

She trailed back to the house through the meadows; the grass was long and brushed against her skirts, giving off puffs of pollen. At Longbourn, the young ladies were out on the lawns, taking the air. There had been a resumption of summer finery, of lace and muslins;

there were new summer bonnets to be worn: the ladies looked light and delicate as butterflies. Sarah, though, trudging up the driveway, felt as though she had been chained to a rock, and must drag it along with her, inch by inch, yard by yard.

'When you write next to Miss Lydia, miss,' she asked Elizabeth, 'would you mind asking her, if it is not too much trouble, if there is any news of Mr Smith at Brighton?'

Elizabeth was looking through her letters, and had brightened beautifully at the sight of the envelope from her favourite aunt. She paused now in breaking its seal.

'Mr Smith?' she asked.

'I thought perhaps he might have gone to Brighton too, or been – took. I thought perhaps Miss Lydia might have heard tell of him there, or seen something of him.'

Elizabeth frowned, half shook her head. 'I'm sorry. Of whom?'

'Mr Smith. You must remember him?'

Elizabeth's eyebrows crept up; Sarah had moved closer, her hand was reaching out: she had forgot herself. She remembered now, and brought her hand back to clasp the other.

'I am sorry, miss. I really am, but he was here just a little while ago, and so much in our lives. A fine young man, your father said so. Everybody said so. A fine, upstanding young man.'

Elizabeth's expression cleared. 'Oh! *Smith*! You mean the *footman*!'

'Yes.'

'You called him *Mr* Smith, that's why I misunderstood you; I thought you meant someone of my acquaintance. I thought you meant a gentleman.'

'I am sorry I was unclear.'

'Yes. He did leave quite abruptly. Perhaps he heard of more remunerative work. But you think for some reason he has maybe gone to Brighton?'

It was something, Brighton: it was a word, a place, a possibility. 'He may have.'

'Well then, I shall mention it as you ask, when next I write to Lydia.

And I shall let you know if she has anything to report of him. But I fear her thoughts are so occupied with officers that it will be unlikely she would spare much notice for a footman.'

CHAPTER VII

'Adieu to disappointment and spleen. What are men to rocks and mountains? Oh! what hours of transport we shall spend!'

On Midsummer Day, Mrs Hill betook herself into Meryton to settle the accounts, and bring back something cold from the pork-butcher's for dinner. She went in much state, with a very proper bonnet on her head, the ribbons knotted with her own particular firmness, and her old linen fichu pinned underneath her chin, so that no unnecessary eighth-of-an-inch of skin would be exposed to sunshine or view. She marched along the path, a stout and upright figure with a solid tread, under a hand-me-down parasol. She was a respectable sort of a person, was Mrs Hill. They knew it in the kitchen; they knew it in the household. And the whole world knew it, on quarter days, when she went into Meryton to settle the accounts.

Sarah, though, was now able to see through the matter of fichus and bonnets, to the flesh and its betrayals. While Polly and Mr Hill slept, the housekeeper and housemaid had stumbled their way through the truth of it, hands reaching out to clasp across the scrubbed table. Sarah's shock had soon melted into understanding – she knew of course what it was to be young, and wanting, though it was hard to imagine Mr Bennet so – and then bubbled up to anger: *all those years.*

'But you, Sarah—' Mrs Hill had rubbed her nose, and sniffed. 'Are you likely to be – in the breeding way yourself, do you think?'

Sarah had run a nail along the grain of the tabletop, where the pith had been scrubbed away; she shook her head: she had already bled.

After a moment, Mrs Hill spoke. 'It's probably for the best.'

*

With Mrs Hill absent on her seasonal migration, the kitchen was briefly shining and quiet. The ashes were sinking in the grate, and the flour and lard were laid out on the table for the making of scones, and Mr Hill was off elsewhere on the estate about his unfathomable business. Sarah and Polly sat silent, caught up in their own thoughts, and unwilling to shatter the peace. Sarah gnawed at her finger, thinking, I should just go looking for him; I should pack a bag and go – and then, equally pressingly – I must just sit tight and wait for him; here is the only place he knows that I will be; where he will, when he can, come looking for me.

These thoughts churned and tumbled, refusing to curdle into anything of substance.

'I miss him too, you know,' Polly said.

Sarah nodded; she knew.

'What will you do?'

Sarah shunted herself away from the table and set to work, bundling a couple of muffins, left over from breakfast, into a tea-cloth, paring slices from a cheese. She went into the still room and filled a bottle with small beer, and corked it.

'Right,' she said. 'Get your bonnet.'

Polly, who had watched all this activity blankly, suddenly brightened. 'Where we going?'

'We're going for a walk. I want to go and see something. See if it's still there.'

Polly grinned.

They ambled down the track, and Polly was soon chattering happily, gathering flowers. She exclaimed over dog roses and bees and butterflies, and the rabbits that flitted away at their approach. The track took them downhill, and then across a wooden cattle bridge over the river. Then they climbed up the far hillside, and through the woods, right up to the edge of the trees, and the tip of the hillside down into the next valley. A wide sweep of pasture lay before them, and clusters of sheep; the whole was fenced around with willow hurdles.

'This used to be common land,' Sarah said. 'There were houses here.'

Sarah climbed the fence, digging her toes into the slats; then she took Polly's hand to help the girl down. Beyond, the sheep had cropped the grass to a short nap, and there were dry lines in the turf, where the soil was thin over stone. Sarah traced her way along the marks: four tumbled walls, a line across that divided the dwelling in two; a gap that used to be the doorway, where the hens had scratched.

'I was born here,' Sarah said.

Polly looked up from her posy of wild geranium, and buttercups, and dog daisies. 'What, here?'

'At least, I think so. One of these. I remember the line of the hills. The edge of the woods. These were weavers' cottages. My father was a weaver.'

'Well,' said Polly, 'there's nothing here now.'

The two girls climbed back over the fence, and walked a little way, and then sat down on a bank, and toed off their boots, and Polly lay back and gazed through the flicker of leaves and laced branches up at a sky as blue as forget-me-nots. Then she curled onto her side, head pillowed on an arm, and blinked slowly, and fell asleep. Sarah sat awake for a long time, with the sound of bees and flies buzzing through the woodland flowers, haunted by the memory of happiness, of the woman in a faded red dress, who walked away from her through the long grass, against the wide blue sky.

Chapter VIII

The Gardiners staid only one night at Longbourn, and set off the next morning with Elizabeth in pursuit of novelty and amusement.

M RS GARDINER SEEMED, by anyone's reckoning, to be very ready to abandon her children to other people's care, and to other people's servants her infant's stinking nappies to scrub. It was to be a three-week tour for her husband, her good self and her niece Elizabeth. They were to see Derbyshire from the comfort of the Gardiners' carriage, and examine the celebrated beauties of Matlock, Chatsworth, Dovedale and the Peak.

Elizabeth left without a word for Sarah; either she had not yet written of the matter to Lydia, or she had not yet had any reply, or the reply had conveyed nothing pertinent to Sarah's plight, or, simply, she had forgotten all about it. Sarah chewed her nails, and watched the carriage roll away.

Mrs Hill did what she always did when things were difficult: she buried herself in her work. And there was plenty to be had of it, for all they were rid of two young ladies and their laundry. What with the there-and-back of it, there was to be the best part of a month with the Gardiner children in the household, and that meant a deal of extra trouble, and noise, and meals, and washing. The shitty nappies, the wetted beds: the *work*.

Life was, Mrs Hill had come to understand, a trial by endurance, which everybody, eventually, failed.

CHAPTER IX

*. . . neither her virtue nor her understanding would preserve
her from falling an easy prey.*

THE EXPRESS CAME at midnight. The boy hammered at the bolted
door, bringing Mr Hill down the back stairs with a guttering
candle, sucking his few remaining teeth and grumbling; Mrs Hill followed straight behind with her hair in long grey braids. Sarah flew
down, scudding past them, night rail streaming, a shawl falling loose
where she had thrown it about her shoulders, her feet bare on the
boards.

It must be James. It must be news of him at least.

Polly crept down after them, blinking sleepily.

They found Mr Bennet standing in the lobby with his bedside
candle and an opened letter in his hand, his face white as his nightcap,
and his wife hanging off him. Kitty, Mary and Jane were ranged
upon the stairs; the Gardiner children, high up in the old nursery, had
slept through the noise. Beyond the open front door all was moonlight
and blue shadows. The express – a young lad of maybe twelve with a
mop of dusty blond hair – leaned sleepily against the flank of his tall
horse.

'Pay the boy, would you, Mrs Hill?' asked Mr Bennet.

Mrs Hill ran to the console for the purse; she counted coins onto her
creased palm; all the time, Mrs Bennet was pulling at her husband's
arm, asking what Sarah, though she burnt to, could not.

'What is it, Mr Bennet? Oh, pray make haste and tell me! Oh, is it one of my dear girls?'

On the gravel, Mrs Hill handed the boy his money; he pocketed it, and clambered back up into the saddle, and turned his horse's head. He clopped exhaustedly away into the dark, easy prey for thieves and highwaymen. A nightingale sang. It was a beautiful night. Mrs Hill came back in and shut the door on it.

'Who is it from? What is it, Mr Bennet? Is it Lydia? Or Lizzy? Oh, if some thing has befallen them I don't know what I shall do! I cannot bear it if they are harmed.'

Mrs Bennet buckled at the knees, clutching at her husband.

'It is from Colonel Forster,' he said.

Sarah moved forward, eager. 'What does he say?'

Mr Bennet noticed her then, and Polly, and Mr Hill: all the servants gathered there, all witnesses to this disgrace.

'Assist your mistress, Mrs Hill; help her back to bed.'

'But then it is my Lyddie! My little girl!' Mrs Bennet was desperate to know; she shrugged Mrs Hill away. 'What has happened to her? Oh, pray tell me, do!'

'I do not think,' Mr Bennet said, 'that we need share this with the whole household.'

He folded up the letter.

'Sarah, Polly, get back to your beds. You are not wanted here.'

Lydia was gone. She had thrown herself upon the mercy of that villainous young man. Whatever was she thinking? Mrs B.'s words came out choked and broken by sobs. Mrs Hill just held her mistress for a while, murmuring the words you murmur to a child. It will be all right, shhh, all will be well, things will seem better in the morning, just you wait and see. She let go of Mrs Bennet only to pour water, and drop laudanum into the glass, and then, when that had left her distress still unsoftened, to half-fill a glass with Cordial Balm of Gilead, and hold it to her mistress's lips. The lady sipped the brown liquid, with its whiff of brandy and herbs. She looked so broken. Mrs Hill had not seen her like this since the time of her mishap, all those long years ago. Fogged by poppy and by grape, she grew quieter. Mrs Hill drew a blanket over her, and left her slumbering on the sofa.

Polly dragged herself back up to bed, but Sarah, rather than returning to the hot closeness of the little attic room, and the stale smell of the shared bed, trod her feet into her boots, and shuffled out across the yard, and climbed up to the stable loft where James no longer was, and huddled down in his bed, and pulled his sheets up to her face, and tried to catch the last scent of him there.

CHAPTER X

. . . *the impudence of an impudent man.*

JANE SCRIBBLED A note, folded and sealed it with a yellow wafer. Sarah had been summoned from her morning chores; the dew was not yet burnt off the lawn: this was urgent.

'Would you take this to the post office, Sarah, dear, and send it? And, in a general fashion, ask if there are any letters waiting for us there?'

Sarah looked at the little packet. It was addressed to Miss Elizabeth, in Lambton, Derbyshire.

'Yes, miss. I always ask, miss.'

'Good girl; thank you.'

Jane gave Sarah one of her sweet smiles, and touched her on the shoulder. They were all still pretending that nobody actually knew about Lydia. From Jane's queasy look, it could be guessed that she had some uneasy half-suspicion of what men and women might do together, if they were but given the opportunity: there was disgust there, as well as distress. Sarah, leaving her mistress, fetching her shawl and clattering down the servants' stairs, realized that she was quite alone in envying Lydia: but it was something, it must be something, to be with the man you wanted. Even if it was just Wickham, there must be joy in it.

The postmistress shook her head at Sarah's enquiry; there was nothing for the family yet today. Were they expecting something in particular?

She could have the boy run over with it if a packet came on the later coach. If Sarah would just let her know from what direction they expected it, she would know it straight away, and would send it straight on to Longbourn, at only a little extra charge—

'That's quite all right, thank you, missus. I can come back and check in the afternoon. Is there anything, though—' Sarah fumbled the words, knowing how strange they must sound, coming from her. 'I wonder, do you happen, by any chance, to have anything for me?'

A snort of laughter. Sarah said nothing; she watched from under knitted brows as the woman's expression changed. Realizing that the question had been seriously intended, she composed herself, and became business-like again.

'I'll just go and see.'

Sarah thanked her; the postmistress turned to check the pigeonholes. It took barely a moment: she turned back again, empty hands turned palms up, like a stained-glass saint.

'There's always the late coach, of course; as you say, come again in the afternoon. Though where are *you* expecting letters from now, I wonder?'

'You are a good girl, Sarah,' Jane told her, when she returned without the longed-for missive. 'Thank you for your trouble. You may go now, and get on with your work.'

Sarah curtseyed. She closed the door softly behind her, leaving Jane to her dreadful imaginings.

CHAPTER XI

He did trace them easily to Clapham, but no farther . . .

'YOU ONLY HAD to look at him to know that it was bad. He was grey, he was. Positively grey.'

Polly was doing her best to be grave, but all attempts at solemnity were in vain; she was giddy with excitement. She had rushed to open the front door when Colonel Forster thumped on it, and had been thrilled to usher him into the house and show him to the breakfast room. She had remained in the hallway outside – just in case she was needed; that would be her excuse – listening brazenly while Colonel Forster delivered his news.

It had not been received with much restraint; Mrs Bennet was not one to tiptoe around the edges of disaster, with one eye to the abyss and another to her own comportment: she plunged headlong in, and as she fell, took pains to enumerate the discomforts and inconveniences of the fall. Polly had, as a consequence, heard a good deal of what was said on the matter, and was quite ready to extrapolate the rest.

'So, what did the colonel say?'

Eyebrows arched, Polly whistled out a scandalized breath. 'Well, it turns out Lydia—'

'No, but—' Sarah cut her off. 'Was there any news of Mr Smith?'

'Does the colonel know James?' Polly frowned. 'How does he know James?'

'I was just wondering, maybe, that he might have heard, since he's been asking around anyway—'

'Well, you'll have to ask him yourself. What I heard was only about Lydia, 'cos it seems they are not gone to Gretna at all, but actually to London . . .'

There was a time when London had seemed the summit of all desires to Sarah, and now it seemed to matter not at all. What mattered now was that Colonel Forster was here, at Longbourn, and might have direct and immediate knowledge of James. One word from him could confirm her worst fears, or disperse them entirely to the winds. She might, this very day, come to know the truth of him. If he was a prisoner of the Militia, if he had been taken with them to Brighton. If he had been pressed back into the Army. If he had been flogged again.

If they had killed him.

But she would go to him, in a fingersnap, if he was still alive. If she could but find out where to go.

'So they are not married, because you can't get married in London just like that, you don't go there to get married like you do in Gretna!'

Mrs Hill nodded along, chewing her lip.

'The colonel said that Lydia and Wickham changed carriages at Clapham, but he could find no trace of them after that, though he asked at every turn-pike, he said, and at all the inns in Barnet and Hatfield.'

'And then what?' Mr Hill asked.

'Well, the poor man, what a time he's had of it, all that trouble looking for them, and then to have to suffer all the trouble here! He handed over a note Lydia had left for Mrs Forster; they read it, Mr B. and Mrs B. did, and then Mrs B. gave out this great big scream, and then there was the most almighty kerfuffle, and I thought I'd better hoof it—'

A pause. Polly looked from one to the other, delighted with her own importance.

'You should have seen Kitty, though! I saw her when I brought up the tea. She's in *so* much trouble. It's like she's shrunk, actually shrunk.

And then Jane rang for me to take this – *another* letter to the post . . .' Her voice dropped to a significant whisper. 'And do you know! I do not think Mr B. has spoke a single word since he read that letter of Lydia's, that she left for Mrs Forster.'

'Mrs Hill,' Sarah said suddenly. 'I shall ask the colonel. About James.'

The housekeeper went still, her top lip bit hard between her front teeth.

'I really don't see why James would have anything to do with the colonel.' Polly was cleaning her nails with a corner of Jane's letter. 'He hated the soldiers.'

'Shut up, Polly. I should ask him, though, shouldn't I, Mrs Hill?'

Mrs Hill was still a moment longer. Then she reached out and tweaked the letter out of Polly's hand.

'I'll take that.' She knotted her shawl sturdily around her. 'Sarah—'

'Yes?'

'Let me know how you get on.'

In the post office, Mrs Hill handed Jane's letter to the postmistress, who looked it over, and frowned.

'That's ill wrote, that is. Where's that going to? Is that an L? Is that Derbyshire? Is that to Lambton again?'

Mrs Hill nodded.

'I can hardly make it out. I won't vouch for that making its way there straight. Why two letters there today, anyway?'

Mrs Hill was not in much of a position to judge the quality of the script. She was used, however, to the postmistress's spinning of fine threads into substantial yarns of gossip, and did her best to snap her line of thought straight off.

'Oh, you know how it is, with sisters, when they are close.' She shrugged. 'They do need to keep up their confidences, don't they?'

'Secrets, eh.'

'No! Not secrets. They are good girls, my young ladies are.'

'Ah yes,' said the postmistress, leaning forward on the counter, resting her bony frame on her folded arms. 'Yes, yes, of course they are, the Bennet girls, aren't they? But that's only half the point now; the other half is the young fellows, and you can't be certain there at all.'

'I don't know what you mean.'

'Don't you? You've not heard of the accounts left unsettled all over town, the gambling debts? Or that there's barely a tradesman's daughter who has not been' – here she dropped her voice to an insidious whisper, leaning so close that Mrs Hill could almost taste her eggy breath – '*interfered with.*'

Mrs Hill stiffened and stepped back. 'I think that kind of talk is best left unrepeated—'

'Now, Wickham, that great favourite of the Bennet misses—'

'—because that kind of talk, it reflects well on no one; not the officers, nor the tradesmen, and certainly not the daughters, or, indeed, on the folk who do repeat it—'

'Well, I hope you are not suggesting—' She pushed herself upright.

'—because I always say, "Let them without sin, let them cast the first stone."'

'Is that right, Mrs Hill?' The postmistress folded her arms under her meagre bosom, with the manner of someone clinching an argument. 'Is that what you say, now, is it, Mrs Hill?'

No, she would not pass it on. It would help no one to hear it; it would only serve to worsen the general distress. So Mrs Hill kept mum all that day. The postmistress was a wicked gossip, and knew nothing about anything, and everybody knew it. But that would not stop the story being repeated, and smoothed with handling, so that it seemed to acquire a patina of truth. One thing was certain, though: Mrs Hill would not contribute to that handling. She would not gossip.

She would, however, partake of something of her mistress's grief, though in quieter measure. Mrs Hill had changed Lyddie's nappies, wiped her snotty nose, had nursed her through colic and croup and chickenpox, all those childhood illnesses – and she was still just a child, a girl with a brown birthmark on her calf, a sweet tooth, a bold eye and an infectious laugh. Mrs Hill felt at once desperate for her, and furious: what a poor, poor bargain she had made of herself.

When Mrs Bennet began to stir and fret again, Mrs Hill put an extra drop of laudanum, and then another, into Mrs Bennet's water, and helped her drink the mixture down, and she soon became quiet. Mrs Hill stroked the faded ringlets off her mistress's face, and then left her to attend on the gentlemen. She was a wearying, anxious being, was Mrs B.; she was always so eager to solicit interest in her sufferings. But if her husband had loved her as a husband should – contentedly, generously, and without reserve – would she then have found it necessary to keep on seeking proofs of love, only to keep on being disappointed?

When she responded to the library bell, she found Mr Bennet crumpled in his chair; Colonel Forster stood upright by the fire, an elbow on the mantelpiece, a picture of frustrated vigour.

'Will you pack for me?' Mr Bennet asked.

'You are going to London, then.'

'Epsom, first, which is where they last changed horses. I shall speak to the postillions, and then . . . go onwards.'

'To find Lydia.'

'They must be married. I must make him marry her.'

Mrs Hill nodded. 'A week's worth of linen?'

'I will find a laundress there, if my stay is prolonged beyond that.'

Her throat aching, Mrs Hill dragged her old bones up to his dressing room, and packed his shirts and stockings and neck-cloths and included with them a sprig of rosemary, so that when he pulled out a clean shirt in whatever London lodging he happened to wash up in, the little scented twig would fall out, and cause him to remember, and consider the gap between what he was prepared to do for Lydia and respectability, but was not prepared to do for others, whom he had also professed to love, at other desperate times.

When Colonel Forster emerged from the library, Sarah was instantly at his elbow, pocketing her duster. He had a lost, enquiring air, so she dared to speak first.

'Can I help you, sir?'

'Ah, yes. I was looking for the, eh, necessary—'

'Round the side of the main house, sir, and across the gravel. This way, here, let me show you.'

'There's no need, no need, I can find my way.' He brushed past her.

'Sir—'

He stopped, glanced back.

'Sir, we had a footman here, sir, you might remember. James Smith, his name was; he had dark hair, and hazel eyes, and he was about this tall . . .' She held up a hand, marking the air beside her, six inches higher than her own head. And for just a moment she had conjured him up – the length of him, the curve of his arm, the angles of his face – the urgent elastic pull towards him that made her unsteady on her feet.

The colonel frowned. 'What?' he asked. 'What did you say?'

She brightened: a ripple of hope. 'Our footman here, James Smith, sir, he left the night you left for Brighton and I—'

'What is this you are asking me?'

He came up close to her now; she was faced with his red coat, gilded buttons, braid. He smelt of horse and sweat and smoke.

'Sir, thank you, sir. If you have seen anything of him. If he was in . . . in company with you, or—'

'What do you take me for?'

'Sir, Colonel Forster, I—'

'That, when a young lady under my protection – puts herself in peril, that I would have the time, or the interest—'

'Sir—'

'That you dare solicit my assistance?'

'Sir.'

'You forget yourself.'

'I am sorry, sir.'

She muttered it at her feet, so that he would not see her face.

Back in the kitchen, she picked up a cream dish, held it at arm's length, and let it fall to the floor. It crashed into shards, which scattered and span across the stone flags. Then she got out her broom, and dustpan, and began to sweep the pieces up. If the old blusterer had known anything, he would have told her, wouldn't he? He would have enjoyed telling her.

The colonel himself, as much astonished as offended, marched away down the hall, and stepped out through a side door into the summer day. He wandered around a while, looking for, and failing to find, the necessary house: Polly passed by some minutes later, with a basket of peas from the kitchen garden, and saw him pissing in the shrubbery.

CHAPTER XII

In this perturbed state of mind, with thoughts that could rest on nothing, she walked on . . .

ROOMS WERE HUSHED and had a breath-held air; there were too many obvious absences about the place. Though they did their best to make things normal for the Gardiner children, it was clear they were picking up on it, the poor little things: they went about with puzzled, placatory expressions, uncertain as to how they were at fault.

Mrs B.'s sister, Mrs Philips, stayed some days, and Lady Lucas called to offer her support. All other visitors were deflected by Mr Hill at the door.

The Gardiners returned from their travels with Elizabeth, who was pale and fatigued; no doubt it was moving, all this sisterly distress, but somehow Sarah could not manage to feel for her quite as she should: Elizabeth had not a word to say about the footman, Mr Smith.

Relaying trays to and from Mrs Bennet, running into Meryton to leave or collect letters, brushing past the neighbours and the neighbours' servants in the street, all of them looking for a nugget, a crumb, some little thing to help sustain the lumbering gossip-golem that Lydia's actions had conjured into being, and all the time with the loss of James gnawing at her: this had all become quite normal.

'No one even mentions him at all now,' she said, one day, to Mrs Hill. 'He may as well have never been here at all.'

'That is certainly not true.'

'But he was somebody. He was.'

'Sarah, I know.'

'But you won't do anything.' Sarah pushed back her chair. 'I'm going looking for him.'

'Don't be silly.'

'It makes perfect sense. I'm going to go round all the villages, and knock at every door—'

'No, Sarah.'

'Someone will have seen him. I can just keep on going till I find that person, and then—'

'Sarah. You cannot. You must not.'

'I have to—' Her voice cracked. 'I cannot bear—'

'Don't be so bloody stupid!' Mrs Hill slapped her hand down on the table, making Sarah jump, and the crocks rattle. 'You have no idea at all yet what you can stand!'

Sarah stared. Mrs Hill breathed, calming herself.

'Look, Sarah. You have a home. You have work. You are safe and warm and fed. And you are spoilt – no, no, hear me out – you must be, if you don't value any of that. But if you leave now, you'll have nothing, not a bean. You'll just be one of the multitude of young folk out of work, wandering the roads, and who will take you in then? You couldn't come back here, after you've broken your word to your master, and left in the middle of your term. You won't even have a good word from him then, no one will give you a character. You'd be throwing your life away.'

'But,' Sarah said, 'what about love?'

'I love you. Polly loves you. Mr Hill does too.'

Sarah nodded. She looked away, eyes brimming. Mrs Hill reached out and touched her hand.

'You forget, honey; these are bad times; these are lean years. The troubles, they don't touch us here; they never have yet. But if you leave, sweetheart, I am afraid that you'd just . . . disappear.'

Sarah rubbed her forehead. 'I must do something.'

'Do what I do.'

'What is that?'

'Work,' Mrs Hill said. 'And wait.'

Sarah's chin crumpled, her head in her hands. It was not to be borne.

'But, you see . . . He knows where you are, if you are here. He will write to you, I am sure he will; or he will come back and find you . . . if he can.'

Jane and Elizabeth confided with each other in anxious virginal huddles, whispering over letters, scandalized by the gossip that was now leaking back to them, despite Mrs Hill and Sarah's best efforts to stem its flow.

'I don't know why everyone is so hard on Mr Wickham,' said Polly, while she and Sarah were picking raspberries. 'He was nice.'

'Do you think so?'

Polly pulled a face, popped a raspberry into her mouth.

'Well, it's not like he locked Lyddie up in a trunk, is it! She wanted to go, because he's *nice*.'

'I'm not sure what you mean by "nice".'

Polly ignored this. She pushed raspberry canes aside, exploring deeper into the bushes to get at the fruit.

'He would've bought me sweets, you know.'

'Is that right?'

'He wanted to. All I had to do was be sweet to him first.' A pause, thoughtful; then: 'What do you think he meant by that?'

Sarah looked at her a long moment, and then she shrugged. 'I don't know, Polly.'

She turned away, and lifted a sprig, and bent to hunt for berries. Whatever happened with Lydia, at least Wickham would not be welcome here again, at Longbourn.

Mr Bennet returned from London without his daughter: Lydia was not yet discovered. Mrs Gardiner took the children home: her husband was to continue the search from their home in Gracechurch Street. But the worst must be prepared for: Lydia would be found debauched, unmarried and abandoned, and come upon the town, or she'd be living under the protection of another man. A retired life in a distant farmhouse was the best that could be hoped for, given how far along the primrose path Lydia had already skipped.

But this cause was not to be abandoned, no matter what the inconvenience, no matter what the expense. This child was to be recovered, no matter her condition on discovery. It did not seem to matter that the girl had made her bed, and leapt eagerly into it; she would not be obliged to stew in it for ever. If she could be detached from her debaucher, she would still be supplied with a home, a companion, an allowance. To live out her days in some quiet, comfortable place would perhaps be a torture to her, but it was an unattainable luxury to others.

There were hushed voices, swollen eyes, curtains drawn against the sun. This is what it will be like when Mr Bennet dies, Mrs Hill thought, though then the family could quite reasonably expect their neighbours' sympathy, and not their thinly veiled contempt.

And Mr Bennet had become suddenly quite old; he was worn out by all the exertion, and by the endlessly circling blame and guilt. The evening of his return he hid in the library and rang the bell for Mrs Hill.

All he wanted was to hold her hand. She let him.

'I am sorry,' he said.

She nodded. This was something, after all those years.

Chapter XIII

'It is enough to know they are discovered, I have seen them both—'

THE BENNETS SURFACED, gasping from grief. Lydia was found, and then shortly afterwards, in London, was married to Mr Wickham; the thing was managed with such dispatch that it was to be hoped that people would conflate the rumour of the elopement with the fact of the marriage. In the kitchen, they had a bowl of punch to drink, in honour of the event.

'How much do you suppose it would have cost, to fix up the thing like that?'

Mrs Hill glanced up from her sewing. Her husband was seated on the other side of the ashy fire, with his cup of punch balanced on the armrest. He had been, between sips, chewing a leather strap with his remaining back teeth, to soften it, preparatory to tackling it with an awl.

'A small fortune, I should think,' she said.

'I heard, ten thousand pounds.'

Her sewing fell into her lap. 'Money like that—'

'Half as much. A quarter. A tenth. A hundredth.'

She shook her head.

'Could be comfortable,' he said. 'Could be happy as a pair of pigs in muck with just a hundred pounds, we could, the two of us.'

She smiled, a real natural smile, not one of her pretend ones. He had not seen her smile like that in . . . well, he could not think how long. He returned the smile, all gaps and gums. It had been a hard and stony furrow she had been obliged to plough, the poor creature.

'What would we do with it?' she asked. 'What would we find to spend a hundred pounds on?'

He whistled. 'Oh, what wouldn't we? Wine and parmesan and an upholstered chair for each of us. A silk scarf and comfits for you, and two ounces of tobacco every blessed Friday for me.' He laughed. '*We* would invest it wisely, not like some people I might mention.'

Polly called over from the kitchen table, where she and Sarah were buffing the pewter: 'Things will be back to normal, then, I suppose.'

'Mm?'

'With Miss Lydia married. Things will go back to how they were before, I suppose.'

'Yes,' Mrs Hill said. 'Yes, I suppose so.'

Mrs Hill could feel the ripples of Lydia's actions spreading and becoming fainter. Things would, as Polly said, go back to how they had been, or at least some semblance of it. As with Lydia, so with James, though their circumstances were so different: everyone would just keep on keeping on, pretending that nothing much had happened, and the pretence would become habitual, until, eventually, the lie would seem more real than the truth. There was no footman now, there had not been for a while; Sarah was right – he was never mentioned any more; it would soon become as though he had never been.

Having softened the leather, Mr Hill was now repairing the tack, with his stitching-awl and thread. He squinted fiercely down at it, his old eyes straining, the lower lids falling slack and pink.

'And Mr and Mrs Wickham, they won't be back here now ever, I suppose?' Sarah asked.

'Oh no, I shouldn't think so,' said Mrs Hill. 'Not after that. The master would never allow it.'

Chapter XIV

*'I will not encourage the impudence of either, by receiving them
at Longbourn.'*

SOME PEOPLE CAN, it seems, be redeemed. The blots on their characters can be sponged off, and though the mark might never be gone
entirely, it can pass unnoticed by all but the keenest-sighted, or those
who already know the stain is there, and know where to look for its
traces. These people can pass muster in a crowd, or amongst strangers;
they can be made good enough again for everyday use.

Little Lyddie pressed a bare and grubby hand into Mr Hill's old thin
one; a gold-and-diamond ring glittered. Her cheeks were flushed, her
eyes bright as he helped her down from the coach, and she seemed very
much the girl that she had been. He was reminded of the farmyard ducks,
the way they gabbled and jostled, the way that water beaded up and
rolled right off them. He did not know what to say, but it hardly mattered, since she didn't pause long enough in her chatter to let him speak.

'To think, Hill, when I last saw you, I was still a girl of fifteen and
unmarried, and now I am a married woman. It seems an age since I last
saw you, and yet here you are, not changed at all! Nothing here is
changed, indeed, this old inn is just as I left it, and I wager Longbourn
will be just the same too—'

'Don't rattle on at the servants, Lydia.'

Wickham climbed down from the coach behind her, in a light-blue
dress coat, which he tugged fastidiously straight.

She turned to him, anxious. 'My dear?'

'It is a country habit and I do not like it.'

She looked from her shiny new husband to the lined old face that she had known all her growing life, and then back to Wickham. 'But it is a fine thing, is it not, to be married, and only just sixteen?'

Mrs Hill peeled out the few chemises and petticoats and nightgowns that Lydia had bundled away with her from Brighton: she tried not to look too directly at them, or inhale the odours of cheap lodging houses, sweat and sex.

She steeped the soiled linen – blood and sweat and spunk and travel dust, and the shiny grubbiness of things that have gone too long between washings – in lye, prodding at it with the laundry tongs, swirling it through the murky grey water. And all the time bitterness, like the eating-up acridity of the lye, welled up in her, though she kept pushing it down and pushing it back and nailing boards down over it. If Mrs Hill had the ruling, and not just the maintenance, of Lydia, the little madam would be obliged to wash her own dirty linen just this once, and see what other people saw of her.

In the yard, Polly was set to clean the baggage. She wiped down the inside of the boxes and bags with camphor, to get rid of pests; she was at it so long that the lining paper smudged and bled along the seams. Lydia, when she finally came to unpack properly in her new lodgings in Newcastle, would exclaim at Polly's carelessness. But every time Polly saw fit to stop, Sarah would gesture vaguely and say, 'Think you missed a bit.'

After dinner, Lydia galloped down to the kitchen to show off her wedding ring to Mrs Hill and the housemaids, and boast of being married. Polly looked on, wide-eyed, lips parted; Mrs Hill peered at the plump little hand and the flower of tiny diamonds, and murmured along with Lydia's talk, and then, when she could bear it no more, gave her a stick of barley-sugar to shut her up, all the while thinking that if the girl did not run back off upstairs she stood a good chance of getting a proper slap. Sarah, barely glancing at the ring, wanted to ask,

What of Mr Smith, the footman, did you see him at all in Brighton? But it was like an ulcer in her throat, and eating inward: what if Lydia *had* seen him? What if she had seen him in manacles, dragged through the camp, and flogged raw before a crowd? What if he were shot for what he'd done? And then Lyddie was off back upstairs in another flurry of excitement, and Sarah had not asked her, and it was too late, for now at least.

Mrs Wickham wafted a fashion plate at Sarah.

Sarah set the curling-irons to heat at the fire, then peered at the picture of a baby-featured, heavy-limbed woman squeezed into a flounced evening-gown; the hair was braided high at the back, and thick ringlets hung about the face like bundled sausages, or like those clags of wool that get stuck around sheeps' backsides.

'Shall do my best, ma'am.' And she began raking through Lydia's heavy hair.

Lydia squirmed in discomfort as Sarah braided and pinned. 'I wish you could have seen it, Brighton.'

Which meant Lydia wished to talk about it: she might mention James.

'Oh yes, ma'am. I think it must be very fine.'

Sarah folded a curling-paper into place, lifted the hot curling-irons and scissored them around a lock. She twisted tight; there was a huff of smoke, the smell of singeing hair.

'What a sight, I can tell you!' Lydia spoke awkwardly, her head dragged sideways by the pull on her hair. 'A whole camp full of soldiers, officers as far as the eye could see, and my dear Wickham the finest of them all.'

'How lovely.'

'Let me tell you: it is just the place for getting husbands. You should go, you know, since you won't ever find one here.'

Sarah swapped the irons for the hot ones from the fire, and slid the papers around another lock. Lydia's heedless, blithe expression was mirrored in the looking glass. Lydia did not possess much in the way of an imaginative faculty, and so did not construct possibilities, or look beyond her immediate moment, and the immediate moment was, to Lydia, very pleasant indeed, and so she was content. And this being so, she would not look for intrigues, or suspect a soul of anything, and she would not withhold anything, and she would not lie. Lydia was honest.

'And did you see . . . anybody . . . we know there, madam?'

Sarah unwrapped a curling-paper; a lock fell loose, lank, with just a hint of a curl.

'The officers, of course, all the officers, Denny and Pratt and Chamberlayne.'

Then Polly, who was supposed to be locked up safely in the scullery with the silver and the silver-polish, now sidled into the bedchamber. Sarah scowled round at the younger girl, mouthed: *Go away.*

Polly pretended not to notice. 'Did you go to the sweetie shop in Brighton, madam?'

'Oh, I went to all the shops, I'm sure of it.'

'Haven't you got work to be getting on with?' Sarah asked.

'Oh, I've done it all.'

This must be a lie. But Polly sat down on the floor, and drew up her knees, ankles crossed, big eyes fixed on the exotic splendour that was the new Mrs Wickham; Mrs Wickham picked up a little pot from the dresser, unstoppered it, and swirled rouge onto her cheeks. She touched her lips with it, too, and peered at herself in the mirror, and smiled. She looked glittery and hot, and not entirely well. She might have picked up something else in Brighton, or London, besides rouge and a husband.

'Did you see, did you hear of, the footman . . . ?' Sarah tried. 'Mr Smith, who left—'

Lydia tilted her head. 'Oh, I have not thought of him in an age – my goodness now, did he leave us?'

Elizabeth had not written. Or Lydia had not read.

'He did, and it was the same night that you – and the Militia—' But Sarah was cut across.

'What a pretty picture you do make.'

They turned as one, and saw Wickham lounging in the doorway, regarding them all with a complaisant smile.

'The young wife,' he said, 'and maids in quiet reverie. It could be a print: *Loyalty*. Or *The Young Mistress*.'

'There he is, my dear, handsome Wickham!'

Lydia got up, papers scattering, and went over to fling her arms around him. Sarah looked away. The flesh of him, the sheen of him: it seemed almost indecent. She scooped up the hair-papers, briskly tidied the dresser. She saw, in their mirrored reflection, how Mr Wickham, his arms wrapped around his sixteen-year-old wife, smiled over her head at Polly, and how Polly scrambled to her feet, and curtseyed, and stared, smiling, bare-faced and innocent, back at him.

'You should bring one of them with you, to Newcastle.'

'You are all thoughtfulness, but Mama could not spare them.'

'Just the little one. Pop her in your trunk.'

Sarah, the papers and pins in their box, the hot irons gathered up and hanging from their handles, went to take Polly by the wrist.

'Come along now.'

Polly whispered, 'I want to see if there are sweets.'

'Come *along*.'

Sarah, clutching the hair things to her, bundled Polly past the newly-weds, and out of the door.

CHAPTER XV

. . . for, of course, they were to have a son.

Mrs Hill found him, where she knew that she could always find him, in the library, having slunk away from the gathering. He was old and tired and drunk. He had scarcely opened his lips in company since the Wickhams' arrival, and had avoided what he could of the engagements made in honour of the newly-weds. He felt the disgrace most sharply now, now that everybody else, it seemed, no longer noticed it at all.

'I hope you've brought a fresh bottle of brandy.'

She closed the door behind her, showed her empty hands. A slow, red-eyed blink from him, a nod; and then, hearing laughter from the other room, a flinch. She drew a chair up to the desk, but just stood there, a hand resting on the top slat of the ladderback.

'I don't know which is worse,' Mr Bennet said. 'My daughter's disgrace, or my wife's blindness to it.'

'Mrs Bennet is . . .' Mrs Hill hesitated. 'Perhaps it is better that she is as she is.'

'It is hardly respectable.'

'That's not quite the sum of it, though, sir, is it?'

He lifted his glass clumsily. 'I fail to understand you, Mrs Hill.'

'For someone to be quite respectable,' she said, 'I think they must be shown respect. We build ourselves like the caddis flies in the river do, out of the bits and pieces that wash around us.'

He raised his eyebrows at this. Then he nodded.

She drew out the chair and sat down.

'Now it is settled,' she said, 'and she is married, I just want note made. I want it noticed, between the two of us at least, what you would do for your daughter, that you would not do for your natural son.'

He wiped his face with his hand. He poured more brandy into his glass. 'If you knew, if you knew what I have suffered, Margaret . . .'

The intimacy of her name on his lips: the years fled like starlings. She leaned forward and took his hand.

'I thought about it every night,' he said. 'All the time that he was gone. Every night till the night that he came back.'

She pressed her lips tight.

'All I wanted, from when he was little, from the moment you told me you were – all I was trying to do was be practical.'

She nodded.

'But there was no practical solution, was there?' he said. 'Being practical didn't solve anything.'

After a moment, Mrs Hill spoke again: 'I realized why he did it, you know. Why he took it; the King's shilling.'

Mr Bennet blinked up at her, his eyes sore; he nodded for her to go on.

'No one ever seemed to care, so he didn't really care either. He didn't know that he could be loved. That's why he didn't think twice about throwing himself into harm's way.'

Mr Bennet screwed up his mouth, his features blurred. He drew another glass towards him, slopped in brandy, and slid it across the desk to Mrs Hill. She took it by the stem. She touched the wet from her eyes. They drank.

CHAPTER XVI

'. . . she has got over the most trying age.'

THEY GATHERED THE sweet green plums in silence, Sarah on a high rung of the ladder, plucking them from their twigs, Polly standing at the ladder's foot to receive them and lay them gently in the basket. The Wickhams were gone; gone without imparting the slightest scrap of useful news, but also without any further harm done. He had brought no sweets with him for Polly, and gave her no more half-pennies or farthings – and so Polly now thought of him as a man who made empty promises, and could not be trusted, and was much less fun than she had remembered him to be. In the event, the Wickhams did not press for a maid to accompany them to Newcastle. For the sake of those northern scrubs and skivvies, it was to be hoped his young wife would be enough for him, for the time being.

From her perch high up in the greengage tree, Sarah glimpsed movement, and pulled aside a branch to peer out. Two gentlemen approached on horseback; they leapt the fence into the paddock, and the Longbourn horses joined them for a little canter, and then one after the other they leapt the nearer paddock gate and rode up the track towards the house.

'Mr Darcy and Mr Bingley,' Sarah said.

Blue coat, black horse: that was Mr Bingley. The great tall fellow in the green was Mr Darcy again. They clipped past the orchard, in profile and oblivious to the housemaids: Sarah felt herself fade. She could see the leaves and branches through her hand; the sun shone straight through her skin.

They had had early rumours of Mr Bingley's return to Netherfield. Mrs Philips had had the news off Mrs Nicholls, and had relayed it in short order to Mrs Bennet. Sarah and Polly were then detailed to keep an eye out for the Bingley carriage, since it was vital that Mrs Bennet have the earliest information of its arrival. Sarah had bobbed and said, 'Yes, ma'am,' but her thoughts had been scattered like seed – Mrs B. would surely miss her footman now, and as her every slightest thought found its way into speech, Sarah expected her mistress to bewail the inconvenience of the situation loudly and at length. But Mrs Bennet just wafted Sarah away, to go about her business, and did not say a word about James. That they had ever had a footman here at Longbourn, was, it seemed, already quite forgot.

'Was it my fault?' Polly asked, calling up from the base of the ladder.

'What?'

'Was it my fault that James went when he did? Was it to do with Mr Wickham liking me and giving me pennies, and all that? Should I not have took them? Was it because he promised me sweets?'

Sarah scrambled down the ladder, and, at its foot, wrapped her arms around the girl's thin body. The basket of greengages swung precariously on Polly's arm; the girl laid her head on Sarah's shoulder, and sobbed.

'It is my fault. I know it is. He said we must steer clear of the officers, but—'

Sarah's anger – at James, at Polly, at Wickham and Elizabeth and Lydia and Colonel Forster, at Longbourn and Fate and the whole world in general – melted away in the face of the child's misery. Sarah rubbed her back, and soothed her.

'It was not your fault, my sweetness. Don't believe that even for a moment.'

Ptolemy Bingley arrived on Tuesday, when the gentlemen came to dine at Longbourn. He stayed smoking in the yard, throwing dice with his companions, whilst the party dined upstairs. It had not even occurred to Sarah that he might still be in service with the family.

With all the business of a large party to dinner – sundry neighbours had to be invited for form's sake, along with the desired gentlemen, and there was much roasting of venison and simmering of soup and broiling of partridges – there was no possibility of absenting herself, as Mrs Hill had instructed her to, half a lifetime ago. But there was also no cause to speak with Ptolemy that afternoon, and, for that, Sarah was grateful.

But from time to time Ptolemy must have glanced at her; Sarah kept catching the tail of his gaze as he looked away; he was undeniably beautiful. She felt ashamed of herself, of the callow selfishness of her behaviour towards him. And then she thought of James standing there, on the drovers' road that cold night, and her cheeks grew hot and she fell still. She stroked her lips with a thumbnail in recollection of his kiss.

The Bingley carriage was ordered soon after dinner, while Sarah was still clearing the dishes from the dining room. She made no haste to complete the task; indeed she lingered over it rather longer than necessary, so that they all might get clean away.

After four days' worth of dinners and shooting and teas and suppers, Jane was engaged to be married. The noise her mother made at the news was correspondent to the relief she felt. But, of course, Mrs Hill told herself, such joy and noise were not unreasonable, because now Mrs Bennet knew her baby girl was safe. Other good things could only follow this.

Mrs Hill was as pleased for them all as she could be. She congratulated her mistress, and kissed Jane, and wished her all the luck in the world.

'She doesn't need luck! She will have five thousand pounds a year!'

'Well,' said Mrs Hill, 'a bit of luck will do her no harm.'

Though really Jane had only got what she deserved. She was a good and pretty girl, and so deserving of good and pretty things. As everybody knew, Mrs Hill thought as she dusted off the wine glasses for a toast, the girls who did not get good and pretty things were them-selves somehow deficient, either in their goodness or their prettiness.

The engagement was made three days before Michaelmas; Ptolemy Bingley was frequently at Longbourn. He accompanied his master whenever he drove there in the carriage, or he came on foot to deliver notes, and then he lingered downstairs, awaiting a reply. He was like a hawk in the autumn air: hanging still, distanced, but his interest fixed – and as with a hawk, this stillness was achieved only with constant effort and adjustment to the changing currents.

The inevitable moment came, when they two were alone, and she could not leave the kitchen before he stopped her with a look, a word.

'You came to London, I think.'

'Oh, I—' He must have heard about Jane's stay there.

'But you did not look me up.'

'I never had the chance—'

'I am sorry for it.'

She looked down at her boots, dragged a toe across the flags.

'I think you would look the part, you know, in London,' he said. 'Dressed up to the nines, out strolling of a Sunday, in the Park.'

'I do not, I would not know, anything about that, Mr Bingley.'

She turned away. Mrs Hill came in, and went over to examine the soup, doing her best to look as though she had not noticed anything. Sarah took this chance to slip out to the stables, where she picked up the currycomb, and rubbed down the horses for a while. The farmhands did not bother with it, not the way that James had.

On Michaelmas Day, Mr Bennet doled out the servants' wages in the library with all the usual ceremony. Sitting at his old black-oak desk, he recorded each payment in his ledger, and let each servant, both domestic and agricultural, make their mark, and those that could sign, sign. Sarah, coins clamped in her palm, carefully printed out her name.

'We find ourselves sadly diminished this quarter,' her master observed.

'Indeed so, sir.'

'What is life but constant change? Did not Heraclitus say—' He paused, and thought better of it. 'Well. Well. You are a good girl, Sarah; thank you for all your hard work.'

'Thank you, Mr Bennet, sir.'

She bobbed a curtsey, and took her money up to her room, and put it away in her wooden box, along with the previous quarter's pay. If she could find it, and it was writ in English, she would borrow Heraclitus from the library, at the next opportunity, since Mr Bennet had not told her what he had said. She locked the box, and shoved it back under her bed, and then got up and went to her window. The moon was up, a pale wafer in the daytime sky. It was more than a year now since James had first come to Longbourn, and four months since he had left. How long could she wait without a scrap, a crumb?

The household was thrown into panic that Saturday morning by the arrival of a chaise and four, which had travelled fast: the horses were clearly post. On Mrs Hill's answering the front door, the passenger, a lady, demanded to know where the family were gathered, then swept past her without waiting to be announced. Stunned, Mrs Hill ran back to the kitchen to boil water for tea, since some courtesy must be shown, however discourteous the visitor.

It was the old lady from Kent, Sarah was able to explain, back in the kitchen, having heard the description of the traveller. It was Mr Collins's patroness, Lady Catherine de Bourgh, who peered at your sewing and told you what you were doing wrong.

Sarah, crossing the yard a little later with the pig-bucket, saw Elizabeth passing the side of the house in Lady Catherine's wake. They disappeared into the little wilderness. Sarah shifted the bucket from her right hand to her left, ran her sore palm down her apron, and then carried on towards the sty, where she would stay and watch the piglets play and scratch the sow's ears, till she heard the chaise crunch away down the gravel, and could be sure that Lady Catherine had left.

And this was what money could do – it was a sort of magic. It turned thoughts into things, desire into effect: Lady Catherine had, for whatever reason, wanted to come here, and so she had just rung a bell, and spoken some words, and everything flowed from this. How many quarters' pay would Sarah have to save, before she could turn any of her desire into anything at all?

Mrs Hill watched Sarah drag herself and her empty bucket back across the yard, and felt for her. Work was not a cure; it never had been: it simply grew a skin on despair, and crusted over it. And the thing was, Sarah was still so very young, younger than even Mrs Hill had been when she had lost her happiness. Sarah had, God willing, a good many years left yet to haul herself broken-winded through.

Something must be found for Sarah; something must be done.

Mrs B.'s nightgown was warming at the dressing-room fire, and in the adjoining bedchamber, Mrs Hill had already turned back the bed and slipped in the warming-pan. Mrs B. held up her arms for assistance with buttons and laces. She had had a few celebratory glasses of claret. It made her calmer and more self-contained than usual.

Then there was a soft knock on the door, and Elizabeth slipped into the close little room. Mrs Hill bobbed her curtsey and moved out into the bedchamber, leaving mother – only a little unbuttoned at the back – and daughter to their confidences.

The mistress at first struggled to comprehend what Elizabeth was saying, but Mrs Hill, quietly tidying the bedchamber, understood perfectly. Elizabeth had made a spectacular deal, and the household was to contract still further. With three girls married, and the elder two becoming, on their marriages, suitable chaperones for unmarried sisters, the younger pair would soon hardly be at home at all. The Longbourn household was shrinking apace.

She and Mr Hill were safe there, she knew: it was part of her own deal. The two of them could get old, and die there, and with no fear of being forced to go upon the parish. But the girls: they would not be kept on at Longbourn, not both of them, not when they were no longer needed.

'To Mr Darcy?' Sarah asked, on being told the news.

Mrs Hill had steered her into the scullery. 'Yes.'

'Right. And is she happy?'

'Her mother says, a house in town, and a house in the country, and everything that is good. Carriages and the Lord knows what. Jane's match, she says, is nothing to it.'

'But is she happy?'

'I think so. She says so.'

Sarah nodded. 'Well, then. Good for her.'

Sarah went back to her work, her jaw tight. She would have been content with so little. She would have been content with just his company.

When Ptolemy Bingley next appeared in the kitchen, one morning before breakfast, and cast his beautiful eyes around, and found the room lacked Sarah, and therefore also lacked interest, Mrs Hill was minded for the first time to overlook the misfortune of his breeding, since he could not help it, and look on him with some measure of compassion. She would enquire a little deeper into his prospects and his intentions. It could do no harm. It made sense to consider every possibility. One must – though the word grated even in her thoughts – be practical.

She had not expected him to open up to her the way he did, like a daisy in the sun.

'You have been almost a parent to her, I see that. You wish to protect her, which is admirable. I had myself hoped to win your good opinion.'

He had missed Sarah more than he had thought possible, he confessed. London and its amusements had afforded him but little pleasure, after that first brief stay at Netherfield. His thoughts were always returning here, to Hertfordshire, and to Sarah. Sweet, unworldly Sarah. There was not a girl like her to be found in all of London town.

He really had not expected it. It had not been part of his plan.

Mrs Hill made him tea, and poured him a cup, and gave him milk and sugar too. He sipped his drink, and disclosed to Mrs Hill the depths of his attachment, the heights of his hopes, the scope of his plans, and the steep trajectory that a woman, his wife, could expect to climb with him.

Because he would not be a footman for ever, oh no indeed.

Mrs Hill watched him carefully. His manners were those of a gentleman: service at that level rubbed the rough edges off a fellow. She had no doubt that he would get on in the world. So in purely practical terms, in terms of security, he would be an excellent match for Sarah. With his charm and her industry, the little enterprise he proposed must thrive; they would put money aside; they would, by dint of effort and economy, become persons of substance, and have their names written up over the shop door: *Mr and Mrs Bingley, Props.* How fine that would be. They would themselves keep servants. It would be a match, in its own way, almost as brilliant as Elizabeth's, in the degree to which Sarah would be raised up by it.

Mrs Hill offered this all up to Sarah over breakfast later, like it was a present.

'He is quite, quite smitten.'

Polly slowed in the buttering of a muffin, looked from the housekeeper to the housemaid and back again.

Mr Hill's chewing ceased. He swallowed. 'Shop?' he asked.

'He has it all arranged by now, I suppose,' Sarah said.

'That boy has a shop?' asked Mr Hill again.

'Not yet. But he will have. He told you already, I take it, Sarah?'

'When he was last here. Before you forbad me seeing him.'

'He has his eye on a particular spot,' Mrs Hill said, ignoring the latter remark.

'I forget where.'

'Spitalfields.'

Polly scraped at the butter with her knife, pulled a face. 'Spittle!'

'Spital. As in hospital. Not as in slobber.'

'Oh.'

'He has money saved—' Mrs Hill continued.

'Does he now?' Mr Hill spoke around a new mouthful.

'Twelve pounds!' She leaned back from the table and folded her arms, and stared at Sarah, as though this clinched it. 'Twelve pounds, three shillings and sixpence, to be exact.'

'Twelve pounds, three shillings and sixpence?'

'It will be more than that, come Lady Day; that's when he plans to leave the Bingleys' service and start out on his own.'

Mr Hill whistled, spraying moist crumbs.

Polly, watching one intent face and then another, helped herself discreetly to a second muffin.

'He is a man of ambition,' said Mrs Hill. 'He is a man who knows what he wants. He is a man who has twelve pounds, three shillings and sixpence, and he wants you, Sarah, dear.'

Mrs Hill reached across the table, between the teacups and the plates, and took Sarah's hand. 'You must know that it would be such a comfort, to see you well settled, and safe in your own establishment. Whatever else we may have hoped for once. And, Sarah, consider this: think what it would be like to have your own home, and not to be ordered about, or be dependent on anyone's goodwill.'

'Except my husband's.'

'Yes, of course, except your husband's.'

The library bell rang. They all flinched, then looked round at it, jangling there on its spring. Mr Hill wiped his mouth and scraped back his chair. Mrs Hill also started up, but he held up a hand to still her.

'You stay there, Mrs Hill. Rest yourself a little longer.'

He made his tired old way out of the kitchen, and the door swung closed behind him. Unnoticed, Polly drew the greengage jam towards her. Mrs Hill turned back to Sarah.

'My dear. Consider it, at least. It would be a – practical – solution to all this.'

Practical. There it was again, that gritty word; it made Mrs Hill's mouth feel unclean.

Polly dug the spoon deep into the jar, and lifted out a dripping heap of translucent green-gold preserve. She let it fall onto the upturned face of her muffin, spread it around with the back of the spoon, then popped the spoon into her mouth to clean it.

Sarah folded her arms, leaning back, a mirror of Mrs Hill.

'Would you, Mrs Hill?' she asked. 'In my place? Would you marry him, knowing what you know now, having lived as you have lived?'

Mrs Hill hesitated a moment, then lips pressed together, she nodded.

'No—'

'Yes. I would.'

'No.' Sarah faltered. 'But – what about—'

'Love?' Mrs Hill looked at the girl's sore-looking, determined face. She lied: 'You'd be surprised how little it matters in the end.'

'You can't mean that.'

'He loves you. Isn't that enough? He would be good to you. He is a good man.'

'But he is not James.'

Mrs Hill closed her eyes, and let a breath go, and could argue no longer. Her boy James, there and gone, lost and found and lost again: a treasure far too precious for her to keep. The hopes that Ptolemy's confidences had engendered in her now fell clean away.

'They'll let one of you go,' Mrs Hill said. 'You know that, don't you? We can't go on like this for ever. There soon won't be work enough for all of us.'

Polly bit into her over-laden muffin, looking from one to the other. She wedged her mouthful into her cheek. 'Is that true?'

Sarah glanced at her. 'You have jam by the corner of your mouth.'

Polly wiped at her lips ineffectually, swallowed. 'You stay, then. You wait for James here. I can go and work for the Wickhams.'

'No, sweetie, you can't.'

'It'll be all right.'

'No it won't.'

They sat there, in silence, each alone.

Chapter XVII

. . . he had yet to learn to be laught at, and it was rather too early to begin.

PACKAGES NOW ARRIVED daily for Jane and Elizabeth. It fell to Polly and Sarah to collect them from the post office – they went together when they could. These were quiet, companionable walks, through mist on the low fields and drifting autumn leaves.

Many of these parcels contained fine fabrics for the young brides' trousseaux – silks and muslins and velvets, ordered by their mother from the London warehouses. Two new bonnets came in smart band-boxes from Mrs Gardiner, who had been charged with their commission at a London milliner. One small square box, however, addressed to Miss Elizabeth, came straight from Nottingham. The paper was peeled apart, the pasteboard lid lifted with eager fingers; a beautiful silk-lace bonnet veil, with a pattern of falling leaves, and a delicately scalloped edge, lay inside.

'From Mr Darcy,' Elizabeth said.

This must be tried: immediately was not too soon. The tissue-paper fell away. Laying it out on the bed, Sarah fastened the drawstrings around the crown of the bonnet, and settled the lace over the peak.

'It's quite heavy,' Sarah said, lifting the bonnet and veil together, the drift of lace lying over an arm.

'The best stuff always is.'

Sarah set the bonnet on Elizabeth's head, and let the veil fall; she bent to arrange its folds. Elizabeth's neck stiffened.

'It's beautiful.'

'Mr Darcy is very generous,' said Elizabeth.

'He is.'

To Sarah, Elizabeth seemed a world away, and icy cold, with the veil hanging over her face. Elizabeth must have felt something of this too, seeing her reflection in the mirror – because she reached up and started to fumble the veil away. Then she paused, realizing the risk to the lace.

'Would you do that for me? Take it off, please.' Elizabeth folded her hands in her lap to keep them still. 'I don't want it spoilt.'

'Of course.'

The lace draped over one arm, Sarah lifted off the bonnet while Elizabeth sat stone still.

'What do you think it will be like, Sarah, to be married?'

Sarah's eyes met Elizabeth's in the glass. She could see her own reflection, standing behind the young mistress, a raw hand resting on a delicate shoulder, the other holding the lace and bonnet; her own mousy dress, her hair in need of a wash and scraped back under a work-cap.

'I dare say it shall be very pleasant indeed.'

Elizabeth nodded, her silky curls slipping up and down the nape of her neck.

People said that Mr Darcy was marrying down, but Sarah could not see it that way at all. It all seemed to work out neatly, like the columns in a well-kept ledger: his wealth, property and standing were equal to, and offered in straightforward payment for, her loveliness. When you considered it like that, he did not stoop in marrying her at all. And when you considered it like that, it was no wonder to Sarah that she had nobody.

'I can see little glimpses of it,' Elizabeth said. 'I mean, marriage; me being married and living there at Pemberley; Christmas, I can imagine that, and dear Jane and Mr Bingley visiting in the spring perhaps. And I can see me, seated at the pianoforte with his sister.'

'It does sound pleasant.'

'But what I can't see, what I have no idea at all of, is what it will be like day to day, day after day, just him and me. I am not certain of it – I find I am a little . . . nervous.'

Elizabeth's soft fingertips rested on Sarah's red hand.

'I want you to come with me.'

'What, miss?'

'To Pemberley. I want you to come too. You will, won't you?'

'I don't know, I—'

Elizabeth spoke hurriedly: 'You see, I shall want something from home about me. It would be such a comfort. Mr Darcy sees no harm in it, and Mama says that once Jane and I are married, she will not need you here any more.'

Sarah set the bonnet down on the bed and untied the drawstrings, loosening the fine creases in the lace. Everything had, it seemed, already been decided.

'The work would be light compared with what you are used to here; Pemberley is already well equipped with servants. You will not have to lug buckets or light fires. You will not have to mend stockings there. At least, not for the whole household. Just your own, perhaps, and I suppose mine.'

Sarah lifted the veil away, folded it, and laid it back in its box.

'You are afraid that you will miss your friends, of course you are, this is what you are used to. But at Pemberley, Mrs Reynolds, the house-keeper, she would like you; she would be kind to you when she sees how proper and good and well trained you are. And you would see a little more of the world, and you know you have always wanted to do that.'

The veil lay square in the box, like a sheaf of unwritten paper. Sarah shut the lid on it.

'So, is it settled? Are we agreed?'

Sarah turned back to the dressing table. Her mistress, expectant, watched her in the mirror. Sarah nodded.

'Oh, I am happy to know it. You will like it there, I am certain that you will.'

Sarah touched Elizabeth's curls back into order. Her mistress had brightened, but now faded again, and was thoughtful. Perhaps it was not an easy thing, to be so entirely happy. Perhaps it was actually quite a fearful state to live in – the knowledge that one had achieved a complete success.

There were tears in the kitchen when she told them. Even Mr Hill had to clear his throat and turn away and make himself busy, picking at the dripped wax on a candlestick. Just because they had seen this coming down the road at them – this dissolution – did not mean that any of them were really prepared for its arrival.

'If you hear anything,' Sarah said. 'If you ever get word of him – if he returns—'

'I will write to you that same moment.'

'Polly, too – take care of her. Make sure she has some time to study. And to play with the village children.'

Mrs Hill nodded, swallowed down the lump in her throat.

'She is very young,' Sarah said.

'I know.'

'And a proper little cuckoo.'

'Hey!'

She picked Polly up, squeezed her, pressed her face into her neck. 'You are so gorgeous that I want to bite you.'

'Don't,' said Polly, and wiped her eyes with the side of her hand. 'Write to me, though, from Pemberley. I have got quite good at deciphering, you know.'

Chapter XVIII

To Pemberley, therefore, they were to go.

THE STAGECOACH DEPOSITED Sarah, along with Elizabeth's trunks and portmanteaux, at the inn in Lambton, and then bundled on its way. She could see a few glowing windows, a church spire against the stars, the open dark of the green – then she was hailed by an old, angle-faced man carrying a candle-lamp. He gestured to a wagon, which the inn servants were loading with Mrs Darcy's things. She climbed up, and waited for him there, while he shook and tugged the canvas covering into place and lashed it down.

When he joined her, he talked incomprehensibly, and smelt of malt and horse, and they were out again in the wide dark, the wheels rumbling along the well-made roads. After a while, he fell silent, and that was a relief; Sarah had nodded, smiled, but had no idea what she had been agreeing with all this time. A while later – it was hard to gauge the passing of time, after so long on the road – there was a cross-roads, and he slowed the wagon, and they turned. The lane brought them into woodland; they turned again, this time at a gate lodge that loomed pale in the night. The driver exchanged a few words with the lodge-keeper who swung open the gates for them. Sarah could make neither head nor tail of what they said.

The lamp swung from its stand, illuminating the wagoner's sharp features and the weave of the blanket over Sarah's lap, and the rumps and tails of the two drays, but little of the world beyond. The pain had

337

become familiar by now; she felt that she accepted it; the long drive up to Derbyshire had given her time to become accustomed to the completeness of her loss. Everything that she had ever known, everyone she loved, every fond association that she had formed had been stripped entirely away, and all that was left was the raw and tender pith of herself. It had, of course, been her heartfelt wish for as long as she could remember, that she would see something of the world beyond Longbourn; she should, she thought, have been more precise in her wishing. She should have wished for happiness in which to see it.

The wagon had been ascending for a half-mile or so through the woods, and Sarah's head was nodding, drooping to her chest, when the bony elbow of the wagoner jolted her alert. He jutted his chin, indicating where she should look. She looked.

They were out of the woods, and there was a wide stretch of sky, and the moon bald and white and cold above. The house stood on rising ground at the far side of the valley, backed by a ridge of wooded hills. The façade was skimmed silver with moonlight; its reflection glimmered in a spreading pool at its foot. Pemberley. It was beautiful, and vast, and strange.

The wagon trundled on, but Sarah's gaze was stuck; she twisted round in her seat to keep the house in sight. It was so extraordinary: how did it all start, property and wealth and beauty like that? Who staked out a fence, strung out lines and said, This is my land and nobody else's; these fields are mine, these woods are mine; this water, reflecting the white moon, is mine; and all the fish that swim in the water are mine; and all the birds that fly and roost in the woods are mine; and the very air is mine while it moves over my land; and all of this will be mine, and after I am gone, it will be my son's; and it will never leave our hands, not while there are still sons left to inherit it. Because there was, there *must* have been a time before, when the fish swam and the fowl flew and were not anybody's at all, and the world was young, when Adam and Eve staggered out of Eden all baffled and ashamed.

And then the view was gone, the wagon turning into deep shadow, and the moonlight was cut off and they were confined to the narrow circle of the lamp, and a long cavern of trees, and the sudden flap and flurry of a startled bird. From the view-point she had seen the road twist up towards a bridge and the grand front door; they were not following that road: she looked to the wagoner, the haze of stubble on his cheek and the shadowed eyes.

'Why do we go this way?'

He cleared his throat, and spoke carefully: 'Servants' and suppliers' way.'

She huddled deeper into her old pelisse. She had been three long days on the road, but all this time the idea of arrival had seemed to retreat as she approached it. She wished the journey over, but she did not want to arrive.

They crossed the stream on a narrow rumbling wooden bridge, just wide enough for the wagon; there was another brief glimpse of the house, in three-quarters profile, and the water spreading out into a mirror. Then they were back in the woods, and the track wheeled round, and they approached the working part of the house.

The wagon rolled into a courtyard. A stable lad came up to the horses, and a pair of liveried footmen approached the wagon, carrying lanterns. Inside, figures darted past the narrow barred windows like shuttles through a loom. There was a burst of noise as someone came outside; the door fell shut and it was cut abruptly off. One of the footmen reached up a gloved hand to her. She took hold of it and, stiff from her journey, climbed down from her seat.

The wagoner slung her box down onto the cobbles; the footmen unloaded Elizabeth's luggage. Sarah moved out of the way, behind the growing bulk of boxes and trunks. She pressed her eyes with the heels of her hands, her fingers cold against her forehead. What to do? Where to go? The whole world was wide and dark and empty, and no corner of it was hers.

A woman bustled over; Sarah tugged her sleeves down, straightened herself, and tried a smile.

The housekeeper was fifty perhaps, and had a lawn cap and a nice clean collar. She carried a lantern. She spoke first to the footmen, about the destination of the trunks. She then asked the wagoner to go in and partake of some refreshment, and offered him a bed for the night in the manservants' quarters, since otherwise he faced a long cold road back to town tonight. The stable lad had unhitched the drays, and now led them off for fodder and rest. Every act, every instruction, seemed to signal that this was an expansive, accommodating place; that its inhabitants were hospitable, and mindful of the responsibilities of high rank.

Sarah stood, her one box at her feet, while all around her was returned to order and quiet: the luggage was spirited inside, the horses disappeared into the stables, doors were shut, and there was only the muffled hum of the kitchen, as work continued inside. Only then, when all was calm, did the housekeeper turn her attention to Sarah.

'Is that you there? The mistress's maid?'

'Yes, ma'am.'

'I'm Mrs Reynolds, I'm the housekeeper here.'

Sarah curtseyed.

'Well, come on, then,' she said. 'Let's get you settled in.'

Sarah crouched to lift her box.

'I would have had that carried up for you. You should have said.'

'Sorry.'

She followed Mrs Reynolds and her candle through the flagged, echoing entrance and down a hall, lugging all her possessions with her. Fatigued, it was a struggle just to keep up with the housekeeper's quick tread, and to pay attention to all that she was being told.

Mrs Reynolds kept naming rooms as they passed. The boot room. The gun room. The still room, the pantry, the butler's pantry, the cheese store. Then she pushed a door, and they stepped into a wall of heat. The kitchen; a flurry of activity, a man cook barking orders, kitchen maids and boys jumping to comply, chopping and stirring and basting and sweating.

The housekeeper negotiated all this with calm indifference, skirting patches of activity and nodding to the cook, and smiling at a kitchen maid who caught her eye. Sarah, following in her wake, was jostled out of the way and chivvied along, and felt her colour rise.

They were skimming along a corridor; candles burnt in sconces at intervals along the walls. Sarah swam through a patch of candlelight, dropped into a pool of darkness, and then back out again into the light, again and again, following the flickering burn of Mrs Reynolds's candle. She was mesmerized by the housekeeper's swishing skirts, the tap of her shoes on the stone flags, and the stream of information flowing from her about the workings and the hierarchies and the layout of the household. She must memorize her way, so that she might find it again, but there was nothing to fix on – scrolling walls, the flares of candlelight and plunging darkness, and all so fast – it blurred and blotted.

They turned up a flight of bare stone stairs, and swept along lime-washed corridors, and up more stairs, wooden now, climbing up and up, her box heavy under her arm, her skirts gathered in a hand, her head light. They came out into a narrow landing and an attic hallway; there was a strip of matting on the floor, and a row of little wooden doors, endlessly repeating down the length of the hallway, till all was lost in dimness.

'This way.'

The servants' attics stretched – Mrs Reynolds informed her, as door after door slipped past them in the candle's glow – the whole length of the wing. Then the housekeeper stopped suddenly, bringing Sarah up short; they stood outside one of the doors. It was just the same as every other they had passed.

Mrs Reynolds twisted the little doorknob, and pushed. 'Here we are.'

Sarah followed her in. Narrow wooden beds stood on either side of the room; there was a worn rag-rug on the floor between them; there was space for little else, beyond a deal washstand at the end of the room, beneath the sloping window, with a candlestick and an earthenware bowl-and-ewer. A stranger's locked box was tucked under the right-hand bed.

'There is water for you to wash. And there, that's what you wear.'

She gestured to a neat pile of black flannel and white linen on the left-hand counterpane.

'You may need to make adjustments to the garments; feel free to do so in your own time. There is a small sewing box under the washstand you may use. But I think it will fit you well enough for now. I should say you are much the same size as Miss Darcy's maid.'

Sarah set her box down on the left-hand bed, crumpling the counterpane. Mrs Reynolds lifted the candle from the washstand, lit it from her own, and set it back.

'You'll share with Anne, that's Miss Darcy's maid; she has been doing for Mrs Darcy till you got here, she can instruct you in the differences of the work here at Pemberley. And if you come down to my rooms once you are washed and changed, I will give you supper, and then show you the way to Mrs Darcy's dressing room. Anne will have started the unpacking by then; you can assist her.'

'Thank you, ma'am.'

'I think you will do very well here,' she said. 'You seem a decent, good sort of a girl.'

'Thank you, Mrs Reynolds.'

The housekeeper seemed to be about to go, but then she paused.

'We were, as you might imagine, anxious as to how you would turn out. Not knowing anything about you, but knowing the household that you come from. Longbourn is a small sort of a place, and the standards there may be very different. But I think we shall find you quite acceptable.'

Then she left, taking her candle with her.

There were hours still to be got through. Hours and hours and hours.

Sarah sat down, took off her bonnet and laid it down on the counterpane. She had a bed to herself now. She undid her pelisse and shrugged it off, looked down at her familiar old boots on the strange rug. A rug made by unknown hands, out of rags she didn't recognize: back at Longbourn she would have recalled an old spencer, coat or blanket that had been shredded up to make it.

But there was no point in dwelling on any of that now.

She heaved herself up, and soaked a washcloth, and wrung it out, and scrubbed her neck and face and washed behind her ears and then cleaned her nails. When she was clean and dry, she fished her key out of the pocket hanging inside her skirt, and unlocked her box. She got out her best cap, which Mrs Hill had trimmed for her with a new ribbon, and put it on, and tucked all her hair away into it. She put on the maid's uniform, which hung loose around her waist and arms and bosom. She tucked in a kerchief. She wished that she could change her shoes, because her feet ached, and the boots were clumsy old things, but there was no help for that. She lifted her candle, and closing the door behind her, counted the doors till she reached the top of the stairs, so that she might find her way back there again.

Sarah really did try to be happy at Pemberley. As she had been promised, the nature of the work was light in comparison with what she had been used to at Longbourn. At Pemberley, there was an army to cart water and wood and coals, to cook and scrub and polish; she never saw a pig-bucket, nor a pig, from one week to the next, though of course there must have been such things, even at Pemberley. She was left only with the care of Mrs Darcy's person, its clothing and adornment. But this had become, all of a sudden, a labour of Hercules.

Elizabeth, being naturally very lovely indeed, had hitherto possessed only a healthy degree of interest in her appearance; a ball was worth dressing for, but she had never concerned herself particularly with her day-to-day toilette, and had been quite prepared to go muddy-hemmed, rosy-cheeked and shiny-nosed into the family breakfast, and could take tea with the neighbours quite happily in a faded outgrown gown of her sister's. But now, her time at the dressing table took on all the solemnity and self-scrutiny of prayer.

'Will I do?'

'You will do very well.'

'Do you really think so?'

Sarah was threading a ribbon through Elizabeth's curls, in preparation for the young lady's descent to breakfast. 'Of course. You will very much more than do. You look lovely.'

Elizabeth did not even smile. 'You must understand that I am anxious to be quite as he would wish me.'

'I'm sure you are.'

'You do not understand, Sarah. You really do not understand a thing at all.'

That afternoon, Sarah returned to Mrs Darcy's closet to dress her hair again before dinner. She found Anne was already there, armed with fragrant pomade and pearls; Sarah was not required. Miss Darcy's maid did, of course, have a better understanding of the current fashions, having spent time at Bath, and London, and Ramsgate, in the course of her employment.

Pemberley was beautiful, no doubt of that. With Christmas approaching, the grounds and trees were rimed with frost and, if you could go out walking in them, and collect holly for the mantelpieces and ivy to twine around the picture-frames and mistletoe to hang from the chandeliers, they must seem very lovely indeed. But what was that to Sarah, confined to Mrs Darcy's closet with her sewing? She could not stir abroad. Once Mrs Darcy was dressed for the morning, and had sat down for Anne to do her hair, Sarah was dismissed, and did not see another soul until dinnertime.

It became apparent almost immediately that she was not to be trusted with anything beyond the simplest work. Fabrics arrived in parcels; Sarah unfurled the cloth and checked it over for flaws, and inhaled the scents of London shops – exotic, spicy, faintly unclean – before folding them and leaving them aside to be taken to the mantuamaker's in town; she did not have dealings with them again until she hung the finished dresses up in the closet and was done. She was kept at mending, and the making of underthings. She worked with fine white lawn and silk, which she would once have thought a pleasure, but either it was tiny and fiddly, hard on the fingertips and eyes, or it was simply dull: she stitched on ribbon and lace; she re-sewed fallen hems; she joined up the slipped seams of shifts and petticoats. It was novice-work, and it gave her little satisfaction. She would surface to find herself gazing out of the window, with its view out across the side lawns, towards the countryside beyond. Sewing abandoned in her lap, she would stare across the frosted park, to the wooded hills, and the wide expanse of sky.

Her hands grew softer with the softer work. The hours languished. The days ticked by.

More parcels arrived from London, little, lightweight parcels: darned stockings and mended shifts were crumpled to the back of a drawer.

Her body grew soft too: she had never eaten so well in all her life. Eggs at breakfast, meat or fish at dinner, something sweet and comforting at suppertime. Mrs Hill had been a good plain cook, but this was a different order of a thing, a whole course served in the great cavern of the servants' dining hall, where she ate carefully and without speaking and did not know where to look, and could make out little of her fellow servants' thick Derbyshire accents. Tea was brought up to her by a housemaid, with a tray of clinking servants' china and a filthy look, because no one wanted to play servant to the servantry. Sarah, conscious of this, blushed when the maid clattered the tray down in front of her, and said, 'Thank you so much, Lucy,' and then was not sure that the girl was called Lucy after all.

But there was some consolation to be found, in having her own little china pot of hot tea, and her own jug of milk, and there was even a little bowl with three lumps of sugar in it. She slipped a couple into her pocket, and later sent them off to Polly, carefully wrapped in tissue-paper, in her next letter.

The Gardiners came to stay at Christmas. Sarah sat by the window of Mrs Darcy's dressing room, and sewed, listening to the distant sounds of the family gathered in the grand parlour below. She could hear voices, and the pianoforte, and the laughter of the Gardiner children as they spun and raced around the expansive apartments.

Beyond the confines of Mrs Darcy's closet, the house stretched open and accommodating: those spacious rooms, their comfortable furnishings, their warmth and the diversions they contained, of art and music and conversation and books. And beyond its walls unfurled the ordered grounds, the well-managed park, the woods and farms, all full of purpose and comfort and prosperity, and all she could do was be here, in this seat, at this window, stitching a ribbon back onto a petticoat that, for all that Sarah knew, might never be worn again.

If she just put her sewing aside, and went out into the corridor, and opened a few doors and looked inside; if she wandered around some of the unused rooms downstairs, examining miniatures and marbles; if she stepped out through the French windows and out into the air, and followed the gravel walks, dawdling along between the frosted box hedges, and then through the shrubbery; if she strolled out across the lawns to the riverbank to gaze at a slothful trout in a patch of winter sun, and then slipped past the gate out into the woodlands, and climbed the paths worn into the hills beyond – how long could she last, how far could she get, how much could she *be* in this place, before she was stopped and sent back to this seat here, this little corner?

This was hers: a view of bare elms, a heap of light sewing, a place to sit, a tray set out with things for her tea.

It was not bad. It was far better than could be expected. But it was not enough.

CHAPTER XIX

'. . . you must be very happy.'

IT WAS A shock – an actual bodily shock like a fall or a stumble, or walking into the edge of a table – to see Ptolemy Bingley roll into the park, that bright morning in March, the day before Lady Day.

Sarah's needle dropped from her grip, swung a moment on its thread, then slipped and hit the floor. She stood up. The Bingley carriage wheeled down the drive; Sarah's breath misted and then faded from the windowpane. There was no mistaking him, even at such a distance. Not his colour, but his bearing, his stature marked him out amongst the other men. She saw, too, how the daffodils were dragged sideways by the wind, and the bare branches tore at the sky, and the clouds bundled up and were teased apart above. The year had turned, and she had not noticed its turning.

Behind her, in the room, the clock struck the half-hour.

'Are they here?'

Sarah glanced round. Mrs Darcy had turned in her seat at the dressing table.

'Believe so, ma'am.'

Her mistress got up and came over to the window. Sarah moved aside to make space. Together, they watched the carriage approach. Sarah had known that the Bingleys were coming – this was a long-anticipated visit – but in her mind's eye Ptolemy had been weighing out tobacco in his gleaming shop in Spitalfields; she had even conjured

347

up a pretty, plump young wife for him: she had assumed he would be happy, but had thought of him as quite, quite gone.

'My India shawl, Sarah, if you please.'

Sarah moved away from the window, slid open a drawer. 'Which one, ma'am?'

'One of the new ones.'

Sarah lifted out a cream cashmere shawl, its ends worked with twining leaves and flowers; her thoughts were quick. The Bingleys' visit was to be of a fortnight's duration: two weeks of anxious dinners in the servants' hall, and nervousness at corners, and in corridors. Ptolemy would avoid her too – it would no doubt be uncomfortable for both of them, but then it would be over. At least, it would be over for now, but who knew what would follow after, down all the years to come?

'I am glad that Jane is come to see me.'

Sarah smoothed the cashmere over Mrs Darcy's shoulders. There was a woman far away who'd worked this cloth, and, stretching, had gone outside into the warm air, and wandered amongst leaves and flowers just like these, under trees that were alive with birds.

Elizabeth turned from the window; she was bright now. 'Well, come along then.'

'Madam?'

'Come downstairs, make haste. You will wish to welcome Jane.'

When Mrs Bingley spotted Sarah, standing in line with the other servants in the blustering March wind, she greeted her warmly, and kissed her cheek, and said she hoped that she was happy, then continued on up the steps, and went into the house, her arm linked through her husband's, and her sister's arm hooked through the other, and did not wait to hear Sarah's reply.

Sarah gathered up the small possessions abandoned in the coach – the gloves and reticules and books – and carried them indoors; as she climbed the steps she watched Ptolemy from the corner of her eye. He was busying himself with the luggage, and conversing only with his fellow footmen, and she did not once catch him looking over towards her. She had no idea if he expected to find her here. It was going to be awkward until she spoke to him, but then it could hardly be otherwise afterwards.

In the event, it was all over and done with more swiftly than she could have hoped. Sarah spoke to Ptolemy that same evening – for they dined fashionably late at Pemberley; it was nearly six o'clock before the family sat down, it was only once they were served that the servants ate – when she found herself seated beside him at dinner in the servants' hall. She was fiercely conscious that she was being observed by Mrs Reynolds, who was a stickler for proper conduct, and by Anne, who was always looking for intrigues and passions, and by Lucy (if that was indeed her name), who always seemed to be looking for trouble, and by a stable boy, who had taken to turning up whenever Sarah happened to be downstairs in that part of the house, and smiling, and talking to her, while she blushed and failed to understand his thick accent, and he hers.

When she had finally mustered the courage to enter the servants' hall, Ptolemy was just drawing out a chair to seat himself beside one of the prettier maids; the only place remaining was to his left. Sarah, hesitating on the threshold, had considered for a moment the possibility of turning and running back to the sanctuary of Mrs Darcy's dressing room, but it was not to be attempted – everyone would see, and everyone would know, and so this must be faced. She drew in a breath, and let it go, and marched across the bare flags towards him. He glanced up at her approach, stiffened, and then looked away, turning to his pretty neighbour, and saying something that made the girl's eyes widen, and her cheeks dimple.

So Sarah found herself sitting right beside him, by his shirtsleeve and collar and his canary waistcoat, and the twist of his nape, and the back of his head, while he kept his attention fixed entirely on the young woman to his right, who blushed now, and stammered a few ungainly words. Sarah had been just the same, she realized – confounded and thrilled to be noticed by a man like him – when he had first come to Longbourn.

After a while, the conversation fell away, as it must, there being so little in common between him and a country girl like that. Sarah was, for a time, obliged to reply to the stable boy seated near her, which was an ordeal all of its own, because he had nothing to tell her that was not about himself, and his old Pa, and the horses, and she could make out only one word in three. Then they too fell into silence, though there was, all around them, a fug of chatter, cutlery on china, chewing, scraping chairs when a bell was rung and someone must go and answer it. She lifted a hand to her hot cheek, her food untouched.

Ptolemy spoke softly, under cover of the general noise; he did not look at her. 'Are you well?'

'Quite well,' she said. 'Thank you.' Then, after a moment: 'And you?'

He nodded.

Then he turned back to the young maid, and asked her if she had had anything to do with the cooking of the beef, because it was excellent, and he had never had such good beef anywhere before, not even in London town itself. It was a valiant attempt, but this topic, too, soon flagged. He was left looking into space, and rearranging his cutlery.

'I did not think to see you here.' She spoke quietly. 'I thought you would be all set up by now.'

'Oh, you know me.'

She turned to look at him now. He was staring straight across the room, at a row of headless hares that hung by their back legs, dripping blood into the dishes set out below.

'Keeping my options open,' he said. 'Keeping an eye out.'

'I wish you all the best of luck, Mr Bingley.'

He huffed a breath, half shook his head: she thought for a moment that he was going to accuse her of cruelty, of destroying his hopes, his happiness. But he just turned his head, and looked at her. His eyes were still beautiful, and black as coffee, but now they were swimming wet. When he spoke next, it was hardly above a whisper.

'I didn't want . . .' he said. 'When I heard you were here, I thought

350

that when I saw you, I could make you feel something. Hurt you. But—'

'Mr Bingley. I am sorry, I—'

He shrugged. 'But it's not your fault.'

She folded her hands together in her lap. She looked down at them.

'That footman,' he said. 'Smith.'

She swallowed, tried to clear her throat, but then all she could manage was a nod.

'And you are quite fixed upon him. No one else will do.'

Her face felt sore; she could not look up.

'I have given up all hope,' she said.

He plucked at his white gloves. 'Have you?'

A slow blink; she nodded.

'But if you knew where he was? If you had a chance of finding him?'

'Mr Bingley. Ptolemy. Please.'

'But it would matter to you, more than all this' – he wafted a hand, taking in her work, the servants' hall, the house beyond – 'more than anything—'

'I think—' she said, and then swallowed, and steadied her voice. 'I think that he is dead. But I do not know.'

'What if I told you, that I do know.'

She looked round at him. The noise and bustle, the other servants, the kitchen, Pemberley – everything – reeled away and all was silence, and stillness. Just his dark eyes fixed on hers.

'Tell me.'

'He's alive.'

'You saw him?'

'Or he was, a few days since.'

'Where did you see him?'

His jaw set, he looked at her a moment longer, and then he turned away. And as he spoke, his hand brushed the tablecloth, gathering up crumbs into a heap, then sweeping them out again.

'We were crossing the sands from Ulverston. Just a few days ago, this was, on our way here, at the end of their tour of the Lake Country. And he, the footman from Longbourn, Smith; he was crossing the sands, only he was going the other way, heading north—'

'You saw him.'

'I saw him. He was with road engineers – a whole troop of them, and all their gear, a trail of wagons crossing the sands. It was just a moment, as we were passing, but I knew it was him, and he knew me too. It was just a moment, and then we were past and gone.'

Her hand came up; it covered her mouth.

'Well,' he said. 'I thought you should know.'

After a moment, she touched his arm. 'You are quite, quite certain it was him?'

He looked down at her fingers, dimpling the white cotton. 'I am. I knew him. I am sure.'

Then he lifted his arm, so that her hand fell away from him. He turned, and cleared his throat, and addressed himself to his other neighbour again, and did not look at Sarah any more, and they never spoke again.

Lady Day. A day of engagements and dismissals, of endings and beginnings; a day when change is woven into the very fabric of the creeping hours; a day that demands the totting up of accounts, the consideration of what has been bought and sold and at what cost; a day when one is obliged to consider if any of it was worth the price that has been paid.

Mrs Darcy's desk had been drawn out from the window into the middle of her parlour. She was already seated behind it, in a sober day-dress and draped shawl. The servants waited their turn at the door, lined up in decent silence. The mistress looked beautiful and nervous and tired. She had a ledger open in front of her. Mrs Reynolds stood a convenient distance away, should assistance be required. This was, after all, just a first attempt.

The accounts of previous quarters were all in Mrs Reynolds's precise hand: Mrs Darcy's handwriting was by no means as neat, but she worked conscientiously at it, the tip of her tongue poking out while she pored over her sums, and wrote out names; she smiled as each servant made their mark, and as she bestowed on them their small stack of coin. Elizabeth was doing her very best, Sarah could see that. She was being what she was required to be.

The weight of Sarah's pay dipped her hand; she bobbed her curtsey.

Elizabeth gave Sarah one of her lovely smiles; jewels glittered on her fingers as her pen moved to make the tick in the Paid column. She made the downstroke for the tick, and Sarah's lips parted, and she spoke.

'Forgive me, madam.'

Mrs Darcy's smile settled in, patient. 'Yes, Sarah?'

'Madam. I hope it won't inconvenience you too much, but I wish to make an end of this.'

'To make an end?'

'To cease employment here.'

'But—' Mrs Darcy's smile stiffened now. 'Why?'

'Is there a problem, madam?' Mrs Reynolds moved closer, peering in.

Mrs Darcy lifted up her hands. 'She wishes to leave!'

Mrs Reynolds turned on Sarah: 'Are you not well-treated? Are you not shown every kindness here?'

'Yes,' said Sarah. 'Yes – you are all very good to me indeed.'

Mrs Darcy sat back; she shook her head.

'Is the work not light enough for you? Surely,' Mrs Reynolds asked, 'this is the most comfortable situation you have ever found yourself in, and are ever likely to?'

Sarah nodded. This was certainly true.

Mrs Darcy seemed amazed, and quite perturbed. 'You are not wanted back at Longbourn, perhaps? Does Mother want you, or Mrs Hill?'

'Even if they did, they should have applied to you first, madam.'

'Are you perhaps' – and with this, Mrs Darcy's countenance darkened, and she leaned closer, and dropped her voice, as if even the possibility of this was shameful – 'somehow, unhappy? Are you . . . homesick?'

'Yes,' said Sarah, 'yes, I think I am.'

She persuaded the stable lad to give her a knapsack in exchange for her old wooden box, so that her belongings would be that much easier to carry. The poor fellow was inconsolable that she was leaving, but thrilled to have her ask a favour of him. He muttered incomprehensibly when he handed it over, and she kissed his smooth cheek to thank him.

A path skimmed the grounds behind the house; it then rose towards the western edge of the park. From there, it climbed up through the woods to join a packhorse route, which trailed out over the hills, heading in a direction that was generally agreed to be northwesterly. Sarah could follow that, from one town to the next, as far as Chester. And from Chester, she could take the long flat road to Lancaster, and thence to the sands, which she could cross on foot to the north country beyond. The Bingleys' coachman volunteered this last nugget of information, having driven this road himself so recently. He looked at her like she was fit for Bedlam, though: a young girl like her off on the tramp, choosing the cold and the empty road and all its dangers over ease and safety, and Pemberley.

Alone in her room, she tried the knapsack on her shoulders. Without the box to weigh them down, her little things seemed to weigh almost nothing at all.

There would be others out there, on the tramp. There always were, around the time of hiring fairs and quarter days; these great tidal shifts and settlings of servants around the country. She would find some other women and girls to travel with, and go in company as far as they were going.

Mrs Reynolds opened the attic door without knocking.

'The mistress wants another word.'

In the morning room, Mrs Darcy was sewing something tiny and white. She dismissed Mrs Reynolds, but did not move from her seat in one of the pair of winged armchairs by the fire. She looked a little pale, and nervous – her hands gripped her work, and for a moment she just looked at Sarah and did not speak, and then she looked away, and said something so quietly that Sarah could not hear it. Uncertain, Sarah waited where she was, in the middle of the complicated carpet. Then she saw to whom Mrs Darcy had spoken: Mr Darcy was sitting in the chair opposite his wife; it was only when he leaned forward, and spoke a word in reply, that Sarah saw him; he had been hidden by the high back and wings of the chair. Now, he rose from his seat, like a statue come to life.

Sarah shrank. Fixed for the first time on her, his gaze made her dwindle to the size of a salt-cellar. He strode briskly up, stopped just a shade too close; she had to fight the urge to take a step back, to get a better angle on him, to make more space between her and his flesh. But she stayed put, and held her head up; she set her eyes on his starched cravat – they washed very white at Pemberley – while he studied her in a puzzled, faintly irritated manner, as if she were an unconsidered household item that had abruptly ceased to function, and on which he now found himself obliged to have an opinion.

'My wife had expected to keep you with her at this time.'

Sarah addressed herself to his cravat. 'I am sorry, sir, to go against her expectations.'

'*I* expect you to remain with her.'

'I am afraid that I cannot.'

'You *cannot*?'

Sarah nodded.

'Am I not a good master? Is she not the best of mistresses?'

'I think you must be, sir. Both of you.'

'Well, then. Sense dictates that you stay.'

'No.'

He loomed closer. 'This is your answer?'

Sarah squared her shoulders. 'You have had it already, sir: I cannot stay.'

'But you are *wanted* here.'

This from Elizabeth, who was getting to her feet, then came across towards them. She moved slowly, without her former elasticity of step. She seemed somehow weighted now.

'You are so good with little ones, Sarah. You always were, with my sisters, even when you were just a girl yourself.'

Sarah looked again at the sewing, still clutched in Elizabeth's hand. A tiny thing, a newborn's cap. There had been no rags to soak and scrub from her, Sarah recalled; not for these past months. If she had thought about it at all, it was to think that it must have fallen to somebody else to clean them. But it was clear now that Mrs Darcy was expecting her first child – her skirts skimmed the cusp of her belly; her breasts, where they rose above her bodice, were full and veined with blue. She was facing her first confinement, and with all the usual fears. Sarah felt a tug of sympathy, but—

'My staying here will not really help you, miss.'

Elizabeth would just have to go through it; every breeding woman did. If she survived this once, then she would just have to do it all over again in the full knowledge of its horrors – and then again, and again, because a man like Mr Darcy would need his sons.

Endure and pray, that was all that could be done.

'I can't help you, miss. I am sorry.'

'Madam,' Mr Darcy said.

'Madam, yes.'

'You are determined, then?'

Sarah risked a look straight up at his big handsome face, the meat of him: the sheen of cheekbone and nose, the gloss of eyes, the smooth rubbery flesh of his shaved lip. He was descended from a race of giants; he must be.

'Yes, sir.'

'Well, then,' he said. 'This is quite baffling.' He turned away from Sarah, and addressed himself to his wife: 'I find there is, after all, nothing we can do about this. If the girl wishes to go, however foolish this might be, however austere and dangerous the life she chooses, and indeed uncertain its continuance, she has every right to choose it. This is England, after all, and she is not a slave.'

Elizabeth came close now, and grasped Sarah's hands, still clutching the sewing; the needle pricked Sarah's skin so that when her mistress came to take up her needlework again, she would see that it was spotted with dark blood.

'But where will you go, Sarah? What can a woman do, all on her own, and unsupported?'

'Work,' Sarah said. 'I can always work.'

She left Pemberley quietly, unattended, by a servants' door. Bag on her shoulder, she crossed the stable yard, and took the path that led from the back of the house, away across the park. It wound along the stream, and soon she was walking past clumps of pale daffodils, and then was climbing up through the woods. She reached the edge of the park, where there were stone steps set into the boundary wall. She climbed up. The treads were glossy with the years.

From here, she could see the path shear away across the open hillside to join the packhorse way. From here, too, when she turned her head, she could still see Pemberley, standing silent and self-contained, its eyes silvered by the cool spring light.

She gathered up her skirts, and stepped over, and slithered down the other side.

Finis

It is not, perhaps, an entirely happy situation after all, to gain something that has been wanted for long years. The object itself, once achieved, is often found not to be exactly as anticipated. It has perhaps become tired and worn over time; flaws that had been overlooked for years are now all too apparent. One finds one does not know what to do with it at all.

This did not apply to Mrs Bennet, however: Mrs Bennet's happiness was pure, perfect and unalloyed. With her elder girls brilliantly well married, her youngest at least convincingly so, Mrs Bennet could find nothing to complain of; indeed, she had so much good news to share over cards and teacake that some of her acquaintance began to find her company rather wearing. The ladies, who had condoled so thoroughly with her during her time of grief, found it rather more difficult to participate in her happiness, which takes a true and proper friend indeed. Mrs Bennet had the good fortune to notice none of this, but if she had, she would have pshawed and waved a hand and laughed and said she did not care a fig: for her, all unhappiness was done away with, and, feeling confident of her children's security, she could now herself be quite content.

Kitty, too, was happy; she now spent much of her time with her elder sisters, and this was much to her advantage and her taste.

Mary, being the only child remaining now at home, found that she became overnight what she had always struggled and jostled to be, which was, quite simply, important. It was Mary's company that was required now by her mother; her opinions were solicited on every subject. And with no other daughters at home to empty her purse for her, Mrs Bennet was now determined that Mary must be bought clothes, and bonnets, and ribbons, and even new sheets of music if she really must have more of the stuff. But she was a clever, talented child, her mother now discovered, and Mrs Bennet was determined to share this revelation with everyone she met. It was extremely provoking, Mary told Polly, who now assisted her with her toilette, that she must be dragged away from her studies so very often, to drink tea, or look at a fashion plate, or drive out on a morning call.

'I don't think you mind so very much, though, do you, miss?'

Mary smiled. 'I shall reconcile myself to it, I dare say.'

And so Mary flourished and was happy in the warm glow of her mother's attention. And to be flourishing, and happy, was to be a good way towards being beautiful. And being flourishing, and happy, *and* beautiful, was a good way towards being beloved – it seemed at least to suggest its possibility to Mary, and this made the world seem bright again. Such another as Mr Collins could indeed be hoped for.

Mr Hill died, as he had been promised that he would, at Longbourn – and died as he would have wished to, in the embrace of his lover, a hard-handed labourer of middle years from the next farm along. This man, wordless with shock and sorrow, brought Mrs Hill to their trysting place in the little wilderness to the side of the lawns. There, between them, they managed to get Mr Hill's britches back on. They both wept, and Mrs Hill rubbed the grieving fellow's back and did her best to comfort him. They carried the old body back up to the house, and all the way to the attic, and laid him in his marriage bed, so that he might die as respectably as he had lived, and with the lie intact.

But they heard nothing from Sarah. After her flit from Pemberley, there was not a word. She might be dead, as the saying went, in a ditch, for all Mrs Hill knew. Or she might have found James, and be settled somewhere with him. Or she might, even now, still be on the tramp, out on the roads looking for him. And the thing was, Sarah *must* know that Mrs Hill would have gladly paid the postage, just to hear a word or two from her. And ink and paper could be got hold of, by hook or by crook; they could be begged from an employer, or a clergyman; a clergyman did not begrudge that kind of thing to a decent girl fallen on hard times, and missing her home.

But letters, in those restless and uneasy days, were often opened; everyone knew they might be scrutinized for sedition, for schemes and plots and threats of revolution. A careless word, a clue, an intimation of a deserter's whereabouts: it was not to be risked. And so, if Sarah *was* with James, she could not risk a letter. And still Sarah did not write. And over time, the idea began to grow, providing a kind of uncertain reassurance to Mrs Hill, that the very absence of correspondence was telling: it seemed to say that all might yet be well.

Polly became, in Sarah's absence, the kitchen's scholar. She raided Mr Bennet's library for books to read to Mrs Hill of an evening, to fill those quiet times, now there were just the two of them downstairs. She grew like a beanstalk too, racing through her hand-me-downs, becoming – almost overnight, it seemed – a woman. The farmhands – at least, those of them that tended towards the liking of women – stopped and stared, mouths hanging open, as she went by in Mary's pretty cast-offs.

Polly, though, would have none of them; men were not for her, nor love, nor any of that nonsense. *She* was going to be a schoolteacher, she told Mary, who clapped her hands in delight and offered her every assistance. (French! Geometry! I have *all* the books. Shall we try to learn a little Latin together?)

Polly would, in later years, come to teach all of these to the gaping rustics' children, when they lined up attentively at the day-school, grasping their slates and chalk. It had been founded by Mr Long, who, it turned out, held the very modern belief that children should be educated five days a week and not just on Sundays, and Polly was the first – and for a long time the only – teacher there, though she had by then been restored to her given name, and had become a well-respected, and in some measure feared, Miss Mary.

For now, though, the fathers of these as-yet-unconceived infants could stare all they liked: she would not be distracted.

And so it transpired that, after all those long years of wanting, Mrs Hill was now possessed of her desired object: she had Mr Bennet almost entirely to herself. Of an evening sometimes, the ladies being out, and Polly absorbed in her studies, Mrs Hill would bring a bottle of Madeira and a slice or two of cake up to him in the library. Mr Bennet, who had been struggling with his book perhaps, his sight and his intellect fading apace, would blink up at her with his rheumy eyes, and say, 'Thank you, Margaret, my dear.'

He'd gesture to the armchair opposite, and she would sit. He would lay his book aside, and pour himself a glass of wine, and break off a fragment of cake, and she would watch the slack flesh moving at his jaw, and the fastidious, fussy brushing of his lapels, and the moist snail-like mouth as he sipped his Madeira. She found that, after more than a quarter-century of keeping silent, there were no words waiting to be said.

And then, once, he asked her, out of nowhere, 'Do you sometimes wish, my dear, that things had been different?'

She considered this. If things had been different. If they had married. She might have had a glass of wine herself. She might have had a slice or two of cake, and someone to bring it to her. She might not have had callouses on her hands, or the swellings that pained her legs, or the bitter pool of grief that still seethed in her, at the loss of James. She might have had him with her; she might have cared for him and watched him grow; she might have had other babies to love and dandle since, who would all be grown young men and women now, with babies of their own to love in turn. And the Longbourn entail – that had once seemed to matter more than anything, and now did not signify at all – it would have melted away, all those long years ago, when James was born.

Still, still, but still: would they not just have ended up here, like this? In Mr Bennet's library, the family gone, and he slumped and slack, sipping wine and eating cake and being old, and needing to be taken care of, and needing her there to take care of him?

No matter how they got there, after all, she thought. The end was all the same.

It was not *the* end, of course; it was just *an* end. Mrs Hill's thread may have become snarled up into an intractable knot, but others were still unspooling. One had wound all the way out through the wild Derbyshire hills, and then along the gentler lanes of Cheshire, and then drifted across to the flat lands by the sea.

The sea. Her first sight of it came with Easter bells and a sharp, blustering wind, and the low call of sheep, and the lambs replying, and the murmuring talk of fellow-travellers, and waiting, clipped salt-marsh-grass beneath one palm, damp rising through her skirts, and the other hand lifted to screen her eyes. It was a sweet brightness in the air that made her feel – despite the fatigues of the road, the nights of ragged sleep in barns and hedgerows, woken by the cold, and the nights of no sleep at all, just walking on and on through the dark, trusting to the road beneath her feet – more awake than ever. It was a sheet of pale brilliance that peeled swiftly away, sucked out of sight by some irresistible persuasion, leaving behind an expanse of silvery mud, miles and miles of it, trenched with glittering rills and scattered with dipping, wheeling, crying birds. Beyond the bay, the lake-country hills stood stark against the sky. They were deep blue, and still creased here and there with snow.

'Is it time?'

Eyes shaded by the brim of his cap, the guide nodded. She scrambled to her feet, shouldering her bag, and paid him his penny. The silt gave under her feet, skinning itself with water; across the sands, a tracery of footsteps filled and faded out behind them. The crossing was brisk, of necessity, between the racing tides. Her feet bled.

On the far side, she changed her stockings and wadded her boots with moss.

She bought a bun and a cup of milk at a baker's shop in the town there. She mentioned – as though it were something, and nothing – that she'd heard a road gang had come that way recently. The shopkeeper nodded. The cup stilled at her lips; where were they headed, did he know?

North. Kirkstone. Up over the tops, away past Windermere.

She swallowed the milk, stuffed the bun into her pocket. The bell jangled as the door fell shut behind her.

This was baffling country, veiled by rain that did not fall so much as hang in the air, and made distances impenetrable; the roads twisted like staircases up and down the hillsides, and every summit was a false one, and every lake or tarn that lay like grey stone underneath the lowering sky must be skirted round, and nothing could be approached as the crow flies, but must be sidled up on, and swerved away from, with only inching progress made.

So she could not have said how far it was, or how long it took. Time itself had become indistinct; nights shaded into day and out again, and sleep was an hour on a stone bench in a patch of sudden sunshine, or curled between the tree-roots of a spreading beech, her cheek on her arm; waking, she was back up on her feet and away, since there was no virtue at all to be found in stillness. But one day she found herself upon a new road, climbing out of the tree-line, the limestone chippings fresh and chalky and coating her broken boots with white, the land falling sheer to her left and climbing abruptly to her right, the steep pasture studded with crags and fallen scree and stands of bracken; the road took her through the peaty wastes of the watershed, and the calls of curlews, and up into the cloud.

She heard voices then, coming out of the mist: men singing to the heave and thwack of work. She rounded one bend, expectant, but there was nothing – then the road swung past an outcrop, and the land fell away, and a green valley and a brilliant blue lake and sunshine opened out beyond. And there were figures silhouetted against this sudden light. Pickaxes hefted and swung, hammers dinged on rock, shovels shunted into the broken stone. They were not fifty yards ahead of her now, where the gravel petered out and stopped: the end of the road.

She put a hand out, touched nothing, her head adrift like dandelion seed. Because there he was. He swung a pickaxe high over his shoulder; it jarred onto rock; he swung again, and again, and again; dust puffed, grit flew. She watched as he paused, and set the pickaxe down; it rocked on its head. He unknotted his neckerchief and wiped his face, then reached round to the back of his neck, and looked up. She saw the moment that he saw her, how he went entirely still.

She picked her way down to him; the slope caught her; stones slid and rolled out from underneath her feet.

He was stripped to his sweat-sodden, filthy shirt. He was bone-thin, hard, and weather-burnt. She noticed this all as she came close, and how his face was deeply lined, and how he looked years older, and how he seemed withheld, hidden inside himself, as though he accepted now that this was all there was, and all there ever could be.

But she was close now. She reached out, rested her fingertips against his chest. The rise and fall of his breath under her fingertips, the wet of his sweat, the warmth of him. She could see a pulse throb in his throat, and his eyes brightening. He reached out to touch her. She shoved his arm away, and grabbed handfuls of his shirt. She shook him.

'Don't you ever, ever, *ever* dare do that again.'

Threads that drift alone will sometimes simply twine themselves together, without need for spindle or distaff: brought into each other's ambit, they bind themselves tight with the force of their own torsion. And this same torsion can, in the course of things, bundle the resulting cord back upon itself, ravelling it up into a skein, returning to the point of its beginning.

Some years had passed – Mr Hill was already mouldering in his grave, but Polly was yet unfixed and unfinished and still had much left to strive for – when the travellers made the turn from the drovers' road, and strode down the lane between high hedges. These were years filled with work, and moving on when work was done, and finding friends and leaving them behind, and borrowing books and passing them on, and keeping quiet, and keeping their heads down, and doing their best to go unnoticed, and waiting for the peace that was to come; and always, always moving on.

There were long blue autumn shadows, and the trees were on the turn. In the fields, cows stood motionless; rabbits scudded through the grass, then stopped and disappeared. Smoke rose from the high chimneys; she caught the scent of washday fires. She breathed it in.

'D'you know what Heraclitus said?'

He plucked a green cobnut from a bush in passing, and cracked it between his palms. 'I don't recall.'

'He said,' she scuffed a stone, sent it rolling, 'you can't step into the same river twice.'

Nodding, he picked away the shell and pith, conscious of the small neat shape of her, the rustle of her skirts as she walked beside him; the simple fact of her was every day a miracle. He offered out the kernel on his calloused palm; the nut was green-white, and milky, the first of the turning year.

'Here.'

She took it, was about to thank him; but then movement caught her eye: she stopped in her tracks; cobnut curled inside her palm, she brushed her knuckles against his arm – white linen stirring down on the washing lines, and Polly, oh my goodness, was that *Polly* – a young woman now, pegging out a petticoat, who, noticing something going on up there in the lane, paused in her work, and stared, and then let the petticoat fall to the ground, and blundered right over it; hitching up her skirts, now racing at full tilt across the green paddock, towards them.

Sarah laughed, skipped a step, then broke into a dash herself, hurrying to meet her. But the sudden shift in movement proved unsettling; inside her tight-bound shawl, a small, still bundle now began to stir and mewl. Sarah stopped and peered down into the folds. The baby, newly woken, gazed up with wide and startled eyes.

Sarah touched the perfect brow with a fingertip. 'It's all right, sweetheart. Not far now.'

She cupped the child's head to her, steadying, and glanced back round for James. He ran a few steps to catch up with her, old canvas backpack bouncing. She smiled up at him; he took her hand. Together, they strode down the lane to Longbourn.

AUTHOR'S NOTE

The main characters in *Longbourn* are ghostly presences in *Pride and Prejudice*: they exist to serve the family and the story. They deliver notes and drive carriages; they run errands when nobody else will step out of doors – they are the 'proxy' by which the shoe roses for Netherfield Ball are fetched in the pouring rain. But they are – at least in my head – people too.

Longbourn reaches back into these characters' pasts, and out beyond *Pride and Prejudice*'s happy ending; but where the two books overlap, the events of this novel are mapped directly onto Jane Austen's. When a meal is served in *Pride and Prejudice*, it has been prepared in *Longbourn*. When the Bennet girls enter a ball in Austen's novel, they leave the carriage waiting in this one. I have interfered only so far as to give names to the unnamed – the butler, footman, and second housemaid – and to bestow on Mrs Hill the role of cook as well as housekeeper, since such an arrangement was not uncommon in this kind of household. But what the servants get up to in the kitchen, unobserved, while Elizabeth and Darcy are busy falling in love upstairs, is, I think, entirely up to them.

One final note: in *Pride and Prejudice* the footman appears just once in the text, when he delivers a note to Jane (page 31 of Volume One, in my Penguin Classics edition). After that, he is never mentioned again.

ACKNOWLEDGEMENTS

I can't remember when I first read *Pride and Prejudice*. It seems as if I've always loved it. Jane Austen's work was my first experience of grown-up literature, and has supplied a lifetime of pleasure: it's the only book that, as an adult, I re-read. Even after all these years, all those re-readings, and even after unpicking the backing to look at the underside, I still love it. I still admire it. And to inhabit it in this different way has been an unalloyed pleasure.

But there are other books, too, to which I am particularly indebted. Maggie Black's *A Taste of History* and *The Jane Austen Cookbook*, edited by Maggie Black and Deirdre Le Faye, provided me with ideas for dinner; Charles Esdaile's *The Peninsular War*, Robert Harvey's *The War of Wars*, Richard Holmes's *Redcoat* all supplied essential detail – both military and personal – for James's experiences in Spain and Portugal. Jane Austen's *Letters*, edited by Deirdre Le Faye, Carolyn Steedman's *Labours Lost: Domestic Service and the Making of Modern England*, Amanda Vickery's *Behind Closed Doors: At Home in Georgian England*, Andrew White's *Life in Georgian Lancaster*, and Ben Wilson's *Decency and Disorder 1789–1837* offered invaluable insight into domestic and social life in this fascinating and unstable period.

And there are people to thank, as well as books. Daragh, for twisting my arm. Saleel, for keeping lookout. Diana, Jane and Marianne, for nudging me along. Clare, for staying put. And my mum and dad, for not thinking twice about letting me play out all day, when I was little, in the ramshackle outbuildings of a nearby Georgian house, where there was a big, echoing kitchen, a disused necessary house, and empty stables with a ladder at the back, which led up to the sunlit stable loft above.

Jo Baker was born and grew up in Lancaster, and educated at Oxford and Belfast. She lives in Lancaster with her husband and two children, aged ten and five. *Longbourn* is to be published internationally and is due to be made into a film produced by Focus Features.